Praise for bestselling author Leslie Kelly

"Sexy, funny and a little outrageous,
Leslie Kelly is a must read!"
—*New York Times* and *USA TODAY* bestselling author
Carly Phillips

"Leslie Kelly introduces characters you'll love
spending time with, explores soulmates you'll dream
about, open honest sex and a hero to die for."
—*RT Book Reviews* on *Naturally Naughty*

"The perfect blend of sass and class!"
—*New York Times* and *USA TODAY* bestselling author
Vicki Lewis Thompson

"*Wicked & Willing* [is] a terrific story with a
refreshingly earthy and outspoken heroine."
—*RT Book Reviews*

"Leslie Kelly is a rising star of romance."
—#1 *New York Times* and *USA TODAY* bestselling
author Debbie Macomber

LESLIE KELLY

has written more than two dozen books and novellas for Harlequin Blaze, Harlequin Temptation and HQN Books. Known for her sparkling dialogue, fun characters and depth of emotion, her books have been honored with numerous awards, including a National Readers' Choice Award and three nominations for the RWA RITA® Award. Leslie resides in Maryland with her own romantic hero, Bruce, and their three daughters. Visit her online at www.lesliekelly.com.

LESLIE KELLY

Naturally Naughty

Wicked & Willing

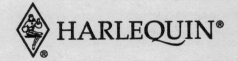

HARLEQUIN®

TORONTO • NEW YORK • LONDON
AMSTERDAM • PARIS • SYDNEY • HAMBURG
STOCKHOLM • ATHENS • TOKYO • MILAN • MADRID
PRAGUE • WARSAW • BUDAPEST • AUCKLAND

Recycling programs
for this product may
not exist in your area.

ISBN-13: 978-0-373-68803-6

NATURALLY NAUGHTY & WICKED & WILLING

Copyright © 2010 by Harlequin Books S.A.

The publisher acknowledges the copyright holder of the individual works as follows:

NATURALLY NAUGHTY
Copyright © 2002 by Leslie Kelly

WICKED & WILLING
Copyright © 2003 by Leslie Kelly

This edition published by arrangement with Harlequin Books S.A.

For questions and comments about the quality of this book please contact us at Customer_eCare@Harlequin.ca.

® and TM are trademarks of the publisher. Trademarks indicated with ® are registered in the United States Patent and Trademark Office, the Canadian Trade Marks Office and in other countries.

www.eHarlequin.com

Printed in U.S.A.

CONTENTS

To Jill Shalvis—a great critique partner, an even greater friend. Thanks for always being there. And, as always, to Bruce. Thanks for the Christmas gifts/ tax write-offs. Research has never been more fun.

NATURALLY NAUGHTY

PROLOGUE

Ten Years Ago

HOLDING HER PINK taffeta dress up to her knees, Kate Jones trudged toward home wishing the ground would open up and swallow her. Live burial seemed better than spending one more night in Pleasantville, Ohio. Her cousin's favorite expression came to mind—*This town's about as pleasant as a yeast infection.*

Without a doubt, this evening would have a place on Kate's list of all-time worst experiences. No, it wasn't nearly as bad as when her dad had died, or when her mom had brought her here to live, a town where their family was treated like dirt. In terms of teenage experiences, however, tonight was bad. Kate had been resoundingly dumped. On prom night no less.

You should have stayed, a voice whispered in her brain.

Kate snorted. "Stayed? After being jilted by Darren McIntyre for Angela Winfield, wickedest witch on earth? Right!"

Cassie wouldn't have run away. No, her cousin would have popped Angela one, kicked Darren where it counted, and told them to stick it where the sun didn't shine. Too bad she'd left early.

She passed another dark house. Its inhabitants were probably cozy in their beds, reflecting on their *pleasant* days.

They wouldn't think twice about her trudging in the street. Who'd expect anything else from a trashy Tremaine? Her last name might be Jones, but no one let her forget her mother's maiden name. In spite of being a straight-A student who'd never gotten into any real trouble, people here believed Kate must have hit every no-good branch on her way down the Tremaine family tree.

Turning off Petunia onto Pansy Lane, Kate grimaced for the half-millionth time at the dumb street names. *I'd love a giant bottle of Weed-B-Gone.* She could think of a creeping pest she'd like to zap. Darren.

"Darren's a conceited jerk." Kate knew she shouldn't have gone with him, especially since his mother hated her. But just for one night she'd wanted to be part of the in crowd. She'd wanted to be cool and popular, instead of the nice, quiet girl who tried to disguise her family's poverty by getting good grades and working harder than anyone ever expected.

Tonight at the prom Angela had pawed all over Darren, urging him to ditch Kate and leave with her instead. The whole school knew Angela put out. And despite being a trashy Tremaine, Kate did not. Hmm, such a tough choice for Darren—Angela the tramp from the most respected family in town? Or Kate the pure, from the trashiest one? What was a horny eighteen-year-old boy to do?

He'd left so fast Kate's head had spun.

Kate was nearly home when the rain started. "What did I do to deserve this?" she said as drops hit her face. She was long past the point of caring about her panty hose. Nor did she worry about her makeup smearing—her tears had accomplished that.

The rain was just one more insult in a rotten night.

Spying her family's duplex, she prayed her mother was asleep, and Cassie home in the adjoining unit where she and Aunt Flo lived. If Cassie was home, Kate would knock on her bedroom wall, which butted right against Cassie's in the next unit. They'd communicated by knocking on it since they were little girls. She'd signal her to sneak out back for one of their late-night gab sessions and fill her in about her lousy prom night.

Then she noticed a parked car out front. When her mother emerged from it, Kate wondered who Edie could have been out with so late. As a man exited she said, "Mayor Winfield?"

Yes, Angela's father. Rich, jolly John Winfield who kept her mother busy cleaning his fancy house on Lilac Hill. Once again the mayor thought nothing of working Edie late in the night, as if she didn't already spend forty hours a week scrubbing other people's toilets. Kate raised a brow as the mayor played gentleman and walked her mother to the door.

Walk away, her inner voice said. But she couldn't. Moving closer, she'd reached the steps when they began to kiss.

Kate moaned. Her gentle mother was having an affair with the very *married* mayor? John Winfield was the patriarch of the town, a family man, father of Angela and of town golden boy, J.J., who'd gone away to college years ago and hadn't returned.

After their kiss Winfield said, "I don't know what I'd do without you. You've made life bearable for me all these years."

Years? Mr. Mayor, the pure saintly leader of Pleasantville, has been having an affair with his cleaning woman for years?

"Here," Winfield continued, reaching into his pocket. "Your paycheck. I'm sorry it's so late, sugar, you know how she is."

A sweet smile softened her mother's face. "I'm okay, John. If she's overspent again and you're in need, I can wait a bit."

Kate shook her head in shock. The phone bill hadn't been

paid. They'd had canned soup and tuna sandwiches for dinner all week. And her mother was giving back her paycheck to the richest man in town? Worse…the son of a bitch took it.

Blinking away tears as she acknowledged her respectable, much-loved mother was the willing mistress of a married man, she darted around back. Kate instinctively headed toward the ramshackle tree house where she and Cassie had played as kids, seeking comfort like a child would seek her mother's arms. Kate whimpered as she realized she no longer had that option. Her mother wasn't the person she'd always thought she was.

Looking up as she approached, she saw a glow of light from within and the burning red tip of a cigarette.

Cassie. Kate paused. She simply could not tell her cousin what she'd witnessed in front of the house. Cassie and Kate had long ago accepted the truth about their mothers. Cassie's mom, Flo, was the wild charmer who'd let them have makeup parties at age seven, and bought them their first six-pack. They loved her, no matter what the town thought of her outrageous clothes and numerous affairs. But Edie had been the real nurturing mother figure, the kind one who'd dried their tears and encouraged their dreams.

For Kate, Edie would never be the same. How could she destroy Cassie's image of Edie, too? In spite of her outward toughness, Kate knew Cassie would be very hurt by this. As hurt as Kate had been. So no, she couldn't tell her. Not now. Maybe not ever.

"Kitty Kate, you down there?"

Wiping away her tears, she climbed the rope ladder. Inside the tree house, Cassie's golden hair was haloed by candlelight. "Hi."

"Hey." Cassie took another long drag of her cigarette.

"Got another one?" Kate sat next to her cousin, noting the

way their dresses filled up nearly every inch of floor space in the tiny house. Hers a boring pink. Cassie's a sultry black that screamed seduction and showcased her curvy figure.

"Last time you smoked you ralphed all over the bathroom."

Feeling sick enough already, Kate didn't risk smoking. "You okay? You skipped out on prom pretty early."

"Yeah. I'm sure the gold-plated set missed me real bad."

Kate ignored the sarcasm. "I missed you. What happened?"

Cassie gave a bitter laugh. "Biff said we were going to a party. Turns out he had a two-person, naked party in mind."

"Perv."

"Total perv. Then he gets pulled over for drunk driving."

"You were drinking?" Kate raised a surprised brow, knowing Cassie thought alcohol made guys stupid and mean.

"No. He wanted to get beer, so we stopped at the store before the prom. He said I should buy it since I look older. Friggin' moron. Like the clerk wouldn't notice I was wearing a prom dress."

"What'd you do?"

"I pretended I couldn't. He found somebody else at the prom who gave him some." Cassie squashed out her cigarette and leaned her head against the wall. "Look, Katey, I don't want to talk about this. Why are you here? Shouldn't you and Darling Darren be celebrating as king and queen of Pea-Ville High right now?"

Kate told her everything, leaving out what had happened when she got home. "Guess we both had disastrous prom nights."

Cassie took Kate's hand. "Did I say Darling Darren? I meant Dickless Darren. I hope you told him to eat shit and die."

"I told him he deserved a girl like Angela, and took off."

Frankly, she liked Cassie's comeback better. If she'd thought about it long enough, maybe she could have come up with it. But Kate was so used to being the sweeter of the Tremaine cousins, she generally refrained from mouthing off out loud, as she often did in her brain, or when alone with Cassie.

"Good for you."

Cassie opened an old, dusty Arturo Fuente cigar box in which they hid the stashes of stuff they didn't want the moms to find. It held candles, diaries, even a *Playgirl* they'd dug out of Flo's trash can a few years ago. "I hate this stinking town."

Remembering the way she'd felt as she watched Mayor Winfield and her mother, Kate completely understood. "Ditto."

"I'd give anything to get outta here. Make it big, make lots of money, then come back and tell them all to stuff it."

Kate had the same fantasy. Hours spent in the old Rialto Theater had introduced her to places she wanted to go, people she wanted to meet. Women she wanted to become. Far away from here. "Wouldn't that be something? The trashy Tremaine cousins coming back and stirring up some serious trouble," Kate said. "You know what I'd do? I'd open up a shop right next door to Mrs. McIntyre's Tea Room. And I'd sell…dirty movies!"

Cassie snickered. "Go all out, triple-X porn, baby."

"And sex toys. Darren's mom could really use a vibrator."

"You wouldn't know a vibrator if it fell in your lap. *Turned on.* So, first stop in the big city, we buy sex toys."

Kate giggled. "And when we're rich and famous, we come back here and shove 'em right up certain people's noses."

Cassie reached into the box, grabbing Kate's diary. "I've been sitting here listing all the things I'd do to get even with some people in this town. Why don't you make one, too?"

"A list?"

"Yep. We each list the things we'll someday do to the cruddy populace of Pleasantville, if we ever get the chance."

The idea made perfect sense to Kate. "Publicly humiliate Darren McIntyre and Angela Winfield," she said as she wrote.

As they wrote Kate watched Cassie's smile fade as she thought of something else. Kate couldn't stop her own thoughts from returning to her mother. John Winfield.

She ached, deep within, at the loss of her own childhood beliefs.

Tears blurred her vision as she secretly added one more item to her list. *For Mom's sake, get even with the Winfield family...particularly John Winfield.* She didn't know how, but someday she would do to that family what they'd done to hers...

Cause some serious heartache.

CHAPTER ONE

Present Day

AS SHE PULLED UP in front of the Rose Café on Magnolia Avenue, Kate Jones took a deep breath and looked around at the heart of Pleasantville. Heart. Probably the wrong word. The town hadn't possessed that particular organ when she'd left ten years ago. Judging by what her mother had told her in their last phone call, she feared it hadn't grown one in the intervening decade.

The street appeared the same on the surface, though was perhaps dirtier, its buildings grayer than she remembered. Warped, mildew-speckled boards covered some of the windows of the once-thriving storefronts. Very few people strolled along the brick sidewalks. The cheerful, emerald paint on the benches lining the fountain in the town square had faded to a faint pea-green. A reluctant grin crossed her lips as she heard Cassie's voice in her head. *Welcome back to Pea-Ville.*

Hers wouldn't be an extended stay. She had a job to do, then she'd drive away forever. Reaching for the door handle of her SUV, she paused when she heard her cell phone ring. "Yes?"

"Kate, I'm going crazy. Tell me you're on your way home."

"Armand, I've only been gone one day," Kate said with a

laugh, recognizing the voice of her high-strung, creative business partner. "Besides, you were crazy before you met me."

"Crazy and poor. Now I'm crazy and rich and I can't take this kind of pressure. You are going to pay for leaving me in charge. Nothing that happens at Bare Essentials while you're gone is my fault. Understood?"

"Nothing's going to go wrong in two or three days. Tell me what happened so we can fix it."

"The shipment didn't arrive from California. We're down to *one* Bucky Beaver. And he was featured in the ad this weekend."

Oh, yes, the world would indeed stop revolving without their bestselling special toy. "I don't think it's a problem of catastrophic proportions. We sell lots of other products."

"None that were featured in the ad. I can see an entire girl's college softball team coming in to stock up for an out-of-town game, and finding the shelves bare." She heard Armand groan. "I see riots. Stampedes. Ten-inch rubber dildoes lobbed at my head until I am knocked unconscious. Imagine having to explain that to the handsome young police officer in his tight blue suit with his jaunty black cap when he comes in response to my frantic call." He paused. "Hmm…maybe this isn't such a crisis after all."

"Definitely not, but just call the supplier anyway."

"Maybe I should ask your cousin to use her connections…"

"Cassie's still in Europe. I think." Kate wasn't quite sure where her famous model cousin was working this week. She'd tried to track her down after getting her mother's news and had left messages with Cassie's agent and publicist. So far, no word. Cassie almost seemed to be in hiding. Another worry.

"So how's business today?" she asked.

"As thriving as ever," he replied. "Two different bridal parties came in this morning, hence the shortage of Buckys."

"I do love those wedding showers."

"Dewy brides and do-me bridesmaids. A delightful, money-spending combination."

"Absolutely. Now, have there been any calls for me?" She wondered if Edie had tried to reach her again from her new home in Florida. Their last conversation had ended somewhat abruptly.

Edie hadn't told her all the details of what some people in this town had put her through during her last weeks of residence. What she did say had made Kate wince. She gave her full opinion on the matter, though never revealing she knew the truth of Edie's relationship with Mayor Winfield.

"None that matter. But I warn you, if Phillip Sayre calls again, I'm stealing him for myself. So you better hurry your pretty fanny back here to Chicago."

"You're welcome to him. One date was quite enough for me. The man has a huge ego."

"You know what they say, big ego, big…"

"I think you mean big hands. Or big feet. In any case, I don't have any interest in finding out when it comes to Phillip. Who needs a big, sloppy real one attached to an arrogant, untrustworthy man, when a small, clean vibrating one with no strings attached is sufficient?"

Armand tsked, though she knew he wasn't shocked. After all, he was one of the few people with whom Kate felt comfortable enough to reveal her occasional less-than-nice-girl qualities.

"Playing with the merchandise?" he asked.

"Ah, you caught me. How can I sell it if I can't attest to its effectiveness?"

"As long as you paid for it first and weren't sampling the wares then putting them right back on the shelves."

Yuck! Kate snorted a laugh. "Okay, you win, you nasty thing." Armand always won in games of sexual one-upmanship.

"Besides, small vibrating ones don't have hands or mouths."

"Some have tongues," Kate pointed out with a grin, remembering one of their more popular models of vibrator…a wagging tongue. Cassie had seen it during her last visit to the store in Chicago and had declared it the most disgusting thing she'd ever seen. When Kate had turned it on to show her what it could do, Cassie had bought two of them.

"I'm hanging up now. Be good," Kate said.

"Impossible. Don't you be good, either. It's bad for you."

Kate smiled at Armand's kissy sounds as she cut the connection. She remained in the driver's seat, missing Armand. He was the only man in her life she had ever completely trusted.

A shrink might surmise that it was because Armand was gay, and therefore not a romantic possibility, which allowed Kate to open up and trust him.

The shrink would probably be right. Trusting men had never been her strong suit. One more thing to thank Mayor Winfield for, she supposed. Not to mention the few men she'd dated over the years, who had never inspired thoughts of true love and Prince Charming. More like true greed and Sir Fast Track.

"So, do I get out or restart the car and drive away?" she asked herself, already missing more than just her friend and partner. She also missed her apartment overlooking the water. She really missed her beautiful, stylish shop with its brightly lit, tasteful decor, such a contrast to some of the more frankly startling products they sold.

Two stories high, with huge front glass windows, soft lemony-yellow carpet and delicately intricate display cases, Bare Essentials had done what everyone had sworn couldn't be done. They'd taken sex and made it classy and elegant enough for Michigan Avenue.

Yes, she wanted to be home. Actually, she wanted to be *anywhere* but here.

Could she really go through with it? Could she walk along these streets, enter her mother's house and go through her childhood things so her mother could list the place for sale?

Well, that was the one good thing. At least Edie had finally gotten out, too. Though Edie had taken frequent trips to the city, she'd resisted moving away from Pleasantville for good. No, it had taken Mayor Winfield's death, his subsequent will and some vicious gossip to accomplish that feat.

Kate thought she'd outgrown the vulnerability this place created in her. She wasn't the same girl who used to hide in the tree house to cry after school when she'd been teased about her secondhand clothes. She was no longer a trashy Tremaine kid from the wrong side of town. She and her cousin had bolted from Pleasantville one week after high school graduation, moving to big cities—Kate to Chicago, Cassie to New York's modeling scene—and working to make something of themselves.

Kate had long ago learned the only way to get what you wanted was to work hard for it. Being smart helped, but she knew her limitations. She wasn't brilliant. And as much as she hated to admit it, she wasn't talented enough to pursue her teenage dream of a career in theater, though she'd probably always fantasize about it.

No, common sense and pure determination had been the keys to achieving her goals. So she'd worked retail jobs by day and gone to school by night, taking business and accounting courses, sneaking in a few acting or performing credits when she could.

Then the fates had been kind. She'd met Armand, a brilliantly creative lingerie designer, at exactly the time when

Cassie's career had taken off and she'd had the means to loan Kate the start-up money for a business.

An outrageous, somewhat *dramatic* business.

Combining her need to succeed, her innate business sense and her secret love for the flamboyantly theatrical, she'd dreamed up Bare Essentials. Though originally just designed to be an upscale lingerie boutique to feature Armand's creations, bringing in other seductive items—sexy toys, games for couples, seductive videos and erotic literature—had really made Bare Essentials take off like a rocket when it opened.

The fabulously decorated, exotic shop had taken Chicago by storm. With the right props, location and set design, what could have been a seedy, backroom store was instead a hot, trendy spot for Chicago's well-to-do singles and adventurous couples.

Coming back to Pleasantville should have been absolutely no problem for the woman who'd been featured in Chicago's *Business Journal* last month as one of the most innovative businesswomen in the city. Still, sitting in the parked SUV, she felt oppression settle on her like two giant hands pushing down on her shoulders. The long-buried part of her that had once been so vulnerable, made to feel so small and helpless and sad, came roaring back to life with one realization.

She was really here.

Taking a deep breath, she opened the door. "Home lousy home," she whispered. Then she stepped into Pleasantville.

AS HE SAT gingerly on the edge of a plastic-covered sofa in the parlor of his childhood home, Jack Winfield considered committing hari-kari with the fireplace poker. Or at least stuffing two of the cow-faced ceramic miniatures his mother collected into his ears to block out the sound of her chewing out the new housekeeper in the next room. *Sophie, the luncheon salad was unacceptably warm and the pasta unforgivably cold.*

As if anyone cared about the food's temperature when its texture was the equivalency of wet cardboard.

"She'd never forgive me if I got blood on the carpet."

He eyed the poker again. Maybe just a whack in the head for a peaceful hour of unconsciousness? At least then he could sleep, uninterrupted by the prancing snuffle of his mother's perpetually horny bulldog, Leonardo, who seemed to have mistaken Jack's pant leg for the hind end of a shapely retriever.

"Sophie," he heard from the hall, "be sure Mr. Winfield's drink is freshened before you start clearing away the dishes."

"Sophie, be sure to drop a tranquilizer in his glass, too, so Mr. Winfield can get through another day in this bloody mausoleum," he muttered.

He rubbed a weary hand over his brow and sank deeper into the uncomfortable sofa. The plastic crinkled beneath his ass. Sick of it, he finally slid off to sit on the plushly carpeted floor. Grabbing a pillow, he put it behind his head and leaned back, wondering how long it had been since he'd relaxed.

"Three days. Five hours. Twenty-seven minutes." Not since he'd returned home to Pleasantville for this long weekend.

Jack didn't like feeling so caged-in. He needed to be home, in his own Chicago apartment, away from grief and the smell of old dead roses and talcum powder. Away from his mother's tears and his sister's complaints.

Actually, when he thought about it, what he really needed to bring about sleep and a good mood was a seriously intense blow job. Followed by some equally intense reciprocal oral sex. And finally good old, blissful, hot, headboard-slamming copulation.

He hadn't been laid in four months and was feeling the stress. It almost seemed worth it to call his ex and ask her to meet him at his place the next day for some we're-not-getting-back-together-but-we-sure-had-fun-in-the-sack sex.

Home. Chicago. Late tonight. And not a moment too soon.

Jack supposed there were worse places to visit than his old hometown of Pleasantville, Ohio. Siberia came to mind. Or Afghanistan. The fiery pits of hell. Then again...

"You're sure you have to leave tonight?" his mother asked as she entered the room. "I thought you were going to stay longer than three days. There's so much to do."

"I'm sorry, Mother, you know I can't."

Tears came to her eyes. If he hadn't seen them every hour or so since his birth, they might have actually done what she wanted them to do—make him change his mind.

Sadly enough, his mother simply knew no other way to communicate. Honest conversation hadn't worked with Jack's father, so she'd relied on tears and emotional black-mail for as long as Jack could remember. His father had responded with prolonged absences from the house.

Dysfunctional did not begin to describe his parents' relationship. It—and his sister's three miserably failed walks down the aisle—had certainly been enough to sour Jack on the entire institution of marriage.

Relationships? Sure. He was all for romance. Dating. Companionship. From shared beer at a ball game, to candlelight dinners or walks along the shores of Lake Michigan on a windy afternoon, he thoroughly enjoyed spending time with women.

Not to mention good, frantic sex with someone who blew his mind but didn't expect to pick out curtains together the next morning. Someone like his ex, or any number of other females he knew who would happily satisfy any of those requirements with a single phone call. Not calling any of them lately had nothing to do with his certainty that he wasn't cut out for commitment or happily-ever-after. It had everything to do with his father's death. Work and his obligation to his family had been all he'd thought about for several months.

"Why can't you?" his mother prodded.

"I've got to wrap up the mall project I'm working on. You know I've planned some extended vacation time in July. I'll come back and help you get things settled then." *Unless I get hit by a train or kidnapped by aliens...one can hope, after all.*

Nah. Trains were messy. And after watching the "X-Files" for years, the alien thing didn't sound so great, either. He really couldn't get into the whole probing of body orifices gig.

So, a summer in Pleasantville it would be.

Thinking of how he'd originally intended to spend his long summer vacation—on a photographic big-game safari in Kenya—could almost make a grown man cry. Pampered poodles instead of elephants. Square dances instead of native tribal rituals. The chatter of blue-haired ladies sitting under hair-drying hoods instead of the roar of lions and the crackle of a raging bonfire. Small town, pouting blond princesses with teased up hair instead of worldly beauties with dark, mysterious eyes.

He sighed. "I think I'll take a walk downtown. To walk off that great lunch." What he really needed was to escape the stifling, decades-old, musty-rose-tinged air in the house.

"Just be careful, J.J."

Jack cringed at the nickname that his mother refused to give up. No one but his parents had called him J.J.—or John Junior—in twenty years. Still, he supposed he could put up with it if it made her happy. She could probably use some happiness right about now; she'd taken his father's death very hard.

"And it looks like it's going to rain. Take your rubbers."

He almost snorted. If she knew how badly he wanted to use a few rubbers—though, not the kind she imagined—she'd faint.

Kissing her on the forehead, he shrugged away a pang of guilt. He needed a brief break from her sadness to deal with his own. Besides, he wanted to get out of the house before his sister got back. With the three of them together, the absence of the fourth became all the more obvious.

His mother would sob quietly. His sister would wail loudly. And Jack would remain strong and quiet. He grieved for his father, too. But always alone, always in silence.

No, they hadn't been on very good terms lately. His father had never forgiven Jack for accepting a scholarship and moving to California fifteen years before. Even after grad school, when he'd gotten a job with an architecture firm in Chicago, he'd managed to avoid all but a handful of visits. The most recent, four months before, had been to attend his father's funeral.

He'd always figured there would be time to mend that fence, to try to make his father understand why he couldn't stay here, couldn't continue the family tradition and become king of Nowhereville. He'd never said that, of course, knowing the old man would have been cut to the quick at an insult to his town. He'd reminded Jack at least once a week growing up about his ancestors, who'd lived here since before the Civil War.

His mother's roots ran even deeper, a fact she enjoyed bringing up whenever his father had started pontificating.

Funny. Walking past his father's study, eyeing the brandy decanter and the old man's favorite glass, he realized he'd have gladly listened to his father pontificate if it meant seeing him once more. Amazing how there always seemed to be time for one more conversation right up until time ran out. That realization had helped a lot lately in dealing with his emotional mother.

He considered it a new life's lesson. Tomorrow might not ever come, so don't put off what you want to do today. Grab it now or risk losing the chance forever. John Winfield, Junior…Jack to his friends…planned to stick to that mantra.

Starting today.

THE FIRST THING Kate noticed during her walk downtown was the absence of the pungent odors of the Ohio General Paper Mill. The unpleasant aroma used to hang over the town, which had once seemed appropriate to Kate and Cassie. The mill had closed three years ago, according to her mother. That had caused the town's bad economic situation. Kate couldn't even conjure up any satisfaction about it. She felt only a sharp tinge of sadness, particularly when she saw the sorry condition of the town square and the courthouse. Pleasantville might not have been pleasant for the Tremaines, but it had actually once been pretty.

As she walked, she got a couple of curious looks. No one recognized her, not that she'd expected anyone to. She was no longer the pretty-in-a-quiet-way, nice girl she'd once been. That was one good thing about her move away from Pleasantville. She no longer felt the need to always be the good girl. Without Cassie around to be so flamboyantly bad, Kate had become free to speak her mind. She sometimes went out of her way to shock people, even if it was really only a defense mechanism to keep others from trying to get too close, as Armand claimed.

There were one or two people she wouldn't mind seeing. Some of her mother's friends had been kind. And Kate's high school drama teacher, Mr. Otis, had been one of the smartest people she'd ever met. She imagined he was long retired by now.

Feeling hot, Kate went into the deli for a drink. She didn't know the couple who ran the place, and they were friendlier than she'd expected. She began to relax. Maybe ten years of dislike had created an unrealistic anxiety about her trip back here.

After the deli, she continued her stroll. Heavy gray clouds blocked all but a few watery rays of sunlight and kept the unusual spring heat close to the ground. The soda helped cool her off, but her sleeveless silk blouse still clung to her body, and her ivory linen skirt hung limply in the thick humidity.

A few buildings down, in what used to be a record shop, she noticed a new business. A nail salon, judging by the neon hand in the window, which beckoned customers inside. From an angle, the middle finger on the hand appeared abnormally long, almost as thought it was flipping the bird to everyone on the street. Then she saw the name—Nail Me. "Well, now I've got to go in."

"Pull up a chair, angel face," she heard. "You want your fingers, your toes or both? I'm runnin' a special."

Kate had to grin in response to the welcoming smile of a skinny girl, who looked no more than eighteen, sitting on a stool in the empty shop. "Uh, I don't actually need a manicure."

The young woman, who had bright orange hair and at least a half-dozen pierced earrings in one ear, sighed. "You sure?"

Kate nodded and held out her hands, knowing her regular manicurist would throw a fit if she ever went to someone else.

The girl whistled. "Nice." She then pointed to some chairs in a makeshift waiting area. "Have a seat anyway. You're a stranger, I can give you directions to anyplace you need to go."

"I'm familiar with this town. I've been here before."

"And you came back voluntarily?"

Kate chuckled. "You're not a fan of Pleasantville?"

"It's all right," the girl said, shrugging. "Could be a decent place, if it would move out of the 1940s and into the new millennium. Just needs something to shake things up."

The return of a trashy Tremaine could do the trick…not that Kate would be here long enough to renew any acquaintances.

"I wanted to see how the place has changed. I really should go now, though." She'd seen enough of downtown. Time to stop putting off the inevitable and to go out to her mom's house.

Bidding the girl goodbye, she exited, crossing Magnolia Avenue to walk back to her parked SUV. She'd only gone a few yards when someone across the street caught her eye.

A man. Oh, without question, a man. A tiny wolf whistle escaped her lips before Kate could stop it. *Mister, you are definitely in the wrong place.*

No way did this blond god belong here. He should be in Hollywood among the beautiful people. Not in this Ohio town where some men considered changing from crap-covered work boots into non-crap-covered work boots dressing up for a night out.

She sighed as she realized even her thoughts had regressed. Kate Jones, successful business owner, did not generally think about crap-covered anything.

Unable to help herself, she looked across the street at the man again. He appeared tall. Of course, to Kate, most people appeared tall since she stood five foot four. The stranger's dark blond hair caught the few remnants of sunlight peeking through the gray clouds. It shone like twenty-four-carat gold. Though she wasn't close enough to determine the color of his eyes, she certainly noted the strength of his jawline, the curve of his lips. And a body that would moisten the underwear of any female under ninety.

Knock it off, Kate. He's going to catch you staring.

She couldn't stop herself. She had to look some more,

noting the tightness of his navy shirt against those broad shoulders and thick arms. Not to mention the tailored khaki slacks hugging narrow hips and long legs.

They hadn't grown them like this when she'd lived here.

From behind her, she heard a man shout, "Hey, Jack!"

The blond man looked over, probably searching for the person who'd shouted. But his stare found Kate first.

She froze as he spotted her. So did he. Though several yards of black paved street separated them, she could see the expression on his face. Interest. Definite interest. A slow smile. A brief nod.

The person who'd called to him was a man, so she figured Mr. Gorgeous—Jack—was smiling and nodding at *her*. And staring just as she had at him. An appreciative stare. An I'd-really-like-to-meet-you stare. A totally unexpected stare, considering her frame of mind since she'd pulled into this place a half hour ago.

She smiled back, simply unable to help it. Damn, the man had dimples. Someone needed to come along with a big street sweeper and clean her up, because, unless she was mistaken, she was melting into a puddle of mush from one heartbreakingly sexy grin.

"Hi," he said, though she couldn't hear him. She could tell by the way his lips moved. Those lips… Lord save her, the man had to kiss like a sensual dream with a mouth like that. And those thick arms to wrap around her. The hard chest to explore.

An old, seldom-heard voice of doubt mentally intruded. *He must be talking to someone else. Why would he be talking to me?*

Once Kate had reached Chicago, it had taken her a while before she'd begun to accept that men might really want to look at *her*…even when her stunning blond cousin was in the room. She almost couldn't get used to it, even now. Sure, she knew she had always been pretty. Sweet Kate. Quiet Kate. Smart, dark-haired, petite Kate with the pale, delicate face and the boring chocolate-brown eyes who'd always been too easily wounded by the meanness of others. Nothing like show-stopping bombshell Cassie, who was every 36-24-36 inch a Tremaine, with a mile of attitude and a ton of confidence.

Yet this Mount Olympus-bound hunk had stopped to flirt with *her*? He tilted his head to the side and raised one eyebrow. When he pointed to her, then to the sidewalk on which he stood, she knew what he was asking. *Your side or mine?*

Remembering where they were, she stiffened and shook her head. *Forget it. No way are you going to even say hello. Do what you have to do and get outta Dodge, Katherine Jones. You've got no time to get all drooly over the local Don Juan.*

He stepped closer, toward the curb. By the time his feet hit the street, Kate realized he was coming over, though not to talk to the man who'd hailed him. No, his stare had never left Kate's face. She forced herself to move, hurrying down the sidewalk.

She peeked over her shoulder only once. A mixture of relief and disappointment flooded through her as she realized the man who'd hailed him had planted himself firmly in the path of the blond hunk. He couldn't follow her even if he wanted to.

Did he want to? *Doesn't matter.* She kept on walking.

A plop of rain landed on Kate's shoulder. She experienced an instant of déjà vu, remembering walking the streets of Pleasantville on a rainy night when the raindrops had warred with her tears to wash away her makeup.

Seeking shelter, she turned toward the nearest doorway. Somehow, without realizing where her steps had carried her, she found herself standing outside McIntyre's Tea Room. "Oh, no."

The Tea Room, owned by Darren McIntyre's mother, had been the worst spot for any Tremaine ten years ago. The old guard of Pleasantville—the Winfields and the other Lilac Hill set, considered this "their" territory. Kate's mom and her friends had been more comfortable at the beauty parlor in the basement of Eileen Saginaw's house, so it wasn't until Kate had gotten friendly with Darren that she'd ever even been in the Tea Room.

"Still the same," she mused, looking at the small, discreet sign in the window. Next door, though, Mr. McIntyre's menswear shop was gone, closed, dark and empty.

Don't, Kate. Just don't. Casting one more quick look up the street, she saw the handsome stranger watching her from over the shoulder of his companion. He wouldn't follow her, would he? Well, he certainly wouldn't follow her into the Tea Room, a notoriously female establishment.

Knowing she must have some liking for self-torture, she walked up the wood steps to the awning-covered porch and reached for the doorknob. Once inside, she had to pause for a moment as sense memory kicked in and her mind identified the smells of her youth. Yeasty bread. Raspberry jam. Spiced teas. Some old lady perfume…White Shoulders? Lots of hair spray. Dried flowers.

She had to stop in the foyer to take it all in.

This place, at least, was hopping, every table full. She recognized some faces, though they'd aged. Physically, nothing had altered. From the white-linen tablecloths to the lilac-tinted wallpaper, the room looked the same as the last time she'd been in it. All it needed was a glowering, frowning-faced Mrs. McIntyre to flare her nostrils as if she smelled something bad whenever Kate walked in, to make her trip down memory lane complete.

No one paid a bit of attention as she stood watching. They were all, it appeared, engaged in a room-wide debate over some poor soul they kept calling shameless and shocking.

Things hadn't changed here at all.

Knowing there was absolutely nothing in this place for her, Kate turned to leave. Before she could walk back out the door, however, she heard the only word that could have stopped her.

Tremaine.

CHAPTER TWO

As HARRY BILLINGSLEY, the town's ancient barber, engaged him in conversation, Jack watched every step the brunette took. She walked quickly, almost tripping once on an uneven brick, as if she wanted to escape the rain. He knew better. She wasn't running from the rain. When she peeked over her shoulder at him, he knew she was avoiding *him*.

Something downright electric had happened a few moments ago when their stares had met across Magnolia Avenue. There'd been an instant connection, a shared intimacy though they were complete strangers. It was like nothing he'd ever experienced before.

Obviously she had been just as affected. Only instead of intriguing her, as it had him, their silent, thirty-second exchange had bothered her, scared her even. Her feet had turned cold and she'd run off.

No matter, he'd be able to find her again. The woman stood out here like a bloodred rose in a bouquet of daisies.

A few months ago he might not have let the charged stare across a deserted street affect him. His new attitude toward life, however, made finding the brunette and talking to her a must. No more letting opportunities slide. Now, when Jack Winfield saw a good thing, he was going to go after it. He somehow knew the stranger could be a very good thing indeed.

Jack tried to brush off Harry as politely as he could. "Yes, but I really have to go now. Maybe we can talk in July when I come back for a longer stay."

Harry continued. "Your father made some mistakes. Stirred up a lot of gossip around here with his will and Edie Jones."

Gossip. His least favorite word, and it was used as currency in this town. Jack had never listened to it and never would. So his father had left his maid a small bequest. Only in a town like this could that be considered gossip-worthy.

Watching as the dark-haired stranger in the sexy green blouse went into the Tea Room, he cringed. Of all the places she could have picked, why did she have to go into that hen's nest?

"I'm sorry, I really have to go," Jack said, finally simply walking away in the middle of Harry's long-winded monologue. He didn't care to hear about any old town scandals, especially not if they involved his father, the former mayor.

Following a stranger down a public street wasn't Jack's M.O. In fact, he didn't think he'd ever done it. But something about this stranger…this perfectly delightful stranger…made him certain he could follow her anywhere. He simply had to see her, up close. To determine if her face was really as delicate and perfect as it had appeared from across the street. If her eyes were possibly the same dark, rich brown as her long hair.

Shrugging, he walked to the entrance of the Tea Room and stood outside the door. For a second he wondered if old lady McIntyre would come out and shoo him away. She used to shout at all the boys who'd plant themselves on the stoop, hoping a customer with a take-out bag would hand over some free sweets.

Never happened, as far as he recalled. The snob set of Pleasantville was notoriously tight-fisted with their sweets.

Crossing his arms in front of his chest, he proceeded to wait. "You've got to come out sooner or later."

It took less time than he expected. Before he even realized what was happening, the door to the Tea Room opened and she barreled out, crashing straight into his arms.

Just as if she belonged there.

"OH, I'M SO SORRY!" Before Kate could step away from the person she'd crashed into, she quickly reached up to dash away some angry tears blurring her vision.

That these people could make her cry infuriated her. Somehow, though, anger and sharp hurt for her mother had combined to bring moisture to her eyes while she stood in the Tea Room listening to her family being torn apart yet again by a bunch of small-minded, small-town witches. It was either turn and hurry out or throw a big screaming hissy fit telling them all to jump on their broomsticks and fly straight to the devil.

She couldn't have said which course of action her cousin Cassie would have chosen. But for Kate, who'd become quite adept at maintaining a cool and calm composure, it was think first, react second. Kate didn't believe in hysterical fits—particularly not when she had tears in her eyes. She did, however, believe in well-thought-out retaliation. *Someday.*

Finally turning her attention to the person she'd nailed, she sucked in a breath. "You."

Mr. Gorgeous. Jack. *This is* so *not my day.*

"Nice to meet you too," he said with a sexy grin, as if they were exchanging handshakes instead of being practically wrapped around one another on the steps of the Tea Room.

He made no effort to move away, seeming content that her hand was on his shoulder, her belly pressed to his hip and her leg between both his thighs.

Of course, Kate didn't move, either. Funny thing the sudden lethargy in her limbs. Particularly considering the sharp heat shooting from the tips of her breasts—which brushed against his shirt—down to her stomach. Lower.

"Did I hurt you?" she whispered.

"Only my ego when you ran away from me a few minutes ago."

Kate blinked, but remained still, somehow unable, or perhaps unwilling, to break their intimate contact. Her breaths grew deeper as she watched him stare at her. His gaze studied her long, dark hair, her face, her mouth. His eyes glittered and a smile played about his sensual lips, as if he liked what he saw.

As did she. Up close, he was even more devastating than he'd been from across the street. Tanned skin, square jaw, beautiful green eyes with lashes a cover model would envy. Her fingers tightened slightly into his cotton shirt.

Move, Kate. Put your hands in the air and step away from the hunk.

"Are you married?" he asked.

She shook her head. But before she could ask him why he wanted to know, before she could do anything—including disengaging their much-too-close-together bodies—he moved closer. Kate thought she heard him whisper the word, "Good," just before he caught her mouth in a completely unexpected kiss.

Kiss? A gorgeous stranger was kissing her, in broad daylight, outside Mrs. McIntyre's Tea Room?

That was as far as her thoughts took her before she shooed them away and focused on what was happening.

Yes, the kiss was unexpected. And unbelievably pleasurable.

She didn't try to step back, didn't shove him away and slap his face as she probably should have. Instead she let him kiss her, let this incredible stranger gently take her lips with his own. Soft and tender at first, then more heated as he slipped his hands lower to encircle her waist and pull her even tighter against his body. As if they weren't already so close together a whisper couldn't have come between them.

As the kiss went on, she briefly wondered if she'd fallen asleep, if she was still at the motel where she'd spent the previous night. Maybe she'd popped one too many nickels into the Magic Fingers and they'd gotten her all worked up so she was having an amazingly intense, erotic dream.

Kissing had never been this good in real life. Besides, no man this perfect could exist in this nightmare of a town.

So she could be dreaming, couldn't she? And if it was merely a dream, couldn't she, uh, kiss him back?

She softened her mouth and tilted her head. Feeling the flick of his tongue against the seam of her lips, she whimpered, continuing to tell herself that this couldn't be happening. The beeping of a passing car horn and the musty damp-wood smell of the old porch on which they stood were merely realistic elements of her dream. These weren't real lips now tugging gently at hers, tasting her, exploring her. She hadn't fallen into the arms of a complete stranger…and stayed there quite happily.

Feeling a few drops of rain plop down from the striped awning over the Tea Room's porch onto her face, she focused on their descent down her cheek. Cold water. Warm kiss. Gentle tongue. His clean, male scent. Hard chest pressing against hers. A thrilling bulge in his pants pressing firmly against her lower belly, which made her rise up on her tiptoes to line things up a little better. The sudden hot flood of moisture between her thighs. Definite car horn beeping. Nosy-faced old lady stepping around them to go down the steps to the sidewalk.

The clarity of detail assured her she was not dreaming.

Insanity. She didn't care. His breath tasted minty as his mouth caressed hers, gently, then deeper. She moaned slightly, deep in her throat, no longer able to pretend this wasn't real, knowing she had to either just go for it, part her lips and let their tongues tangle and mate, or else shove him down the steps.

Kate's rational side said to shove. For once she told it to shut the hell up.

Her entire body hummed with energy. She lifted her leg, sliding it against his, delighting in the friction of her stocking against his trousers. As he moaned and pushed closer, she considered how simple a thing it would be to lift her leg to his hip, to let him pick her up until she encircled his waist with her thighs. To slide onto the wonderfully hard erection straining against the seam of his pants.

She wanted to. Desperately. If only there were no car engines, broad daylight…and the minor fact that he was a complete stranger.

He finally pulled away and smiled gently at her. She shook her head hard and gulped, noting the slowness of a passing car, the curious stare of a face in the window of the Rose Café across the street. Finally she took a wobbly step back. "You're insane."

He stepped forward. Following her. "No, I'm Jack."

Kate shook her head, still bemused. "You kissed me."

"I'm so glad you noticed."

"You can't go around kissing strangers on the street. How could you do that? Just…just…kiss me?"

He shrugged. "You said you weren't married."

"What if I were engaged? A novitiate? A lesbian?"

"Engaged isn't married, so I'd say tough luck to the guy." Grinning, he continued, "Novitiate would simply be a crime against mankind, definitely worth ignoring." He glanced down at her trembling body, his stare lingering on the hard tips of her breasts, scraping so sensitively against her blouse. Then at her legs, which she had to clench together to try to stop the trembling. Not to mention the hot, musky smell of aroused woman.

"Lesbian isn't even in the realm of possibility," he finally said, his voice nearly a purr. "You want me pretty badly."

Her jaw dropped. He tipped it up with the tip of his index finger. "Now, introductions. Remember? I'm Jack. It's very nice to meet you. Who are you, and what in God's name are you doing in Pleasantville?"

She ignored the question. "You followed me."

He didn't try to deny it. "Guilty."

That stopped her. "Why?"

He shrugged. "Fate? Instinct?" Then he lowered his voice, almost whispering as he leaned even closer until his body almost touched hers from shoulder to knee. "Or maybe so I could see what color eyes my children are going to have?"

Kate opened her mouth, but couldn't make a sound come out.

The man was unbelievable. Outrageous. Sexy. Charming and heart-stoppingly handsome.

And still standing much too close. So close she could see his pulse beating in his neck and the cords of muscle on his shoulders. His upper arms were thick beneath the tight navy cotton of his shirt, so different from the Chicago health club addicts she sometimes dated. As if he didn't work out for his health, but because he was the kind of guy who just needed to pound something once in a while.

Her breath caught as she imagined his sweaty, hard body pounding something. Pounding *into* something. Into someone.

Focus!

"How do you know I don't already have a live-in guy and three kids somewhere?" she finally asked, hearing the shakiness in her voice. She took another step back, needing air, needing space, needing control of her own mind, which seemed muddled and fuzzy as she examined the tanned V of skin revealed by his shirt. Had she really been kissed by him? Held in his arms? And, damn it, why hadn't she thought to move her fingers to that V to tangle in the light matting of chest hair just below his throat? *Cool it, Kate!*

"Do you?"

Yes. Tell him yes. Then run like hell. "No."

He smiled. "I didn't think so. So, tell me your name, tell me your phone number, and let's go to dinner."

Dinner. Only a few hours till dinnertime and she hadn't even made it to her mother's house yet.

"No. I can't."

"You take my breath away, run right into me, ruin my pants and you won't even tell me your name? Cruel."

"Cruel. Yeah. Welcome to Pleasantville," she muttered.

"Ah, I suspected you weren't a native."

Remembering his other comment she asked, "What's wrong with your pants?" She glanced down, noting the rigid bulge in his crotch, and had to gulp. Yeah, she guessed their embrace had ruined the *fit* of his pants, anyway.

He obviously saw her stare and lifted a brow. Then he turned, pointing ruefully at his taut backside hugged close in the expensive khaki trousers. Expensive, wet and *dirty* khaki trousers. Somehow, during their embrace, he must have leaned back against the soggy wood porch railing.

"You're making it worse," she noted, watching as he tried to brush off the dirt, but only succeeded in smearing the stains around.

"You could offer to help."

Uh, right. Her hands. On his perfect male butt. Brushing against those lean hips. Trying not to squeeze his firm thighs. She swallowed hard. Glancing at him, she saw laughter in his eyes. Green eyes, dimples, thick blond hair, a body to stop traffic and what looked to be a good solid eight inches of hot and ready hard-on just waiting to be let loose.

On a public street. In broad daylight. In *Pleasantville.*

Sometimes life simply wasn't fair.

"Sure, take off your pants and I'll drop them off at Royal Dry Cleaners for you," she finally managed to say, striving for nonchalance.

"That'd cause some eyes to pop, wouldn't it?" he asked with a wicked grin. "You really want me to take them off now?"

She felt heat stain her cheeks. "I mean, you can…go somewhere and change."

He chuckled. "I was teasing you. It's not a problem. Besides, Royal closed several years ago. Pleasantville has no dry cleaner anymore."

"A shame, given this town's dirty laundry," she muttered.

He gave her a curious look, but she certainly wasn't going to elaborate.

"So, are you going to make it up to me?"

"I'm sorry if my running into you caused you to fall head-first onto my lips and then back into the railing to ruin your pants," she said, crossing her arms in front of her chest.

"Apology accepted," he said succinctly, as if he'd had nothing to do with what had just happened.

She found herself almost grinning. Finally she admitted, "My name's Kate."

He brushed a strand of hair off her face, his fingers warm against her temple. Her heart skipped a beat.

"It's nice to meet you, Kate." He somehow made the simple words seem much more suggestive than they were. *It'd be nice to have you, Kate.* And, oh, it'd be nice to be had.

Before she could reply, Kate heard the Tea Room door open. Three women emerged, eyeing them curiously.

"I have to go," she whispered, feeling the blood drain from her face. How this stranger could have made her forget the things she'd heard in the Tea Room, she didn't know. The memory of the vicious gossip came back full force now, though.

Gossip about her mother. Her aunt. And the men in this town who apparently had left them each money or property.

According to the harpies, Edie had been left a fortune by Mayor John Winfield. Which, they believed, had to have been a payoff for a secret, torrid love affair.

Kate mentally snorted. The man had left Edie a measly thousand bucks. As far as Kate was concerned, that didn't even cover the interest on all the late paychecks over the years.

It was almost laughable, really. The town in a tizzy, rumors of a scandalous affair. It could have been downright hilarious...if only it hadn't been true. Kate suspected she was the single person who understood that, just this once, the vicious, mean-spirited Pleasantville grapevine was spreading a rumor actually based in truth.

The old saying about the truth hurting had never been more appropriate. In this particular case, the truth made her ache. She'd never completely gotten over the shock and hurt of that life-altering moment when her childhood illusions had shattered and her mother's saintly image had become all too human.

"Don't leave."

She turned her attention back to the amazing stranger. He didn't plead, didn't cajole or coerce. He simply stared at her, all gorgeous intensity, tempting her with his smile and the heat in his eyes.

"I have to go somewhere. I'm only in town for today." She wondered if he heard the anger and hurt in her voice. Did he see her hands shaking as she watched the audience inside the doorway of the Tea Room grow and expand?

Then, perhaps *because* the audience in the doorway was expanding, or perhaps because she simply wanted to know if he'd really kissed as well as she'd thought, she leaned up on her toes and slipped a hand behind the stranger's—Jack's—neck.

"Thanks, Jack, for giving me one pleasant thing to remember about my visit back to this mean little town." His lips parted as she pulled him down to press a hot, wet kiss to his mouth. She playfully moved her tongue against his lips, teasing and coaxing him to be naughty with her.

He complied instantly, lowering his hands to her hips, tugging her tightly against his body. The kiss deepened and somewhere Kate heard a shocked gasp.

As if she cared.

Finally, dizzy and breathless, she felt him let her go. Somehow, a simple "Up-yours" to the occupants of the Tea Room had turned into a conflagration of desire. She found it hard to stand. Her whole body ached and she wanted to cry at the thought of not finishing what she'd so recklessly restarted.

"I'll be seeing you, Kate," he promised in a husky whisper.

And somehow, not sure why, she felt sure he was right.

AFTER SHE GOT IN her SUV and drove away, Jack stood on the porch for several moments. He ignored the people exiting the Tea Room—his mother's cronies who'd probably already called her. And the men staring unabashedly from the barber shop—his late father's buddies who probably wanted to change places with him.

They'd all watched while he'd done something outrageous. He'd seen a chance, seen something he wanted, followed his instincts and kissed a beautiful stranger. In his years playing the male/female sex/love game, he'd never done something so impulsive. Yeah, he'd probably had a few more women in his life than the average guy. But he'd never been as deeply affected by one, just from a heated stare across a nearly deserted street.

Jack still had the shakes, remembering the feel of her in his arms, the way she'd tilted her supple, firm body to maximize the touch of chest to chest, hip to hip. Man to woman. Her dark eyes had shone with confusion, but had been unable to hide the unexpected flare of passion. "Kate," he whispered out loud.

He felt no sense of urgency to go after her since he knew who she was. As soon as she'd said her name, he'd remembered her face from the picture in the Chicago paper a few weeks ago.

He hadn't read the article, and couldn't remember much—only that she owned some trendy new women's store on the Magnificent Mile. But he definitely remembered her face, and her name—Katherine…Kate—because, with her thick, dark hair she'd reminded him of an actress of the same name. Kate Jackson? No…but something like that. He couldn't place the last name yet, but he felt sure he would.

What on earth she was doing in Pleasantville he couldn't fathom. But tracking her down really shouldn't pose much of a problem at all. A scan of the newspaper's Web site archives and he'd be able to find the article easily enough.

His return to Chicago tonight couldn't come soon enough.

KATE DIDN'T PLAN to spend much time in her mother's house. Edie had packed up everything she really wanted when she'd moved to Florida a few weeks back. The place was immaculate, the cabinets emptied and the furniture covered. All Kate had to do was go through her own personal belongings and load what she wanted to keep into her SUV for the drive back to Chicago.

There wasn't much. Edie was a practical person, not an overly sentimental one. So there weren't scads of toys or Kate's first-grade papers to sort through. Just some precious items. Family pictures. Her first doll. The stuffed bear her father had given her for her sixth birthday—that was a month before he'd been killed in an accident involving his truck.

She carefully packed a carton with those things, rubbing the worn fur of the bear, remembering how she'd once been unable to sleep through the night without it curled in her arms. Leaving it behind when she'd left town had been an emotional decision, not a logical one. She'd left to escape her childhood, to escape the burden of her family name and the sadness over her mother's situation. She'd left everything that might connect her to this place, telling her mother over the years to feel free to get rid of her old stuff. Thankfully, Edie never had. She'd known exactly what to keep. And, judging by the absence of most of her high school junk—with the exception of the programs from plays in which Kate had appeared—what to throw away.

When she'd nearly finished, Kate noticed the old Arturo Fuente cigar box in the corner of her old room. Opening it, she felt a smile tug her lips as she saw two diaries, an empty pack of cigarettes, the stub of a burned-down candle. Even the tattered, musty *Playgirl*. Surely her mother hadn't opened this box—the magazine would have been long discarded, otherwise.

The memory of prom night descended with the impact of a boulder on her heart. That night had marked the end of teenage illusions. It had enforced adult consciousness, made her see her mother as a woman not merely a parent. Over the years she'd come to accept that moment as something everyone had to go through. While she'd been deeply disappointed, it hadn't affected her strong feelings for Edie. She loved her as much now as she ever had. And, deep down, she was thankful for having learned the valuable lesson about the fickleness of relationships and the heartbreak of love by seeing what her mother had gone through. It had saved her from ever having to experience it firsthand.

"Glad you got out, Mom. Now, find some great retired guy down in Florida and grab yourself some happiness."

Flipping idly through the *Playgirl,* she cast a speculative glance at the centerfold. "Not bad." She liked her men long and lean, though not hairless and smooth-chested like this guy. Though flaccid, he definitely had a decent package, reminding her that it had been a long time since she'd had sex. She'd been surrounded by fake penises of all shapes, colors and sizes for so long, she hardly remembered what a real one looked like.

"No big loss," she mused out loud, still staring. She hadn't been kidding when she'd told Armand a small, clean vibrating one was her preference these days. She enjoyed sex. But it seemed to be an awful lot of work for an orgasm she could give herself in five minutes flat. Okay, so she'd never stayed with a man enough to really fall in love and couldn't judge how "making love" compared to sex. Frankly, deep down Kate suspected she would *never* fall in love—since love would have to involve trust and vulnerability. She wouldn't allow anyone to make her vulnerable, not after seeing what it had done to her mother for a couple of decades.

So sex it was. And sex alone had suited her fine for some time now. As a matter of fact, her favorite new toy—and a hot seller at her store, Bare Essentials—was a tiny vibrator that snapped to the end of her finger and handled things quite nicely. Small enough to carry in a tiny case in her purse, it was safely hidden in a side pocket right at this very minute.

She might just have to dig out her small friend tonight at the hotel. An orgasm would help blow off some tension. Though it had been a long time since she'd had sex with a man—more than a year...okay, *two*—Kate certainly hadn't lacked for orgasms. "A woman owns her orgasms," she told the photo. "She can take them anytime she wants and doesn't need to be gifted with them by some guy with a big dick, a little brain and no heart."

Though, she had to admit, sometimes the real thing could be awfully nice. She closed her eyes, thinking of her day. Of Jack. Definitely not a little brain, judging by his quick wit and self-confidence. His friendly charm hinted at a man with a heart.

And, remembering the way he'd felt pressed against her body, he definitely had a big… "Snap out of it, Kate."

But she couldn't. Closing her eyes, she leaned against her old bed. She licked her lips, remembering how his tasted. She moved her hand to her breast, remembering how his chest had felt pressed against hers. She shifted on the floor, aroused again, her thoughts moving back to what she'd felt that afternoon.

She'd wanted him. Still did, judging by the hot dampness between her legs. Remembering she had brought her purse with her up to the bedroom, she reached for it, finding the zippered side pocket. Retrieving the vibrator, she snapped it onto the tip of her middle finger, and moved up onto the bed.

"Maybe it's been too long since the real thing," she said. There were benefits to sex with someone else. Touching. Deep, slow, wet kisses that curled her toes…like those she'd shared with Jack this afternoon. And she totally got off on having a man suck her breasts. Her nipples were hard now, just thinking about it. She envisioned a mouth. *His* mouth.

But her tiny friend would do for now. She moved her hand lower, down her body, under her skirt. Along the seam of her thigh-high stockings.

"Jack," she whispered as she brought the tiny, fluttering device to the lacy edge of her silk panties. "Who are you, really?"

CHAPTER THREE

A SHORT TIME LATER, after straightening herself up in the bathroom, Kate went back to work on her belongings. She grabbed the cigar box, snapped the lid closed and put it with the rest of her things. Loading everything in the car was a simple task, and she was finished a short time later.

Not even suppertime. In and out of Pleasantville in a matter of hours. A simple, unremarkable end to one long, painful chapter of her life. Well, unremarkable except for one thing. "Jack," she whispered. Did he live here in town? He must if the barber knew him. So he was best forgotten. She had no desire to get to know someone from Pleasantville. No matter how amazing a someone he might be.

Judging by what had happened in the bedroom, however, she imagined he'd be starring in her fantasies for a while. Her private interlude had done little to ease her tension. Orgasms were lovely. But she also found herself really wanting some hot and deep penetration. Unfortunately, she hadn't purchased any of the *larger* and more realistic-looking toys she sold at her store. "Might have to do something about that when I get home."

Before she left for the last time, she turned to look closer at the neighborhood. Her old street looked better than it had ten years ago. Obviously some new families had moved in. Most of the duplexes, which had once been considered the wrong side of the tracks, were neat and freshly painted. A rain-speckled kid's bike lay in front of a house up the block. Pretty flowers bloomed in the beds across the street. It appeared the lower- to middle-class residents here refused to give in to the apathy and depression that had sucked dry the downtown area. She smiled, hoping the kids growing up here walked with their heads held high.

Out of curiosity, Kate went back up to the porch to peek into the window of Aunt Flo's duplex. It was, as she expected, empty. Her aunt had hooked up with the rich man she'd always wanted and had gone off to live with him somewhere in Europe.

Good for the Tremaine sisters.

Kate got into her SUV and drove away, fully intending to drive straight out of town. There was nowhere else she needed to go. Yes, she might see a friendly face, such as Mrs. Saginaw or Mr. Otis. But, with her luck, she'd run into someone who'd greet her with a smile, then whisper about her family behind her back. As had most of the people she'd gone to high school with.

But Kate hadn't counted on one last tug of nostalgia. As she pulled off Magnolia onto Blossom, she spied the sign for the Rialto Theater. She sighed over the boarded windows and dilapidated sign. "Oh, no." The one spot in town she remembered with genuine fondness, and it had obviously gone under long ago.

Some demon pushed her right foot against the brake pedal and she brought the car to a stop. The cloudy, murky afternoon had actually begun to give way to a partly sunny early evening. Lazy late-day sunlight flickered off the broken bits of glass and bulb remaining in the old marquis. Casting a quick glance up the street, she saw no one else around. Obviously whatever was left of Pleasantville's prosperity lingered up on Magnolia. Only closed storefronts and boarded-up buildings framed the sad-looking, historic theater.

She got out of the car, telling herself she'd just glance in the giant fishbowl of a box office, but she couldn't resist going to the front door. Rubbing her hand on the dirty glass, she cleared away a spot of grime and looked in. To her surprise, the door moved beneath her hand. Reaching for the handle, she pushed on it, and the door opened easily. It seemed unfathomable to her that the graceful historic building should be left abandoned, but to leave it unlocked and unprotected was downright criminal.

She bit the corner of her lip. It was still light enough out that she could see clearly into the lobby. A ladder and drop cloth stood near the old refreshment counter, along with tools, plywood and paint cans. Someone had obviously been working.

"Curiosity killed the Kate," she muttered out loud.

Then she walked inside.

JACK WASTED A GOOD BIT of the afternoon walking around downtown Pleasantville, looking for pleasant memories. There weren't many. For a town where the Winfield family was considered royalty, he had to say he had few fond re-membrances of his childhood. His father had been mostly busy. His mother had been mostly teary-eyed. His sister…hell, he barely recognized the smiling, sweet-faced toddler in the surly blond woman.

The only real ray of sunshine from his childhood, their *maid*, had recently left Pleasantville and moved away. He wished he'd had a chance to say goodbye to Edie. Maybe he'd ask his mother if she had her new address. Then again, his mother seemed awfully skittish whenever Edie's name came up. He hoped she didn't owe the hardworking woman back wages. His mother had no conception of careful spending and was usually in debt, part of the reason his parents' marriage had been so rocky.

While he walked, he kept his eyes open for a brand-spanking-new SUV. He really didn't expect to see her. Since he knew he'd been looking Kate up when he got back to Chicago, he didn't feel it imperative to find her today. Then he glanced down a side street and saw it. Her silver car. Parked right in the open in front of the old movie theater.

Another opportunity—one too good to pass up. He headed for the theater entrance. When he saw one door was slightly ajar, he figured she'd gone inside, so he walked in, also.

Hearing some loud, off-key singing, he followed the sound through the lobby area. His steps echoed on the cracked-tile floor, the only sound other than the top-of-the-lungs belting coming from the theater. He barely spared a glance at the lobby, beyond noting that someone had been painting and cleaning up.

When he pushed open the door to enter the auditorium, he paused, figuring it would be dark and his eyes would need to adjust. Somehow, though, probably because there was repair work going on, the electricity worked. The theater wasn't dark at all down in front where work lights washed the stage with light. In the audience area, a few side fixtures made things visible.

He could see the rows upon rows of burgundy crushed-velvet seats. The thin, worn carpeting in the aisle hadn't changed; its pattern remained virtually indistinguishable after decades of wear. A pair of vast chandeliers still hung suspended over the audience—not lit, obviously. Even fifteen years ago when he'd come to see movies in this place, the chandeliers had been strictly decorative. The town was too cheap to electrify them, so they remained a sparklingly dark reminder of another era.

Finally he turned toward the stage, at the bottom of the theater, where the organist had played in the silent picture days. And he saw her. Kate. Singing as though there was no tomorrow.

Jack began to smile. Then to chuckle. He approached the stage, remaining quiet. She still hadn't seen him, so he took a seat a few rows from the front, watching her performance.

Lordy, the woman could *not* hold a tune. But what she lacked in pitch, she made up for in volume. The rafters nearly shook and he finally recognized the song. Vintage Pat Benatar. She even had the rocker's strut.

No, she couldn't sing, but damn, the woman had some moves.

"I would *definitely* like to hit you with my best shot," he murmured, knowing she couldn't hear over her own voice.

Her legs looked impossibly long beneath her short ivory skirt as she gyrated. She was bent at the waist, holding an imaginary microphone and singing into her fist. Her thick, dark hair fell forward, curtaining her face. From here, he had a magnificent view of the curve of her ass and hips as she bent lower, with parted legs, rocking on her high white heels. Then even lower, until the hem of her skirt rose higher, revealing the top of one thigh-high stocking.

Jack swallowed hard, knowing another inch or two and he'd be seeing whether Kate favored bikinis or thongs. Deciding to alert her to his presence, he prepared to stand. Before he could, however, she tossed her head back, and stood upright to finish the song. She thrust her chest forward. He shifted in his seat, watching the silkiness of her sleeveless blouse brush against the pronounced curves beneath.

When she finally finished, he simply had to applaud. She heard, obviously, and looked down toward the seats like a kid who'd been caught shoplifting bubblegum. "Who's out there?"

Jack rose to his feet, still bringing his hands together in a slow and lazy clap. "We meet again," he said as he walked down the aisle to greet her.

"Oh, no, did you hear me?" She looked thoroughly disgruntled as she narrowed her eyes and crossed her arms in front of her chest.

He climbed the steps leading up onto the stage. "Yep."

She cringed. "For your information, I know I can't sing. So don't even try to pretend you don't think I sounded like a howling female cat in heat."

Hmm. Interesting image—a female in heat. Particularly with the flush of color in her face, the sheen of sweat on her brow and the clinginess of her damp clothes against her amazing body.

She looked aroused. Sultry. Alive. He'd love to hear her purr. "You didn't sound like a cat."

"Well, then, a mutt braying at the moon," she continued with a surly frown. "Don't humor me."

"Not humoring you. Honey, you really can't sing. But, boy, you obviously know how to dance."

The compliment didn't ease her frown. Instead she practically glared. "So, are you following me? Should I worry I'm being stalked by the kissing bandit?"

"I wasn't stalking. I saw your SUV outside and came to investigate. Besides, I'm wounded. Here I thought you liked our kiss." Her cheeks flushed and she averted her eyes. *Gotcha!* He stepped closer until their bodies nearly touched. "I certainly did, and I've been thinking all afternoon about how much I wanted to see you again."

"You don't even know me."

"We could change that. Come have dinner with me, Kate."

"I'm really not hungry, thank you."

"Just coffee, then. Let's go sit somewhere and talk for hours while we pretend we're not both thinking about what happened this afternoon."

She raised a brow. "Oh, you've been thinking about that? I'd nearly forgotten all about it."

"Liar."

"If it helps your male ego to think so, go right ahead."

He laughed out loud. "I'm not an egotistical man, Kate. But I know when I'm being kissed back." He stepped closer, into her space, but she wouldn't back down. "Admit it. You *definitely* kissed me back."

"Only to give the old biddies something to chew on with their tea and crumpets," she said with a determined frown.

"Ah, ah, you're breaking my heart here." He held his hands out at his sides, palms up in supplication.

"I somehow doubt that. You're a complete stranger. One who accosted me in public this afternoon."

A definite overstatement. "Not accosted. Surprised."

"You surprised me all right. Don't guys like you usually wind up kissing a celebrity or streaking through the Academy Awards, then get committed to the funny farm sooner or later?"

He rolled his eyes. "Do you always keep your guard up? Except when you're singing your heart out in an old abandoned theater, that is?"

"Do you always go around kissing women you see on the street?" she countered.

He shook his head, becoming very serious. "Never. Not until today. Not until you."

She broke their eye contact first, suddenly looking nervous. "Look, this is probably not a great idea, us being here. I don't even know you."

"Would it help if I give my word I'm not a psycho serial killing…or serial kissing…nutcase?"

She shrugged. "If I'd thought that I woulda pushed you into the orchestra pit and run like crazy out of here."

"I'm glad to know you trust me. Now, about the coffee…"

"Don't you ever give up?"

"Not when I'm faced with something this important."

He didn't elaborate, and she didn't ask him to. They both

knew what they meant. There was something happening here, something living and warm and vibrant flowing beneath them. She just wouldn't admit it.

"I won't say I'm not tempted. But I am on my way out of town," she said slowly. "Heading home."

"To Chicago?"

She paused. "How did you…"

"Well, I know there's no way you live in Pleasantville."

"True."

"And I recognized you."

"From where?"

"I'm from Chicago, too." He saw her eyes widen. In interest? Or maybe relief? "I saw the article in the business paper a few weeks back. You own some hot new women's store, right? The picture was striking." He looked down at her body, her chest still heaving as she brought her breathing back to normal. His mouth went dry. "But it didn't do you justice."

She froze as he looked at her, probably seeing the pulse in his temple as he stared. Beneath his gaze, two sharp points jutted against her silk blouse, telling him she was as aware of him as he was of her. "I liked that picture," she said, unable to disguise a shaky tremor in her voice.

"I did, too. For a businesswoman. A Katherine." He watched as she smoothed her skirt with her palms. She then checked the waistband to be sure her blouse was tucked in. "But today, when you landed in my arms, you didn't look like a Katherine. Then…and now…you're Kate."

Almost as if she was unaware of her movements, she slid one hand up higher, up the smooth, soft-looking skin of her arm, until the tip of her finger rested in the hollow of her throat and her forearm on the curve of her breasts.

Her nipples jutted harder now, brought to tighter peaks by the scrape of her own arm across them. Did she realize it?

Was she conscious of the silently seductive invitation she issued? As if she read his thoughts, she tapped her index finger against her throat. Lightly. Drawing his gaze there once again.

"So you read about me." She sounded breathless. Clearing her throat, she continued. "My store. Is that why you followed me? Why you kissed me?"

He shook his head, still watching the pulse tick away in her throat, right beneath the tip of her finger, wondering how she tasted right there. Wondering how she smelled. Wondering if she'd whimper when he gently licked the moist spot. And mostly wondering when he'd be able to take her in his arms again. Though, this time the decision would be hers. As much as she might believe otherwise, Jack didn't believe in *taking* what he wanted. It was much more pleasurable to be given such a gift.

"I followed you because of the way we looked at each other." Like they were looking at each other now. "I kissed you because you landed in my arms." As he wanted her to now. "What can I say? You were a beautifully wrapped present and I couldn't resist. Who could resist a beautiful woman so obviously in need of a kiss?" *Like now.*

She took a tiny, step back. He let her go. Not crowding. Not encroaching.

"You let me leave. You didn't try to stop me."

He smiled. "I let you go because after you told me your name, I remembered your face and the article and knew I could find you again once I got home to Chicago."

Her eyes widened. Tap went the index finger. Tick went the pulse. Down went the heat—through his gut, into his groin.

"So you read the article?"

He shook his head, being honest. "Not really. I just remember your face, your first name and something about a store. You sell women's lotion and things?"

She chuckled, a warm and truly amused laugh that rose from her throat. "And things." Before he could question the naughty twinkle in her eye, she'd turned and looked out into the dark auditorium. "When did the Rialto close?"

He shrugged. "I'm not sure, really. I don't come back too often. But I think it was seven or eight years ago."

"You have family here?" She lowered her voice, betraying her keen interest. "You're from Pleasantville?"

Jack nodded, but didn't offer more information. He certainly wasn't about to reveal who his family was. If Kate had spent time in town, she'd know the Winfield name. The last thing he wanted was someone else bringing up his father's death. And whatever scandal the town gossipmongers had been whispering about any time his back was turned in the past few days.

Besides, he liked the anonymity of this night. It seemed right, especially here, in the old abandoned theater, so rich with atmosphere and antique glamour.

"Yeah. But, like I said, I got out years ago, as soon as I could. And I avoid coming back as much as possible."

Her rueful nod said she completely understood what he was saying. Then she smiled, a small, friendly smile that made him think for some reason she'd let down her guard. Because he'd admitted he didn't like this town?

"I used to love this building. It was my favorite place in Pleasantville." She walked across the stage, her footsteps echoing loudly on the wooden planks. "I used to come for the first showing of a new movie, then hide in the bathroom to stay and watch it again and again."

"Ah, a daredevil," he said with a laugh.

A reminiscent smile curled her lips. "The ticket taker, the old one with the poofy black wig, caught me once."

"Miss Rose?"

She nodded. "Yes! That's it. Miss Rose. She was so funny,

the way she'd talk about the movie stars, as if they were really here, living behind the screen."

"So what'd she do about you hiding?"

"From then on out I didn't have to hide—she always let me stay, but told me not to let on to anybody else." She looked down at her hands. "I'd forgotten about her."

Interesting. She looked happy and sad at the same time, as if it pained her to find positive memories about her years in Pleasantville. He could relate. Since his father's death, especially, Jack had tried to reconcile the kid Jack who'd left town with the man who'd come back.

Seeing a table right behind the partly open, red-velvet stage curtains, he pointed. "Anything interesting back there?"

Kate stepped between the curtains, and he followed her into the murky backstage area.

She picked up her purse, which was lying on the sturdy old wooden worktable beside the curtain. But, thankfully, she didn't immediately turn and try to leave. *"Flashdance,"* she said out loud, looking at a stack of papers lying on the table. "And *Dirty Dancing.* I think I actually saw that one in this theater."

"I could have guessed you liked dance movies."

She grinned. "What can I say? I can't hold a tune, but I can move to one."

"Did you take lessons?"

"Yeah, I started when I was really little, back in Florida."

"Florida? I thought you were from here."

"We moved here when I was six. After that, I took lessons when I could, before the only dance teacher in town got married and moved away."

He winced. "Don't remind me. My sister went into mourning and my mother wanted to sue the teacher for breaking her lease on the studio…just as a way to try to get her to stay."

As soon as he said it, he wished he hadn't. He still didn't want to get into any discussion about his family. Stepping closer to the table, he was easily able to distinguish the names on the old, crinkled, dusty advertisements. It wasn't completely dark back here—after all, the curtain remained open and the stage was brightly lit. Still, it felt very intimate. Almost cocooned.

"I wonder why no one ever took all these wonderful old movie posters. Look, here's Clint Eastwood."

He glanced at the title. "Don't think I've seen that one."

"*High Plains Drifter.* Not one of his most popular." She stared at the poster, looking deep in thought.

"Spaghetti western?"

"Sort of. He's a ghostly man who comes back to a horrid little town to get vengeance on the townspeople." Her eyes narrowed. "They think he's there to save them. In the end, he destroys them and rides away, disappearing into the mist."

He reached around her and pulled the poster away to see the next one. She didn't watch, appearing completely unaware of anything except the Eastwood picture, at which she still stared.

"Here's a James Bond one…from several Bonds ago."

She finally shook her head, ending her reverie, and glanced at the poster in his hand. "Sean Connery. He's still so hot."

"You have a thing for older men?"

She cast a sideways glance at him. "No." Then she studied the poster again. "I think it's his mouth. He's got the kind of mouth that makes women wonder what he can do with it." She looked at Jack's lips, looking frankly interested.

"What he can *do* with it?"

She nodded. "Some men are strictly visual. While women might like being looked at, we're more elemental creatures. Some women like to be…tasted."

Jack dropped the poster, staring intently at her. "Are you one of them? Do you like to be…tasted?" He wondered if she'd dare to answer. If the color rising in her cheeks was brought about by sexual excitement, or simply nervousness.

"Yes, I do," she admitted, her voice husky and thick.

Definitely sexual excitement.

"And you? Do you like to *taste?*" she countered.

Yeah, he *really* did. Right now he wanted to dine on her as if she were an all-you-can-eat buffet and he a starving man.

Which was exactly the way she wanted it. She, the woman, in complete control. He, the drooling male, at her feet. He wasn't sure how he knew, but there was no doubt Kate liked being the one in charge when it came to sex. Perhaps that's why she'd kissed him the second time today. As if to say, "Okay, the first one was yours. Now, here's what *I've* got."

Two could play this sultry game. He shrugged, noncommittal. "I enjoy input from all my senses, Kate. Taste, of course. Good food. Cold beer. Sea air. Sweet, fragrant skin. The salty flavor of sweat on a woman's thigh after a vigorous workout."

She wobbled on her high-heeled shoes.

"And sight, of course. I think men are focused on the visual because we like to claim things. We like to see what we've claimed. Whether it's a continent, a car, a business contract. Or a beautiful woman in a red silk teddy."

She swallowed hard, then pursed her lips. "Some women don't want to be claimed."

He touched her chin, tilting it up with his index finger until she stared into his eyes. "Some women also *think* they don't want to be kissed by strangers in broad daylight."

She shuddered. "Touché."

"I'm a sensory man. I also enjoy subtle smells." He

brushed a wisp of hair off her forehead. "Like the lemon scent of your hair, Kate. And sounds. Gentle moans and cries. Not to mention touch. Soft, moist heat against my skin."

Kate leaned back against the table, as if needing it for support. Her breathing deepened. He watched her chest rise and fall and color redden her cheeks.

"Yes, some men are definitely capable of appreciating all their senses." He crossed his arms, leaning against the table, next to her, so close their hips brushed. "So, Kate, tell me, a man who knows how to use his mouth. Is that really your *only* requirement?"

She licked her lips. "I suppose there are…other things."

"Other things?"

His fingers? His tongue? His dick, which was so hard he felt as though he was going to shoot off in his pants?

"His…" This time she ran her hand down her body, flattening her palm against her midriff, then lower, to her hip.

"Hands?" he prompted, staring at hers.

She nodded. "And one most important thing of all."

He waited.

"His brain."

Jack grinned but didn't pause for a second. "Did I tell you I graduated with honors from U.C.L.A. and have my masters in architectural design?"

She laughed again. A light, joyous laugh, considering they were having a heavy, sensual conversation about oral sex and other pleasures. He found himself laughing with her.

"I like you," she admitted, her smile making her eyes sparkle. Then she paused. Her smile faded, as if she'd just realized what she'd said and regretted saying it. A look of confusion crossed her face. It was quickly replaced by cool determination. As if tossing down a gauntlet, or trying to shock him into backing off, she tipped up her chin and said, "I mean, it's been a long time since I met a man who made me laugh and made me wet in the same sixty seconds."

Whoa. Yeah, definite challenge. Did she think she'd scare him off? Erect a wall that most men wouldn't have the guts to try to broach? He could have told her, had they known each other better, that he wasn't a man who was easily scared. And nothing turned him on as much as a woman who said what she wanted.

Holding her stare, he let a relaxed smile cross his lips, and let her have it right back. "I like you, too. It's been a long time since I've had to jerk off in the shower of my parents' house after meeting a beautiful, amazing, unattainable female."

Kate's heart jumped out of her chest and into her throat, then skipped two solid beats as she took in what he'd said. He'd answered her deliberate challenge with one of his own, without so much as a second's hesitation. Most men would have backed off, intimidated into retreat. A few would have thought about it, deciding whether or not they wanted a woman who knew what she wanted and said so. Some would have figured out a way to see if she really intended to put out. Played the standard game.

Not Jack. *He's too much. He's too much for you to handle.*

But, oh, my, how she wanted to *handle* him.

The realization surprised her. She'd thought she wanted him to back away. She'd figured her natural defense—that being a deliberately aggressive offense—would protect her as it had so many times in the past. It hadn't. Instead it had catapulted her right out of the frying pan and into the fire.

A seductive, intoxicating, all-consuming fire.

He didn't move closer, made no other suggestive comment, didn't try to kiss her or to persuade her in any way. They both knew what was at stake here. Good, hot, completely unexpected sex. A gift of pleasure from an attractive stranger.

She didn't think she'd had a more appealing opportunity in years. She'd never wanted anything so much in her entire life.

There really was no deciding.

"Now why on earth would you want to do something so terribly wasteful in your parents' shower?" His eyes widened as she reached up to touch his cheek, then pulled him close for a kiss. "And why would you possibly think I'm unattainable?"

She felt his shudder as he recognized her answer to his unvoiced invitation. To have him. To take him. To take this, now, to hell with what came afterward.

Yes. This wet kiss. This warm meeting of lips and tongue that stole her breath and rattled her senses. The touch of his hands, sliding around her waist, cupping her hip, then her bottom. He pulled her tighter against him and she ended the kiss, dropping her head back to moan at the feel of his rigid hard-on pressing insistently against the apex of her thighs.

"You're sure about this?" he asked, almost growling against her neck as he nipped at her throat, then lower, to press a hot kiss in the hollow below.

Her answer emerged from both her energized, aroused body, and also from a lonely, empty place in her heart. She wanted to be close to someone. Held by someone.

Taken by someone.

"More sure than I've been about anything in a long time."

He didn't ask again. Lifting her at the waist, he sat her up on the table and continued to feast on her neck. Her earlobe. Her collarbone. Tangling his fingers in her hair. She parted her legs, and he stepped between them, making her hiss as his big erection came directly in contact with her thin, wet panties.

He couldn't seem to stop touching her. Her arms, her thighs, her face. She was just as greedy, tugging his shirt up so she could slip her hands beneath. She felt his washboard stomach, the light furring of hair, then tugged the shirt off.

He was glorious—a woman's erotic dream, with the kind of long, lean body she'd fantasized about earlier that afternoon.

"Can I tell you something?" she asked in a hazy whisper.

"Anything," he replied, pulling her blouse free of her skirt. He began to slip the buttons open, one by one, his fingers creating intense friction as they brushed against her bare belly and midriff. She shivered, lost her train of thought and strained toward his hands. Her breasts felt heavy and full and if he didn't touch them soon, she'd go crazy.

"Tell me, Kate," he said, finishing the unbuttoning and leaving her blouse hanging from her shoulders. He glanced down at her, his eyes darkening with desire.

Kate had never felt such a fierce sense of satisfaction about her own body. She did now, though. She liked herself because of the appreciation in his eyes as he studied her. Her skirt was pulled all the way up to her hips, exposing her thigh-high stockings and her tiny white silk panties. And the curves of her breasts, barely contained in the skimpy lacy bra.

But he still didn't touch them. Didn't caress them as she wanted him to. She whimpered and leaned into his hands. Offering herself. Hissing as her nipples brushed his index finger.

He moved his palms to cup her around the ribs. With his thumbs, he lightly touched her nipples, easily visible behind the lace of her bra. Then he moved them again, a tiny flick, a taunting caress. Knowing why he waited, she admitted, "I wanted you so much earlier today, I had to…to…"

"Yes?" Another flick, too gentle. She wanted more, wanted him to push the fabric away and take her nipples between his lips and suck deeply. Her breasts were ultra-sensitive; it wouldn't take much more than that for her to come.

"Tell me," he ordered.

"I had to touch myself," she admitted.

He rewarded her with a longer stroke, sliding two fingers into her bra and taking her nipple between them. Then he stopped again. "Where?"

"In my old bed."

He chuckled lazily and resumed the all too brief flicks of thumb against nipple, accompanying the touches with tantalizing love bites to her neck. "I meant where on your body?"

She groaned in frustration. "Where do you think?"

"Here?" he asked, covering her breasts with both hands, cupping their fullness.

"Oh, finally!"

"So you did touch your breasts?"

She shook her head, desperate for more. "No, but that's exactly where I want *you* to touch."

"You've got me curious, Kate." He kissed his way down her neck, pushing her back farther on the table until she was nearly reclining. Then he moved his lips down. Over the curve of her breast. Scraping his teeth along the lace, slipping his tongue beneath it to lick her nipple.

She jerked hard, her hot core grinding against him. "Curious? You've got me ready to sing the Hallelujah Chorus!"

"Hey, no singing," he scolded, lifting his mouth from her.

"I promise," she said between harsh pants. "No singing. But please, don't stop touching me or I'll scream."

"I want you to scream," he murmured, staring down into her face, his eyes lit with passion. "I want us both to scream because it feels so good there's no other way to express it."

Finally he deftly undid her bra, tugging it away and catching her fullness in his hands.

"Have I told you yet that I'm a visual man?" he asked as he moved lower to kiss her. "I love looking at these." Then he lifted her nipple to his lips and flicked his tongue over it with exquisite precision. "And feeling them."

"Thank heaven." She clutched his hair in her hands and pulled him closer, silently ordering him to stop fooling around and to get to some serious action. He complied, sucking her nipple deeply into his mouth as he caught the other between his fingers.

She had her second orgasm of the day a minute later. It made the first one in her old bedroom pale in comparison.

"I see we're well matched. You're very sensitive here, aren't you?" he asked, continuing his sensual assault on her chest. The pleasure began to build again, before she'd come down from her orgasmic high. "But we still haven't found the spot you touched yet, have we?" He reached around to unzip her skirt.

Okay. This was good. Her nipples still tingled, but now other parts—lower parts—were ready for some action. She almost purred as he followed the path of skin exposed by the zipper, trailing his fingers down her tailbone until he slipped a hand under her panties to cup her bottom.

"Are you going to show me, Kate, where you touched?"

She nodded wordlessly, wondering how he'd stolen all thought, all will. He eased the skirt down, waiting for her to lift up so he could pull it all the way off and toss it to the floor. Then he stepped back and merely looked at her, clad only in panties, thigh-highs and strappy sandals. He looked his fill. "I'm suddenly starting to hear strains of the Hallelujah Chorus myself. I think I've died and gone to heaven."

Kate twisted and shifted restlessly, loving the way he ate her up with his eyes. Then she reached for the belt of his trousers. "Well, angel, you're not going to get your wings, until you ring my bell."

Chuckling, he pushed her hands away, undid his trousers and pushed them down. Kate bit her lip, watching through a curtain of her own hair as he pushed off his boxer briefs. When she saw his thick, erect penis spring free of them, she moaned out loud.

Vibrating fingertips just can't compare.

She found her voice. "My purse. In my purse…"

He understood what she meant. He grabbed it, handing it to her while he shucked off the remainder of his clothes. Kate dug inside, grabbing one of the small foil packets in the bottom of the bag. She saw his curious expression. "Freebies from my shop. Some stores give away matchbooks. We give away condoms."

He looked as though he wanted to question her, but she wouldn't have that. Ripping open the condom with her teeth, she reached for his penis to put it on, but had to pause, to feel the pulsing heat in her hands, to test the moisture at its tip with her fingers. *It's definitely been too long.*

But what a yummy way to get back in the saddle.

"Let me," he insisted, his voice thick and nearly out of control with need.

She did, turning her attention to her now-in-the-way panties. Pushing them off, she watched as he groaned at the sight of her. Glistening. Open and ready.

"Kate?"

"Yes?"

"Remember the discussion we had about the senses?"

Remember? She could barely remember her own name.

"I don't think I told you…I'm a visual man. But taste really is my favorite."

She only understood what he meant when he bent down and licked at her glistening curls.

Welcome her third orgasm of the day.

Before she'd even recovered from it, he stood, took her by the thighs and pulled her to the edge of the table. "Now?"

"Now," she cried, still heaving from the feel of his tongue inside her. "And, Jack? Don't even think about being gentle."

She had one moment to suck in a deep breath before he plunged into her. No hesitation. No sweet, thoughtful insertion.

Thank heaven.

He was giving her exactly what she wanted. She was being well and truly...

"Faster?" he asked when she jerked her hips harder and tugged him down for another wet kiss.

She couldn't talk, just nodded, delighting in the fullness, in the thick, hard feel of him driving ever deeper into her body. And when he finally dropped his head back and groaned with the pleasure of his own fulfillment, she greeted orgasm number four.

Definitely a personal record.

CHAPTER FOUR

IF THERE HAD EVER BEEN a time in Jack's life when he needed a bed, this was it. He wanted nothing more than to pull her body tightly against his, curl around her and languorously come back to earth after their pounding, exciting interlude. Instead he kept his hands on either side of her, holding himself above her, still connected below the waist. "You okay?"

Below him, Kate lay panting, with her eyes closed and her skin still flushed with pleasure. A sultry smile curved her lips, and he watched her pink tongue dart out to moisten them as she nodded. Though he couldn't imagine possibly having anything left in his body after exploding into hers a few minutes before, he felt a definite stirring of interest. God, she was glorious.

"Is that a gun in your condom or are you just happy to see me?"

She opened one eye and glanced down at their joined bodies.

He chuckled, again delighted by her wicked wit. "I can't seem to get enough of you. But, oh, I could use a bed. Or even a comfortable chair."

"Chaise longue," she said, a purr in her voice. "No sides."

Her suggestion definitely brought to mind some enticing images. Her, on top of him, straddling him and taking as much pleasure as she wanted. He held on to the mental picture, determined to one day make it a reality.

She wriggled beneath him, tightening herself deep inside and wringing a moan from him. "As flattering as this is, I don't think those things are reusable," she said, biting the corner of her kiss-swollen lip, trying unsuccessfully to hide a grin.

He gently pulled out of her. What he really wanted to do was grab another condom and go right back in. Make love to her slowly. Erotically. For hours. But this wasn't the time, place or soft flat surface for slow, sultry sex. *Chicago.*

"Any suggestions on where to, uh, dispose of the evidence?"

"I hadn't thought of that," she said with a giggle.

He chuckled, too. "It's been a long time since my teenage years in the back seats of cars, when this was a real issue."

"Teenage? Tsk, tsk. Don't tell me you were a bad boy."

"Actually, I was the golden boy," he replied, making no effort to hide his own disgust. "Which is why whenever I dated a girl, we'd have to go out of town if we didn't want a full report on our activities phoned in to our parents before our 1:00 a.m. curfew." Not wanting to get into a conversation about his family, he looked around backstage. "Now, I really should…"

"There." She nodded toward the workman's ladder standing in front of the partially drawn curtain. Jack followed her stare, seeing the big trash can standing nearby. Tugging his pants up to his hips, he said, "I'll be right back." He gave her a quick kiss on the lips before he walked away.

By the time he returned, after burying the used condom amid the remains of plastic, paint-speckled drop cloths and food wrappers, she was sitting up on the table, buttoning her blouse.

"So, wanna go see a movie sometime? I'm sure we could find something to do while we hide in the bathroom to sneak into the second show," he said with a grin.

She laughed again, not appearing at all nervous, having no second thoughts or regrets. He liked that, since he felt exactly the same way. Tonight was only the beginning. And he didn't regret one damn minute of it.

"I don't know if I'll ever be able to go into a theater again without thinking of this," she admitted, looking up from her buttoning to fix her brown-eyed stare on him. "I think we definitely made a memory tonight."

"Do you like making memories?"

She nodded. "I guess that's what my impromptu rock concert was all about. Throughout my childhood I'd wanted to get up on this stage. I always hoped somebody would buy it, forget about showing movies here and get down to business putting on some great plays in which I could be the star."

"Hopefully not musicals."

She responded with a light punch on his upper arm.

"I'm kidding," he said. "So, did that have something to do with why you decided to, uh, go for it with me? Not just a memory—but living out some childhood fantasy?"

"I don't know what kind of childhood you had, but I did not spend my third-grade year wanting to be stark naked, having the hottest sex of my life, on the stage of the Rialto."

He raised a brow. "Hottest of your life, huh?"

She looked away to reach for her skirt. "Well, hottest in the past year at least."

He crossed his arms. "Admit it. You haven't had sex in the past year. Have you."

Her face flushed. "How could you possibly know?"

"Let's call it a lucky guess."

"Well, what about you?" she asked as she hopped down from the table and slid her feet into her shoes. "Can I hazard a guess and say it's been a while for you, too?"

"I guess it *was* over pretty fast."

She laughed, low and sultry. "It was perfect. Exactly the way I needed it. One to blow off steam…"

"And the next one?"

She paused. Then, lowering her voice, she said, "I wish there could be a next one."

Her honesty did not surprise him. No coyness, no shyness, no flirtation, just fabulous, forthright, honest Kate. No question, she was the most intoxicating woman he'd met in years.

She bent to hook her sandals, her hair brushing Jack's naked stomach. He heaved in a breath.

"Unfortunately," she continued, apparently not noticing his sudden inability to think a coherent thought, "there can't."

That woke him up and he bent to look at her. "Why can't there?"

She straightened immediately, almost cracking the top of her head into his chin. "You want there to be?"

Seeing the look of uncertainty in her rich brown eyes, Jack immediately took her into his arms. "Yeah. I definitely want there to be. And you're right, I haven't been involved with anyone for several months. I guess you and I met each other at precisely the right moment for volcanic sexual eruption."

She raised a brow. "Lucky us."

"By the way, the movie idea, and my dinner invitation, were very real. I want to see you again, beyond more of…*this*."

She hesitated, leading him to wonder if she really was out for sex and nothing else. For some reason that thought didn't hold as much appeal as it usually would for Jack. Sex and no strings had seemed fine for him up until a few months ago.

Hell, up until today. When he'd met her eyes across a nearly deserted street.

"We'd better go," she said softly. "The workman who left this stuff might remember he forgot to lock up and come back."

Sensing her desire to change the subject, Jack let it go. The subject of what they each were looking for in a relationship could be left for another time. Kate was unlike other women he'd known. She obviously knew what she wanted and wasn't afraid—nor apologetic—about going after it. Her cool exterior and calm demeanor hid a passionate woman with a naughty streak.

"Hope he didn't come back a while ago and quietly watch."

A decidedly wicked grin curved the corners of her lips up. "Well, what's a stage for, if there's no audience?"

Yes, a *definite* naughty streak. He could hardly wait to get to know her better.

After they dressed, they left the theater and stood outside, next to her SUV. Jack hated to see her leave, though he knew he'd see her soon. "So you'll get home sometime tomorrow?"

She nodded. "And you fly home late tonight."

He wished he didn't have to go back to his mother's house to pack. The simple solution to his regret at parting from this amazing woman was to drive back to Chicago with her. But he didn't suggest it. He sensed Kate wanted some time alone to sort things out. He didn't need any alone time. He had not one single doubt about what had happened. He was fully prepared to ride out this incredible wave to see what might happen next.

"I'll call you the day after tomorrow," he assured her.

"We'll see." She turned away, looking down the silent, shadowed street. "You don't have to, you know. You didn't do anything I didn't want you to. So there should be no guilt."

"I'm not feeling guilty." He brushed a strand of hair off her brow, wishing the streetlights around here worked so she could see the sincerity in his eyes. "I'm missing you already."

She shrugged, appearing unconvinced. Leaning forward, he pressed his lips to hers. Her hands snaked around his neck, and she deepened the kiss, as if making one of her memories—this time, the feel of him in her arms. He made one, too.

"I *will* call. So can you give me your number and save me from having to dig through my neighbor's recycling bins, trying to find a month-old newspaper with your name and store address?"

She chuckled. Reaching into her purse, she pulled out a small pink card and handed it to him. He palmed it. "Thanks."

She got into her car, then lowered the window. "I had a great time tonight, Jack. Thanks to you, from now on when I think of Pleasantville, I'll have much more pleasant memories."

He leaned in to kiss her one more time. "I'll see you in two days. I promise." He watched as she drove away.

Still holding the business card in his hand, he headed back to his mother's house. He hadn't even closed the door behind him when she waylaid him in the foyer. "Where have you been? And who were you kissing? Elmira Finley called this afternoon and said you and some stranger made a spectacle of yourselves outside the Tea Room!" She paused only long enough to take a long sip of her drink. Her favorite cocktail—a glass of vodka with a thimbleful of orange juice to turn the thing a murky peach color.

He walked past her. "I wouldn't call it a spectacle."

"How could you? And who was she? Nobody recognized her."

His sister Angela entered from the living room and gave him an amused look. "So, the golden boy gets a turn as black sheep."

"Who, J.J.?" his mother stressed, ignoring Angela.

Jack glanced at the business card, which he'd tucked into his pocket. Jones. Katherine Jones. Of course. Her thick, long, dark hair and name had made him think of Catherine Zeta-Jones when he saw the picture in the paper. "Her name's Kate Jones."

The glass slid from his mother's fingers and crashed to the tile floor, shattering into several sharp pieces.

"Mother?"

She shook her head, saying nothing. Angela, however, didn't remain silent. "You've got to be kidding. Kate Jones is back here? I can't believe she'd show her face in town now."

He narrowed his eyes and stared at his sister.

"You know who she is, Jack. For heaven's sake, she's one of those trashy Tremaine women."

Jack clenched his teeth. "I don't care what her connection is to this town. She doesn't live here now, and neither do I."

"You can't mean to see her again," his mother said, sounding on the verge of tears. "Edie, her mother…"

He instantly understood. Kate was Edie's daughter. He'd forgotten all about the fact that Edie had moved home to Pleasantville as a widow with a little girl so many years ago. He'd been only a kid of eleven or twelve himself.

His instant connection to Kate sure made sense. Edie was one of the nicest people he'd ever known. "Mother, it's fine. Kate's wonderful, honest and open, like Edie. You'd like her."

Angela stepped over the broken glass until she stood next to him. "Honest? Open? Get real. How can you call the woman who'd been banging our father for twenty years honest and open?"

He narrowed his eyes. "You're on dangerous ground, Ang."

"Come on, Jack, the whole town knows it," Angela said.

"Including Mom, who, if I'm not mistaken, was happy about it. Free maid service because Edie felt so guilty, plus you got to avoid any icky sex with Dad. Isn't that what you said, Mom?"

Jack looked at his mother, waiting for her to deny it. He expected her to faint, cry or yell. She did none of these. In fact, there was only one way to describe her expression.

Guilty as sin.

"SO, HE STILL hasn't called?"

Kate looked up from her office computer screen and frowned at Armand. "I don't know who you're talking about."

He waved an airy hand. "Remember who you're talking to."

Kate smirked. "Your sexual preference is showing." Armand hated to be thought of as flaming, though he occasionally was.

"I don't really care, because for the first time in forever, we're talking about your sex life, not mine!"

"No, we're *not* talking about it." She walked past him onto the sales floor. The overhead lights were on, though they wouldn't open for an hour. Pretending she needed to check the bondage section, she busied herself counting leather masks and handcuffs. Big sellers, particularly around the holidays.

"Kate, stop pretending you don't care this guy didn't call. You've been moping for ten days, ever since you got home from Tortureville. Track the bastard down and confront him about it."

"I can't. The last words I said to him were there's no guilt, no regret, and he didn't have to call."

Armand rolled his eyes in disgust. "Well, of course, but you didn't *mean* it. Darling, all men—including the heterosexual ones—know that speech is complete bullshit."

She ignored him. "Besides, I don't know his last name."

"Stranger sex. I still can't believe you went for it."

She wished she'd never told him. But Armand was a sexual bloodhound. He could smell naughty secrets, even days later.

"So, you see, I can't track him down, even if I wanted to."

Which she didn't. Jack's silence in the past ten days spoke volumes. He knew where to find her and he hadn't looked. She'd cared at first. Too much. Then she'd reminded herself she knew what she was getting into. She could have walked away at any time, but she wanted great sex, with him, then and there. And she got it. So she couldn't now hate him for not following up on his promise to see her when he got back to Chicago.

"Please, Armand, let it drop," she said, rubbing a weary hand over her brow. "It was great, now it's done. I'm over it."

"You're such a phony, Katherine Jones," he replied. Then he stepped closer and took her in his arms, hugging her close. Kate allowed herself to be comforted, burrowing into Armand's hard, masculine chest the way she would with an older brother.

"It's really a shame you don't like women," Kate said, looking up at him. "You're funny, loyal and a total hottie."

Armand smiled, a heart-stopping smile that could make women try to reform him and gay men sit up and beg. "I *adore* women. I just don't want to sleep with them. Besides, I wouldn't want to be one of those men you push away as you close yourself up in your prickly, tough shell, keeping out anyone you think could hurt you. This way we can love each other without any sex or commitment stuff getting in the way."

"I love you, too," she said with a gentle smile, not acknowledging his probably all-too-accurate description of Kate's views on trust, love and relationships.

Before they could get any mushier, the phone rang. Kate answered, smiling as she heard her mom's voice. The smile faded as Edie told her some bad news about her Pleasantville house.

"Vandalized? How? Did the Keystone Kops do anything?"

"Sheriff Taggart assures me he'll do everything he can to catch those who did it," Edie said. "Tag's a nice young man, you'd like him. He and your cousin have apparently already met."

Kate snorted, still unable to believe Cassie had gone to Pleasantville. "Yeah, the son of a...I mean, the sheriff, gave her a ticket last night, her first night in town. Sounds like Pleasantville's as pleasant as ever to the Tremaines."

"It's not the whole town, Kate. Only a few bad apples."

"Enough to fill Mrs. Smith's pies for a decade."

Her mother tsked. "Obviously your cousin disagrees with you, since she's decided to spend the summer there."

Kate could have told her the *real* reason Cassie had gone to Pleasantville. But the cousins had agreed not to. Edie and Flo didn't need to know that Cassie was, in essence, hiding out from a troubling situation. A possibly dangerous situation.

At least Pleasantville is better than dead. Kinda.

"In any case, the real estate agent is having a handyman repaint," Edie said. "He also tells me he had a call asking if the house was available for short-term rental. What do you think?"

Kate, the accountant-at-heart, nodded. "Good idea. If you can rent it out to cover the mortgage until it sells, then do it."

After a few minutes' conversation she hung up and told Armand what had happened to her mother's house.

"What a horrid little burg," he said. "Who would paint graffiti on Edie's door? She's the nicest soul I know!"

Kate nodded, agreeing. Her mom was genuinely the nicest

person she knew. Patient and understanding. Sweet-natured, helpful and modest. All the qualities Kate had wanted as a kid—which she now knew definitely had *not* swum across that gene pool from mother to daughter. She'd tried to pretend they had, while growing up in Ohio. But the sweet, modest, quiet genes had eluded her. She had to admit it…she liked herself better now that she was free to be herself. Prickly tough shell and all.

"I can't believe Cassie's vacationing there. Couldn't she have gone *anywhere* else but Nastyville?"

Kate shrugged. Yes, Cassie could have gone somewhere else, but fate and circumstance had pointed her to Pleasantville. There was Cassie's personal situation. Edie's departure. Flo's affair and decision to give Cassie several properties in their hometown—properties left to Flo by some of her more affluent lovers. That had amused Cassie to no end. And the diaries.

Kate had mailed Cassie's diary to her immediately after her return from Ohio, and the two of them had sat on the phone for two hours one night, talking about them. They'd relived all the slights, the hurts and their infamous prom night. They'd even read over their "revenge lists." Then and there, Cassie had decided the best place to hide out was in a town that had never really seen her anyway. It made sense, in a sad, twisted way.

THEIR DIARIES were still on Kate's mind late that night when her phone rang at home. Cassie, needing a friendly voice. They talked for several minutes about the pricey house on Lilac Hill, which Flo had given Cassie. Then Kate asked the inevitable. "So, did you go by Pansy Lane today?"

When Cassie went silent, Kate sighed. "You saw."

"Yeah. Your mom called, and I went to see how bad it was."

"And?" When Cassie hesitated, Kate said, "Come on, Cass, do you think I'll be shocked by anything the people there do?"

"It's pretty bad. Horrible, ugly words, spray-painted across the front of your mom's house." Cassie gave a humorless chuckle. "And a few for Flo's house, just for good measure."

Kate muttered an obscenity. "I'm thinking Pleasantville could really use a High Plains Drifter," she muttered. "Mom says the agent's going to have the damage fixed. Let's talk about something else. Tell me how it's going for you."

Cassie chuckled. "Did I tell you about the other building Flo gave me? It was Mr. McIntyre's shop on Magnolia."

Kate gasped. "McIntyre's? No way! I never knew Flo was involved with Darren's father. No wonder Mrs. McIntyre hated us. I guess that's why the men's shop closed down."

Kate should have expected what came next. Cassie had come up with the crazy idea to give Kate the building to open a store, a Bare Essentials, in Pleasantville! She laughed, loudly, as her cousin launched into reasons why it was a good idea.

They lightheartedly argued about it for a few minutes then Cassie said, "And besides, it's right downtown. Right next door to the Tea Room. Are you following me here?"

While they kept discussing it, Kate's mind was somewhere else. Thinking of Edie. Of the vicious words that day in the Tea Room. Of the spite. Of the silly Clint Eastwood poster. Of the big overstock she had piling up in the backroom of her store, because of the going-out-of-business sale of a sex toy supplier from Texas. Of a big empty building and storefront, which, Cassie said, needed only a little elbow grease to get it ready to open. Which Cassie wanted to provide, if only to keep from going crazy with boredom. She thought of the cute girl she'd met in the nail salon, who'd longed for something to happen.

Mostly, she thought of Cassie. Alone, a sitting duck, in a town that didn't care a rat's ass for any of them and wouldn't lift a finger to help if her trouble followed her to Ohio.

Cassie urged, "Come on, Kate. Opening a porn shop in Pleasantville. It doesn't get better than that."

Kate rolled her eyes. "Bare Essentials is not a porn shop. But you're right, it sure would cross number one off my revenge list, wouldn't it?" Then she chuckled. "And some of the Winfields are still in town to get even with, right?"

Cassie obviously understood. She knew what had happened on prom night, just as Kate knew what had happened to Cassie. They'd shared their most anguished secrets one night a few years ago over a bottle of cheap tequila and an entire key lime cheesecake. Then Cassie gasped. "Oh, I can't believe I forgot. Did your mom tell you someone wants to rent her house?"

"Yeah. I guess *if* I come back to town, I'd better ask her not to so I'll have someplace to stay."

"Don't be silly. You can stay with me. It's too late, anyway, your mom told me she heard from the renter today. It's J. J. Winfield. He's renting her place in a couple of weeks."

Kate reeled. J. J. Winfield was going to be living in her mother's house? Why would he stay on the *seedy* side of town when his family lived on the sunny one? "Impossible!"

"Swear to God. Your mom seemed really touched by it."

Kate wasn't surprised her mother hadn't called her back to tell her. Kate had never admitted knowing about her affair, but Edie knew she couldn't stand the Winfields, anyway.

Kate suddenly saw an opportunity. Mayor John Winfield was gone, but there would soon be another John Winfield in Pleasantville. Could she possibly get vengeance on the late Mayor Winfield through his son? Seduce him, break his heart, get some serious payback on behalf of the Tremaine women?

She wondered if she could really go through with it. Physically, yes. Kate wasn't vain. But she knew something about sex and seduction. It was her stock in trade. So yes, she could do it. It was the emotional part she worried about.

But men did that kind of thing every day, didn't they? Look at what had happened to her in good old Pea-Ville ten days before. A man had taken what he wanted—admittedly giving her some pleasure, too—and walked away without a single word since. Hurting her. Though, damn it, she'd never admit that to anyone!

Her decision was easy. With a few shipments of goods, and some vacation time this summer, she could look out for Cassie, give a major screw-you to the old guard in Pleasantville…and seduce and break the heart of the son of the man who'd broken her mother's. Throw in a humiliating moment for Darren and Angela, and she'd make all her teenage dreams come true.

"Cassie," she finally said, knowing her cousin awaited her decision. "Do you think Flo would let me stay in her old place?"

CHAPTER FIVE

JACK COULD HAVE CHOSEN the master bedroom when he moved into Edie Jones's house. Since he'd be in town for at least a month settling his father's tangled financial affairs, he probably should have made himself comfortable in the larger bed. He didn't, for several reasons, but mostly because of the image of his own father—and Edie—in it. He shuddered at the thought.

He still couldn't believe it. His father and Edie had been lovers for two decades. He hadn't just taken Angela's word; his mother had admitted it. That was when he'd decided he couldn't stay in his parents' house during his trip home this summer.

Most sons would probably have felt as much anger toward Edie as toward his father. Jack felt only pity and regret for the woman, who'd been the kindest part of his boyhood. His parents' marriage had been as convoluted as his father's finances, and Edie had been a victim more than anything else. Looking through his father's records, it became obvious the pittance he'd left Edie in his will didn't come near to covering her paychecks, some of which she hadn't cashed over the years.

His family owed Edie something. Staying here, fixing up her house, doing repairs and maintenance so she could sell the place and make a new life for herself, was the least Jack could do.

"Sleep, Jack." He glanced at the clock, which showed the hour had moved past one. Sleep proved elusive here, especially because Kate had told him how she'd spent her last afternoon in this house. Lying on her bed. Thinking of him. Touching herself. "Knock it off, moron," he said. He couldn't allow himself to think about Kate. Not until he'd figured out how to make up for the damage his parents had caused to her and her mother.

"God, I'm sorry," he muttered. Sorry for Edie, who, he'd learned, had been ridden out of town like a scarlet woman by the old guard of Pleasantville. Sorry for Kate, who'd grown up in this tiny house, on Edie's small income, made smaller by his parents' selfishness. Sorry for himself, because what he wanted more than anything was to find Kate and to tell her how hard he'd fallen for her on the day they'd met, just over a month ago.

But he couldn't. His family had done enough to hurt the Jones women. Until he could find some way to right the wrong, he couldn't let himself see Kate again.

It had been impossible to stay away from her. He'd been drawn to her, easily locating her store on Michigan Avenue. Twice he'd watched her from outside, trying to figure out how to go in and face her. The second time he'd had his hand on the door handle, prepared to go inside. Then he'd seen her in the closed shop in the arms of a tall, dark-haired man. He'd driven away, never finding out whether the guy had been friend or lover. But the image of her with another man had given him some long, sleepless nights.

Like now.

He closed his eyes again, determined to sleep, then opened them as he heard a noise through the wall. A bang. A low curse. Both came from next door, inside what should have been the *empty* half of the duplex, which belonged to Edie's sister.

"Son of a bitch." Jumping up, he grabbed some sweat-pants and ran downstairs, figuring the vandals had returned.

Whoever the vandals were, they weren't very smart. The front door to the adjoining unit was wide open. He easily made out the beam of a flashlight moving around upstairs. Ready to transfer all his unexpended sexual energy into some violence against the intruders, Jack took the stairs two at a time. In the upstairs hall he turned toward the room directly beside the one in which he'd been lying next door. As he burst in, the beam of a flashlight, held by a dark-clothed person, swung toward him.

"Stop right there, you rat bastard," Jack snarled as he tackled the person and took him to the floor.

"Ow, get off me!"

A female voice had spoken. Definitely a soft, curvy female body cushioned his against the hard floor. A mass of thick, dark hair spilled across his hands and brushed against his bare chest. Catching the achingly familiar sweet scent of lemon, he knew even before he saw her who it was. "Kate?"

The flashlight thunked as it rolled out of her hands, swinging around to shine on her face.

She stopped struggling beneath him and stared up, finally recognizing him in the shadowy darkness. "Jack?"

"I'm sorry." He rolled off her. "Did I hurt you?"

She sat up, sucking in deep breaths, but didn't answer. When Jack reached toward her, to make sure she was real and all right, she flinched away as if she couldn't bear his touch.

He probably deserved it. He couldn't imagine what she'd made of his silence since their meeting. "Are you all right?"

"I'm fine," she finally answered, her voice shaky and her breathing still shallow. "What are *you* doing here?"

"I could ask the same of you."

"This is my aunt's house. She knows I'm here, she told me I could stay for a while."

Kate staying right next door? Sleeping in this room, directly next to the one where he'd be sleeping? Moving around in this house behind one all-too-thin wall so he'd be able to hear her sigh in her sleep or step into the shower?

God help him.

"Now, answer my question, Jack. Why are you here in the middle of the night?" She glanced down, as if just noticing his bare chest and loose sweats. Her eyes immediately shifted away, but not before he saw her lips part so she could suck in a deep, shaky breath.

"I'm staying here."

She jerked her attention back to his face. "Staying? *Here?*"

"I mean, next door. I'm renting the duplex next door." He paused. "Your mother's place."

"My mother's…wait, you know my mother?" She paused. "You know who I am?"

"Yes. To both questions."

"How? And what do you mean, you're renting Mom's duplex? That's not possible. You can't be living in her house."

"You didn't know she'd rented it out?"

"Well, of course, but to J. J. Winfield…" Her voice softened. Even in the low lighting provided by the flashlight and the moon shining in through the bare front window, he saw her cheeks go pale and her mouth drop open. "Oh, no. Tell me your name is not J. J. Winfield."

He shook his head, sending a bolt of relief shooting through her body. "No, it's not." Her relief quickly disintegrated when he continued. "No one except my parents and your mother have called me J.J. since I was a teenager. I go by Jack now."

Kate couldn't breathe. Couldn't think. Certainly she couldn't speak. The man she'd had fabulous sex with in the theater several weeks ago was J. J. Winfield—the son of

Mayor John Winfield? The man she'd come back to town to seduce and to destroy was the one who'd already hurt her so badly by breaking his promise to call after their amazing encounter? She covered her eyes. "This is a nightmare."

"Kate, I'm sorry, I had no idea you were coming back to Ohio. Your mother never mentioned it."

She didn't know which was worse. That he was here and she had to face her inattentive lover, or that he was John Winfield Junior. Somehow, the memory of all those long, silent, lonely weeks since she'd seen him last seemed the more devastating now.

"No, of course you didn't know I was coming."

Her mother couldn't have told him, because even *she* hadn't known. Kate and Cassie hadn't told Edie because Kate knew her mother too well. She'd be on the first plane back here if she thought Kate was coming to stay in town.

Cassie was one thing—everyone in the family knew Cassie could take care of herself. With her looks, brains and her self-confidence, Cassie had never really had to rely on anyone for anything. Except love and loyalty, which the Tremaine women were always quick to provide to one another.

But, to Kate's eternal annoyance, her mother seemed to think Kate was too easily hurt, too vulnerable, and in need of protection. Which really sucked when she wanted people to see a hardworking, intelligent, kick-ass businesswoman. Not the girl who'd cried into her teddy bear after so many childhood hurts, the girl who'd hidden in her tree house and made up stories about how her father hadn't really died and would one day come back.

Not the girl who'd been dumped on prom night.

Jack couldn't have heard about her return from anybody else, either. Kate and Cassie had been careful to keep their plans quiet, to avoid the inevitable protests and backlash. She was sure many people had known Cassie had been working in the old storefront for the past three weeks, preparing to open a ladies' shop, but not the exact *nature* of the ladies' shop.

"No, you couldn't have known I'd show up. You never would have stayed here, in this house, had you known," she said. "Because, you couldn't very well avoid me if we were practically roomies. And obviously, you had no intention of seeing me again. Right?" She couldn't keep the accusation out of her voice. She wondered if he heard the tinge of hurt there, too.

She waited for him to run the usual male line. *I meant to call you, babe, just lost your number…forgot to pay my phone bill…broke my dialing finger…was sent away on a deadly, top-secret government mission.*

"I should go," he said, not even acknowledging her justified anger.

His lack of response angered her even more. He couldn't even *attempt* to make up a lame excuse? He wasn't going to be courteous enough to give her the chance to tell him what she thought of him? Wasn't going to try to sweet talk her so she could tell him he could touch her again when hogs started flying over Pleasantville, leaving the appropriate droppings right down the middle of Magnolia Avenue?

That wasn't how the game worked. Uh-uh. No way was he getting off so easily. "Oh, sure, I know you must be a busy man. Too busy to even, oh, I dunno, pick up a phone once in a while?"

"Kate…"

"What, Jack? You expect me to be like your Lilac Hill girlfriends? Like your sister, *Angela?*" She spat out the name, not caring if he heard her dislike. "I'm supposed to be brushed off quietly, like a lady, not bring up the fact that I'm *unhappy* you lied?"

"I didn't lie..."

"You shouldn't have promised, Jack. You shouldn't have made a big deal out of swearing you'd see me in two days. I was willing to let it end right then and there outside the Rialto. But you had to be Mr. Noble, Mr. Good Guy. You made me think of what happened as something more than it was. You hurt me and, damn it, you have no business hurting me!" To her horror, she heard her voice break. If one tear fell down her cheek, she mentally swore she'd poke her own eye out.

"Kate, honey, I'm sorry. Listen..."

"Forget it," she snapped. "Forget I said anything."

"I thought about you all the time," Jack said, his voice low and throaty in the near darkness. "But things got...complicated."

She snorted. "Complicated. Uh-huh." She started to rise. "Look, I don't really care. You shouldn't have said you wanted to see me again if you didn't plan to, that's all." Swallowing hard, she continued. "We're both adults. We both knew it didn't mean anything."

Her words seemed to anger him. He grabbed her wrist and held her, not letting her get up beyond her knees. "Like hell. It meant a lot, Kate, and you know it."

His green eyes sparkled with intensity in the near darkness, and she could almost believe him. Then she remembered his name. His lineage. And knew she could never trust a word that came out of his heartbreaking mouth.

"No, *Mr. Winfield.* It didn't mean anything more than any other sexual encounter between two strangers." She jerked her arm away, stood and brushed off her jeans, wincing as she realized he'd knocked her hipbone right into the floor with his tackle. It already ached.

"We're not strangers." He stood, as well, standing so near she could feel his warm breath against her hair. She bit her lip, trying not to look at him, trying not to remember the feel of his hot, hard chest pressing against hers. Trying to erase the mental picture of him standing above her, his face filled with need and passion, as he thrust into her while she lay on the table at the Rialto.

"We recognized something in each other from the minute our eyes met," he continued. "That's never happened to me before."

From out of the near darkness, she felt his hand move to her cheek. She pushed it away. "Back off, J.J. Don't touch me."

"Ouch. I don't know which is worse, hearing you tell me not to touch you, or hearing you call me J.J. Please call me Jack." His voice moved lower. She realized he'd bent to pick up the flashlight only when he brought it up and shone it on them both.

The light looked pretty damn good on him. His chest. His tousled, right-out-of-bed hair. His thick, muscular arms and broad shoulders. His green eyes, not twinkling with humor now, but dark and confused. His mouth…

She gulped, then crossed her arms in front of her chest, looking for a defense mechanism when there was really none to be found that could halt her physical attraction to him. Finally she said, "What kind of stupid nickname is Jack, anyway?"

"What?"

She knew she sounded like a belligerent kid, but couldn't help herself. Sarcasm was her only defense. "I mean, come on, aren't nicknames supposed to *shorten* your real name? Like Kate instead of Katherine? What genius decided to change a four-letter word like John into a four-letter word like Jack?" *Four-letter word being the operative phrase, here.*

She saw his lips turn up as he shook his head and gave a rueful chuckle.

"Oh, I amuse you now? You break in here, tackle me, almost break my back..." *Almost break my heart...* "And now you're laughing at me?"

"No, I'm actually agreeing with you. It doesn't make much sense, does it? But anything's better than J.J."

"So what's wrong with plain old John? It's good enough for your average, everyday toilet, isn't it?"

"Ouch. You're really pissed."

She clenched her jaw, mad at herself for letting him see her anger, which he would rightly assume had to have evolved out of hurt. She took a few deep breaths, trying to regain control. Where was her infamous control? *Gone, baby. Gone for weeks, since that kiss on the steps of Mrs. McIntyre's Tea Room.*

Finally she forced a shrug. "No, I'm not, not angry at all." A strained laugh emerged from between her clenched teeth. "I'm just tired and cranky from getting knocked on my rear by a six-foot-tall man in the middle of the night."

"I'm so sorry about knocking you down. I had no idea it was you moving around over here. I was afraid someone had come back to cause more problems for your mother. I told her I'd look after the house for her. Both houses, actually."

"Why would you do that?" she asked, still not able to comprehend him being here. "Why would you, a mighty Winfield, care what happens to your trashy Tremaine maid's house?"

He stepped closer, holding her chin and forcing her to look up at him in the semidarkness. She remembered, suddenly, how tall he was. How petite and feminine he'd made her feel.

Their bodies were only inches apart and she could smell his musky, clean scent, and feel warmth radiating from his hard, bare chest. Her body reacted instinctively, getting hot and achy. Her nipples felt incredibly sensitive against the cotton of her sleeveless tank top, and her jeans were suddenly uncomfortably snug. She wanted nothing more than to taste him. All over.

"Your mother was the nicest person I knew growing up," he said, his voice thick with emotion. "And I hated to hear what this town had done to her because of my father."

Kate's eyes widened. Did he know? Could he possibly know about Edie's affair with the mayor? She took a deep breath and carefully asked, "Your father?"

He let go of her face, walking over to stare out the undraped window at the shadowy front lawn. "My father left her a small amount of money, when by rights he owed her more." He cleared his throat and shook his head. "A *lot* more. As usual, the town looked for scandal and decided to crucify her with spite and innuendo because of it."

No. He didn't know. He didn't understand the truth. Kate, Cassie and Edie were still the only ones who knew the Pleasantville gossipmongers really had the story right.

And that's the way it was going to stay.

"Okay, you liked her. You wanted to help her. Why does that equal you living here, in her house, instead of with your mother and Angela at your family's place?" Her voice dripped dislike. "Don't tell me you're not one big, happy, rich Winfield family?" She could tell by the look in his eyes, and the way his jaw clenched, that he was mentally arguing over how to answer. "Come on, Jack, what's the story?"

Finally his eyes shifted away from her face and he muttered, "You know my father died only a few months ago."

She bit the corner of her lip, trying hard to remember Mayor Winfield had actually been someone's father. Swallowing her dislike, she murmured, "Yes, I know. I'm sure that's been painful for you."

"It's been difficult. I never realized..."

"What?" she prompted.

"I don't know. How much I cared about him, I guess?" He gave a sad laugh. "How much I'd miss him, even as I find out day by day how very little I knew him."

Having lost her dad at a young age, Kate could understand that feeling of wishing she'd had a chance to know a parent. "I'm sorry, Jack. I know how it is to lose your father."

"I know you do. You were a kid when you lost yours, right?"

She nodded. "Six."

He shook his head. "Awful. Your mom was so young to be a widow." He lowered his voice. "And she never remarried."

No, Edie had never remarried. She'd instead wasted decades on a man who was married to someone else. Kate rubbed a weary hand over her brow. "No. But we're talking about your father."

"Yes, we are," Jack replied. "He left a mess behind him." *More than you could possibly know.*

"I told my mother I'd come help her out this summer, sell some real estate, get some paperwork taken care of."

"And you can't do that on Lilac Hill?"

"I'm a grown man, Kate. Can you picture me living in my mother's house for a month, being scolded not to let my shoes scuff up her tile floor, and to be careful not to rumple the plastic on the sofa in the parlor?"

She couldn't help it. She burst into laughter. "She has plastic on the sofa?"

A faint smile crossed his lips. "Yeah."

"Does it ever come off?"

He shook his head.

"Not even if the First Lady came over?"

"Well, maybe the current one. But definitely not a Democrat. And certainly it wouldn't come off for me!"

Suddenly his childhood sounded less golden than she'd

always imagined. "Sounds like you were the classic poor little rich kid."

"I did okay. Thankfully, your mother was around a lot."

Kate's smile faded. Yeah, her mother had been around the Winfields a lot more than he knew. She wondered what he'd think about that.

In her heart she knew it would hurt him, just as it had hurt her to learn a parent she loved really hadn't been perfect. Maybe if she were a vindictive person…or maybe if Jack weren't already mourning his father's death…she'd have told him. As it was, she simply couldn't. No matter what he'd done to her, no matter how much his broken promises had hurt her, she couldn't repay him with that kind of spite.

His sister was much better at that, she recalled.

"Anyway, I wanted to be on my own," he continued. "There aren't a lot of furnished short-term rentals around. Your mom seemed happy to let me stay here for a month. End of story."

Kate sensed it wasn't really the end of the story, but she was too tired to think about it tonight. She still hadn't quite absorbed the fact that she was here, back in Pleasantville, this time not only for an afternoon, but for weeks.

And Mr. Gorgeous was her next-door neighbor. Oh, joy.

"You need to leave," she finally said, wanting him out of here before she did something terribly stupid. Such as kick him, kill him. Or even worse, kiss him. "I'm tired and I want to go to sleep."

He looked around the empty room. "Uh, where?"

"I brought a sleeping bag for tonight."

"The power's not even on and it's hot as blazes in here. You'll roast."

"I'll be fine. Just go, please? I'm really beat, it was a long drive from Chicago."

He turned to leave, then hesitated. "Look, your mom's furniture is all still in her house. Why don't you stay over there tonight? It'll be more comfortable than the floor."

Stay there? With him? And give him another chance to use her again? *Do I have I'm A Sucker stamped on my forehead? No, thanks, mister.*

Then she thought about her revenge plan, one of her main reasons for coming back here. Hadn't she intended all along to get involved with J. J. Winfield? Seduce and destroy. Entice and evade. It appeared he was handing her the prime opportunity to do exactly that.

But that was with J. J. Winfield. The spoiled, weak, pale and pasty-faced J. J. Winfield she'd pictured in her mind for so long. Not Jack. Definitely not golden-haired, laughing-eyed Jack with the strong hands, the perfect mouth and the big…

"What do you say, Kate? Just for one night." He raised a brow and gave her a wicked smile. "It could be fun."

One night. One more night like the one they'd shared at the Rialto? She might never survive it. Though, there was no doubt in her mind she'd love every minute of it. Every deep, sweaty, hot, pounding, orgasmic minute of it.

Get your mind out of your pants, Kate! This man could hurt her. She was already too vulnerable to him, too attracted to him. Damn it, she already liked him too much. Or at least she had before she'd decided he was a creep and a user. Another interlude with Jack and she might find herself forgetting she wasn't allowed to like him anymore. She could be the one with the broken heart if she followed through on her seduction idea.

No, there had to be another way—a less dangerous way—to even the score with the Winfields. One that wouldn't risk her own emotions. Emotions she'd become quite adept at protecting over the years. After all, with the examples set by women in her family, emotional self-preservation was a requirement. Nobody else looked after a Tremaine woman… except a Tremaine woman.

"I'll be fine. I can open a window."

"What about the vandals?"

She shrugged. "My mother told me the sheriff caught the kids who sprayed her house. They'd apparently hit a lot of other houses in town with the paint cans, and now they're doing five hundred hours community service each."

"Good. Still, you don't need to stay here. Come on, it makes sense. Your mom's place is furnished, and lit. Aren't you achy from your drive? Don't you feel like taking a long shower?"

"I know what you do in showers," she snapped, remembering his comment from the theater.

He thought about it and chuckled. "I just moved in today."

"Doesn't take too long for some men."

"Zing. Was that another comment about how quickly it was over the first time?"

Quick? Ha! In her memory she could *still* feel him making love to her. Riding her, filling her, rolling orgasm after orgasm over her body. She'd felt him inside her for weeks.

"No," she finally replied. "And I think you mean *only* time. First implies there could be a second." *Or a twentieth.*

But there wouldn't!

He ignored her comment. "I promise the shower's clean, Kate. As for anything happening between us…"

She waited, wondering if he'd make some flirtatious, sexy suggestion that they pick up where they'd left off weeks before. If he did, she'd have to kick him, she really would.

He shook his head. "Don't worry. Strictly platonic."

She found herself wanting to kick him anyway.

As if his silence in the past weeks wasn't bad enough, now he'd basically admitted he didn't want her even though she'd practically fallen right back into his arms? She hated to admit it, but her femininity took a definite hit.

"Well, maybe a shower would be nice," she mused out

loud, suddenly wanting some payback, wanting to remind him what he was missing out on. She tilted her head from side to side to work out some imaginary kinks in her neck, then raised her arms above her head to stretch. Arching her back so her breasts pushed tight against the cotton tank top, she hid a look of satisfaction as Jack stared, long and hard.

"Okay," he finally said, his voice low and shaky. "Do you need any help with your stuff? A suitcase?"

"No, thanks. I'll only need my purse and my toiletry case." Some devil made her add, "I don't wear anything to bed, anyway."

He closed his eyes.

"It'll be funny, going back to sleeping in my old room for one night. At my place in Chicago, I have a huge California King bed." *Liar.* She had a queen. "With black satin sheets." *Double liar.* They were percale. And pink.

Rather than looking even more hot and bothered, as she'd hoped, Jack gave her an amused look. Finally he said, "Sorry, Kate, your room's taken. 'Fraid you'll have to take the master bedroom…or the foldout."

"You're staying in my room? Why?"

He nodded. "You're not the only one who remembers everything we talked about that night at the Rialto."

She didn't follow.

He stepped closer, invading her space again so their bodies were separated by only a bit of air and moonlight. "You might know what I do in the shower," he whispered, reaching out to scrape the tip of one index finger along her shoulder, playing with her bra strap, which had somehow slipped out. His touch made her shake and she could barely keep herself focused on his words.

"But I also remember what *you* did in your old bed."

By the time she understood, and felt hot blood rush into her cheeks, Jack had already turned and left the room.

CHAPTER SIX

OFFERING A SHOWER and a bed to a woman he couldn't have—but wanted so much his nuts ached—had to rank up there among the stupidest things Jack had ever done in his life. Maybe not as stupid as the time he'd tried bungee jumping off a bridge in California, or when he'd scuba dived with sharks in Australia, but pretty stupid all the same.

The house had only one bathroom. It was upstairs, between the two bedrooms, and he listened to every move Kate made in there. He could swear he heard a metallic hiss as she unfastened the zipper of her jeans, followed by a whoosh of air as she dropped her clothes to the floor. Then the rustling of the shower curtain as it opened, the water starting, her tiny gasp as she tested the temperature and found it too hot. Or too cold.

Jack gave up trying to sleep. Sliding closer to the wall in her small, twin-size bed, he listened intently. The gurgling rush of the water from the faucet changed to a sizzling stream emerging from the showerhead. She stepped into the tub, closing the curtain behind her. Then she dropped something—the soap? As she retrieved it, her hand knocked against the tub just inches from his head. He swallowed hard.

She began to hum. Off-key. Not Benatar now, but some other old rock tune he couldn't place.

Soon there was nothing but the pounding cascade of water, muted when her body was beneath it, harder as it struck the tub when she had stepped out of the stream to wash.

That was the hardest. Imagining her rubbing a soapy washcloth, or, better yet, her bare hand, over her skin. Easing the tight muscles of her neck. Kneading the kinks out of her shoulders. He closed his eyes and pictured the slide of her hands down her body. The way her fingers would look on her throat, her breasts, her thighs. And between them.

He shuddered. Probably the only thing he could imagine being as arousing as touching her himself would be to watch Kate's hands on her own body. Giving herself pleasure, the way she said she had here, in this very bed, a few weeks back.

He groaned and pulled the pillow over his face, dying for sleep…for release. Both thoroughly eluded him.

Her long shower continued. *Hurry up, would you?* He had a feeling he was going to need to take a cold one of his own.

Jack imagined sharing one with her. It would be incredible. He'd barely gotten to taste her at the theater and his mind flooded with images of sitting beneath her in the shower. Looking up at her. Holding her hips in his hands and tilting her soft thatch of dark curls toward his hungry mouth to taste her, indulge in her, positively inhale her.

Only after he'd had his fill would he stand up, turning her to face away while he stood behind her. She'd lift one foot, resting it on the side of the tub. He could picture her hand, flat against the tile wall for support, her red-tinted nails a stark contrast to the cream-colored tiles. Her fingers would clench then widen as he stepped closer and she felt his body press against her back, his hard-on slipping between her legs.

He'd have to touch her. He'd reach his hand around, caressing her breast, then her belly. Then lower, until he could slide his fingers into her slick crevice, testing her readiness. Pleased at how wet she was for him.

She'd bend forward slightly, arching her back, turning to look over her shoulder at him with wide, passion-filled eyes that screamed "Take me now." He'd tease her, not giving in to her demands yet, taking time to kiss the tiny little bones on her spine until he heard her whimper in anticipation.

Then he'd give her what she wanted, sliding into her from behind, slowly, until he was so deep inside her they couldn't distinguish their bodies from one another.

They'd pause, the hot water pelting them as they savored the connection. They'd be inundated with the scent of the soap and her lemon shampoo. And the thick, heady smell of sex.

She'd bend lower, tempting him with the curve of her hips and her perfect rear. The visual would join with all his other senses to overwhelm him and he'd have to move. Faster. Getting caught up in her tight heat, having to bend over her, holding her hips and driving them both into oblivion.

"Stop, you idiot," he muttered with a gasp.

He almost came in her bed. It took all his concentration to grab his last bit of control to prevent his body's reaction. Calling himself an asshole, he lay there for a few moments, thinking of prostate exams, Brussels sprouts and wrinkled geriatric patients. Anything unappealing.

It wasn't easy; it didn't help his erection subside, but he managed to avoid having to make a sneaky, middle of the night sheet change as he had a few times during puberty.

Jack couldn't remember the last time he'd come so close to climaxing just from thinking about a woman. Considering Kate was all he'd thought about for weeks, maybe it wasn't so surprising.

He still couldn't believe she was here, not only here in this house, but in Pleasantville at all. From some of the things he'd heard, Kate and the rest of her family hadn't been treated too nicely in the old days. He only hoped she wouldn't hear any of the rumors about her mother while she was in town. He knew she couldn't possibly be aware of the truth…if she were, she'd never have spoken to him once she found out who he was.

If she ever did find out, she'd hate his guts, thinking him just another snobby Winfield out to nail a trashy Tremaine.

Wrong. So wrong. He'd been fascinated by her, wildly attracted to her, dazzled by her, back when he didn't even know her name. He didn't remember another better sexual encounter in his life than the one they'd shared on the stage. Completely spontaneous, passionate, fulfilling. If her last name—or his—had been anything else, he would have spent every night since then in her bed. Guaran-damn-tee it.

And during each one of those nights, he would have worked to remove the sadness he sometimes saw in her eyes, and the anger he'd heard in her voice. Particularly tonight, next door, when her sarcasm hadn't been able to disguise her hurt.

He made it his goal, then and there, to do exactly that. But not here, not in her mother's house, in this town that sucked the soul right out of her. The only place he'd seen her truly happy, passionate and excited was at the Rialto. That was the Kate he wanted to seduce—but he had a feeling he wouldn't find her again until they returned to Chicago.

And until Jack wiped the slate clean regarding his father.

In the meantime he'd control himself, keeping his libido firmly in check. "Yeah, right," he muttered.

Just when he wondered if she was ever going to get out of the shower, he heard the water turn off. "Thank God," he muttered.

The plastic rings clinked against the metal rod as she pulled back the curtain. Then silence, for one long moment, until he heard her voice. "Jack? You awake?"

Was he awake? How could he *not* be awake when three-quarters of his blood supply was centered in his groin? It was a miracle he hadn't passed out from lack of blood flow to the brain.

"Yeah," he said. Realizing he'd spoken in a whisper, he cleared his throat. "Yeah, Kate, did you need me?"

"I don't have a towel."

No towel. Perfect.

Tempted to tell her to stay in there and drip dry—quietly—until he could get control over his raging libido, he sighed and sat up in the bed. Throwing back the sheet, which had felt cumbersome and heavy against his naked body anyway, he reached for his sweatpants. He couldn't find them.

"They're too hot, anyway," he muttered in disgust. Instead, he grabbed a pair of gray boxer briefs and tugged them on. It wasn't as if the woman hadn't seen him naked already.

They were uncomfortably tight. Too damn bad.

Walking out of the bedroom to the small linen closet out on the landing, he grabbed the top two towels on a stack and knocked on the bathroom door. "I've got two for you, just in case."

"Great. I don't have a robe, so I can wrap up in one."

Jack gritted his teeth.

"You can leave them on the counter," she continued.

Pushing the door open several inches, he reached in, intending to drop the towels and go. The shower was behind the door, no way would he see anything. He figured she was hiding in there, fully covered by the flowery plastic curtain, and certainly didn't consider trying to sneak a peek. He was already horny enough, thanks so very much. Even a glimpse at her naked body behind the curtain could have him coming in his briefs.

Jack hadn't counted on the mirror. As he dropped the

towels, he glanced up and met her eyes in the reflection. The cold air from the hall had seeped in when he opened the door. Where it met the glass, the misty steam rapidly began to evaporate. She was *not* cowering behind the curtain, probably having assumed he couldn't see her from around the nearly closed door. But see her he did.

Her brown eyes widened in her creamy pale face as their stares met in the mirror. Her lips were parted, droplets of moisture falling down her cheeks toward them. She slowly licked one away. He had to clutch the doorknob for balance.

Swallowing and taking in a deep, shaky breath, he lowered his eyes, staring at the long, wet hair that hung over her shoulders. Jack couldn't have prevented his gaze from shifting even lower if someone held a gun to his head. So he looked, seeing a few strands of hair draping her breasts, though not completely covering them. Her dark, puckered nipples were easily visible. His mouth went dry as his pulse sped up.

She said nothing, didn't make a move, just watched him watch her. He kept looking, at the curve of her waist, that wet thatch of brown curls between her slim thighs.

Then his stare shifted to her hip where a purplish bruise marred the pale perfection of her skin. "What happened to you?"

She seemed to awaken from her daze. Snatching the edge of the curtain, she pulled it over herself, until only her face was visible. He wondered what she'd do if she knew he had a perfect view of one breast and puckered nipple peeking between the leaves of two roses on the plastic curtain. He thought it wise not to point it out. "Tell me."

"You can leave now."

"I mean it, Kate, what happened to your hip? You've got a horrible bruise." He clenched his fists. "Did someone hurt you?"

Obviously seeing he wasn't going to go away until she explained, she said, "You did, you big jerk. When you tackled me earlier."

"Oh, God, I'm so sorry." Pushing the door farther, he stepped inside and turned to face her. "I didn't realize I'd injured you. Let me see it."

She didn't answer. Her attention was firmly fixed low on his body. Her lips parted as she saw the erection he couldn't hide. "I think you should go." Her voice was thin and reedy.

Seeing her injury had nearly made him forget the almost painful urge between his own legs. He could only imagine what she thought. He thrust the concern away, not caring right now if she wondered what he'd been doing in her old bedroom while she'd showered. "Let me see your hip."

She shook her head, slowly, not saying anything. But she didn't resist as he gently pulled the edge of the shower curtain from her fingers and tugged it over a few inches so he could see the side of her body. She still said nothing as he dropped to his knees to examine the reddish-purple bruise on her hipbone.

The size of his palm, it must have hurt like hell. "I'm so sorry. Can I get you some ice for it?"

"No," she whispered. "I'll be fine. Thanks for the towel."

"Why didn't you say something?"

"It's not a big deal, Jack. I'm fair-skinned, I bruise easily." Her voice still sounded shaky. "I can barely feel it."

He touched the bruise with the tip of his index finger. When she winced, he yanked his finger away. "Liar."

Then, almost unable to resist, he leaned forward to place a gentle kiss on the bruise. When she moaned, he pulled back. "Did I hurt you again?"

"No. You didn't…hurt me."

He leaned forward again to gently kiss her skin. He avoided the tender bruised area. Instead he kissed her all around it, caressing her waist, her upper thigh. Unable to resist, he moved to that vulnerable hollow of flesh between her pelvic bone and the still-concealed dark thatch of curls hiding her feminine secrets. The curtain shifted slightly, as if she'd let go of it. When he glanced up, he saw her eyes closed, her head tipped back and her hand on her throat.

"Better?"

She groaned. "You're trying to kiss it and make it better?"

He nodded, his lips still brushing her skin as he inhaled her, breathing in the smell of her clean skin. And the unmistakable, musky scent of aroused woman. "Is it working?"

"I can't tell yet."

He chuckled, knowing she wanted more. He gave it to her, now kissing her more deeply, flicking his tongue over her moist body, licking the water off her hip and thigh. She shuddered and he moved his hand up to steady her. He held her leg, then higher, to cup her rear. Her scent filled his brain, drawing his mouth closer to the edge of the plastic curtain, which barely concealed her curls. He remembered the hot, sweet taste of her on his tongue, the tenderness of that beautiful pink flesh between her legs. He wanted to taste her again. Wanted to feel her, touch her, have her. He pulled her tighter against him, unable to resist the feel of her skin against his cheek, fighting a battle deep within himself.

His mind told him no even after his body had decided yes.

When she hissed, he realized he'd pressed too hard against her bruise. "I'm sorry, you really are in pain." He looked up and saw her flushed face, her parted lips.

Well, she didn't look *entirely* pained. She also looked very aroused, very…*close.* Hot satisfaction at having brought her to the brink swept through him. He'd seen her this way in his dreams. Every night since the night they'd met.

Shit.

Unless he was prepared to forget all about his decision to

be a decent guy and not make love to her again while they were here in Pleasantville, he needed to exit stage left. Immediately if not sooner.

He stood, trying not to notice that the curtain had moved farther to the side, completely baring one perfect breast and delicious puckered nipple. Remembering how sensitive she was there made his feet freeze and his hands clench.

"I'm going to get you some ice," he finally said tightly. He somehow found the strength to turn and walk out of the bathroom.

Kate watched him leave, then let out a long, shuddery breath. "Not one of your brightest ideas, Kate Jones."

No. Not smart. She'd come into the bathroom knowing full well there were no towels. She'd had one thing in mind. Okay, two, if she counted washing away the grime of several hours' worth of driving. Even more than cleanliness, however, she'd wanted payback. Just a tiny bit of satisfaction by way of some brief shower exhibitionism. The way Jack had walked away from her next door—after commenting on how she'd had to pleasure herself in her bed the day they'd met—had pricked her ego. Not to mention her libido.

Damned if she hadn't wanted to prick his, too.

Hence the naked-in-the-shower-without-a-towel bit. Okay, so it was sneaky, though, she really hadn't intended for him to see her reflection completely. She'd figured there would be only a foggy image to get his imagination racing and give him some sleepless hours tonight.

Once their eyes had met and she'd seen the heat in his stare, her will had fled as quickly as the steam on the mirror.

She'd certainly been repaid in full. Because, man, oh man, she'd been the one left shaking and unfulfilled. Yes, she'd brought him to his knees, literally. But looking down, seeing him with his mouth and tongue on her body, so warm, so tender, so *close* to where she'd wanted him to be—had been agony.

"I can't believe you just left," she whispered angrily as she got out of the tub, grabbed one of the towels off the counter and began drying off.

His quick departure rankled. No, she wasn't going to sleep with him, she'd already decided. Getting further involved with him would be about as stupid as sitting in a tub full of water and turning on the hair dryer.

Good analogy. He could fry her brains and she knew it.

Of course, that didn't mean she didn't want him to want her. She had to admit, if only to herself in the quiet bathroom—it bugged her that he'd walked away, that he'd been *able* to walk away. If the fit of his briefs was any indication, he had not been physically unaffected by her.

Which meant he didn't want her mentally.

"Well, doesn't this suck eggs," she muttered. The first guy she'd had sex with in two years, and it wasn't even good enough to make him want seconds, not even when she had been wet and naked right in front of him.

Frowning, she moved faster, drying her body in quick, almost rough strokes. She winced as the cotton scraped across her bruised hip. Biting her lip, she looked at it in the mirror and winced. *Okay, yes, an ice pack would be good.*

Tucking the towel around her body, sarong-style, she reached for the other one and used it to dry her hair.

"I can think of a better use for an ice pack," she muttered. If she truly wanted to feel better, she should put the damn thing between her legs to try to cool herself off where she was *really* aching.

But cold, hard ice wasn't what she wanted between her legs. She wanted hot, hard man. One big, hot, hard man.

"No way, Kate. It's a Hugh Jackman fantasy and a vibrating fingertip for you tonight," she muttered as she bent to wrap the towel around her hair.

"Vibrating fingertip?"

Still bent at the waist, she winced, hoping those weren't Jack's sexy bare feet she spied right outside the partly open doorway. Praying that hadn't been his voice and he hadn't heard her comment about needing to get herself off with an actor fantasy and a vibrator.

She squeezed her eyes shut. When she opened them, the feet were still there. And she was still bent in front of him like some kowtowing servant. He'd heard.

Kate knew she had three choices—ignore him, pretend he'd misunderstood or be bold and shameless about the whole thing. Knowing what Cassie would do—what any self-respecting Tremaine woman *should* do—she took a deep breath. *Brazen it out.*

"Yeah, a vibrating fingertip," she said, standing and twisting the towel so it would stay on her hair. Her upraised arm caused the towel wrapped around her body to loosen. As it began to slip, she caught it at the tip of her breasts, and tucked it back together. Then she risked a glance at Jack. His chest was moving rapidly, as if he had to struggle to breathe.

She had a feeling it wasn't the lingering steam in the bathroom making him gasp.

Thank heaven.

"It's actually a clever little vibrator that slips over your finger and feels…mmm…so good." She licked her lips. "I have it right here in my purse, and can take care of myself anytime I want," she added, not knowing how she could be stupid enough to step even closer to the fire in which he could consume her. But step she did. Then even closer. "Would you like me to show it to you?" She lowered her voice. "I remember you're the kind of man who appreciates visual images."

Jack's jaw clenched and his eyes narrowed. "Sit down."

"Excuse me?"

"You heard me," he said, his voice low and thick. "Sit down, Kate."

He stepped closer. Not waiting for her to obey, he instead pushed her with the tip of his index finger until she backed up against the bathroom counter. Sliding up to sit on it, she held her breath, wondering what he would do next, wondering what she'd begun…and if she dared to finish it.

Had she gone too far? Her intention had been to taunt, to arouse, then to walk away leaving him to imagine her touching herself in another room in the house. Somehow, though, things had changed. He'd taken control of the situation.

She didn't pause to evaluate why she didn't care.

He reached for her thighs, tugging her closer to the edge of the counter. Then he gently eased her knees apart.

She shuddered. "Jack, I…"

"You don't have to take care of yourself."

Her eyes widened and her heart pounded with the primal rhythms of a tribal drum in her chest.

"I'm going to take care of you this time," he whispered.

She held her breath as he reached for her towel, tugging it open at the bottom, exposing one thigh all the way up to her hip. The other flap of the towel remained over her lap, caught almost coyly between her thighs. He made no effort to tug it free, instead trailing his fingers on her flesh in a slow, gentle caress.

Kate closed her eyes, waiting for a voice to scream in her head, telling her to stop, to not be taken in by him again. *Great sex and a whole bunch of earth-shaking orgasms won't cancel out the hurt of his disinterest later.*

Who the hell was she kidding? Right now, at this very moment, great sex and a whole bunch of orgasms would be worth just about anything, including a kidney or her firstborn child.

It was only when she felt the frigidly cold water splash on her leg, and the colder ice pack connect with her aching bruise, that she realized what he'd meant by *taking care* of her.

"You're taking care of my hip."

He nodded. Only a tiny twitch of his lips told her he knew what she'd been picturing him taking care of.

Touché. Score one for Mr. Gorgeous. She almost groaned out loud. But she didn't. This game wasn't over yet. Especially because he did not simply leave the pack in her capable hands and walk out of the room. No. He stayed, holding it against her skin, still standing between her knees. His jaw remained rigid as he sucked in deep breaths, as if he were trying to control himself by sheer force of will.

She dared a quick glance down. *Those tight briefs can't lie, sweetheart.* She almost purred with satisfaction at the sight of his immense hard-on. A small spot of moisture on the gray cotton tempted her beyond belief. She wanted to touch it, taste it with her tongue. Wanted to have him explosive, hot and wet in her hand. Her mouth. Her body. *All three.*

Smiling slightly, she murmured, "Thank you for the ice."

"I really am sorry I hurt you," he rasped.

Her hip? Her heart? Her feelings? He didn't clarify. She didn't ask.

"Funny thing, ice. So cold, it's almost painful. Yet it's…pleasurable in a way. Makes me feel tingly."

"Tingly?"

"Yeah. Almost…hot. As strange as that sounds."

"Shut up, Kate, you're breaking my concentration."

She grinned. "Uh, sure. I know it takes a lot of concentration to hold an ice pack on someone. I mean, I'm sure that's why there's such a high turnover rate in the candy striper field…all that ice pack holding. Sheer torture."

His bare shoulders—so thick, broad and toned—shook as he chuckled. Darn, he'd succeeded in distracting her. The laughter hadn't changed the way she felt, though. She shifted, not feigning her discomfort on the hard surface of the small counter. She was wet and throbbing, sensitive and needy, and the countertop didn't help things. "This isn't the most comfortable place to sit. It's almost as hard as that table at the Rialto."

His eyes narrowed as he continued to stare at the ice pack, holding it steady. Now and then, though, she'd feel his fingers shift, feel him touch her, just the tip of an index finger on her hipbone. So light and fleeting at first she thought she'd imagined it. Now she ached for it.

"So, you never answered my question, Jack."

"What question?"

"About whether you want to see my little toy."

"I thought you were joking."

Reaching for her purse, she unzipped a side pouch and pulled out the small carrying case.

"You weren't kidding," he said, staring at the plastic pouch. His stare never wavered as she flicked the snap open with her thumb.

"One of the hottest sellers at Bare Essentials."

"Your store?"

Nodding, she ran her fingers along the tip of the vibrator, knowing he paid very close attention.

"You *sell* vibrators in your ladies' shop?"

She tsked. "You never did go back and find that article, did you, Jack? If you had, you'd know that Bare Essentials isn't a typical ladies store. We sell intimate items for women."

"Like that," he said, nodding toward the vibrator.

Smiling lazily. "Like this. And other things. Lots of delightful…other things."

He raised a brow. "So, you own a porn shop?"

She sniffed. "Bare Essentials does not sell pornography.

We have lots of fun, sexy toys for ladies and couples. People come from other cities to shop for our lingerie, which is designed by my partner. We have a media section, with tasteful, instructional books. Plus erotic videos geared for women and couples. But nothing X-rated."

"I'm not criticizing, Kate," he said, obviously sensing her defensive reaction. "I'm fascinated. You have obviously made a big success for yourself. It's not often you see the owner of a sex shop on the cover of the Chicago *Business Journal.* You should be very proud."

Sensing he really wasn't being judgmental, and finding herself refreshed by his attitude, she relaxed slightly. "We found a niche. A clean, tasteful, brightly lit place for women and monogamous but adventurous couples—who are our biggest client base—to shop for special items. Bringing sex out of the seedy dark rooms or brown-paper-wrapped catalogs, and into the bright light of Michigan Avenue." Some demon made her add, "Complete with guest sex therapist lecturers, and the best selection of dildoes and cock rings in the state."

"Oh, so we're back to that, are we?"

"What?"

"This game of up the ante again. Trying to shock and tempt me some more."

Heat rose in her cheeks. "I don't know what you mean."

A slow smile spread across his lips. "Sure you do. The way you're running your fingers over that thing, like you don't know I'm watching, as if you don't think I'm picturing you touching yourself like that." His voice lowered. "Turning it on and moving it over every sensitive inch of your body."

Taking in a shaky breath, she pulled the vibrator out of the pouch. "Are you?"

"You know damn well I am."

She clipped it onto her middle finger.

He continued. "Just like you knew how I'd react to you naked in the shower. The forgotten towel. The vibrating finger comment."

"I really didn't know you were there when I said that," she murmured. Turning the vibrator on, she ran it across her shoulder to her collarbone, then her throat. Lower, over the curves of her breasts. Goose bumps rose on her skin. Beneath the towel, she felt her nipples grow even harder, until they scraped almost painfully against the cotton fabric.

Heat, stark and intense, flashed in Jack's eyes as he watched her. He silently dared her on, and she answered his challenge. Running the tiny device down the edge of the towel, she followed the seam down to her stomach. Lower. Until her hand rested on her lap and the vibrator kissed the inside of her thigh. Its hum was the only sound in the room, other than the faint rasp of Jack's labored breathing. And her own.

Pausing, she curled her lips into a sultry smile, warning him that she wasn't going to stop. Not unless he stopped her.

He didn't move a muscle.

Kate slid her hand beneath the towel.

"Mmm." She moaned as she scraped her fingertip across the curls between her legs.

"Enough." He dropped the ice pack and caught her wrist in his hand, clenching it tightly.

"I've barely started." She knew he could hear both the challenge and the promise in her voice.

He shook his head. "You've done what you set out to do, Kate. Hell, you did that the minute I saw you next door earlier." He let go of her wrist and took a step back. "You want me to want you. You want me crazy with wanting you."

Well, yeah!

"Mission accomplished."

He didn't try to do anything about it. He'd admitted it, but made no move to kiss her, to touch her.

"You've won. I concede. Now you need to stop."

His lips said stop. His eyes begged her to proceed. She moved her fingertip, letting her lips fall open in a pleasureful sigh as the vibrator skimmed across her throbbing clitoris. She knew he was going crazy, imagining what she was doing, but not really able to tell because of the discreet draping of the towel over her hand. "You're sure you want me…to stop?"

He closed his eyes. "Yes."

Liar. With a quick glance down, she saw that his body was still raring to go.

"The timing's bad on this, Kate," he said. "Really bad."

Obviously his mind was *not* raring to go.

"Bad timing. Right. There's a good reason for me not to give myself the orgasm I'm dying for," Kate said. "This has nothing to do with you, anyway."

"It has everything to do with me." He stepped closer, putting both his hands flat on the counter on each side of her hips. Leaning in until his face was inches from hers, he admitted, "I want to take you right here and now, fast and hard and furious, just like you're *begging* for…like it was that first night." His gaze dropped to her lips, to the towel, which had loosened again and barely clung to her body. As if he couldn't resist, his hands moved closer, until they touched her thighs. His fingers were cold from the ice pack, but it wasn't cold that made her gasp. It was the heat of his touch.

"Then I want to take you to bed, kiss away the pain on your hip, spend hours exploring your body and make love to you in ways you've never even dreamed of," he finally said, his voice ragged and full of need.

His expression told her he could, too. *So do it.*

"But not tonight, Kate. Not now." He straightened and stepped back. "Definitely not *here*."

Once she was able to think again—once her heart started beating again—she told herself it didn't matter, that she had never planned to have sex with him tonight anyway. And he was right, she couldn't imagine a worse place to have sex with Jack Winfield than in the same house where their parents had probably spent intimate time together.

She flipped off the vibrator. "Sure." After tightening the towel around her chest, she slid off the counter. "Look, maybe I wasn't playing nicely. Maybe I was being unfair, trying to pay you back a little for not calling."

"I figured as much. And I'm sorry."

He didn't try to explain. Made no effort to tell her what had happened, what had changed between that night in the theater and two days later when he *hadn't* called her.

She couldn't ask him, of course. She instead relied on false bravado. "It really doesn't matter. I got what I wanted. A little payback." She glanced down at his body, making them both fully aware of his need for her. Then she smiled seductively.

"You go back to bed. Alone." Stepping closer to walk around him and out the door, she continued. "While I go back to bed, too. With the mental image of a shirtless Hugh Jackman." Holding up her hand, she glanced at the vibrator.

"And this."

CHAPTER SEVEN

JACK SLEPT LATE the next morning. That wasn't a big surprise since he'd lain awake in her bed until at least 5:00 a.m., wondering what she was doing. If she was touching herself. If she ached, the way he did. He'd listened for hours, torturing himself, waiting to see if she'd cry out when she came, as she had the night in the theater.

He wasn't sure if he ever heard her cry out, or if he just imagined the cries of ecstasy throughout the long night hours.

Enough of that.

Rising, he pulled on some jeans, then walked down the short hallway to the master bedroom. Though the door was partially open, he knocked quietly in case she was still asleep. When there was no answer, he glanced in and saw the stripped bed.

Kate hadn't slept in her mother's old room.

Curious, he went downstairs and saw the pile of folded linens and a pillow on the living room sofa. Hearing a voice through the thin wall, he stepped out onto the patio and walked over to the open door of the adjoining duplex.

Kate was inside, talking on a cell phone, sounding more than a little irritated. "Look, the power was supposed to be turned on yesterday. I have my confirmation numbers, you already charged my credit card, so why am I sitting in the dark, sweaty, and unable to take a shower this morning?"

He couldn't imagine how she could be dirty after the endless shower she'd taken the night before. She looked fresh and chipper, dressed in tight jean shorts and another of those flimsy, sleeveless tank tops. Red and wicked, it hugged her curves and made his heart skip a beat. There'd obviously been no sleepless night for her. She'd probably slept like a baby with her play toy clipped to her finger, her hand curled in her lap.

"Yes, I know it's a Saturday," she continued. "But please try to get someone out here this morning."

Jack would be willing to pay any after-hour fees the company might charge if it meant getting her into her own place by that night. No way could he take another night like the previous one.

"Problems?"

She almost dropped the phone when she heard his voice. "Hi. Yes, problems. The power company's as efficient as ever around here. They lost the work order to get the electricity back on for me before yesterday."

Without waiting for an invitation, he entered the living room of the small house. It was a mirror image of the one next door, though it held not a stick of furniture. "You never did tell me why you're here, anyway. I had the impression visiting Pleasantville isn't your favorite thing to do."

"I suppose it's better than being buried up to my neck in a red ant nest," she muttered.

He chuckled. "So why're you here?"

"Business."

Interesting, given her line of work. "*Your* kind of business?"

"The private kind."

"Okay," he said with a shrug. "Is this business going to keep you in town long?"

"A few weeks at least."

Weeks. Damn. He'd really hoped she was making a quick trip. If she stayed, he'd be in for lots of long, sleepless nights. Even worse, it would be nearly impossible for her to avoid hearing the gossip about Edie and his father.

Jack suddenly found himself willing to do just about anything to prevent that. As sorry as he felt for Edie, he knew she'd made her choices. She'd dealt with them in her own way.

Kate hadn't chosen to be the target of gossip, scorn and spite from this town. Yet that was about all she'd gotten here as a kid. And, he feared, about all she'd find here now.

If his sister Angela's comments were anything to go on, Kate and her cousin hadn't had the best time in high school. Kate hadn't let that stop her in the least. She'd gotten out, made a life for herself, created a new world where she had the power, the money and the upper hand.

Much as he had done.

No wonder he liked her so much. After all, in spite of their dissimilar childhoods, they had a lot in common. Hadn't they each been put into a mold by this town, and done whatever they could to break out of it? They'd both left after high school—her opening a sex shop and him focusing on career and casual relationships with a lot of different women. And they'd both come back, still wanting to rebel and shock, until they'd found each other and fallen headfirst into a hot kiss on a public street. Not to mention what had happened in the theater.

"Do you want something to eat?" he finally asked, figuring she couldn't possibly have any groceries in the house.

"I already had a donut and a warm diet Coke, thanks."

"How nutritious."

"It's not exactly the breakfast of champions, but it will do."

Glancing toward the floor, she bent to get something out

of her purse. Jack tried not to notice the way her shorts hugged her ass, the way they rode up on her thighs until he could see the hem of her panties.

Well, no, he didn't really try not to look. He just tried not to let it affect him. Which was impossible.

After grabbing a brush, she straightened and gathered her hair into a ponytail at the back of her neck. Her shirt pulled tighter against her curves as she lifted her arms. Jack again wished he'd stayed in bed, avoiding her for the day.

"Did you sleep okay? I noticed you stayed downstairs on the couch. You could have used your mom's room."

She looked away, busying her hands putting the brush back into her purse. "The couch was fine."

"Sure there was enough room for all three of you?"

"Three of us?"

"You know. You, Hugh and your little friend?" he asked, wondering what demon made him bring the subject back to what had happened last night when they'd parted.

She laughed softly.

"So what is it with Hugh Jackman? A mouth, like Connery? Dangerous glint in his eye, like Eastwood? Or that schmaltzy chick-flick-time-travel with him and Meg Ryan?"

She shook her head, licking her lips. "Wolverine in *X-Men*. I just love a lean-looking man who can kick ass." She shrugged, obviously being honest and not trying to torment him sexually as she had the night before. "What can I say? I like men who can move their bodies gracefully while being seriously dangerous."

If he were going to pursue a sexual relationship with her—which he absolutely was *not,* not *yet* anyway—he'd have contemplated inviting her to one of his Tae Kwon Do classes, which he taught three nights a week. Instead he changed the subject. "So, are you planning to sleep on the floor for weeks?"

She glanced around the empty room. "Some of my aunt's old furniture is stored in the garage of her new place. My cousin, Cassie, is going to help me load some up and bring it here."

"Cousin? Your cousin's back in town, too?"

She shot him a look from half-lowered lashes. "She's been here in town for several weeks already. Do you know her?"

He shook his head. "No, I don't remember her at all. But I know the two of you lived here, in these houses. Is she going to stay here with you?"

"No. Her mom owns some other property around here. Cassie's staying at Aunt Flo's other place up on Lilac Hill."

Jack raised a questioning brow.

"Aunt Flo had a lot of admirers in this town. Male admirers. A couple of them liked to give her presents."

He understood. "Someone *gave* her a house on Lilac Hill?" At her nod, he whistled. "Some present. Who was it?"

"Mr. Miller, the banker."

A grin tickled the corners of Jack's lips. "He was old as dirt when I was born."

"Flo's not age discriminatory."

"He was a widower with no family for as long as I can remember." Jack thought about it. "I'm glad your aunt gave him a little bit of happiness. He was a nice old guy. You know he lived only two doors down from us."

Her chuckle was decidedly wicked. "There goes the neighborhood."

Knowing how his mother and sister felt about the Tremaine family, he had to wonder why he hadn't heard anything about this latest insult upon the glory that was Winfield.

"So, Cassie stays on the hill and you're staying here."

"Right. Is there a problem?"

"I'm wondering why you're not staying there with her."

"Let's just say the snob set's not exactly my cup of tea."

"But they are your cousin's?"

Kate shrugged. "Cassie fits in anywhere. She's very successful. You'll probably recognize her when you see her."

"Why?"

"She's a lingerie model. Poses in sexy underclothes for catalogs that pretend they're for women, but which men swipe from their wives and hide in the bathroom to look at."

He shrugged. "And you're a super successful store owner who makes front-page news. Sounds like both of you got away from here and made good." He glanced around the room. "I'm sure you have more expensive tastes these days, too."

"This is fine for me." She raised a hand, gesturing to the small room. "Part of Cassie's reason for staying up there was out of her innate need to be as outrageous as possible."

"I somehow think your cousin hasn't cornered the market on being outrageous in your family."

Rolling her eyes, she sat on the floor, draping her arms on her upraised knees. "No, I'm the smart, quiet, *sweet* one." She sounded thoroughly disgusted.

He couldn't help it—he let out a loud bark of laughter. Her glare told him she didn't appreciate his amusement.

"Honey, I can think of a lot of words to describe you, but something as insipid as sweet definitely isn't on the list."

She frowned at him. "You're saying I'm not sweet?"

"No, you're definitely not sweet, Kate." Stepping across the room, he bent to sit directly in front of her. "Smart, yes. Quiet—well, only in the way that smart people are because they're always thinking. Deciding their course of action before they act on it. Like you did at the theater."

Her jaw tightened. "Get back to the part where you tell me why I'm not a nice person."

He wagged an index finger at her. "Uh-uh, I didn't say you're not a nice person. You're a fascinating, charming, *nice* woman, Kate. But not anything as simple as sweet. There are such depths to you…." He stared intently at her face, losing himself again in those dark brown eyes, wondering what was going on in that beautiful mind of hers. "I'd like to know what makes you tick," he admitted softly.

Color rose in her cheeks and her lips parted. He'd gone too far, treaded back into personal, intimate territory. He backpedaled. "So, tell me, why do you think you're sweet and quiet?"

"Because my family has told me I am for twenty-eight years." She blew out a frustrated breath. "Cassie was the wild, tempestuous child. I was the sweet, good girl. The little ballerina, the straight-A student."

"I imagine you got quite a reaction with your store."

"My mother left during the grand opening reception. Never came back again until after I started sending her copies of my bank statements." She paused. "Of course, my aunt Flo sent a huge bouquet of orchids and told me she never thought I had a wicked streak in me. I guess they thought Cassie and I were destined to be exact replicas of them. They expected it even before we were ever born."

Knowing how difficult it was to break out of the position in which every family tried to paint its members, he nodded in agreement. "I would be willing to bet Cassie is not nearly as wild as she's said to be." He leaned closer to her. "And I know you're not exactly a good girl."

"Really?" She looked at him so hopefully he almost laughed. He didn't, though, not wanting to hurt her feelings.

"No, I don't think good girls own sex shops or carry tiny vibrators around in their purses. Nor do they often go for it when offered the chance to do something as wildly impulsive as what we did at the theater."

He waited for her to look away, to break the stare, but she didn't. Her eyes looked softer, dreamier, as her lips parted. A tiny sigh preceded her reply. "Thank you."

"For?"

"For seeing the Kate I see…not the one everyone else sees. For letting me be myself, not who everyone thinks I am." She paused. "Even if who I am is sometimes a not-so-nice, not-so-sweet person."

Jack leaned close and pressed a kiss to her temple, then brushed her hair away. He saw her pulse ticking in her throat as she looked up at him. "Sweet is boring, Kate," he whispered. "I much prefer spicy…even if I know I'm going to get burned."

Her moist lips parted and she tilted her head back as she took in a deep breath. He'd never seen a more clear invitation to go further. Kissing her temple wasn't enough for either of them. He had to taste her, just once more, or else he'd go crazy wondering if her mouth was as soft as he remembered. He leaned closer, brushing his lips across her temple again, then her cheek, and her jaw. She sighed, but didn't pull away.

"I take it back, Kate," he murmured as he moved lower, to kiss her earlobe and the side of her neck. "You taste very sweet." Then, unable to resist, he moved his mouth to hers. Their lips met and parted as instinctively as the beating of a heart. He licked lazily at her tongue, dipping his own into her mouth to taste her more thoroughly. She kissed him back, curling against him, tilting her head, inviting him deeper.

When they finally pulled apart, neither spoke for a moment. Then she narrowed her eyes. "Don't you do that again."

Her shaky voice held a warning and a challenge. He

wondered if, as usual, she was trying to scare him into backing off. He mentally tsked. Obviously she didn't remember what had happened when she'd tried that at the Rialto.

Finally, Jack smiled. "Yeah, there's definitely both sweet and spicy to you, Kate Jones. I can't decide which side I like better."

Before she could reply, he got up and left the duplex.

WHEN KATE ARRIVED at Cassie's house up on the hill that afternoon, her cousin greeted her with a big hug and a humongous margarita. "A pea-green drink in honor of your return to Pea-Ville." Cassie held up her salt-rimmed glass to clink a toast.

Kate clinked back, then sipped deeply. The electric company still hadn't gotten her power on by the time she'd left the house, and the drink went down like a powerful blast of air-conditioning. Besides, she'd been all hot and bothered ever since Jack had kissed her then walked out. "Ah, perfect. I'd forgotten how hot it is here in the pits of hell in the summer."

"I guess I'm getting used to it."

Hearing an unexpected note of warmth in Cassie's voice, Kate raised a brow. "The heat? Or the town?"

Cassie shrugged. "Maybe a little of both."

"Well, I can see you don't have a scarlet letter on your shirt, so maybe things aren't as bad as I'd expected."

"Believe it or not, I haven't heard one person call me a tramp since I got here." She winked. "At least not to my face."

Her cousin led Kate into the house, then gave her a quick tour, including a stop in Flo's outrageously decorated boudoir.

Going back downstairs, they sat in the kitchen, drinking their margaritas and gabbing for an hour. Kate didn't like the tired, dark circles under Cassie's eyes—though, they certainly didn't distract from her beauty. Since Cassie never brought up the trouble she was in, trouble that involved an over-amorous man who hadn't taken her rejection too well, Kate didn't, either. There would be time enough to talk about it, and to give Cassie her mail, which had been forwarded to Kate in Chicago while Cassie hid out. Kate wanted to put off handing over the dozen or more letters. "So the store's really coming along okay?"

"Absolutely. I've got a couple of high school boys who've helped with the painting and repairs. The shelving units and cabinetry were already there from when the men's shop was open. Carpet goes in Monday, and the stock you sent arrives daily."

"Well, I'm here now to help with the inventory, at least, now that you did the hard stuff. The permit was approved, right? I still don't know how you pulled it off."

Cassie gave her an evil smile. "It's called boobs. A low-cut shirt and a pair of breasts leaning on the desk of a city worker's office can accomplish a lot. Including rubber-stamping an application for a business license."

"Boobs and brains. Cassie Tremaine Montgomery, you're a force to be reckoned with." Kate sipped her drink.

"It's only fair I got the bigger boobs, since you got the bigger brain," Cassie pointed out.

Kate sighed. "But we both got the big hips."

Cassie gave her a Cheshire-cat smile. "Most men who look at my pictures in the catalog like curvy hips."

Kate agreed. "I'll bet the permit guy is a fan."

"Even if he's not, I didn't lie on the business app. We *are* going to open a lovely, tasteful little ladies' shop...."

"With King Kong Dong featured prominently in the front display window," Kate interjected with a snorty laugh.

They clinked their glasses again.

Cassie got up to make them a couple of sandwiches for lunch. "Speaking of King Kong Dong, or dongs in general, have you met your new neighbor yet?"

Kate didn't answer right away, drawing a curious stare from Cassie. In spite of how close they were, Kate hadn't told Cassie about her interlude with Jack at the Rialto. So she couldn't exactly explain what had happened the night before when she'd discovered he was really J. J. Winfield. "We've met."

"And?"

Kate got up to wash lettuce for the sandwiches.

"Come on, what gives? Aren't you going to make him your love slave, then trample all over his heart with the heels of your six-inch-high, slut-puppy boots?"

"I don't own slut-puppy boots."

"You sell them."

"I sell a lot of things that I don't own or use myself," she said as she sipped.

"Aw, gee. Here I figured you gave a personal testimonial with every dildo, clit ring and butt plug you peddle."

Kate laughed so hard some of her margarita spilled from the corner of her lips. "You are as bad as Armand."

"So tell me about the Winfield prince," Cassie said.

"I don't know about Jack—J.J. He's not what I expected."

"Meaning?"

"Meaning he might be more than I can handle."

Cassie lifted a brow. There probably wasn't a man alive who her cousin couldn't handle. But Kate wasn't Cassie.

"Maybe I'd better start out a little easier. Focus on some of my other goals. Like the shop. Or Angela and Darren."

"Hmm, yeah, I forgot about them. I saw Angela one day, walking out to her car. She and her mom live up the street."

"Please tell me she's fat."

"Sorry, hon. She looks pretty good. Still looks like a total bitch, but not a Jenny Craig-bound one."

Rats.

"What about Darren?"

"Works at a car dealership and lives downtown in an apartment over the Tea Room. Did you know he and Angela were married for a while right after high school? The rumor mill says she got knocked up on prom night. They married that summer. Then when she lost the baby, he divorced her and went into the army."

Kate winced. "Maybe I should thank her for stealing him on prom night." She couldn't imagine how her life might have ended up if she'd been the pregnant teen. Probably she'd be living here, bitter and sour with a poochy belly, saggy breasts and four kids who looked like moon-faced Darren clinging to her skirts.

Kate met Cassie's eye, knowing she was thinking along the same lines. They exchanged shaky smiles. "Here's to what *didn't* happen to us on prom night," Kate said softly.

Cassie nodded. "Hear, hear."

JACK LUCKED OUT and arrived at his mother's house after she'd left for her Saturday hair appointment. Closing himself in his father's office—to the chagrin of Leonardo the bulldog—he spent two hours balancing bank statements, sorting out documents. He heard his sister Angela moving around, once stopping to have a long phone conversation in the next room.

He didn't get his sister. Angela was pretty and had been given every advantage. She'd been the apple of their parents' eye, and had once had a genuine sweetness to her personality. Sure, she was spoiled. She'd shown signs of that, even as a toddler. But at least before, when she'd been a kid, she'd had an infectious laugh and a beautiful smile. In the fifteen years he'd been gone, she'd lost them both. Probably three failed marriages and two miscarriages could do that to a person.

Resolving to get along better with her, he forced a look of welcome to his face when she walked into the office. "Hi."

"You busy?"

He nodded and rubbed his weary eyes. "Dad left a mess."

Her laugh could only be described as bitter. "Yeah. As usual." She sat on a chair next to the window. "I don't suppose you've changed your mind and plan to stay here."

He shook his head. "I'm sorry, Ang. I don't know how you can stand it. I can't breathe in this place."

"Even after he died Dad still managed to drive you away."

Jack pushed his chair back. "What are you talking about?"

"I mean, you took off fifteen years ago because of him. Because of how he pressured you to follow in his footsteps."

"Most fathers do."

Angela continued as if he hadn't spoken. "And as soon as it looks like you're going to come back, you find out about his dirty little secret and won't stay here now, either."

Jack shook his head. "It's more complicated than that. How did you find out about Dad and Edie, anyway?"

She glanced out the window. "I saw them kissing once. Not long after you'd gone away to college."

She'd been thirteen. He swallowed, hard. "What'd you do?"

"Nothing. I didn't confront him, or tell Mother, or anybody else. I was afraid if she found out, they'd get a divorce and I'd be shuffled back and forth between them forever."

A wave of guilt washed over him as he acknowledged he'd left her here without an ally in his hurry to escape from home. "I'm sorry, Angela. But maybe now it's time to move on. Have you thought about getting out of here, too?"

"I've been dying to move out, get my own place downtown, but Mother plays the guilt card whenever I mention it."

"I meant, maybe it's time to get out of Pleasantville."

"I can't. I don't want to leave him…I mean, leave here."

Him? He didn't think Angela was seeing anyone, though she'd been divorced from her third husband for over a year.

She stood abruptly. "I have to go. I have a nail appointment. Be sure to lock up when you leave, okay? Mother doesn't trust Sophie to secure the house." Her jaw clenched. "After all, she's not nearly as trustworthy as *Edie* was."

Judging by the way she spat out the other woman's name, Jack surmised his sister had not been able to forgive and forget.

As Angela left the room his parents' ever-hopeful dog, Leonardo, slunk in and strolled over to the desk. At Leonardo's longing glance at his jeans-clad leg, Jack shot him a suspicious glare. "Dog, how many years is it gonna take for you to figure out you've got no balls?"

Leonardo gave him a sheepish glance from his wrinkled face. Walking around in circles once or twice, he appeared to be looking for something—or someone. He finally curled up at Jack's feet and looked up at him with sad eyes.

"Okay," Jack said with a sigh. "I guess you miss him, too."

A half hour later he straightened up to leave, determined to get out before his mother got back. After making sure the mutt had enough water, he locked up and headed for his father's pickup truck, which he'd been driving during his stay.

As he drove down the street, he glanced toward old Mr. Miller's house and saw a shapely brunette in a red tank top trying to drag a big mattress across the driveway.

He immediately stopped the truck. "Kate, are you trying to break your back? Put that down."

She dropped the end of the mattress and frowned at him. "You distracted me. Do you know how long it took to tug that thing out of the garage?"

He trotted across the driveway to her side. "I thought your cousin was going to help you."

"She is. She's had a bunch of phone calls to deal with. Problems with her agent."

"And Miss Have-To-Do-It-Now can't wait for her?"

"I'm not helpless. I've gotten a bunch of other stuff by myself." She gestured toward her SUV, which already held a couple of chairs. And, judging by the upraised legs that nearly reached the interior roof, a small kitchen table.

He couldn't believe she'd done it all alone. "I suppose you plan to unload all this stuff without help when you get back home, too?"

She scuffed the toe of her sneaker on the driveway and mumbled, "Well, I kinda figured you'd be back sooner or later."

"Back to help you unload it, or to make you another ice pack and take care of you again after you slip a disc?"

Wrong thing to say. They both instantly remembered how he'd taken care of her the night before. Awareness hummed between them, as always, now not below the surface, but right out in the open again.

She bit the corner of her lip. "Look," she finally said, "I'm almost done, are you going to help me or criticize me?"

He glanced at the open hatch and the mattress. "Honey, I hate to tell you this, but you've got a size problem here. I don't think something this big is going to fit in there."

"You sound like a conceited teenage boy about to get laid for the first time."

Not recognizing the sultry voice of the woman who'd spoken, he turned and saw a shapely blonde standing just behind them on the driveway. She had her head cocked to the side and her hand on one hip, smiling wickedly. With her eye-popping build, sunny-blond hair and outrageous words, he immediately assumed she was the cousin.

Frowning, he ignored her comment. "I hope your call was important, since your cousin nearly gave herself a hernia out here."

The blonde's brow shot up. She immediately turned to Kate. "Katey, I told you to wait for me. Good grief, how'd you carry all that stuff by yourself?"

Kate didn't answer. She was too busy looking back and forth between Jack and Cassie, a confused frown scrunching her brow.

Jack grabbed the end of the mattress. "Let me throw this in the truck and take it for you, Kate. I'm going home anyway."

"Home?" the blonde—Cassie—asked. Then understanding crossed her face. "Oh, my, you're J. J. Winfield, aren't you?"

He swallowed a groan. "Jack. Jack Winfield."

The blonde didn't reply, just looked him over, head to toe, very intently. Smiling, she extended her hand. "Hi, Jack. I'm Cassie. The truck's a great idea. Can you take a few other things, too?"

"Sure," he said, still wondering why Kate looked so befuddled and hadn't said a single word since her cousin had come out of the house. "Is that all right with you, Kate?"

After she nodded, he hoisted the queen-size mattress up with both hands. He saw Cassie's eyes widen as she stared at his arms, chest and shoulders. As he walked away, he heard her whisper, "Too much to handle, indeed. But oh, Kate, wouldn't you have fun trying?"

They loaded up his truck with the few remaining pieces of furniture and were finished within a half hour of his arrival. Cassie disappeared into the house again, after thanking Jack once more for his help.

"Are you heading back now? Or do you want me to drive this stuff back, then wait for you to get there to unload it?"

"Let me say goodbye to Cassie and I'll come back so we can unload it this afternoon." She turned to go into the house, then paused. "Jack? Thanks a lot for stopping to help. I really do appreciate it."

He shrugged. "Just being neighborly."

She glanced up and down the block, at the manicured lawns, the gated driveways that were filled with expensive cars. "Yeah. Right. I'm sure there were bunches of other neighbors lacing up their deck shoes to come out and help when you stopped. I bet they're still peering out their windows, waiting for the chance to lend a hand."

He followed her stare, figuring she was probably right, but not admitting it. "It's not all bad here."

"I guess Cassie likes it. But I wouldn't be able to stand the quiet sense of knowing everyone on the block is watching every move you make." She brushed an errant, damp strand of hair off her brow. "It'd be like living in a goldfish bowl, some big fat cat always waiting to pounce on you if you leap out of the safe waters where you belong."

"Yeah, that's exactly what it was like growing up."

Their eyes met. She looked surprised that he agreed.

As for Jack, he thought it remarkable how quickly Kate had nailed what his childhood had been like on this block. In this town.

"Can I venture a guess that living on Pansy Lane was something like a fishbowl, too?"

Her slow nod was his only answer.

He reached out to brush away the blowing strand of hair again. His fingers connected with her temple, sending heat through his body. Heat that had absolutely nothing to do with the blazing sunshine overhead.

"Then I guess it's a good thing we both like to live a little dangerously."

WHEN THEY GOT BACK to the duplex, Kate first went inside to check the power, then leaned out to give him a thumbs-up. "Yes! Houston, we have ignition."

"Good, now you can take a shower in your own bathroom tonight," he muttered.

They unloaded the truck, making several trips.

"So," she asked as they carried some chairs into the kitchen. "Did you get a lot done at your mother's house today?"

She seemed to be making an effort to be polite, social and absolutely impersonal. He followed her lead. "Barely made a dent. My father had accounts all over the state, with at least a dozen banks. He owned property I didn't know about, held mortgages my *mother* didn't even know about. I haven't even gotten to the stuff in a file marked Private that I found in his desk drawer."

"Well, if you need any help, I do have some accounting background." At his look of surprise, she hurried on. "What? I mean, I do owe you one for helping me today."

"I'll keep that in mind," he said with a smile. "Though, maybe I'll choose the way you repay me."

They left the queen-size mattress for last. It would be the trickiest, since it had to go up the narrow staircase to the bedroom. "Hope you sleep really well to make it worth lugging this thing all over town," he said as they hoisted the thing through the doorway. They dropped it right on the floor as Kate hadn't bothered with a bed frame.

"At least it's not a twin," she said with a smile, obviously referring to the way he spent his own nights. "Nice and roomy."

He frowned. "You're not planning on sharing it, are you?"

"Huh?" She looked truly puzzled and he felt like an idiot for his instant of jealousy. "Wait a second." She pointed an index finger at him. "You want to know if another man is going to be staying over here occasionally."

He crossed his arms, not saying anything. She chuckled. "Uh, I don't think so, Jack. In spite of what you might think, given the way I acted on the day we met, I'm not a bed hopper." She paused. "I don't think I could even be called a bed crawler, these days."

Good.

"Not that it's any of your business."

"No, of course not." *Damn right it was his business.*

"If I did choose to bring someone here, you'd have absolutely no say in the matter," she continued, almost challenging him to deny it.

He stepped closer, tipping her chin up with his index finger until she met his eye. "I wouldn't say a word." Her lashes lowered as she tried to look down. "I can promise I wouldn't say anything to him as I threw him out the window, Kate."

She bit her lip, looking both confused and a little bit pleased. Unable to resist, he bent to kiss her mouth. Lightly. Playfully.

"What was that for?" She brought her shaking fingers to her mouth when he ended the kiss and stepped away.

"Just to remind you."

"Remind me of what?"

He walked toward the door, but glanced over his shoulder.

"That I'm the only man you want."

CHAPTER EIGHT

KATE DECIDED to spend her first few days in Pleasantville devoting all her thoughts to the new store. And none to her love life, such as it was. That didn't count her dreams, of course, over which she had no control.

Jack starred in them every night, damn it.

On Saturday night, after Jack had helped her unload some furniture at the duplex and given her the playful kiss that had left her reeling, she went downtown to see the shop for the first time. Cassie and her high school helpers had done a great job. Sure, there were some lighting problems, but the old dressing room area was perfect, with lots of mirrors so customers could get addicted to Armand's luxurious lingerie. And the store had adequate air-conditioning and plenty of display shelves, with discreet alcoves for some of their more risqué items. If this store were in some other town, she could envision it thriving.

Kate and Cassie enjoyed eating pizza, listening to loud music, drinking wine and examining sex toys until late Saturday night. At least until the sheriff, Sean Taggart, showed up.

As soon as Kate saw him, she understood why Cassie got such a strange look on her face whenever his name came up. The man was pure, rugged manna from tough-guy heaven. Maybe not movie-star gorgeous, like Jack, but with his lean body, thick brown hair and dangerous smile, she could see why Cassie might find him distracting. So distracting that Kate immediately decided to leave the two of them alone. After all, it wasn't often she saw her cousin nearly blushing around a man.

It also wasn't every day she came across a man who did not turn into a tongue-tied, drooling idiot around her cousin. Jack hadn't. On Saturday, when Cassie had been at her Cassie-est, all blond, leggy and saucy, he'd barely glanced in her direction.

She hadn't known whether to kiss him or to take his pulse to see if he was still alive and breathing. In any case, she could almost love him for it. "Love him?" Insane. She barely liked him.

Well, she conceded, that was a big lie. She did like him, she'd liked him from the minute they met, in spite of who his father had been. He was charming and sexy, playful and self-confident. She liked that he didn't swagger, and he felt no need to play tough guy. He was a flirt, a man who liked women. Right now he liked her, she knew it, in spite of his failure to call. She could see the heat in his eyes when he looked at her. He wanted her every bit as much as he had their first day. But something was holding him back.

If his last name were different, and if he'd come up with a reasonable excuse for not calling her, she might have tried to find out what was stopping him. And maybe she would have tried to change his mind.

The realization floored her. How strange that for the first time in nearly forever, she'd found someone who tempted her to let him get closer. She could conceive of lowering some of her guard, taking a chance on what could be a fabulously erotic, exciting relationship. But he'd erected barriers even taller than her own.

She supposed it was just as well there were insurmountable walls between them right up front. Jack obviously liked to play.

A lot. He wasn't the stick-around type and she knew it. While Kate believed if there ever did come a time when she found that one right guy—her true love—she'd be a goner for life.

Much like her mother had been, unfortunately.

Over the next couple of days Kate refrained from pumping Cassie about her problems—either her old ones, or her new one, in the form of the hunky sheriff. Somehow, while they priced, ordered and set up displays, she found herself getting excited as she had before the opening of her shop in Chicago.

Knock it off, this isn't the same thing at all!

Nope, it definitely wasn't. In Chicago, she'd wanted her shop to be a wild success. Here, she fully expected it to be a grand failure. But at least they'd have fun failing, doing it publicly, right on the main street of Pleasantville. And, as they failed, she'd be right here in case Cassie needed her. She knew her cousin too well...if Kate had stayed in Chicago, Cassie would never have come to her if things got bad. Here, she couldn't very well avoid it!

She managed to avoid Jack for the most part—not an easy feat considering their close living quarters. But he was usually gone during the day, and so was she. That suited her fine.

Nights were tougher. They slept mere inches apart, separated only by the width of one slim, interior wall. There were times when she thought she heard his hand brush the wall behind her head, when he'd roll over in her old bed next door. She knew from childhood experience that at times she and Cassie had heard each other's late-night bad dream cries.

On Wednesday morning she stepped outside on the porch as soon as she got up, glad for the fresh early-morning air. Down the block, a mother rode a bicycle, with a toddler in the child seat. The woman waved as she rode by.

A nice, peaceful morning. She didn't remember those from when she'd lived here, though, she supposed there must have been some. At least for Edie. Otherwise, why would her mother have ever come back here when Kate's dad died?

Hearing sounds coming from next door, she stepped closer and peered into the front window of her mother's duplex. She wished she hadn't. Jack stood in his living room, bare-chested, wearing only a pair of loose white pants. He was stretching, moving his body with fluidity and grace. And power. It took a second for her muddled brain to realize that he was running through some type of karate moves.

He had no idea she was there. So she watched for several minutes. The sweat gleamed on his bare chest and thick arms as he swung and kicked and arched. He moved his body like a sleek animal, a finely tuned—but dangerous—machine.

Walk away before he sees you. She couldn't, though. She couldn't turn and walk into her house. Just one more moment of watching…. One moment stretched into five or ten minutes until finally, inevitably, he glanced up and saw her there.

He immediately stopped. They stared at each other through the glass for a minute, then Jack lifted his hand and pointed toward her with his index finger, wagging it back and forth like a parent to a kid who'd done something naughty.

Act innocent. She gave him a "Who me?" shrug.

He crossed his arms and raised his brow, waiting for her to admit she'd been spying on him.

"Oh, all right," she muttered. As she entered the front door she immediately launched into an explanation. "I didn't mean to watch you working out. I just stepped out for some fresh air, and couldn't help noticing."

"Uh-huh," he said as he began to stretch his arms out, slowly rolling his shoulders as if cooling down from his workout.

"I mean, the curtains were open. I just caught a glimpse."

"Right."

His one-word answers did nothing to hide his amusement. "Really, Jack, I do respect your privacy."

He finally stopped moving all those yummy muscles long enough to meet her eye. "Kate, you've been standing there for almost ten minutes."

She fisted her hands and put them on her hips. "You saw me?"

"No," he admitted. Then he grinned. "But I heard your front door open, and that board on the front porch really creaks."

She was surprised he'd been able to hear anything except his own churning pulse as he'd flexed and stretched all those lovely, hard muscles. She forced herself to look away, wondering if she'd been drooling while she'd watched from the window. She surreptitiously lifted her fingers to her chin to check.

"So, uh, were you doing some kind of karate?" she finally asked, wanting to fill the charged silence. "I've thought about taking some self-defense courses."

"Tae Kwon Do. If you're serious, I teach at a studio in Chicago. I can give you the address."

That implied they'd see one another after they left Pleasantville, something Kate hadn't really allowed herself to consider. "Well, I don't know…."

"If you don't feel comfortable in a class," he said with a cajoling smile, "I'd be happy to work with you one on one."

Work with her. One on one. How about one you on one me?

She gulped. "I'd better go."

He grabbed a white towel and draped it over his shoulders. "Don't go. I'll make you some breakfast. I can't promise gourmet food like diet Coke and donuts, but I can do a decent omelet."

Considering she hadn't bothered to do a grocery shopping trip, and had been living off fast food and 7-Eleven burritos for the past few days, Kate's stomach overruled her brain. "Great."

"Lemme change."

You don't have to on my account!

While he was upstairs, Kate went into the kitchen, glad to see Jack was keeping the place spotless, just as it had been when her mother had lived here. Kate, unfortunately, was more the slob type. And the world's greatest chef—or even a competent one—she was not. She did, however, know how to crack an egg and was hard at it when he returned, dressed in jeans and a T-shirt.

"So tell me why you want to take self-defense courses," he said as he began making their breakfast.

"I dunno, I live in a big city and run a rather infamous store. I got a few wacky phone calls after that article."

Jack's shoulders stiffened. "Did anyone threaten you?"

"Oh, no. I just got asked on some unusual dates—to strip clubs, S and M hangouts and the Circus."

"Circus sounds pretty normal."

"I thought so, too, at first. Turns out there's a sex show called the Circus where the animals are all people in costume who offer rides to members of the audience."

"I think I'd rather not have known that," he said with a groan as he diced some ham for the omelets.

"Me, too." She made herself at home, finding his coffee supply and filling the coffeepot. "I guess some people heard about my shop and instantly thought the worst of me."

He put the knife down to study her. "You've had to deal with that before, haven't you?"

She knew he meant here, in Pleasantville. "Ancient history."

"So how does it measure up now? How has the town treated you these first few days?"

So far, she had to admit, things had been okay. Then again, she hadn't been out too much, staying mostly at home, at Cassie's place or at the store. "Fine, actually. How about you? Has the red carpet been rolled out for the return of the prodigal son?"

"I'm keeping a low profile, though one of my father's friends asked me to move back and run for mayor next year."

"Will you?" She held her breath waiting for his answer.

"Not on your life."

She nearly sighed in relief. *Why would it matter to you if he came back here, married the local big-haired town princess and stayed forever?* She didn't know why, she only knew it would matter.

Somehow, even though she'd told herself nothing was going to happen between them, Kate couldn't imagine being in Chicago, knowing Jack wasn't there somewhere, in that big bustling city, stopping traffic on the street with his smile and teaching his Tae Kwon Do classes. Tackling intruders and doing fix-it work on a needy woman's house.

Their eyes met, and somehow Kate knew Jack had read her thoughts. He knew she liked him, and she felt drawn to him.

Kate's eyes widened as Jack stepped close, until she was backed up against the kitchen counter, and he pressed almost neck to toe against her body. "I'm looking forward to a lot of things changing when I get back to Chicago, Kate." He lifted a hand to her face, softly caressing her cheekbone, then touching a strand of her hair. "Changing for both of us."

Before she could ask him to explain, he'd turned back to the stove. Kate clutched the counter and sucked in a few deep breaths, trying to regain her composure. By the time breakfast was ready, she felt completely calm and relaxed, or at least she thought she looked that way—no point in wondering if he knew she was still edgy and aware, and now very curious about what he'd meant about things changing between them.

"So, Jack, what else do you do in your real life. You're an architect. Ever designed anything I've actually heard of?"

He answered with a question. "Like to go shopping?"

"Does Imelda Marcos like shoes?"

He chuckled. "My firm designed the new Great Lakes Mall. I managed the project."

She gave a little whistle of appreciation. "Nice. Anything else?"

He named a few more buildings Kate instantly recognized, particularly the stores and shopping centers. "Sounds like retail's your niche."

"Mmm-hmm. If you ever decide to open a new Bare Essentials, let me know."

If only you knew…

"How'd you get into architecture? Didn't Daddy want you to follow in his footsteps and become a lawyer?"

"I prefer to build things, not tear them apart, which is what lawyers seem to spend a lot of their time doing." He flipped their omelets onto two plates and carried them to the table. "I really built things when I was going to college. I worked for a construction company in L.A. every summer."

"I somehow pictured you surfing your way through college."

"Ha! I tried it once and the damn board almost tore my ear off. After I wiped out, it hit me in the head. I still have the scar." He turned his head, pushing his hair up with his fingers. Kate bit her lip. Unable to resist, she stepped closer, until the toes of her sandals nearly touched his bare feet.

His hair was still slightly damp with sweat from his workout, and his skin still glowed with energy. She gulped, trying to ignore her response, and examined the thin scar that ran from just under his earlobe into his hairline.

If she wasn't mistaken, she might have kissed that spot during their interlude at the theater. Her heart skipped a beat.

"Ouch," she murmured.

He seemed to notice her sudden intensity, and her closeness. Her face was inches from his neck, and she inhaled deeply, smelling his musky warmth. She closed her eyes briefly, remembering what it had been like to kiss him. To touch him.

Lord help her, she still wanted him so much she could barely stand up. She wanted to nibble on his neck, to taste his earlobe, to feel his body get all sweaty again—preferably while it was on top of hers. Inside hers.

"You ready?" he asked, letting his hand fall to his side.

She nodded dumbly. "Uh-huh." Ready for just about anything.

"Do you like it spicy?"

Spicy? Oh, yeah, she loved it spicy. "Yeah. Real spicy."

"I think there's Tabasco sauce in the fridge."

Tabasco? Kate shook her head, hard, and realized Jack was watching her with an amused, knowing look on his face.

He'd been talking about hot and spicy eggs.

She'd been thinking about hot and spicy sex.

Please, floor, open up under me and swallow me whole. "Kate?"

She raised a brow, trying to pretend she hadn't been picturing some of the spicy things the two of them could do on the kitchen table. Or counter. Or floor. "Huh?"

He reached for her, his hand brushing past her hip as he touched the handle on the refrigerator door. She jumped out of the way, noticing the way his hand tightened on the handle, as if he were exerting some great effort. Possibly for control? Was he as affected as she by their closeness?

There was only one way to find out. She reached out and touched the thin scar on his neck. He flinched and glanced at her. "It must have hurt," she said softly.

Jack didn't pull away as she moved closer, standing on tiptoes until her lips brushed his neck. Remembering the way he'd kissed her hip in the shower, she couldn't help kissing that hot, damp, male skin. Slipping her tongue out, she savored the faint salty flavor of sweat from his workout. She sighed at how good he tasted to her. Her touch elicited an answering groan from him, but he didn't move away. "I'm sorry I wasn't there to kiss it and make it better," she murmured as she moved her lips higher, kissing a path up to his earlobe. She stepped closer, for better access, sliding one foot between his, until his thigh was nestled between her legs. Kate closed her eyes briefly at the very intimate contact.

He muttered a soft curse, as if he could take no more. Catching her around the waist, he lifted her higher, pressing his leg tighter against her sex as he lowered his mouth to hers. Their kiss was explosive. Hot and wet. Deep and hungry. Kate met every thrust of his tongue, loving the way he tasted, the way he explored her mouth as if he couldn't get enough of her. She jerked her hips, needing the strength of his hard thigh against the crotch of her jean shorts.

When they finally broke apart, Jack stared down at her, warmth and tenderness shining through the passion of his gaze. "I invited you to breakfast. I didn't intend to leap on you at the first opportunity."

To be honest, she'd done the leaping. But she didn't point that out. "I wasn't playing any get-back-at-you games," she admitted softly. "Like Friday."

"Good. I wasn't playing games, either. But I think we should probably sit down and eat."

Nodding, she took a few deep breaths, trying to forget the way he'd kissed her, the way the strong muscles of his thigh had felt against her still-aroused body. She was too thankful that he wasn't going to tease her about her momentary lapse into mindless lust to argue.

As they sat to eat, Jack apparently looked for a quick way to change the subject. "Hey, I know what I forgot to tell you. I heard some news about the Rialto yesterday."

"Really?"

"Apparently the city now owns it, due to a loan default. It's sat there empty for years, but now a group of concerned citizens has announced they're going to work on renovating it, then open it as a public playhouse."

She smiled. "Wonderful."

"It gets better. Rose Madison is leading the effort."

"Miss Rose?"

He nodded. "She's the one who told me about it. I ran into her. I mentioned we were both happy to see some work being done on the old place."

"Did she remember me?"

"Yes. She said if you want to pay for those free movies, you're welcome to come down anytime with a paintbrush."

"I think I can wield a paintbrush."

"Hopefully better than you can crack an egg," he said with a grin as he picked a tiny white piece of shell off his tongue.

"You got me. I'm a lousy cook. But if you want me to tell you how to save money at the grocery store, I'm your woman."

"Absolutely," he said softly.

Absolutely? What did that mean? Absolutely he wanted to learn how to save money grocery shopping?

Or…absolutely, she was his woman?

Too chicken to ask which he meant, since she wasn't sure what she wanted his answer to be, Kate finished her breakfast, thanked him and then left.

But she wondered about his comment all day long. Not to mention their kiss.

JACK SPENT THE AFTERNOON out of the area, visiting some of his late father's properties in nearby towns. They were mostly rentals, small tract houses for young families. His father hadn't been a slumlord, but some of the buildings were old and in need of repair. The agent who was handling the sales told him he'd take care of it.

When he got back to Pleasantville that afternoon, he found the duplex empty. Kate's SUV was not parked outside. She'd probably gone back to her cousin's place on Lilac Hill, which was the reason Jack decided not to go to his mother's house.

He told himself he wasn't avoiding *her.* No, he was just trying to avoid temptation. He hadn't been kidding in the kitchen when he'd said he wanted things to change between them once they got back to Chicago. That day couldn't come soon enough for him, particularly after that kiss they'd shared.

He had also been fully aware of her desire for him. Hell, she'd worn it as if it were perfume, oozing from her every pore. So staying away from her seemed to be the smart choice.

Needing something to do, he remembered Rose's request for help at the Rialto. He'd developed a real affection for the old theater, particularly since the day he'd met Kate. Changing into some old clothes, he drove downtown and pulled up outside the Rialto.

Right behind a silver SUV.

Drive away. Of course he didn't. Seeing her might be foolish, since he already spent way too much of his time thinking about her, but he parked and got out of his truck, anyway.

As he entered the building he heard loud music blaring from a boom box and saw a pair of bare legs, complete with paint-speckled sneakers, dangling from a scaffold. "What do you think you're doing?" he asked, recognizing the curve of Kate's calves.

He realized he probably should not have startled her only after he saw her drop the paintbrush. Right toward his head.

A quick step back saved his skull, but not his shorts.

"Jack," she cried as the brush careened down his leg, leaving squishy beige marks in its path.

"I'm really sorry," she muttered. She shimmied on her hands and knees across the wood plank of the scaffolding, doing very interesting things to her black gym shorts. Well, black and beige gym shorts, considering all the paint stains.

She reached the built-in metal ladder on the side of the scaffold and swung around to it. Not wanting her to drop anything else—including herself—Jack went over and steadied her as she descended.

"Did you get any paint on the walls?" he asked her, looking down at her speckled clothes. And her skin. Not to mention her face and hair. "You are a complete mess."

"That's what long showers are for."

Oh, great. Kate was taking another long shower. Maybe he should just shoot himself now.

Looking around the empty lobby, he said, "You here alone?"

She nodded. "Miss Rose and her brother were here when I arrived. They were just getting ready to go for a dinner break, but said if I wanted to I could keep working on this wall."

Jack followed her gaze and looked at the interior wall that she'd been painting. It extended up all the way to the top of the open, two-story lobby. Where Kate had been working, he saw a big circle of paint. "Didn't anyone teach you to do the trim first?"

"Since you're the construction genius, why don't you do it?" She bent, grabbed another brush and tossed it to him. Though not paint covered, the brush was wet and as he caught it on the bristle-side, it oozed beige-tinged water between his fingers.

"Nice," he said as he shook the moisture off. "I think

you've been selling body paint at your store too long. This kind doesn't come off so easily."

She stepped closer, a laugh on her lips. "Oh, so you're saying I shouldn't do…this?" She lifted her completely white hand and cupped his cheek.

He cringed, then realized he didn't feel moisture against his skin. "If that paint on your hand had been wet, I'd be turning you over my knee and spanking you right now."

Her eyes widened. "Oooh, sounds kinky. I didn't know you were into that sort of thing."

"I'm not," he replied. He had to know. "Are you?"

She turned her head slightly and peeked at him through lowered lashes. "Light S and M? Well, lots of my customers are."

He couldn't resist asking, "*Light* S and M? How, exactly, would that differ from the heavy variety?"

She shrugged. "It's more playful, not for seriously weirded-out people. We don't sell whips, belts or paddles. But some couples enjoy the occasional black leather domi-natrix outfit."

He had a sudden mental picture of her wearing black leather and clenched his jaw.

"And, of course, there's also light bondage. Handcuffs, silk scarves, blindfolds. It's all part of the fantasy."

"Fantasy?" God help him. Even though it might give him another long, sleepless night, he really wanted to know her fantasies. "Like?"

"Like being overwhelmed," she admitted softly. "Letting yourself be overcome by passion, even made helpless when you're with someone you can trust." She bit the corner of her lip, as if deciding to continue. "Exploring every possibility, going as far as your body can go, without being able to stop, because someone you know would never hurt you is in complete control."

Kate was nearly covered with paint from head to toe. Her thick, dark hair was pulled haphazardly into a ponytail at the back of her neck. She wore no makeup and she held a drippy paint roller plopping little drops of paint on the plastic drop cloth every time she moved it.

He'd never wanted her more.

Jack had walked hip-deep into this conversation, so he had no one else to blame. And he couldn't quite find a way to get out of it. Nor was he sure he wanted to.

"Is that your fantasy?" He heard the thick tone in his voice. "Being overwhelmed? Letting someone you trust give you pleasure without any mental barriers, any restrictions, taking because you have no other choice but to take?"

"I think so," she murmured. "Being free to wring every ounce of gratification you can because it's beyond your control to stop it."

In twenty seconds Kate had just made him understand the appeal of silk scarves and handcuffs.

"You must be really good at your job," he said softly. "Though, I still don't get the whole spanking thing."

She gave him a wicked grin. "Well, I don't particularly care for pain, but I have to say you are *very* good at kissing and making all better."

Remembering kissing her hip in the shower the other night, he knew exactly what she meant. His body reacted instinctively, another sudden rush of heat rushing southward from his gut to his groin. "Now, I *could* take that the wrong way and be offended," he said, stepping closer.

"Oh?"

He nodded. "You just basically told me to kiss your ass. I could take it as an insult." He lowered his voice to a whisper. "Or a really tempting invitation."

Her lips parted and her tongue snaked out to moisten them.

"Which do you think it was?"

Unable to resist, he lifted a hand to her throat, running his finger down and touching its hollow. "I think if this were a week ago, it'd be an insult. Today, I'm not so sure."

She closed her eyes, tilting her head back as he traced a path around her neck, to her collarbone, touching her only with the tips of his fingers. "Me, neither," she admitted.

Needing to feel her in his arms again, Jack tilted her chin up and caught her mouth with his own. She moaned, parting her lips, inviting him deeper, and he accepted her invitation.

He loved kissing Kate. Every time was better than the last, hot and sweet, carnal and tender. He made love to her mouth, tasting her, drinking of her, making no effort to step away to disguise his body's reaction. She pressed against him, moaning again as he moved his mouth to press kisses on her jaw. "It's hard to find a clean spot," he said with a chuckle.

"Here's one," she whispered, pushing the sleeve of her tank top, and her bra strap, to the edge of her shoulder. A naughty invitation, which he immediately accepted. He kissed down her neck, to her collarbone, and right below it.

"Where else?" he asked, nudging the cotton top down even lower. She answered with only a soft sigh and an arch in her back, telling him to proceed. He did, scraping his tongue down to the top curve of her breast, then sliding it lower to flick at her pebbled nipple.

She quivered in his arms, and leaned back against the old refreshment counter. Appropriate. He wanted to completely gobble her up. But first he wanted to see her.

As if he had no control over them, his hands moved to the waistband of her shorts and tugged her shirt free. He lifted it up, slowly, watching as the toned, creamy-colored skin of her stomach was revealed inch by inch. Until finally he saw the lace of her bra and the bottom curves of her breasts. His mouth went dry with hunger. "You are so beautiful," he whispered as he moved his hands higher. She didn't reply, just arched into his touch, twisting until he slipped his fingers beneath her bra. She hissed when he touched her nipples, tweaking them lightly, stroking and teasing the way he knew she'd liked when they'd made love before.

"I have to taste you," he muttered.

Before Kate responded, Jack heard the front door of the theater open. Footsteps echoed on the tile floor. Acting instinctively, he yanked Kate's shirt down, and turned to shield her behind him while she put herself back together.

"Get a lot of work done?" someone called. Wincing, Jack watched as Miss Rose and her grinning brother entered the lobby. The older woman gave Jack and Kate a pointed glance. "If Jack wants to be covered with paint, he's welcome to get on the scaffold and make a mess of himself, just like you have," Rose said with a chuckle. "There was no need to share yours, Kate."

Kate scrunched her eyes closed, obviously embarrassed as hell. Jack chuckled and reached for a paint tray. "Okay, Kate, you were good enough to teach me one or two things this afternoon." He winked. "How about I teach you how to paint?"

THROUGHOUT THE NEXT DAY, as Kate worked in the store with Cassie and some high school boys who followed her cousin around like puppy dogs, she kept wondering if she should move and stay with Cassie up on Lilac Hill. Even after everyone else left, leaving her alone in the shop to finish up some paperwork and cleaning, she thought about it. Cassie's house would be safer. Having Jack next door was impossible, especially now, after what had happened yesterday. Their kiss in the theater had been intoxicating. If Miss Rose hadn't come back when she did, they might have ended up rolling around on the floor, covering their naked bodies with the specks of paint littering the drop cloth.

She should move. Jack was simply too tempting. Too disturbing. Sooner or later they were going to end up back in bed together, and she didn't know if either of them was prepared for the consequences of that.

One other thing disturbed her about being back in town.

"Hiya, Kate! How's the store coming along?"

Friendliness. Damn, she really couldn't get used to that.

Pausing with her hand filled with the paper towels she'd been using to clean the front window of the store early Thursday evening, she turned around. Diane. New owner of the Downtown Deli, whom Kate had met during her one-day trip to town, then again when she'd gone in for lunch Monday. "Good, thanks."

"I remember when we were gearing up to open," the sweet-faced strawberry-blonde continued, as if not noticing Kate's less-than-welcoming reply. "We got a chilly reception from some of the other merchants, let me tell you." She cast a critical glance toward the Tea Room. "You'd have thought we murdered Mr. Simmons, instead of just buying the deli from him."

"I can't believe he finally decided to retire. He was as crusty as his sub rolls." Kate chuckled. "I bet he wanted you to promise never to put mayonnaise on an Italian sub, didn't he?"

Diane's eyes widened. "Yes, he did!"

"He called it a sacrilege whenever I ordered one for Mom."

"Well, I waited on your mother more times than I can count, and I never once deprived her of her mayonnaise," the other woman replied. "How's she doing down there in sunny Florida, anyway? We sure do miss her at the Bunko Club."

Kate's eyes widened. They missed her? At the Bunko Club? And what the hell was a Bunko Club? "I didn't realize you knew her."

Diane snorted. "Darlin', you've been gone a long time if

you've forgotten that everyone knows everyone here. Edie was the first one at my door with a home-made apple pie when me and Will moved into the apartment above the deli. She's a real doll."

From behind Diane, Kate heard another voice. "Edie? You bet your life she is. Although, it sure was a nightmare getting her raggedy nails fixed all up. The woman worked too hard!"

Kate looked past Diane to see the young woman she'd met her first day in town. The friendly one from the nail salon. She looked different—her hair now being purple instead of a reddish orange. And the number of earrings had increased. But the welcoming grin was the same.

"Hi, again," Kate offered, unable to resist the smile.

"I sure never expected to see you here washing windows. Get in there and get some gloves on before you ruin that manicure."

Kate glanced down at her hands.

"On second thought, don't. Come by my shop after you're done and we'll fix you right up. And we'll have a long gab. Okay?"

"This is Josie," Diane interjected. "Don't make any pussycat jokes or she'll use too much glue on your acrylics then refuse to fill 'em. You'll have to pry them off with a crowbar."

Josie stuck her tongue out at the other woman, then turned her attention to Kate. "And you're Kate Jones. Edie's long-lost, super-successful daughter, cousin of the supermodel who has Sheriff Taggart going around in circles."

She talked so fast Kate had a hard time keeping up.

"Oh, really?"

Diane nodded. "His ex-girlfriend, Annie—she's the dispatcher—says Tag starts acting like a grizzly bear with a burr in his butt whenever he has a run-in with your cousin."

He hadn't looked like a grizzly Saturday night when he'd

come to the shop at 1:00 a.m. No, he'd looked more like a panther. Dark and dangerous. She hoped Cassie knew what she was doing.

"Uh, can I ask a stupid question?"

"Anything," Diane replied.

"What's Bunko?"

The other woman linked her arm in Kate's. "You've never played Bunko? It's the woman's version of poker night. The Lilac Hill types have their bridge club. We prefer Bunko. A dice game, rotated among the homes of the club members. Twice a month we meet to talk, laugh and play. The hostess provides the prizes."

"The members provide the bourbon," Josie added helpfully.

Kate laughed out loud. "Sounds like fun." Surprisingly, she meant it. She could see how her mother would have enjoyed something so simple yet charming.

"Then it's settled, you come to our next game, which happens to be tomorrow night at Eileen Saginaw's house."

Kate's smile widened in genuine pleasure. "Eileen is my mom's best friend. I'd love to see her again."

And as easy as that, Kate found herself committed to a social event with some of the women of Pleasantville.

What is wrong with this picture?

"Now, tell us what you're going to sell in your store," Diane said. "Pretty please? Nobody knows anything more than it's a ladies' shop, and everybody's going crazy trying to find out."

Kate bit her lip. These two were the nicest people she'd met so far in Pleasantville, but that didn't mean they were going to welcome sex toys on the main drag of town.

"It's gotta be something good," Josie said. "Tell me it's real shoes. Real, decent shoes that don't have rubber soles and plastic uppers. If you say you're gonna carry Dr. Martens

I'll get down on the ground and kiss your toes. And I'll give you a free pedicure while I'm down there."

Kate shook her head. "Sorry. Not shoes."

"Clothes. Oh, please let it be clothes," Diane said. "The closest store to buy a decent dress is twenty miles away. And that's not even one of those new super Wal-Marts, it's just a plain old regular one."

Kate bit her lip and shook her head at Diane's genuine consternation. "Sorry. Not clothes." *Not unless you counted crotchless panties and leather bustiers!*

Josie bounced on the toes of her chunky black boots like a kid waiting in line for Santa. "Then what?"

"You'll have to wait until our grand opening to find out."

"Grand opening?"

She recognized that voice. Wincing, Kate turned around to see Jack standing right behind her. The man was quiet as a cat—she'd never even heard him approaching.

Obviously neither had the other two women. Because she felt sure she'd have noticed those matching holy-cannoli-take-me-big-boy looks on their faces.

"Hi, Jack," she murmured. Her voice didn't even shake. Amazing, since her heart had started racing like an out of control freight train speeding toward heartbreak junction.

The man was too handsome. His smile too adorably sexy to be real, the twinkle in his brilliant green eyes too charming. He made women want to hug him. Then *do* him. Including Kate. Especially Kate.

Diane and Josie spoke in unison. "Introduce us."

After she'd made introductions all the way around, and listened to Josie and Diane pump Jack for information about why on earth he'd waited so long to come back for a visit to Pleasantville, she tried to slide away. Evening was approaching, though it was still light out. She wanted to get inside and lock up. Mainly she wanted to get away before Jack started asking any more questions about her store.

Just when she thought she might make a clean getaway, however, an old, beige Cadillac pulled up on the street and parked one building down, in front of the Tea Room.

"Great," Jack muttered. "It's my ex-brother-in-law."

"Which one?" Josie said under her breath, her voice holding a definite note of sarcasm. Obviously she knew Angela.

As Kate watched the man emerge from the Cadillac, she answered softly, "Darren."

CHAPTER NINE

DARREN HADN'T CHANGED a great deal, though his face was rounder and his hair thinner than it had been in high school. His belly was rounder, too. He wasn't fat, just soft and mellow-looking. Like a salesman.

He nodded to Diane and Josie, barely glanced at Kate, then noticed Jack. His face paled and for a second Kate thought he was going to get back in his car and drive away. Then his shoulders straightened as he locked the car and walked around it to the sidewalk.

Okay, so the jerk wasn't a complete wimp. He wasn't going to try to avoid his ex's brother.

"Hello, Jack, Josie. Diane." Then he glanced toward Kate, as if waiting for an introduction. His eyes narrowed as he tilted his head. "You...my God, it's Kate Jones."

"Hello, Darren."

"I had no idea you were back in town."

"Well, you know what they say about bad pennies."

"You look...wow, you look *great,*" he said, his eyes wide as he stared her up and down.

Next door, the door to the Tea Room opened. Darren glanced past Kate, his face growing red. She knew darn well who stood there. "It was *so* nice seeing you, Darren. Be sure to say hi to your mom for me, okay?"

She turned around. Mrs. McIntyre stood on the porch next door, all stiff-necked, righteous indignation. Another woman, one Kate didn't recognize, stood with her. The two of them immediately started speaking in low voices. She couldn't hear their words, but she got the message loud and clear.

Kate gave them a forced but saccharine-sweet smile as she strode inside her store, as if she hadn't a care in the world.

Jack watched Kate leave, and made no attempt to stop her. He'd seen the silent exchange between Kate and Darren's mother. The glassiness in her eyes and the quiver of her lush, beautiful bottom lip, said she was holding on by a thin thread.

He'd also read the tension between his ex-brother-in-law and the woman he now considered his. He didn't stop to evaluate that, knowing Kate would resent the hell out of him thinking that way. Particularly since he'd wondered if it was best to stay away from her, for his own sanity and reproductive health. He'd come to the conclusion that walking around with a hard-on eighteen hours a day could really be bad for his future children.

Josie and Diane seemed to notice the tension in the air, as well. Telling Jack how nice it was to meet him, they both walked down the street, their heads close together as they talked.

Once they were gone, Jack eyed his sister's former husband. "How's it going, Darren?"

Darren was still looking at the door to the building that had once belonged to his father. "I can't believe Kate came back. I haven't seen her since graduation."

"You knew her in high school?"

Darren nodded. "We dated for a while, during senior year. She was my prom date."

Prom night. The night, if he wasn't mistaken, when his kid sister had gotten pregnant by this little prick, who'd walked out on her as soon as she'd miscarried their baby.

Jack's teeth clenched. "I thought Angela was your prom date."

"Oh, no, we just left together afterward..." Darren seemed to realize who he was speaking to, because his face went redder. "I mean, well, Angela and I had dated the year before. And we kind of got back together that night at prom."

"What about Kate? You know, your *date?*"

Darren stood there looking hopeless, helpless and regretful. He finally shrugged. "High school, man. I was a kid."

Jack shook his head. "Some people don't have to wait till they grow up to become dickless assholes." He prepared to walk away, but paused. "Darren?"

Darren finally looked him full in the face.

"If you like breathing, you'll stay away from Kate." Not waiting for an answer, he turned to follow Kate into her shop.

The doorknob didn't jiggle in his hand, she'd obviously flicked the lock when she went inside. He knocked, figuring she wouldn't answer. To his surprise, the door moved. Pushing at it, he watched as it swung open. The lock was apparently broken, lucky for him.

After he got inside, and closed the door firmly behind him, Jack noticed the smell of paint and new carpet. The overhead lights in the shop were off, but recessed ones above the shelves cast illumination throughout the shadowy store. A bit of late-afternoon sunlight peeked in through the sheers on the windows.

He didn't see Kate. He did hear a voice, however. Following the sound of a radio, he walked through the sales area and back to the offices and storage rooms. He found Kate sitting in the center of a cement-floored room, surrounded by boxes, staring mindlessly into the air.

"Kate," he said softly. "Are you okay?"

She slowly nodded. "How'd you get in? I locked the door."

"Something's obviously wrong with the lock. You should have someone look at that. Are you all right?"

A small smile widened her lips, and surprisingly, no tears marred her cheeks. "I'm fine, Jack. Just wondering…"

"Wondering what?"

She hesitated, and he thought for a moment she wouldn't answer. Finally she admitted, "Wondering whether it's right to go on resenting someone for doing only what you yourself have done for much of your life."

He waited but she didn't explain. He somehow suspected she had no intention of talking about whatever it was she was thinking. "So you're really okay?"

She nodded. Rising, she brushed some dust from the floor off her butt, calling his attention to the miniscule white shorts she wore. He closed his eyes briefly. No wonder Darren had been unable to stop staring. Kate looked amazing. "I see you got all the paint washed off."

She nodded. "For now. Though I promised to go back and help some more tomorrow at the Rialto."

"Me, too," he admitted. "Now, you want to tell me what grand opening you were talking about." He glanced around the storage room at all the boxes. "Are you going into business here?"

"Yep," she replied as she grabbed a box and moved past him, exiting the storage room.

He followed her through a short hallway, into the store area. She continued, through an arched doorway toward the dressing rooms and a mirrored alcove. She dropped the box near several others already lined up beneath rows of shelves.

"Your kind of business?" he asked, repeating his question from Saturday.

She tilted her head and gave him an arched glance out of the corner of her eye. "What do you think?"

When she bent and retrieved a filmy white bra from one

box, then what appeared to be a black leather bustier from another, his eyes narrowed. "I think you've decided to play Clint Eastwood."

He'd nailed it. He saw by the shock in her eyes, and the way she gasped as she dropped the two pieces of sexy lingerie, that he'd hit the truth dead-on.

"You're out for a little revenge."

"How could you possibly…"

"Come on, Kate, opening a new Bare Essentials right here in Pleasantville? Next door to the Tea Room?" He paused, letting the concept sink in, then reluctantly began to chuckle. "Damn, you really are something."

"You…you're not shocked?" she whispered.

Shocked? No. He'd already learned that Kate Jones was like no woman he'd ever known. He shook his head. "Not shocked. I think you're crazy, and you're going to lose your shirt." He cast a heated glance at her body. "I mean figuratively speaking. Literally, I wouldn't mind in the least."

She rolled her eyes.

"If you ever open your doors, that is. I'm sure there'll be a protest from certain quarters. You could lose everything you've already put into this place."

"Which wasn't much. It cost only some sweat equity—mostly Cassie's—and shipping charges to ship stuff here." She shrugged. "Besides, it's not about money."

"Of course not."

She stepped closer and her smile faded. "It's not some silly revenge plot, Jack. I had to be here…I needed to come back to town this summer."

He couldn't imagine what could possibly be important enough to bring Kate back to a place she quite obviously hated, and told her so.

"I can't really talk about it," she said. "A lot of things

happened all at once." She crossed her arms in front of her chest and rubbed her hands up and down, as if chilly.

"Kate, whatever is going on, whatever this is about…"

"Yes?"

"Just be careful. Sometimes things don't work out the way you think they will."

"I somehow think this will," she said, "because I don't have unrealistic expectations. I fully expect to fail here."

He raised a brow.

"We'll open, we'll cause a lot of chest-clutching, a lot of scandalous whispering, and then, when Cassie's safe…" She cleared her throat. "I mean, when Cassie's ready to leave…we'll close and go away. Cassie will sell this building and everything else she owns here and we'll never come back. No ties, no bad memories, just a laugh when we think back on our one last hurrah."

"Cassie's in trouble?"

"No. Forget it, okay? Cassie's fine." She looked at her nails, obviously feigning nonchalance. "Did you like her?"

"Like her? I barely spoke to her."

"Most men don't have to *speak* to her to form an impression."

Jack shrugged. "She's beautiful, of course. Flamboyant and probably too sexy for her own good. She'll drive any man who loves her to the verge of insanity."

She waited. When he didn't continue, she prompted, "That's all? You weren't…interested?"

He shook his head. "Do you think I'm a total scumbag? What kind of guy would lust after the cousin of the woman he's involved with?"

"We are not involved."

"Bullshit. We are very much involved," he admitted, confirming that not only to her, but to himself.

He waited for her to deny it. She couldn't. Who could

deny the inevitable? They might not have done much about their relationship since they'd been back in town, except for a few hot kisses and that one close encounter yesterday. But there's no question they would. Sooner or later.

Judging by the look in her eye, and the expectancy in the air, he suspected it was going to be sooner.

He waited for a mental voice to tell him no, waited for his feet to instinctively turn toward the door. Waited to hear from the nice-guy voice of reason who'd been whispering in his ear for weeks.

That voice had been growing weaker as each day passed. He'd been listening to her from the other side of the duplex, seeing her shining, dark hair as she left in the morning, hearing her off-key singing as she showered. Every day another chunk had disappeared out of the wall of willpower he'd tried to erect between them. And after yesterday, it had come down like the last remnants of the Berlin Wall.

Sure he'd had good intentions, but all the good intentions in the world couldn't stop what was happening between them. No more than a surfer could stop a wave on which he was riding.

Sometimes he had to ride it out to see where it took him.

"So are you going to tell me what's wrong? Is your cousin in some kind of trouble or not?"

"Jack, let it go, okay?"

He didn't press her on the Cassie issue, sensing she wouldn't tell him what was going on, anyway. "So, back to your shop and your revenge plan. Anything else on the agenda?"

"No, I think I've summed it up."

"Not much revenge there. I mean, you're not having the population paint every building red?"

She chuckled. "You rented *High Plains Drifter.*"

He nodded.

"Okay, so it's not the greatest revenge." Her smile was mischievous and it made her brown eyes sparkle. "Must be that rotten sweetness everybody says is somewhere inside me. I'm great at fantasizing, just not so great at execution."

Hearing her laugh at herself, Jack found her as captivating as she'd been the day they'd met. As if here, in a shop like the one she owned in Chicago, she was free to be herself. She'd let the negative elements of Pleasantville—her hurts, her misgivings, her sarcasm—disappear.

He found himself doing the same. As if nothing outside the building mattered. They could have been meeting for the first time in Chicago, as far as he was concerned.

She sighed. "Our plan seemed a lot more dramatic and outrageous when we fantasized about it as teenagers."

"You fantasized about opening a sex shop in Pleasantville?"

"Yep, we even wrote it down in our diaries on prom night."

His smile faded. "I heard about your prom night."

"It's fine. Water under the bridge," she insisted. But she wouldn't meet his eye.

"Should I even ask who else was on that revenge list you made that night?"

She pursed her lips. "No, you probably shouldn't."

As he'd thought—his own sister had probably been a pretty large target. Not to mention Darren.

"So, can I assume this shop will satisfy your need for revenge? I mean, I don't have to worry bodies are going to start flying out the upstairs windows over the Tea Room, right?"

She sidestepped the question. "Oh, look, the store's not even revenge at all. It's more…I don't know…like the old song. They talked about us throughout our childhoods, well, now we'll *really* give them something to talk about! And they'll never forget the Tremaines."

"What if you fail to fail?"

"Excuse me?"

"You know, what if the store's a big fat success? What then?"

Her laughter echoed in the small alcove. "Not a chance. That'll never happen."

"You never know. Your store is a big hit in Chicago."

"This is *so* not Chicago." She bent, opening a box at her feet. "Can you see Mrs. McIntyre buying one of these?"

She pulled out what looked like a foot-long hot dog. Then he realized it was a dildo. "Now, there's something you don't see every day in Pleasantville," he mused out loud, not at all shocked, as she'd obviously intended.

"Gee, ya think?" She giggled like a kid as she grabbed something else out of the box. "I'm thinking of these in the display case right by the cash register."

He raised a brow. "Anal beads?"

Holding the strand of beads between her thumb and index finger, she swung them around, a wicked look in her eye. When he said nothing, she dropped them, reached back into the box and pulled out something else. He instantly knew what the black, rubbery circle was for.

The playful laughter faded as she caught the heat in his eyes. It was answered by her own aware expression.

His groin tightened as he imagined using the item during sex with Kate. The way she'd slide it down his dick, her cool hand holding his balls as she tightened the cock ring around him. Then climbing on top of him and riding him, letting the ring keep him engorged and rock-hard. Building the pressure until he'd have to grab her by the hips and thrust up into her until they both came together in one strong, fiery blast of sexual pleasure.

"Ever used one?" she finally asked.

He wondered if she'd be shocked by his reply, and decided to find out. "Yeah. Have you?"

Her lips parted as she sucked in a deep, shuddery breath. She obviously hadn't expected that, hadn't been prepared for him to answer with blatant honesty. Even from several feet away, he could see the goose bumps on her chest, and the sudden jut of her nipples against her tight blue T-shirt.

"No," she finally answered. "I, uh…don't try everything we sell in the store."

His stare shifted to the huge dildo.

She shook her head slowly, as if dazed.

He reached over and picked up a pair of handcuffs from a pile on a nearby shelf. Remembering their conversation from yesterday, he asked, "What about these?"

She shook her head again.

"Just as well," he murmured as he put them back. "They'll chafe your pretty wrists when you thrash around on the bed."

He wasn't speaking in general terms. And felt sure she knew it. This wasn't an *if* conversation—it was a *when*.

The inside of the store began to feel steamy hot.

"We do sell faux-fur-lined ones," she admitted, her voice shaky and breathless.

Did she even know she'd issued him a blatant invitation? Of course she knew. This was Kate, after all.

"What *have* you tried?" he asked, unable to stop this sensual self-torture. "I know you've got your little finger vibrator. But what else can you personally recommend for your shoppers…based on your own experience?"

She hesitated.

"Come on, Kate," he said as he stepped closer and dropped his voice to a whisper. "Show me your wares."

He wondered if she'd leave, if she'd back away from the sultry atmosphere into which they'd once again fallen together.

He should have known better.

"There's a nifty vibrating tongue…"

He groaned softly.

"It's not wet enough, though," she continued slowly, obviously knowing full well what she was doing to him. "Not like a real one. But powerful. It doesn't get tired, doesn't veer off at the last second and ruin everything just before climax."

Neither had he. Not that he reminded her of that.

"What else do you like? Any other replicas of body parts?"

She shook her head. "Not really. My favorite thing we sell is probably the lingerie. My partner has real talent. Bare Essentials goes well beyond your average teddies, thongs and push-up bras."

He managed not to come in his pants at the image of Kate in any or all of these seductive items. "Oh?"

Nodding, she pointed to a stack of folded cloth. She picked up something off the top and shook it out. It took him a moment to realize what it was. "Crotchless tights?"

"A big hit in Chicago in the winter. It's too cold for thigh-highs, or even regular panty hose. And, for some reason, men seem to get off on women in tights." She shrugged. "I think it's the same reason men like blondes on trampolines."

He understood. "Or cheerleaders. It reminds them of that whole teenage thing where boys are one six-foot-tall pile of testosterone and the girls know it."

She laughed.

"So, do you wear them?"

She gave him a coy look out of the corner of her eye. "Maybe. Most women who do like the naughtiness of it. They like knowing that even if it's twenty degrees outside, they can go for something outrageous in the back of a limo if the right man happens to be around."

His smile tightened. "Speaking from experience?"

She didn't try to lie. "No." Raising her hands, palms up, she shrugged. "What can I say? I live a pretty boring life in

Chicago, in spite of being the sex toy queen of Michigan Avenue."

He was damn glad of that. He hated even thinking of Kate with another man. His own possessiveness surprised him. Jack had been involved in enough casual relationships to know women had as much sexual drive as men. Where they chose to fill that need had never been any of his business, once they'd left his bed.

Kate was a different story. He had a feeling he could get damn near violent thinking of her with anyone else.

Which completely floored him.

"There are some pieces of lingerie I've used." She bent at the knee, almost kneeling at his feet. Looking down, seeing the top of her head about level with his groin, Jack had to fist his hands to try to gain control.

She hunted around in a box, then said, "Aha." Standing, she showed him what she'd found. "My favorite."

She held a pretty, lacy, pale blue bra. It had straps, underwire, a satiny strip of material to go beneath a woman's breasts—but nothing to cover the rest. A front-less bra.

"You, uh, wear those things?"

"Sometimes. Especially when I'm wearing cotton or silk."

They both glanced at her cotton T-shirt.

Though almost afraid to ask, he had to. "Why?"

"The different textures of fabric feel amazing against my nipples," she admitted, something dark and erotic flashing in her eyes. "It's empowering to give yourself a thrill throughout the day, without anyone ever being aware of it. Like the tights."

He swallowed. Hard. Then he stepped closer, until their bodies nearly touched from neck to knee. Looking down at the sharp points of her breasts, he finally managed to ask, "Are you wearing one of those bras now?"

"Maybe." She didn't step back. Instead, she reached for

his hand and pulled it toward her body. Dropping her voice to a purr, she said, "Why don't you see if you can tell?"

Dangerous. Like reaching out to touch a blazing red burner on a stove…you know you're going to get burned, but you just can't shake yourself out of the spell.

Jack didn't care.

He touched.

CHAPTER TEN

"YES, I THINK YOU MIGHT be wearing one now," he murmured.

Kate didn't reply, couldn't even speak as he traced the tips of his fingers across her sensitive nipple. Then he moved his hand lower, to cup her breast. Stepping even closer, until their hips brushed, he brought his other hand up. When he passed his open palm against her other breast, making the fabric of her top scrape the other distended nipple, she shuddered.

"Jack…"

"Shh," he whispered, his mouth so close to her hair she felt the warmth of his breath. "I'm not sure yet. I think I need to test some more before I decide if you are."

"Please do," she said with a tiny whimper.

He did, cupping, squeezing lightly. He caught her nipples between fingers on each hand, tweaking them, making sparks shoot from there straight down to her crotch. Her legs shook as heat and moisture flooded her shorts.

"Yes, you are," he finally said. Thankfully he didn't pull his hands away.

"So, Kate, let's recap. You wear seductive lingerie for your own pleasure. You carry a vibrator in your purse and use a battery-powered tongue whenever you want an orgasm."

She nodded mindlessly, agreeing, anything as long as he continued the stroking of her breasts.

LESLIE KELLY 171

"There's one thing you haven't mentioned. Something I know you like."

She instantly knew what he meant and whimpered.

"Penetration," he continued, dragging out the word as if it were a caress. "Deep, hard, erotic penetration."

"Yes." She arched her back, offering more of herself, her fingers itching to grab the bottom hem of her shirt and lift it so she could get even more of his intimate attention.

His hands moved away, caressing her waist, her back, her hip. "Can you get that from your toys or playthings?" he asked, as if he didn't know she was about to crawl out of her own skin out of sheer, undiluted need.

"No." Aroused to the point of pain, she shifted, pushing her pelvis toward his and grinding against the huge erection she could easily feel against her body. The moisture between her legs doubled, the electric awareness thrumming through her body quadrupled. Not questioning the impulse, knowing she had to touch him or die, she slipped her hand between their bodies to cup him through his jeans. "Nothing compares to this."

He hissed as her fingers tightened around him.

He suddenly got serious, obviously realizing she wasn't playing sexy games anymore. "You're sure?"

"Oh, yeah."

"Here?"

"Uh-huh. But there's no table," she said as she continued to caress him.

"Floor'll do," he muttered before catching her mouth in a wet, carnal kiss. She melted against him, rapidly refamiliarizing herself with the taste of his mouth, the sweetness of his tongue. The feel of his long, hard body pressed against hers.

One hand slipped from her breast down to the waistband of her shorts. He tugged it free, stroking her belly, her waist, then higher until his fingers were inches from her nipples.

No cloth barrier this time, she knew it wouldn't take much and she'd be coming right then and there.

That would be lovely. But this time she didn't want to be the only one completely out of control, brought to ever higher peaks of ecstasy by Jack.

She wanted to be the one turning *him* into a raging, living, breathing hormone.

"I love kissing you," she said with a whimper when their lips parted. "I want to kiss you *everywhere*."

His eyes widened in understanding as she dropped to her knees in front of him. "Kate…"

"Hush."

Her hand trembled as she unbuttoned, then unzipped, his jeans. He wore white boxer briefs, which did little to hold back his erect penis. Her mouth watered, then went dry as she savored that long moment of anticipation that probably lasted no longer than a few erratic beats of her heart.

Finally, once again, she would see him. Touch him. Taste him. Working the briefs down, she held her breath, watching as his hard-on was revealed. She moaned at the sight, remembering how it had given her such pleasure their first time. Knowing he'd give her more pleasure tonight.

But not yet. Not until he was completely out of control.

Jack didn't want her to proceed. He'd been walking around in a state of arousal for weeks, and as she leaned closer to his cock, her lips brushing the sensitive skin at its tip, he nearly lost it. "Kate…" he said with a moan as her tongue flicked out, just a touch, a tiny caress to taste the moisture there.

"Remember what you said that day on the stage, Jack? Well, fair's fair. I like taste, too."

Then she moved her lips over him and took him into her mouth. "Ah, Kate." He moaned, dropping his head back. He clenched his fists, let her suck him, surrounding him with hot, wet sweetness and gentle pressure. When he felt her hand slide between his legs to cup his balls, his eyes shot open and he looked down at her.

Her head moved slowly, back and forth, sucking him deep, then pulling away until she'd almost released him completely.

"Kate, please, you've got to let me…"

"Watch," she murmured between one smooth stroke of her mouth and the next. When she tilted her head and glanced to the right, toward the mirror, he followed her gaze.

And nearly lost his mind.

Feeling her wet strokes. Hearing her coos of pleasure that said she really *liked* what she was doing. Seeing part of his body disappearing between those beautiful lips of hers.

He couldn't take another second.

"Enough," he growled, taking her by the shoulders and pushing her back.

Their clothes—with the exception of Kate's front-less bra—were gone within twenty seconds. He was between her upraised legs ten beyond that.

"Condoms are in there," she muttered, pointing to a box near his hip.

Jack didn't even look as reached for it, feeling around with his hand while he kissed Kate senseless. "You knew what that would do to me," he whispered against her lips.

"I kinda hoped," she said with a sultry chuckle. "I wasn't ready to stop."

"Not now," he told her. She panted as he sucked her earlobe, and hissed when he caught her breast in his hand. "Our first time back together…we'll go at the same time."

She gasped and arched up, grinding her hips into him. "Go at the same time? Do you mean…in the *numerical* sense?"

It took him a second to grasp her meaning. When he did, the image she suggested—giving each other oral pleasure at the same time—flooded his mind, making him even harder. Even more frantic.

"Hate to have to break it to you, but you're definitely *not* sweet, Kate Jones," he said with a ragged laugh.

"Thank heaven."

He ran the flat of his palm down her body to her hip. Then he slid his fingers into her curls, into the slick, hot crevice, knowing she was ready. "Except maybe here," he whispered as he slid his finger into her.

She tightened around him, moaning and bumping against his hand. He gave her what she wanted, flicking her tight little clit with his thumb until she cooed, then inserting another finger into her, stroking her G-spot from within. "Yeah, you're very sweet here." He could tell by her cries she was within seconds of climaxing.

"No fair. We're supposed to go together this time," she said with a whimper.

Before he knew what she was doing, she'd pushed him, rolled him over so she could straddle him on the floor. "Better."

Looking up at what had to be the most glorious sight on the planet, he had to agree.

Kate stared down at him, seeing the passion and admiration he could never have feigned. He was hard beneath her bottom, and close to where she wanted him. She shifted slightly until his penis slid into the wet folds of skin concealing her opening.

He growled.

"What? Not good?" She knew damn well it was.

"You know it's good. It's just not enough."

"Anxious, are we?"

He ripped open the condom with his teeth, showing her how anxious he was. She took a glance at their reflection, amazed at the sensuality of the moment. She slid back and forth over him, using his hardness to stroke her clitoris until she gasped.

"You like watching, too." Jack's stare met hers in the mirror.

She nodded. Then, knowing he watched her every move, Kate slid her hands up her body, until she cupped her own breasts.

"Keep going."

She did, catching her nipples between her fingers. "Mmm. But not as good as your hands."

He complied, replacing her hands with his own, then leaning up to suck one nipple deeply into his mouth.

Kate had her first orgasm instantaneously. She was still shuddering from it as she plucked the condom from his fingers and moved out of the way to roll it down over him.

When he was fully sheathed, she held herself above him. She caught his stare and held it. Then, with aching precision and slowness, she slid down on him, taking him completely into her body, inch by endless inch, until he'd filled her up so much she felt complete for the first time in ages.

"Yes," she said with a contented sigh.

"Yes," he echoed.

She didn't move at first, just sat there, absorbing him, stroking him with muscles deep within her body. She saw him clench his fist and tilt his head back in pleasure.

"More?"

He nodded, reaching for her hips. "Definitely more, Kate."

Then he started to move below her, thrusting upward. She met every stroke with one of her own, amazed at how quickly their bodies synchronized to one another.

It was hot. Energetic. Frenzied.

But also something else. There were moments when they'd meet each other's eyes and smile. When he'd reach up to brush her hair off her sweat-dampened cheek. Or he'd rub his thumb across her lower lip, then tug her down for a slow, wet kiss that somehow felt even more personal than the mating of their lower bodies.

He'd slow the pace, drag out the pleasure, until Kate felt her legs tremble with near exhaustion.

"Let me," he said as he held her around the waist. He rolled her over, staying inside her, his face inches from hers. Another kiss. Another stroke.

She turned her head and saw them in the mirror. Saw him holding his beautifully hard body above hers on his thick, strong arms. Saw his shoulders flex, his back strain, his gorgeous, tight butt move up and down as he pumped into her over and over again, so deep she had to gasp for breath. She clutched his shoulders, wrapped her legs around his hips and met him thrust for thrust.

She sensed the minute he'd gone too far to hold back. And as soon as he had, he braced himself on one arm, bringing his other hand between their bodies. "Come with me, honey."

And, of course, Kate did.

"I'M SORRY I didn't call," he whispered a few minutes later. They lay together on the newly carpeted floor, wrapped in each other's arms, exchanging lazy kisses and slow caresses.

He felt her stiffen against him. Then she asked, "Sorry because you had to wait for this?"

"No, I'm not sorry that way. I mean, I *apologize* for not calling you, Kate. I thought I had good reasons—and maybe I did. But I thought about you constantly and I never stopped wanting to see you again."

She tilted her head back to study his face. "Good reasons. And that's all you're going to say?"

He nodded once, knowing he couldn't elaborate. The truth of the long-term relationship between his father and her mother was tough enough for him to deal with. He didn't want to burden Kate with it. Her mother was still alive—the past needed to die.

"Just tell me one thing, okay? Tell me it wasn't because you're involved with someone else. If I find out you're married, engaged or engaged to be engaged, I won't be responsible for my actions."

He chuckled. "No. I'm completely unattached. Or, rather, I was until I met you."

She smiled languorously and leaned over to press a sweet, wet kiss on his mouth. He held her tighter.

"Can I ask you something?" she asked.

"Anything." Knowing the way Kate's mind worked, she was probably about to ask him something sexual and intense, getting them both hot and ready to go again. His mouth went dry in anticipation, knowing they could play sensual games here all night long. He definitely wanted to try some different positions in front of the mirrors.

"Do you know how to play Bunko?"

"I've never heard of it." He raised a hopeful brow. "Is it some kind of sex game?"

She bit her lip as she giggled. "I certainly hope not." He felt her shoulders shaking as her laughter increased. "Good grief, a sex game. Can you imagine? The women of Pleasantville gathering every other week to play a sex game in someone's living room? Complete with prizes and bourbon?"

"I think you could stock the prizes from right here at Bare Essentials."

She giggled even more. "Oh, my, I can just imagine Eileen Saginaw trying to choose her prize from between the strap-on vibrator or the two-headed dildo."

He rolled onto his back, tugging her with him until she lay on his chest. Her hair blanketed his stomach, flowing all the way down to his groin. He ran his fingers through its silkiness as he caressed her back, hip and bottom.

"So why are you asking about it?"

"It's some kind of dice game. I've been invited to come over to play with some of the women tomorrow night. I don't know much about it. The friends I hang out with in Chicago are more into lunch dates, shopping trips and cocktail parties than Tupperware gatherings or Bunko nights."

Her mention of cocktail parties reminded him of something. Knowing it was a long shot, given Kate's dislike of the Lilac Hill set in town, he asked anyway. "Speaking of parties, I've been asked to attend one at city hall Saturday night. A welcome reception for the new mayor."

She stiffened in his arms.

"I'd like you to come with me, Kate."

He could have predicted her answer. "I don't think that's such a good idea."

"Come on, what's the big deal? You're obviously getting involved with some of the townspeople, anyway. With your big Bunko orgy and all."

She laughed, probably in spite of herself. "It's not the same thing. Those are not the same type of townspeople."

He narrowed his eyes. "Oh, so you're a snob? You choose to associate only with *your* kind of people?"

When fire flashed in her eyes, he knew he'd said just the right thing. He prodded further. "Come on, you know you're every bit as good as any other person here. You're probably worth more than anyone who lives on Lilac Hill. Don't let childhood hurts affect the decisions you make today."

She sucked in a deep breath, staring at his face. He saw a variety of expressions rush across her face…hurt, confusion, then acceptance. "You're right," she whispered.

"That's my girl. The party is at eight."

"I'm sure I have something in my closet I could wear."

"Crotchless tights?" he asked hopefully.

She lightly bit the skin just above his nipple. "It's a little hot for that." As he sighed in disappointment, she whispered, "But probably perfect for crotchless panties."

THE NEXT AFTERNOON, as she stood in front of her closet trying to figure out what one wore to a Bunko night, Kate's cell phone rang. When she heard Cassie's voice, she told her about her plans for the evening.

"Are you sure it's a game, and not some swinging women's party with male strippers and livestock?"

Kate snorted. "Why, would you like to come?"

"Nah, can't do it. I'm on my way outta town."

Pausing with a jean skirt and a red peasant blouse in her hand, Kate said, "Where do you think you're going?"

When Cassie explained she was making a quick weekend trip to New York for her agent's birthday, Kate tried to talk her out of it. Cassie was not to be dissuaded. She was sick of hiding out like a victim. She was going. Period.

"All right, Cass, but please promise me you'll be careful. And call me when you're leaving Sunday afternoon so I can drive up to the airport to get you."

Kate cut the connection before she remembered to tell Cassie about tomorrow night's cocktail party. Just as well. She still couldn't believe she'd agreed to go, and wasn't sure she could make Cassie understand why.

Hell, she barely understood why herself. She only knew something had changed within her. Somehow, from the time she'd seen Mrs. McIntyre outside the Tea Room the day before, Kate had been unable to stop thinking about everything that had happened.

She'd been angry for years because Mrs. McIntyre hated her without reason. Now she wondered—was she any different? Darren's mother hated the Tremaine family because her husband had taken up with Flo. Kate had hated the Winfields because John Winfield had strung her mother along for two decades.

Yes, she had reason to resent Angela because of Darren, and prom night. But, really, who the hell cared what had happened in high school, ten years ago? No, she and Angela would never be friends, but there wasn't any reason they should be enemies, either. John Winfield was dead. His family wasn't responsible for his sins…they didn't even know about them! So what kind of hypocrite would she be to keep blaming them?

The thought rankled.

"And Jack." She had no reason to dislike Jack. Yes, she'd been hurt when he hadn't called her, but she sensed he was being truthful when he'd said he thought he had good reason.

She didn't want to put herself at the same level as Mrs. McIntyre—an angry, bitter person who blamed the wrong people for hurting her. Had she become so focused on self-protection, on not letting herself be hurt or abused, that she'd also denied herself the chance to build genuine emotion with a man?

Maybe it was time to rethink a *lot* of things.

Kate was still mulling over the whole revenge plan when she arrived at Eileen Saginaw's house that night. The older woman, who'd raised five kids and now had ten grandkids, gave Kate a hug and immediately asked her a bunch of questions about Edie.

"Last time we talked, she was determined to learn how to play golf so she could join a club in the retirement village," Kate said, pleased at the fondness in the other woman's voice.

Every woman at the party sounded just as regretful that Edie had left. There were no whispers here. No one acted as though some deep, dark scandal had forced Edie out. Not one person made Kate feel—in the three hours she stayed—the way the biddies in the Tea Room had made her feel in three minutes during her first visit back to town.

These were the real women of Pleasantville. And she was shockingly grateful she'd found them.

"Kate, I'm telling you, stop shaking the dice so much. That's why you keep getting snake eyes," Diane informed her as Kate prepared to take another turn late in the evening.

Kate blew an impatient, frustrated breath as she reached for her drink. Not bourbon—she didn't do bourbon. But thankfully someone had brought beer. "How can it be called snake eyes when there are three dice?" she muttered as she lost yet again, with all ones. "Snakes have two eyes, not three."

"Well, don't forget, there *are* snakes with one," Josie said with a suggestive wagging of her eyebrows.

When Kate gave her a confused look, Josie explained, using a bad Australian crocodile hunter accent. "I'm face-to-face with the deadly, one-eyed trouser snake, known to lead men into dark, dangerous places, and to enslave women with its potent power."

After a five-second pause all twelve women seated at the three card tables in Eileen's living room whooped with laughter.

It was, of course, inevitable that with each roll of the dice, the conversation degenerated into some outrageous sex talk. Kate figured it was standard operating procedure, given how freely the women spoke to one another, though, she had a really hard time picturing her mother here as part of it.

"You know, it'd almost be worth it to test that Viagra stuff, just to see if it'd be noticeable if I put it in Hank's coffee every morning," one woman introduced as Viv said.

"You mean, slip it to him, like a mickey? But how would you know if you gave him enough?" another asked.

Eileen reached for the dice. "Just keep pouring until the kitchen table starts rising off the floor right over his lap."

Josie snickered. "Yeah, I can see you explaining it to the doctor when Hank has a heart attack 'cause all his blood's trapped in his winky."

"At least he'd die happy," Diane pointed out.

"Please don't tell me I have to wait till my husband's a corpse before I can see him with a decent hard-on again." Viv poured herself another drink.

When the laughter died down, Kate spoke up. "Have you tried seducing him? Letting him know you're interested?"

Viv grunted. "Sure. Unfortunately, after he drinks the six-pack of Bud I've bought him to warm him up, he doesn't notice I've shaved my legs and I'm not wearing my period underwear."

Kate chuckled. "I mean it. Sexy lingerie, candles, scented massage oils. Then you tell him you've rented a special movie."

"The only thing he likes is Arnold Schwarzenegger blowing up stuff. Which isn't exactly my idea of romance."

"I meant something a little more...titillating."

"Oh, sure," Viv said with a groan. "I'll drive over to Emmitsburg to the Triple-X video store, fight off all the winos hanging around near the nickel booths, and rent some big-boobed-lesbians-in-love flick. Sounds like a real romantic evening."

"I didn't mean porn," Kate explained patiently. "There are erotic videos made for women and couples."

Hot sellers at Bare Essentials.

"Yeah, but I bet they don't show penises, do they?" This from Josie who sounded indignant. "I mean, every erotic movie for couples I've seen—back when I lived in a town that had heard of such things—is camera-shy below the waist on the guy."

Kate shrugged. "Is that so surprising? Isn't the point to get your man worked up—not yourself? I don't think many men are into seeing the competition, and women don't need as much visual stimulation, which is why adult movies are geared toward men."

The women all thought about it. Then Viv sighed again. "You may be right, Kate, and if this were Chicago, I'm sure I could stroll to the neighborhood store to stock up on erotic movies. But this sure ain't Chicago."

Her disappointed sigh was echoed by every woman in the room. Right then and there, Kate started wondering if maybe Jack had been right. Maybe, just maybe, opening a Bare Essentials right here in Pleasantville wasn't such a crazy idea after all.

As the evening drew to a close, Kate found herself one of the last women there. She'd tried to leave earlier, but Eileen had put a quiet hand on her arm and asked her to stick around. Finally, after Diane and Josie exchanged hugs and one last round of man jokes, they said goodbye and left.

"Let me help you clean up," Kate said, though the room wasn't too bad. Part of the rules of Bunko night—hostess's house didn't get left in a shambles.

Kate helped Eileen take the tablecloths off the card tables and began to fold them. "I can't tell you how much I enjoyed tonight. I appreciate all of you making me feel so welcome."

Eileen gave her a sweet smile, which made her gray eyes twinkle. "Katey, I am so glad you're here, even if you don't plan to stay—and I guess you don't."

She shook her head.

"Anyway, I wish you'da come back sooner. Not that I'm criticizing. Three of my kids left, too. This town can be awfully hard on its residents sometimes."

"Yeah." She wondered if Eileen knew how hard. No, Eileen didn't live on Lilac Hill, but she was married to a nice, well-liked gas station owner, and her beauty parlor, down in the basement, was a hot spot for most local women. So she probably hadn't experienced the worst Pleasantville had to offer.

"I guess you know it was hard on your mom and that's why she left. I wish she hadn't, it wasn't but a few nasty people."

Kate laid the folded tablecloth on Eileen's dining room table. "I'm sure you're right."

Eileen held her eye, gauging how much to say. Then, obviously seeing something in Kate's expression, she said, "You know, don't you. You know about Edie and John."

Kate's jaw dropped. "I'm surprised you do."

"Oh, darlin', your mom and I have been friends since eighth grade. I was there the first time she saw him, the first time he asked her out. Heck, we double-dated to our senior prom."

"Wait…you mean Mom dated John Winfield in high school?"

"Well, sure. Didn't you know that? The two of them were quite the talk of the town in those days, what with your mom being a Tremaine and all. He didn't care a bit. The two of them were crazy about each other."

Shocked, Kate leaned against the table. "What happened?"

Eileen sighed. "They had a fight about something stupid. John went and did something even *more* stupid with Pat Pickering. She told him she was pregnant the day after graduation."

Pregnant? With Jack? She quickly calculated—no, couldn't be right, that would make Jack close to forty.

Eileen ushered her into the kitchen, putting on the kettle to make tea. "Edie found out, broke it off with John and left town. John married Pat. When there was no baby several months later, he came to me asking where Edie was. I told him the truth. She was happy with her new life in Florida. He stayed married to Pat and they made a go of it, I guess."

"Years later, Dad died and Mom came back," Kate whispered.

Eileen poured some tea, then sat. "First loves never die. John was so sad, trapped by Pat, his job, the town." Eileen shrugged. "Edie made him happy…they made each other happy. But she would *never* have let him leave Pat and those children."

A half hour later, after one of the most shocking and revealing conversations she'd ever experienced, Kate hugged Eileen goodbye and headed home. She wanted more than anything to call her mother, just to hear her voice. Edie seemed so different to her now, not a victim anymore, but a woman in love who did the best she could with what she was dealt.

Kate didn't know whether to applaud her or to cry for her.

When she arrived home, she immediately looked toward Jack's side of the duplex, to see if any lights were on. He'd told her he'd wait up, saying he wanted the full scoop on the Bunko orgy. Judging by all the lights, he'd kept his word.

She pulled into the driveway, surprised when she saw a rental car parked there. Unsure who would be visiting at this late hour, she walked up to the porch and glanced in the window.

When she saw the dark-haired person sitting on the couch, and realized who it was, she hurried into the house and launched herself into his arms.

CHAPTER ELEVEN

IF JACK HADN'T ALREADY figured out that Kate's business partner was gay, he might be feeling seriously concerned right now. The two of them hugged and chattered with the easy camaraderie of long-time companions. They acted as if they hadn't seen each other in months, rather than a week.

"Armand, what are you doing here? I can't believe you came all this way," Kate said.

"I missed you. I had a fabulous new design I wanted to show you, and since we seem to have a decent staff for a change, I figured we could both be gone for a day or two." Armand sat on the couch, pulling Kate down to sit beside him.

Jack, who'd taken a seat on the other side of the small living room, couldn't help smiling at Kate's obvious excitement.

He hadn't quite known what to think when he'd seen this tall, dark-haired man knocking on Kate's front door an hour ago. When Jack had stepped outside to see what he wanted, the other man had asked about Kate. Jack's first instinct had been to tell the guy she'd left town and had left no forwarding address. Then, when he'd recognized the stranger as the one who'd been hugging Kate at her Chicago shop all those weeks ago, he'd invited him into his place to wait for her.

The first rule in any battle—know your competition.

He'd figured out the man's sexual preference within five

minutes. Not that Armand had tried anything—if he had, he sure as hell wouldn't still be sitting in his living room, friend of Kate's or no friend. No, what had tipped Jack off was Armand's reaction upon learning his name.

He'd acted just like one of Kate's gal pals.

"Oh, so you're Jack." He'd looked at Jack's arms and hands, raised a falsely surprised brow and said, "Hmm, no broken arms or fingers, did your building simply lose phone service for a month? Is that why you never called her?"

Yep. Definitely gay.

Once they'd gotten past those first awkward minutes, with Armand trying to punish him for not calling Kate, and Jack trying to change the subject, they'd actually enjoyed an interesting hour of conversation. The guy had even brought a six-pack of beer, two-thirds of which they'd already killed off.

Armand was part of Kate's other life. Her Chicago life. The life Jack fully intended to share when they both finished up what they had to do in Pleasantville and closed this door behind them. He wanted to see her through Armand's eyes.

Most of what he learned did not surprise him.

She loved the theater and saw nearly every touring production that came through town. A given.

She hated snow. Unusual, considering her Chicago address. But she did like long walks on windy days.

She'd put herself through college at night while working any job she could get, not finishing up her bachelor's degree until a few years ago. That reinforced what he already suspected—everything she had, she'd worked damn hard for. Nothing had been handed to her; she relied on her talent and her perseverance to succeed.

Her cousin Cassie had financed their Chicago shop, but, mostly due to Kate's excellent management, Bare Essentials had already earned enough to pay off the loan.

One more intimate little detail Armand let drop—Kate hadn't dated any man more than twice in over two years, and he doubted she'd slept with any either. *Well, praise the Lord and pass the ammunition.*

"So, how was Bunko night?" Jack asked when he could finally get a word in edgewise.

Kate grinned. "Wonderful. I loved it. And, I tell you, there might actually be a client base in this town for Bare Essentials."

Armand raised a surprised brow. "Get *out!*"

She told them about her evening, then said, "I know a woman named Viv who would probably adore seeing your new designs."

"It sounds like Tortureville hasn't quite lived down to your expectations," Armand said.

She didn't answer for a moment, looking deep in thought. Something seemed different about Kate tonight. She looked less pensive, much more relaxed. Jack didn't think it was only because of her friend's visit. Nor did he think it was entirely because of what had happened between them last night.

And again this morning in her bedroom next door.

"I think we both had a few surprises from our returns to Pleasantville," Jack murmured.

She looked up and met his eyes, a soft smile curling her lips. Next to her, Armand looked back and forth between the two of them. "Okay, it looks like somebody has forgiven somebody for his telephone-itis."

"Not *entirely* forgiven," Kate said.

Jack raised a questioning brow.

"But he's getting closer."

Seeing warmth in her gaze, Jack gave her a slow, steady look, telling her without words that he'd keep doing whatever he had to earn her forgiveness.

"I'm suddenly feeling very third wheel here. Kate, I do

hope you have room for me to crash at your place, because I didn't make a hotel reservation or anything."

"I think the hotel in Pleasantville only rents by the hour anyway," Kate said with a grin. "Of course you'll stay with me. I don't have an extra bed, or very much furniture at all. But I do have a sleeping bag."

"You can stay here." Jack's tone allowed for no argument. "There's an extra, fully furnished bedroom." Two, really, since Jack fully intended to sleep in Kate's bed, anyway.

"Wonderful, thank you." Armand turned to Kate. "And tomorrow you take me downtown to show me the new store. Plus all the horrible places you remember from your teenage years. Your high school, the predictable barber shop, movie theater and fire station where they host pancake breakfasts. And you must introduce me to Viv. Does she have poufed-up blond hair, tacky plastic shoes and like to crack bubblegum?"

Shaking her head, Kate chuckled. "Nope. Sorry to disappoint you, she's a pretty, forty-something housewife with an uninspired husband. I think you've been watching too many movies about small-town life."

"I was raised in a town just like this, by my father the fire chief and my mother the former dairy princess."

"Interesting background, considering your name," Jack said.

"Arnold Dettinger didn't work for me in Chicago," Armand explained with a shrug. "And since I haven't been home in twelve years, I'll consider this my trial run. Who knows? If no one starts dragging out the tar and feathers, I might follow your lead and plan a trip back to Milltown for Christmas."

Jack saw Kate squeeze her friend's hand. "I'm sure your parents would like that."

Armand gave a resigned shrug. "My mother, maybe. My

father would be too busy ordering me not to embarrass him in front of the guys at the fire house to have time to be pleased."

Jack cleared his throat. "He might surprise you." Seeing Armand's doubting expression, Jack continued. "I have to believe that deep down fathers always want their sons to come home. Just don't wait until it's too late to find out."

LATER, with Armand settled into Kate's mother's old room, Jack followed Kate into the other duplex and up to her bedroom.

"So, you going to tell me the truth about the Bunko orgy?" he asked as she reached for the bottom of his shirt.

"You really want to hear?"

"Uh-huh."

"Well," she said, her voice a sultry whisper. "All the women were blondes except me, and they all had *really* big breasts. When we got there, we all took off our shirts and compared."

He snorted with laughter.

"Then, we squirted each other up with scented oils and gave each other massages, until we were just rolling around on the floor, one big mass of naked, squirming female bodies."

"You're evil."

"Isn't that every guy's fantasy orgy?"

"Well, no, actually he'd need to be there. Preferably on the bottom of the pile of naked, squirming female bodies."

"Men are so weird." She rolled her eyes. "What is the attraction of more than one woman at a time?"

"I have no idea," he explained, trying hard to retain a serious expression. "I personally find that type of thing shocking and sordid."

She punched him lightly in the stomach.

"Oh, come on, you're buying into the male stereotype. It's at most a fantasy—the old 'me Tarzan, you Jane, you Janet' thing. Caveman-must-propagate-the-species genes rearing their persistent heads." When she crossed her arms impatiently, he continued. "Most men don't know what the hell to do with one woman and certainly couldn't handle two and they know it."

"True."

"Besides," he continued, "don't women fantasize about being with two men, too?"

"Not this woman. I would never want to be in bed with a naked guy who didn't mind being in bed with another naked guy."

Jack's shoulders shook as he laughed.

"Besides," she continued, "if a man likes other men enough to be naked with them, then there's one or two things I'm lacking that he's bound to notice."

"I'd rather notice the one or two very nice, feminine things you have," he said with a definite leer.

As he reached out his hand and traced the tip of his fingers along the top hem of her loose blouse, she gave him a languid smile.

"One is more than enough for me," she murmured. "Though, two yous might be nice."

He paused, giving her a mock frown. "Did you say two Hughs?"

She rolled her eyes and shoved him onto the mattress, falling on top of him. They rolled across it, wrapped in each other's arms exchanging laughter and hot kisses.

"I said two *yous*. Two Jacks. Two sets of these amazing hands." She brought his hand to her lips, kissing the tips of his fingers and sliding her mouth over his pinky. "Two perfect mouths on my body." She leaned up to press her lips against his. "Two tongues to taste me."

He tasted her, nibbling, kissing and licking his way down her neck, across her collarbone, to the hem of her shirt. She lifted up so he could tug it out, and Jack tossed it over his shoulder to the floor. "No bra at all this time," he murmured, his voice thick with appreciation as he saw her beautiful breasts and pert nipples. When he moved his mouth over one, flicking his tongue across the puckered tip, she jerked against him and groaned.

"Two mouths would be useful here," he murmured as he went back and forth, from one breast to the other, sucking, nibbling and stroking her into a frenzy beneath him.

Sitting up long enough to yank off his clothes, he helped her unfasten her jean skirt, then pulled it off her. Her flimsy panties followed, then he had to pause, to look at her naked body, bathed in the soft glow of the hallway light. She looked at him, as well, her eyelids heavy, her lips parted as she took in deep, ragged breaths.

"Would you prefer two of anything else, Kate?" he asked, as he bent to kiss her again, letting her feel his hard-on against her thigh. She instinctively arched toward it in an age-old signal of welcome from female to male.

"Hmm, no, I think I can stay quite busy playing with this one," she whispered as she reached for him.

She proceeded to play. Stroking him, cupping him, running her hands up and down his dick as they exchanged lazy, wet kisses and he fondled her breasts. He didn't think he'd be able to stand it when she bent to take him into her mouth. He had to lift his arms over his head and press his fists against the wall to try to hold on to his sanity. The way her long, thick hair spread across his body, draping between his thighs to caress his balls, felt almost as good as her hot, wet mouth wrapped around him. Almost.

After a few moments she kissed her way up his body to his lips, then slid one leg across his hips. She rubbed against him, letting her juices spread over his erection, and it felt so good, so damn good to be close to her, without the barrier of a condom, that he nearly came right then. He would like for there to be no barriers between them, of any kind. Ever.

"You amaze me," he admitted as he stared up at her.

"Even though there's only one of me?"

"One's all I want, Kate," he murmured. "One you."

She leaned down to kiss him, their tongues swirling languorously. Her breasts brushed his chest and her warm mound remained tantalizingly close to his penis.

"Not yet," he told her when she retrieved a condom from her purse on the floor next to the mattress.

Raising a curious brow, she stared at him. He smiled as he cupped her hips. Tugging her forward, he slid down to meet her. She watched him, her eyes wide and excited as she understood what he wanted. What he had to have.

"Are you sure you…"

"Oh, yeah," he replied as he positioned her bottom on his chest and her beautiful, sweet, wet opening right in front of his hungry mouth. Then he tasted her, holding her hips as she bucked in delight at the intimate contact.

The position gave him the perfect access to pleasure her, and himself. He licked, stroked and suckled her until she came right in his mouth, her body trembling and hot as she leaned against the wall above his head for support. And that wasn't enough. He kept tasting her, sliding his tongue into her, demanding that she give him more until she cried out as a second orgasm ratcheted through her body.

Only then did he let her go, rolling her onto her back and reaching for the condom she'd dropped.

"I guess two *is* better than one sometimes, isn't it? Twice the pleasure?" he said with a chuckle, referring to her orgasms. Sheathing himself, he plunged into her even before she'd stopped panting from her orgasms.

"Oh, yes," she cried.

He didn't move at first, just savored the wet heat in which he was enveloped. Looking at her face, he saw her parted lips, the flush in her cheeks, the long lashes on her lowered eyelids.

She began to move beneath him, her body telling him what she wanted. He gladly gave it to her. Slowly, with deep, steady, sure strokes, he moved in and out of her until she began to moan and roll her head back and forth on the pillow.

"More, Jack, please," she whispered, bending her legs even higher and tilting her hips up, inviting him deeper inside.

He knew what she wanted and how she wanted it. Faster. Harder. Mind-numbing and scream-inducing.

Kate didn't want sweet. Kate wanted hot.

He complied with a groan, tugging one of her legs over his shoulder and plunging harder than before. Her eyes flew open.

"Good?"

"God, yes," she muttered through choppy indrawn breaths. "I want you so deep inside me that I don't know if I'm feeling your body or my own."

"Oh, I think I can guarantee you're going to know it's mine," he said with a chuckle as he ground against her.

She hissed and met his every move, smiling as he gave her what she wanted.

He watched as she moved her hands up her legs, reaching for her own breasts. She plucked at her nipples with her fingertips, sexy little pants still coming from between her lips. "Four hands might be good right now," she said.

Remembering her incredible sensitivity right there, and wanting to give her everything she desired, Jack slid out of her.

"What are you…"

"Shh," he whispered, giving her a smile that said *Trust me*.

She watched, wide-eyed as he reached for her hip and gently rolled her onto her belly. He heard her moan into the pillow, obviously realizing how he wanted to take her.

"Oh, yes, absolutely," she said as she lifted her curvy bottom and hips, offering herself. The most tempting offer he'd ever had.

"Up, baby," he whispered, pulling her to her knees.

She complied, rising to all fours, moving back to meet him as he slid into her from behind, then leaned forward until his chest touched her back.

Perfect. The position left his hands free to pleasure her, to tweak her sensitive nipples, to stroke the curves of her breasts and the soft flesh of her belly. Then lower, to play with her sweet little clit as he rocked into her until she came close. Damn close, judging by her cries.

"Now," she ordered. *"Now."*

He knew what she wanted—she wanted him to come with her. Straightening, Jack took her hips in his hands and drove into her with a few powerful, body-draining thrusts.

"Now," he agreed.

The moment she screamed in climax, his own overtook him and they both collapsed to the mattress. He instantly rolled onto his side, tugging her close to nestle against his chest. He pressed a kiss to her brow, then to her cheek. Then to her mouth, still open and panting.

"That was amazing," she finally managed to whisper between deep, shuddery breaths.

He nodded.

"But, you know, Jack, now you've got me spoiled."

He lifted a brow.

"I suddenly want two of everything."

Smiling, knowing by the way his body began to react to

her all over again, he whispered, "Let's not set any limits, okay? Why stop at two?"

He caught her mouth in a deep, slow kiss as they began all over again.

ON SATURDAY, Armand took Pleasantville by storm, chatting easily with each person he met and seeming to really enjoy the small-town atmosphere.

He raved over the shop, and gave Kate some good suggestions on layout. He also helped her straighten up the dressing room area, asking once why there were crotchless tights strewn all over the floor. Thankfully, he hadn't questioned her blush.

Nor did he tease her too unmercifully about the thinness of the walls at the duplex, other than to say he'd heard some wild animals howling in the middle of the night, and wondered if there were coyotes in Pleasantville.

Later, during lunch at the Downtown Deli, he'd met Diane and Josie, charming them both completely. Josie had enough innate street sense to recognize his preferences in spite of his sexy charm. She seemed to like him all the more for it.

But the real highlight of the afternoon came when they walked out of the deli and straight into a couple, who stood exchanging heated words on the sidewalk.

"Angela and Darren," Kate whispered, instantly recognizing Jack's sister. "The banes of my teenage existence."

Surprised she hadn't run into Jack's sister before now, she forced herself to take a deep breath and to remember that she was completely over any childhood hurts.

"High school tormentors, hmm?" Armand whispered as they walked within a few feet of the two.

"Hi, Kate," Darren said. He looked at Armand, then stood a little straighter. Armand, with his height and elegant sophistication, had that effect on men.

Angela's face turned red as she stared at Kate, her mouth opening but no sound coming out. She looked not only flustered by Kate's appearance, but also annoyed at the interruption of her conversation with Darren.

"Hello, Darren. Angela," Kate replied, her voice sounding much calmer than she'd have expected.

Darren gave her a big, friendly smile. "I'm sorry I didn't get to talk to you much the other day. It's great to have you back, Kate. I'm really glad things have gone so well for you."

Surprisingly, he sounded sincere.

Angela didn't speak to her; she was too busy glaring at Darren as he talked to Kate. Then, when the other woman finally noticed Armand, an appreciative expression lit up her face.

Funny, when she actually smiled, Angela didn't look quite so much like a cast-iron bitch.

"Introduce us to your friend," she murmured.

After the introductions Armand stepped into his role as if it had been created for him. He flirted with Angela until the woman was practically melting into a puddle on the sidewalk. Once or twice Kate tried to tug him away, knowing he was trying to get a little payback on her behalf by stringing the other woman along. He'd probably be dashing off some scathing rejection at any moment now. The second time Kate tried to hurry him away Angela shot her a dagger-sharp glare. *Well, to hell with helping you, lady!* She stopped trying to lead Armand away.

"So, you're here visiting your *friend* Kate?" Angela asked.

Armand shrugged. "We're business partners. We own a store together on the Miracle Mile in Chicago."

Angela's eyes widened. "Really?" She glanced at Kate.

"Is it the same kind of store you're opening here?" Darren said, stepping not-so-casually between Angela and Armand.

Kate noticed and wondered if things were heating up again between the ex-spouses. It would explain why Darren looked anything but pleased about Angela's interest in Kate's partner.

"Yes, but now, we really have to go. I have things to do before tonight's party."

Angela frowned. "The party at city hall? You're coming?"

"Yes." Kate couldn't resist adding, "As Jack's date."

The other woman's face paled. "How…nice." Turning toward Armand, she said, "And you must come, too."

"Will you be there?"

Angela nodded.

"Then I wouldn't miss it for the world," he said, looking at her with a sexy, promising grin.

Kate kicked his ankle.

"Okay, I guess it's time for us to go," he said with a grimace. If he bent to kiss Angela's hand or anything, Kate swore she'd shove him in front of the next oncoming car.

As soon as they were out of earshot of the other two, Kate said, "That was really bad of you."

"Oh, come on, I know something about high school tormenters, babe. You're telling me you never fantasized about getting a little payback?"

If only you knew!

"Just don't, okay? Angela is Jack's sister!"

Armand whistled. "Whoops."

When they got back to the duplex, Armand insisted on helping pick out something for Kate to wear. She'd brought a few nicer dresses and was now glad she had.

"Red," Armand said as he pulled out a tight spaghetti-strapped cocktail dress with a band of glittering sequins right above the breasts. "Perfect. And it'll match. Wait here."

When he returned, he was carrying a bundle of tissue paper. "My latest design. Here you go."

Kate opened the packet, seeing a tiny pair of red, lacy

panties. She dropped the paper and held them up, looking for the trick. No zipper. No slit. Not a thong. And they had a crotch.

The only thing unique about them was their weight. They felt heavier than they should, given the minute amount of fabric.

"Very pretty, and you're right, they will match."

He rolled his eyes at her lack of enthusiasm. "Go into the bathroom and try them on," he said, shooing her out.

Following his orders, she went into the bathroom and took her shorts and underwear off. As she pulled the new underpants up, she noticed the extra weight seemed centered in the crotch area. When she pulled them into place, she realized why.

"Oh, my God," she whispered with a shocked laugh.

The panties were padded with a spongy, soft middle, covered with a feathery fabric that cupped her private area quite deliciously. A firmer, ridged section toward the front pressed against her clitoris. "You've got to be kidding me," she yelled.

"Walk in them," Armand ordered through the door.

The bathroom was too small, so she wrapped a towel around her waist and walked out into the hallway. Armand stood there, waiting for her reaction. As she walked, she had to admit it, the little ridge felt pretty damn good. Not to mention the soft middle, which made it feel like wispy, downy kisses were being pressed all over her opening.

"Nice?" When she nodded weakly, he practically bounced on his toes. "Try the stairs."

She did. "Oh, very nice," she admitted, almost purring at the pleasure of it.

"Good. You're wearing them tonight. And every time some pissy small-town matriarch wrinkles up her nose in your direction, you stroll right by her with a secretive, delighted smile on your face."

Sounded like a pretty good plan to her.

CHAPTER TWELVE

As HE PULLED KATE'S SUV into the parking lot outside city hall, Jack could tell by the look on her face she was still uncertain about this evening's party. She wasn't frowning, but she looked deep in concentration, as if thinking of something else. Every once in a while, she even wriggled in her seat. "You okay? You're awfully fidgety."

From the back seat, he heard Armand snort a laugh.

She gave Jack a quick guilty look. "Uh, fine. I'm fine. Why do you ask?"

He shrugged. "You just seem distracted." Taking her hand, he squeezed it and said, "But you also look amazing."

She did. Her body turned the red fabric of her dress into pure solid sin. Though petite, Kate had curves men dreamed about. Curves *he'd* dreamed about many nights since they'd met.

Not to mention the fullness of her lips, the sparkle in her deep brown eyes. Her confidence, intelligence and attitude appealed to him even more now than the day they'd met. Especially since they'd become so intimate.

He got the shakes just thinking about the things they'd done together the night before in her bed.

He simply couldn't get enough of her. Kate was the woman he'd been casually seeking and had never really thought he'd find ever since he'd left home fifteen years ago. How funny that he found her right here in Pleasantville, the very place he'd been trying so hard to escape.

She'd pulled her hair back, letting cascades of curls drop over her bare shoulders. The dress was not too short, ending a few inches above the knee, but below it her legs were bare. Her strappy, red high-heeled sandals had caught his eye several times during the short drive from the house.

"I'm fine. Now, who is going to be at this thing? Should I have worn body armor?"

He shook his head. "My mother's not coming. She wasn't feeling well. Frankly, I think it's driving her insane to give up the title of First Lady of Pleasantville. She doesn't want to see her replacement holding court."

Kate chuckled. "But your sister will be here."

"Yeah."

"Ah, your sister, such a charming little thing," Armand murmured from the back seat.

Jack saw Kate shoot her friend a warning glare, but didn't have time to question it.

They made their way into city hall, blending into the crowd of people in the atrium. In a far corner a band played jazzy music and an area had been cleared for dancing. A bar had been set up on what was usually an information desk. Armand immediately beelined for it, offering to get a round of drinks, leaving Kate and Jack to circulate.

He felt her tension, the stiffness of her body. Her hands were like ice, though she maintained an expression of complete calm. Jack wondered again what it must have been like for her growing up here, if it could still make her so anxious all these years later. But she never flinched, never let anyone see a single sign of nervousness, not even when one of his mother's cronies glanced at her, sniffed rudely, and turned away.

He saw Kate's face grow pale. Leaning close, he brushed a kiss against her temple and whispered, "Ignore the old bat. Did you know she wears a wig?"

At Kate's surprised expression, he continued. "My mother told me years ago. Seems she's got a nervous habit and pulls her own hair, so she thought it would be easier—and less painful—to just buzz-cut it and wear wigs."

Kate giggled. "That's her story and she's sticking to it, huh? I think she was rude to the wrong person and someone just snatched her bald."

"That's my girl." Right there in the middle of the crowd, he pressed a soft kiss to her mouth. Her tension seemed to ease as he took her arm and continued to lead her through the crowd.

Finally they came face-to-face with the new mayor and his wife. Kate's eyes widened in shock. "Mr. Otis?"

The elderly mayor, who, Jack remembered, used to teach drama at the high school, squinted and looked at her more closely. "Why, Kate Jones, how you've grown up!"

The mayor then proceeded to sweep Jack's date in his arms and give her a tight hug. "You've gone off to the big city and done quite well for yourself, haven't you?"

"Yes, I have. I had no idea you were mayor. I figured you'd retired from teaching and were off fishing some-where."

"Fishing for trouble at city hall," he said with a wink.

While Kate and Mr. Otis chatted, Armand returned, care-fully balancing three drinks. Jack took his beer, and Kate's wine, holding one glass in each hand.

"By the way," Armand said, speaking in a near whisper, "I meant to give you something before we left the house."

"What?"

Instead of answering, Armand removed what looked like a small black box from his jacket pocket. "You don't have the hands, I'll drop it in your pocket." He did so, then said, "Just something fun to ease Kate's tension."

Since Jack's hands were still full with the drinks, he

couldn't reach in to see what Armand had put there. "You going to explain this?"

Armand shook his head then grinned. "Remember, roll the dial slowly and never take your eyes off her."

Then he strolled away, leaving Jack very curious.

Kate had never actually conceived of enjoying this evening, but as she chatted happily with her favorite high school teacher—now interim mayor of Pleasantville—she realized that she might. When she spied Diane walking around with a tall, red-haired guy who tugged at the collar of his suit as if it was itching him, she felt more certain of it.

"Well, I suppose I have to mingle," Mr. Otis finally said as someone tried to lead him away for a photo op. "It's so nice to have you back here, Kate. I hope you'll visit more often."

"Wow," she said to Jack when they were once again alone in the crowd of elegantly dressed people. "I never imagined Mr. Otis would be the new mayor."

Diane and her husband joined them. "He's been on the city council for a few years," she explained. "So's Will." She introduced her husband. Kate instantly liked the man, who looked as though he'd rather be anywhere but here, dressed in anything but his plain brown suit.

Jack, on the other hand, looked delicious in his dark blue one. Elegant, expertly tailored, it showed off his hard, lean form to perfection. With his thick, blond hair, vivid green eyes and sexy grin, he had the attention of every woman in the place.

He fit in with this crowd easily. But he was just as at ease with Will and Diane, who obviously lived far from Lilac Hill.

Throughout the next hour Diane introduced them to several other newer members of the town's business community, all of whom went out of their way to tell Kate how happy they were about her opening a new store in the downtown area. Kate began to feel torn. Yes, she'd decided to open the store as revenge. But if that were the case, she'd be punishing these nicer people she was meeting, too.

Or maybe not. Ever since last night at Eileen's house, she'd had to wonder if maybe her store wasn't exactly what this town needed. New, fresh, daring—like a lot of these younger people circulating amid the old highbrow set.

The highbrow set increased by one when Mrs. McIntyre walked into the room. Kate, standing close to the door, had turned to throw away her cup, and nearly ran into her.

The woman's face went rigid enough to crack. She made a sound that was a cross between a groan and a harrumph before she turned her back on Kate and walked away.

Taking a deep breath, Kate glanced around to see if anyone had noticed the snub. Jack stood several feet away, pretending to listen to an older woman chatting his ear off, but his attention was focused directly on Kate. His sexy smile was conspicuously absent, his eyes tender and concerned. She felt his silent support as though he'd put his arm around her.

She gave him a little nod, trying to assure him that she was okay, knowing he'd never believe it. He murmured something to the woman, who walked away, then gave Kate a slow smile. His green eyes shone with interest as he reached into his suit pocket.

Before she could step closer to see what he was up to, Kate's panties came alive. "Oh," she said with a sharp gasp.

She froze, her mouth falling open as she focused on the sudden, completely unexpected sensations in her private area.

"Good Lord," she said with a breathy sigh.

Armand had outdone himself.

The spongy middle slowly undulated against her rapidly swelling and quickly aroused mound, while the harder nubbins began to flicker against her clitoris with incredible friction.

She closed her eyes, taking deep breaths, quite unable to move. Around her, the crowd chattered. Someone asked her a question, and she nodded dumbly. Someone else handed her a drink. She lifted it to her lips and gulped without even looking at it, only realizing it was champagne when she felt a tickling sensation in her nose and throat. Of course, that couldn't match the tickling sensation between her legs.

The slow vibration picked up its pace, increasing in speed. She even swore she could hear a tiny hum and almost gasped as she wondered if anyone else heard it. As she cast a quick glance around to see, she met Jack's eyes. His pleased, boyish grin told her he was responsible for what was happening. "More?" he asked, though she couldn't hear him. She read the word on his lips.

She shook her head and gave him a scolding look, unable to believe he was doing this to her in a huge crowd of people.

The look in his eyes as he reached into his suit pocket could only be called wickedly anticipatory. She shook her head again, not able to take any more, but not able to stop it. His hand kept moving, slowly, as he dragged out the tension. And, if she were to be honest, the anticipation.

Kate shot a quick look around the lobby where the party was being held, gauging the distance to the ladies' room. Too far. No way could she make it when her legs were already weak, her breaths choppy and her heart racing out of control.

Jack's hand had finally reached his pocket and as it slipped inside, she sent him one more pleading glance. At this point, she really couldn't have said what she was pleading for.

If the vibrations got much stronger, she'd go right over the edge and have a shattering orgasm in the middle of this crowd of elegantly dressed people.

If they stopped, she'd die.

The heat in Jack's stare as he cranked up the pressure was almost enough to make her come anyway. She shuddered as the intensity of vibration rose yet another notch. Reaching blindly for support, she found herself grabbing the corner of an information desk and her fingers sunk into some creamy substance. A quick glance down told her it was a slice of cheesecake topped with strawberries, but she couldn't bring herself to care.

The waves of pleasure began to roll through her, signaling her climax, and she leaned her hip against the desk. She heard someone say her name, but couldn't even turn her head. Her eyes were glued to Jack's and he nodded with encouragement, knowing even from several feet away that she was close.

"Yes," she whispered, closing her eyes as an intense bolt of pleasure shot through her. Her hands clenched, oozing strawberries and cheesecake between her fingers. Dropping her head back, she gasped for breath as the orgasm sent electric pleasure racing through her body.

Finally the vibrations between her legs slowed, then stopped. When she opened her eyes, she saw Jack watching her, looking hot and ready, as if watching her reach her climax had pushed him close to the edge, too. She was about to walk over to him when she heard Diane's voice.

"Good God, I've eaten cheesecake I'd consider orgasmic, but I never got off just from *touching* one."

"THAT WAS REALLY BAD of you," Kate whispered as Jack curled her tighter in his arms in the back of her SUV an hour later.

They'd escaped the party as quickly as they could, after ensuring Armand could get a ride home with Diane and her husband. By silent consent, they'd avoided going back to the duplex, instead driving up to a popular lake on the outskirts of town. Their clothes had come off a minute after Jack had engaged the parking brake and they'd barely made it over the back seat into the cargo area before he was inside her.

They'd been frenzied and ravenous. Now they lay quietly, exchanging slow, lazy kisses and caresses that were going to lead to sweet, long lovemaking. Jack didn't know how he could want her again, already, but he did.

"I thought it was your fantasy," he finally answered.

"My fantasy?"

"Being made helpless. Having to accept pleasure because you are powerless to stop it."

She laughed. "Yeah, but I meant something more along the lines of being tied to the headboard, not being brought to a shattering orgasm in a room filled with a hundred people. I can't imagine what Diane must have thought."

"I think she went to look for the chef to ask for the recipe for that cheesecake."

She giggled. "Maybe we should sell it at Bare Essentials."

He stretched to work a kink out of his neck. "I haven't had sex in the back of a car in years."

"This is my first back seat experience ever."

"Uncomfortable, isn't it?"

She nodded. "But exciting. I keep picturing a cop knocking on the window and telling us to get our clothes on." She arched closer, sliding her arm around his waist. "Or an ax-maniac with a hook. You know, the kind who always slaughters the teenagers when they run out of gas on lover's lane?"

"I'm fairly certain the parents of a teenage girl made up that story the night before her first date."

"So, was this your make-out spot when you were a teenager?"

He shook his head. "No way. Everyone in town knew my father and I never dared to bring a date out here."

He felt her tense in his arms at the mention of his father.

"I know what it's like to have everyone in town know your family," she admitted.

Leaning down, he pressed kisses on her temple, her cheekbone, then her lips. He kissed her lazily, gently coaxing her mouth to open. When it ended, he whispered, "I'm sorry I didn't know you then. I'm sorry I wasn't around to stop it when you were being treated so badly. By my sister or anyone else."

He wished he had been. He hated like hell to think of anyone hurting her. Ever.

"It was a long time ago, Jack. And you know, being back here has made me remember some of the better times, too. I guess I should be thankful for that. I'd been angry for a long time and let that anger color my memories. It's good to have some of those nicer moments back."

He believed she meant it. Hopefully, no matter what else happened, Kate wouldn't regret this time spent in Pleasantville. Seeing the town through adult eyes had evened out her feelings, much as it had his. "So you think you might come back someday? For a visit?"

She shrugged. "Anything's possible."

Before he could reply, they heard the sound of crunching gravel. The bright sheen of headlights washed through the windows of the SUV.

"Oh, my God, someone else is here," she cried.

They scrambled for their clothes like a couple of kids caught making out by their parents. He tossed her the magical little red underwear she'd worn at the party, watching as she shimmied into her dress. She was giggling hysterically. "Please be the cops and not a guy with an ax and a hook."

"You got your wish. It's the cops," he replied.

Jack was having as hard a time containing his laughter as Kate appeared to be. His first time going parking in more than a decade and they get caught by the town sheriff. Thank heaven it hadn't been ten minutes before or he doubted they'd have even noticed the approach of the other car.

He'd just zipped his pants when he heard a knock on the driver's side window, Thankfully, it was tinted. Recognizing Sean Taggart, with whom he'd gone to high school, he slid into the back seat, then opened the door. "Hi, Tag," he said as he jumped out. He shut the door behind him, giving Kate more time.

"Jack," the other man said with a nod. Tag pushed his sheriff's hat up on his head with the tip of one finger, trying unsuccessfully to hide a grin. "You out for a late-night drive?"

"Yep. Enjoying the view over the lake."

"Well, I can see why you felt the need to take off your shirt. Musta been awful hot with all that steam on the windows." He glanced at the lake. "But wasn't it hard to see the view considering you're parked facing the road, instead of the water?"

Before Jack could reply, Kate stepped out. "Hi, Sheriff," she said, her face awash with color.

Tag's eyes widened as he obviously noticed her crooked dress, bare feet and wildly tangled hair. "Kate, isn't it? Cassie's cousin?" When Kate nodded, Tag said, "Where is she? I heard a rumor she left town for a few days, which I couldn't believe since that'd be so incredibly stupid."

Sensing Tag knew about whatever trouble Cassie was in, Jack waited for her answer, as well. When Kate admitted her cousin had gone to New York for the weekend, and would fly home the next day, Tag swore under his breath. "When does her plane get in?"

"She's supposed to call me and let me know when she's leaving New York so I can go pick her up at the airport."

"Tell you what," Tag said, his calm tone not hiding his obvious anger. "You call me in the morning and tell me what flight she's on so I can go pick her up, and I won't arrest you both for public indecency."

"We weren't exactly in public," Jack said.

"Maybe not. Then again, I've just heard an interesting rumor about some mighty strange behavior by the two of you at the mayor's party, which was *very* public. Now, do we have a deal?"

Kate nibbled on her lip, then finally nodded. "Cassie's gonna kill me."

"Not if I kill her first," Tag muttered as he turned on his heel and strode away. He got into his car, but before leaving, he rolled down his window. "Next time, cut your lights before you pass by old lady Millner's place. She's a quarter mile up the road and calls every time a car comes down here late at night."

Then he drove away, leaving them standing alone.

"Sounds like he's speaking from experience," Kate said with a chuckle.

"Tag never had much problem with the girls back in high school."

"With those looks and that body? I can definitely see why he'd cause a sigh or two." She gave him a look out of the corner of her eye that screamed mischief.

Okay, Kate wanted him jealous. No problem. He grabbed her arm and tugged her close. Lowering his voice, he whispered, "I'm surprised you can sigh, or even talk at all, considering the way you were screaming ten minutes ago. Your throat must be sore."

Then he caught her mouth in a hot, wet kiss designed to drive the thought of any other person on the planet out of her mind. Her gentle moans and pliant body told him he'd succeeded.

When they parted, she sucked in a few deep breaths. "You're definitely scream-worthy, Jack," she said. "And you certainly know how to show a girl a good time." She started to giggle, then to laugh out loud. "Oh, my gosh, if Tag tells Cassie about this, she'll never let me live it down. We made a pact to never go parking with guys when we were in high school. We pinky swore and everything."

"You mean I was good enough to break a pinky swear for?" he said with a pleased grin. "Wow. I don't know if anyone's ever broken a pinky swear just for me."

She lightly elbowed him in the ribs. "Don't go getting a swelled head." She leaned back against the car, crossing her arms and letting out an audible sigh. "I'm going to be dead meat when I'm not the one who shows up tomorrow to pick Cassie up at the airport."

"Something's going on between your cousin and the sheriff?"

"I think so."

"Tag's a nice guy. And a patient one, which is good, since I suspect your cousin could try the patience of a saint."

"Good thing that doesn't run in the family," she said, giving him a deceptively innocent look. When he raised one skeptical brow, she rolled her eyes. "Okay, okay, I guess I can be a pain in the butt, too."

"Nah," he said with a deliberate shrug. "In spite of a deplorable lack of sweetness, you're not so bad."

Her grin widened. "Do you know how nice it is to be with someone who doesn't expect me to be sweet?" She straightened, stepped away from the SUV, and put her arms out to her sides. Spinning around, she almost yelled, "God, tonight was *fun*. Outrageous and naughty, and definitely not sweet!"

"Yeah, it was," he admitted, remembering how aroused he'd been by her at the party. He loved watching her again now as she almost danced in the moonlight, her hair swinging wildly around her face. "But I hate to break it to you, babe. I suspect you really are kinda sweet, deep down."

She stopped. "Keep that up and you'll be walking home."

He jiggled his pants' pocket. "I've got your keys."

She stepped closer, laying her hand flat on his bare chest and giving him a limpid look. "Wanna place a bet on how fast I can get into your pants and get them back?"

He shook his head. "I think we've already proved you hold the world's record on getting into my pants, Kate."

"Ditto," she admitted, trailing her hand across his bare chest to his stomach. "So does that make us both cheap and easy?"

"Only with each other." He swallowed a groan as her hand moved lower, brushing across the front of his pants.

"Fair enough."

Jack liked the humor on her face and the sparkle in her eyes. He liked seeing Kate happy. He'd seen her that way much more often lately. The angry, mistrustful woman who'd come back to Pleasantville for revenge had been erased.

He hoped he'd had something to do with that. Because there was no question in his mind Kate had changed him. For the better. He doubted she'd believe it, he had trouble believing it himself, but he was falling in love with her. Falling hard and fast.

He'd started the slide the first time he'd laid eyes on her across Magnolia Avenue. Making love to her that same day had strengthened the feeling. Every day they'd spent together since then had been better than the one before.

"Come on," he said, tugging her by the hand. "Let's go down to the lake."

Though she wore an obviously expensive dress, Kate didn't hesitate. They walked hand in hand down to the edge of the lake, moving across the cool sand until they reached the shore. The warm water, lit by the bright, star-filled sky, lapped at their bare feet in a gentle rhythm. Not caring about his pants, he pulled her in deeper, until they stood almost knee-deep. He tugged her close, sliding his arms around her waist. She came into them easily, curling against his chest, tucking her head beneath his chin.

"I used to come up here to swim late at night," he said as he gently slid his fingers into her hair.

"It's warm enough," she replied. "But I don't really want to swim."

"Me neither. I'd rather stay just like this."

With Kate wrapped securely in his arms.

That seemed to be exactly what she wanted, too.

THE NEXT DAY, before Armand left to go back to Chicago, Kate asked him if he'd had a good time at the party after they'd left. He'd simply smiled and said, "It was a night that won't be forgotten for a long time."

Thanking him for the panties, she'd admitted she felt the same way.

The night before had been magic. Not only the party, not just the frantic sex in the back of her car. But standing there, wrapped in Jack's arms as they stood in the moonlight, simply enjoying each other's closeness. They'd exchanged long, languorous kisses, sweet, delicate touches. They hadn't talked much, nor had they made love again. Somehow, though, the night felt like the most intimate one they'd shared.

At some point Kate had even been able to admit the truth to herself. Not only did she no longer distrust Jack, she was falling in love with him.

Not intentionally, probably not wisely, but there it was. She loved the son of the man who'd broken her mother's heart.

"Maybe it's fate," she told herself. "Maybe we can have the happy ending in this generation."

She told herself not to hope too much. After all, she'd gone through most of her adult life not believing she could ever trust someone enough to experience real love. Somehow, though, he'd worked past her defenses and captured her heart. She was simply unable to help it.

Cassie called Monday morning, and, to Kate's complete surprise, didn't even scold her for not picking her up from the airport. She did act very strange, though. Something had obviously happened between her and the sheriff after he'd picked her up, but Kate wasn't about to pry. After all, Cassie didn't question her about being caught having sex up at the lake with Jack. Kate had to figure it was because Tag hadn't told her. Cassie would never have let something that juicy go without comment if she knew. She'd instead been much more interested in hearing all about the Bunko party and the mayor's reception, seeming surprised to hear about the friendliness of so many of the women Kate had met.

When her cousin called again at noon, Kate instantly knew Cassie was in one of her wild moods. She sounded ready for something to happen. From experience, she figured that meant Cassie wanted something *dangerous* to happen.

Still, she had to admit, Cassie's idea was a good one. "You're saying we should have a pre-opening, private party for women only in the store tomorrow night?"

"Think of it as a very naughty Tupperware party."

It sounded ridiculous, outrageous and impossible.

And Kate loved the idea.

Their store would open in exactly one week. How better to test the waters than to invite some of the women Kate had met recently for a test run? They'd seemed modern and open about sex and relationships, and also starved for the type of products the store would carry. Deep down, she suspected they'd welcome Bare Essentials. The party would be the perfect time to find out.

That didn't mean she wasn't a nervous wreck. She liked

these women, she really did, and she hated to imagine how she'd feel if they couldn't look past the titillation factor and see the potential for the store.

She wanted them to like Bare Essentials.

More importantly, she didn't want them to *dislike* her.

Kate did not pause to wonder when her goals had changed—she only knew they had. She no longer wanted only to cause controversy. Damn it, she wanted to succeed. She wanted the women of Pleasantville to be glad the Tremaine cousins had come back.

Thirty-six hours later, standing in the middle of a crowd of laughing women, she realized she needn't have worried.

"Oh, my God, Kate, no wonder you know so much about seduction!" Viv said as she greedily dug through the racks of erotic movies in the store.

"I never thought I'd say this, but these might be even better than Dr. Martens." This from Josie as she stood in front of a mirror, holding a jade-green silk teddy up against her body.

Diane went for the sex toys. "Anyone know which end is up?"

Crossing her arms and nodding in satisfaction, Kate met Cassie's eye from across the room. They exchanged a long, knowing look, each realizing that in spite of the way they'd started out, they were witnessing the birth of a bona fide success.

Who'd have ever believed it?

Soon the store was overflowing with chattering women. All the Bunko players came, and they brought friends. Cassie had also invited one woman, Stacie, who was a relative newcomer to town herself and seemed thrilled to meet all the others. Cassie and Kate could barely keep up with the sales, chatter and laughter. They passed around wine and hors d'oeuvres, and as the evening wore on, the sales added up.

"Well, all I know is, I want to buy whatever it was Kate had on under her dress at the party Saturday night," Diane said, fisting her hands and putting them on her hips. "Come on, show me. No cheesecake in the world is that good."

"Sorry," Kate said with a rueful shrug. "It's still in the testing phase. Armand is working on it, though, and I'm sure the store will be carrying them before too long."

"Armand," Diane said with a snicker. "He cracked me and Will up the other night. I don't know what he said to Darren and Angela, but I thought they were going to shit bricks."

Not knowing what she was talking about, Kate raised a brow.

"Oh, gosh, you and Jack had already left, hadn't you?"

"I know where they went," Annie the dispatcher said with a grin. "We got a call about a silver SUV at the lake."

Cassie jerked her head around to listen, giving Kate a curious stare. Feeling a blush stain her cheeks, she ignored the question in her cousin's eyes. "Get back to Darren and Angela."

"I don't really know what happened, just that Angela was dancing with Armand, getting all grabby and touchy-feely. Darren came up, Armand said something to them both, and they took off like bats outta hell in two different directions."

Kate winced. She had a feeling she knew what Armand had said. Probably something along the lines of, *Sorry, Angela babe, Darren's much prettier than you and he's the one I want. Kiss me, big boy.* Armand specialized in cutting down homophobics.

Suddenly very glad they'd left the party early, she made a mental note to strangle Armand when she got back to Chicago.

Well, maybe she'd kiss him first. Then, for sure, she'd strangle him.

CHAPTER THIRTEEN

"SO THE PARTY WAS A BIG success and the rumors are already spreading throughout town about how fabulous your store is. Tomorrow's grand opening will be a hit, I guarantee it. What'd I tell you? You're going to fail to fail." Jack couldn't keep the smug tone out of his voice as he and Kate brushed another coat of varnish remover on the old concession counter at the Rialto on Sunday afternoon.

She stuck her tongue out at him. "Anyone ever told you it's not nice to say I told you so?"

"Anyone ever told you it's not nice to stick your tongue out at people? Unless, of course, you're issuing an invitation." He caught her mouth in a quick, hot kiss that left them both breathless.

When they reluctantly parted, she looked down at the plastic drop cloth beneath their feet, which was splattered with liquid. "Paint washes off. I think varnish remover would sting, though."

"There's no work going on down on the stage," he whispered. "And our table's still there."

"Miss Rose will be back from the hardware store any minute now." She sounded disappointed. Just like he felt.

They couldn't seem to get enough of each other. No matter how many times he made love to Kate, it was always exciting, always amazing. Like that first time had been, right here in the theater all those weeks ago.

Jack had a hard time believing how much things had changed since then. In the past several days he and Kate had spent hours and hours in each other's company. He'd told her about his plans to open his own firm, she'd talked about her desire to expand her store. They'd gone through the past relationship comparisons, each trying to one-up the other with stories about some really bad first dates.

They'd even talked about their families a little. She'd told him what it was like growing up without a father. He'd told her of his regrets at leaving Angela alone in a house with his very unhappily married parents.

She'd grown uncomfortable when he mentioned his parents. "I think we ought to change the subject."

Though he knew she was right, he wished he could tell her what he'd discovered Friday. He could hardly believe it himself and had no one with whom to discuss it.

Dealing with his father's bank records had been nearly impossible from the beginning. But suddenly, the other day, he began to make sense of things. For the first time in weeks, Jack started to realize that his father had, in his own way, tried to do right by Edie.

For each and every month when there had been an uncashed paycheck made out to Edith Jones, Jack had found a subsequent payment to a mysterious account at a state bank. Some digging had revealed the truth. His father had made several sizable payments against Edie's mortgage. He doubted she'd even realized it was happening.

No, his father hadn't wiped the slate clean by any means, but it was nice to know he had not completely taken advantage of Kate's mother. He'd obviously cared about her, enough to help her even when she refused to take his help.

It didn't make things right. But at least it made them better. It also made Jack wonder if he would ever really understand the truth about their relationship. It seemed now it had been more about emotion than just sex. Sex wouldn't have taken the older couple through nearly two decades. There had to have been love.

Somehow that made it a little easier to deal with.

"So, what are you going to do now that your store's on the road to success? You can't just shut it down," he asked.

She shook her head. "I've been thinking a lot about that. Cassie and I have worked there a lot lately and we've been discussing some options. At least she'll be here until the end of the summer. And who knows what she'll want to do then."

He laid his brush down and stared. "No way would Cassie stay here long-term."

She shrugged. "I don't know if she actually would, but I don't think it's a bad idea. I kind of suggested it to her."

He raised a brow. "I can only imagine how she reacted."

"After she stops laughing, maybe she'll really think about it. She's got a great house. And she seems to have found some things she likes about Pleasantville." She snickered, obviously thinking about Tag.

"So you really think she'd stay?"

"I honestly can't say. But it's a possibility. We'll see how tomorrow's grand opening goes."

"Then in a week or two you'll go back to Chicago."

"Right. And you will, too."

He nodded.

"I'm going to miss having you right next door," she admitted. "Who'll nearly kill me when he bursts in to tackle me in the middle of the night?"

"I only hurt you the *first* time I tackled you in the middle of the night. Admit it, every other tackle since then has been painless." He gave her a suggestive look, telling her he meant their more amorous tackles. "Don't forget, I did kiss it better that first time."

"Oh, yeah, you definitely did."

Though he hadn't planned to bring it up, figuring Kate might not have realized yet that she was falling in love with him, he couldn't help himself. "Besides, we don't have to give up on having each other around once we get home. I have a big apartment. And if it's not big enough, I can design us something better. Closer to your store."

Her eyes widened. "What are you saying? You mean, you want us to…"

"Move in together," he said. "I know it's kinda fast, but we're practically living together now. Why don't we just make it official when we get home?"

She lowered her eyes, looking away. Jack called himself ten kinds of fool for bringing it up. *It's too soon.* Hell, he knew they hadn't been together long enough to start talking about cohabitation. But he was already picturing little dark-haired Jacks and blond-haired Kates! Marriage, happily-ever-after, all the stuff he'd once sworn wasn't for him.

Now he understood. He simply hadn't found the right woman yet. Until Kate. His future. The woman he wanted to spend the rest of his life with.

The one who'd gone silent and white as a sheet at just the mention of them moving in together. If he told her he wanted to marry her someday, she'd probably faint face-first into the bucket of varnish remover.

Kate was an unusual woman and she wouldn't approach things—including her love life—in the usual way. A compli-cated mix of modern vixen and smart businesswoman, she'd wanted the sex first, then the relationship. He couldn't forget that, because she might never have even thought about the future or long-term plans. Talk of those things might scare her off.

It killed him to wonder if she'd figured their involvement would end once they left Pleasantville behind. Because it wouldn't. It *couldn't*. He was never letting her go. Though she might not be ready to admit it, he knew damn well she felt the same way.

She couldn't hide the way she looked at him, particularly when he held her in his arms. There was love in her eyes.

"Let's talk about it later, okay?" he said, quickly back-tracking. "We still have some time here, and I know you need to focus on the grand opening tomorrow morning."

She looked troubled; her eyes were bright, as if she had tears in them. He silently cursed himself again for putting her on the spot, pressuring her too soon.

Before he could say anything, or even think of what to say, a woman's voice intruded. "Speaking of the grand opening, Kate, I need you to set something aside for me tomorrow morning."

They both looked up as Rose joined them, her arms loaded with bags of supplies from the hardware store.

"I want one of them Kama Sutra sheet sets, so I can honestly say my bed has had every sexual position known to man performed on it."

Kate's worried expression faded as she ruefully grinned. "You got it, Rose."

KATE FIGURED the grand opening of Bare Essentials in Pleasantville would be discussed by its residents for years to come. Old-timers would reminisce about it the way they did the big snowstorm of '73, the high school girls' state championship team of the early eighties. Even Flo Tremaine's striptease and skinny-dipping session in the town square fountain thirty years back would take a back seat to this day.

The newest generation of Tremaine women were definitely giving them something to talk about.

The line to get into the store Monday morning wound down the cobbled sidewalk, blocking the entrance to the Tea Room. That obviously ticked Mrs. McIntyre off royally, because she'd posted a snippy little sign saying Do Not Block Stairs on her porch railing.

Kate heard later that a few of the Tea Room biddies had made rude comments about the store. They'd been overruled by the people in line, including Mayor Otis who declared Kate and Cassie worthy of a civic award for their efforts to revitalize Pleasantville's downtown shopping district.

A neighboring city had even sent in a news truck. Sure, it was a teeny cable station, with a viewership of about eight, but it was exciting, nonetheless. The reporter conducted interviews with the customers, many of whom were the Bunko women who'd come to the pre-opening party last week. Their husbands were even more enthusiastic in their support of the new shop.

Singles, couples, young and old, the populace of Pleasantville chatted and laughed, lauding the store as an asset to the town while they shopped their hearts out.

Armand's lingerie was a huge hit, with sexy books and fun-and-naughty gifts doing well, too. Kate suspected the hotter items—dildoes, vibrators and the like—would sell better when there were no throngs of townspeople present. Or TV cameras.

If Kate hadn't already changed her mind about wanting this store to fail, she might be feeling pretty upset about its obvious success. Now, since she wanted it to succeed, she should be feeling at least triumph, if not downright jubilation.

Depressed better described her mood.

Stupid. It was stupid, juvenile and girlish, but she was depressed about Jack asking her to move in with him yesterday.

The modern woman who carried a vibrator around in her purse should have been thrilled, recognizing Jack had really been offering a sort of commitment in today's day and age.

A deeper, more vulnerable part of her had been very hurt.

Did he want her to serve the same function as her mother had? The woman who was good enough to mess around with, but not the one you married, not the one you had children with?

Men from Lilac Hill didn't marry trashy Tremaine women. They had sex with them in secret and left them stuff in their wills, but they certainly didn't introduce them to their mothers or give them wedding rings.

She knew her reaction was unfair. She'd seen motives and desires he might never have intended. And it wasn't as if Jack knew about his father's relationship with her mother, so he couldn't possibly have realized how she might take it.

Kate was intelligent enough to know her own deep-down insecurity had made her tense up when he'd asked. That didn't lessen the feeling, though.

At the end of the day, a few minutes before closing time, Kate found herself alone behind the cash register. Cassie had run an errand, most of the shoppers had left. There were one or two people in the dressing rooms, she believed. She was ready for them to get out so she could go take a long, hot bath. When the bell jingled over the door, she glanced up and saw, to her surprise, Darren McIntyre.

"Still open for business?"

She glanced at the clock. "You've got two minutes. Tell me what you're looking for. I'll point you in the right direction."

He shrugged. "How about the apology area?"

Kate dropped her pencil. "Huh?"

Darren walked over to the counter, not able to disguise his interest as he studied the various items on the shelves. He chuckled. "Bet my father never pictured this display case being used for *those* when he had it installed." When Kate didn't reply, he said, "Look, Kate, I came to apologize. I know it was years ago, and I'm sure you've forgotten, but I was a jerk to you in high school and I'm sorry."

Well, indeed, a day of surprises. "That's nice of you, Darren. I appreciate it. I know it's probably not easy for you to walk in here, remembering your dad and all."

He shrugged. "My father had every right to do with this building whatever he wanted to. I'm sure he'd rather see it open as a ladies' shop than sitting here moldering away. My mother on the other hand…"

Kate snorted. "Yeah, I can imagine."

"Divorce can be tough." He glanced away. "On everyone. You marry someone you think you know, think you love, then you find out you don't really know them at all."

She figured he was referring to his marriage but didn't ask. After a minute of small talk Darren said, "I'd better go. I just wanted to wish you luck and to say I'm sorry. Your, uh, *friend* Armand reminded me the other night that you might have a score to settle."

Kate shook her head, putting aside not only Darren's doubts, but any of her own. "No, Darren, I don't." *Not anymore.*

Darren had no sooner left, shutting the door behind them, when Kate heard someone emerge from the dressing room area. She sensed her long, hot bath was going to be further delayed when she recognized Angela. "I didn't know you were here."

"Stay away from Darren," the woman said. "You got your revenge. Your friend made a big fool out of the both of us the other night, so leave him alone."

Seeing tears in the other woman's eyes, Kate had to wonder whether Angela had ever given up on her first marriage. Any sympathy she felt for Angela evaporated when she saw the book she held. Her diary. The last time she'd seen it, it had been in a drawer in a desk in the storage room. "Snooping?"

Angela didn't even have the grace to flush. "Stay away

from my brother, too. I won't let you hurt him in some nasty plot."

"You don't know what you're talking about." Suddenly so tired, Kate rubbed her eyes. She didn't want to have this conversation. Ever.

Angela slammed the diary on the counter, open to the page with Kate's revenge list. "Yes, I do. Didn't you write this? 'For Mom's sake, get even with the Winfield family,'" she read. "'Particularly John Winfield.' My father isn't around to hurt anymore, so you've decided to focus on my brother. A different man, but who cares, the name's the same, right?"

Kate took a deep breath, trying to remain calm enough to deal with Jack's sister, trying to have sympathy for her, given the way Jack had described her childhood. "Angela, that was years ago. I don't have any intention of hurting Jack."

The other woman crossed her arms. "Just like you didn't want revenge on me and Darren, by setting us up to look like fools at the mayor's reception the other night? Like you didn't want to hurt the town by opening up this shop? Don't give me that. You want to hurt my family the way your mother did."

Then it hit her. Angela didn't seem the least bit surprised her diary had spoken of Edie and John. She tilted her head and stared at the woman. "You knew. About their affair."

Angela nodded. "Of course I knew. I've known for years. Everyone knows, even my mother."

Everyone? Including Jack?

"The point is, Kate, your secret's out. I'm going to tell Jack all about this little revenge list of yours, which you've been crossing off since the day you hit town."

Kate shook her head. "You're wrong. I care about Jack."

She smirked. "Won't matter. Jack doesn't care about you. You've been about one thing to him from the very beginning. He doesn't love you. Winfields don't marry trashy Tremaine women who own sex shops or work as maids. He won't marry you any more than my father married your mother."

Kate's anger made her reply so quickly her mind barely registered the ringing of the bell over the front door. "Thanks to *your* mother." At Angela's puzzled look, Kate said, "She made sure of it. Trapping him into marriage with a fake pregnancy just to get him away from *my* mother, who was his girlfriend throughout high school! That's probably just what you did to Darren, only he didn't stick around like your father did after he found out. So don't talk to me about families being hurt. If anyone deserves some payback, it's the Winfields."

Angela had grown pale and looked utterly shocked. Kate regretted the words as soon as she said them, angry with herself for letting the woman goad her so. Kate regretted them even more when she realized who had walked into the store.

Seeing the late-afternoon sunlight shining through the front windows onto a familiar—and very dear—blond head, she felt the blood drain from her face. "Jack."

"Do I even want to know what's going on here?" Jack forced a note of calmness in his voice as he walked across the store to the counter, where Kate and his sister both stood. They looked equally as disturbed by his appearance.

"This is a misunderstanding…"

"She came here for one reason. To get revenge," Angela said at the same time. His sister thrust a small book in his hand, obviously a diary. "She's been plotting it for years. Against me and Darren—we were both totally humiliated by her gay friend the other night. But she's not satisfied yet, she's out to get the whole town, including *you*."

He didn't look at his sister, focusing all his attention on Kate. "Angela, would you please leave?"

He thought she'd argue, but she didn't. Looking confused

and upset, more than angry, Angela grabbed her purse and hurried out of the store. As soon as they were alone, Jack put the diary back on the counter.

"It's not like she said…"

"I know about your revenge list, remember?" he interrupted softly. "You don't have to explain it to me."

She looked relieved. For a moment, anyway.

He continued. "I once asked you if it would be bad for me to see the list. When you said yes, I figured it mentioned Angela. Was she right? Was there more to it than that?"

Kate took a slow, deep breath, then nodded.

"You knew about my father and Edie."

She crossed her arms tightly. "I found out on prom night."

He absorbed her words and said a silent curse. Both Kate and his sister had learned as teenagers of their parents' affair. He again kicked himself for leaving town, for not being around when he might have been needed.

"When did you find out?" she asked softly.

"The night I met you," he admitted. "*After* I left you at the theater. I had absolutely no idea who you were until then. I didn't even know your last name, remember?"

She glanced away, her face growing even paler.

As a heavy, uncomfortable silence fell between them, Jack mentally replayed what he'd heard of the conversation. He still had trouble believing it. Not that Kate had written a revenge list, he'd known about it before, after all. He just hadn't known his entire family was part of the plot. Somehow, it had been easy to imagine she'd gotten over any high school hurts, so he'd accepted her assurances that she really wasn't opening her store for revenge. Now, however, he had to wonder.

"I have to know," he finally said, "was your list on your mind when you came back here? When we got involved?"

She stared at him, not answering.

"Tell me, Kate. When you decided to come back to Pleasantville, did you think about a little payback? Getting involved with me, then breaking my heart, like you thought my dad did to your mom?"

She countered with a question of her own. "You tell me something, Jack. The night we met, when you found out who I was, that Edie *Tremaine* was my mother…is that the reason you never called? The reason you decided we couldn't get involved?"

He answered easily. "Of course."

She stiffened, as if offended by his honesty, though he didn't know why. He opened his mouth to elaborate, to tell her how hurt he'd been for Edie, how he'd wanted to make it up to her and not take advantage of Kate.

Before he could say a word, however, she picked up her purse and keys. "Thanks for being honest. Now, you want the truth? Here it is. I came back here with every intention of seducing J. J. Winfield." Stepping around the counter, she met his stare steadily with her own. "I planned to get him to go crazy over me, then stomp his heart into the dust with the heels of my six-inch-tall slut-puppy boots."

Without another word, she turned and walked out of her own store.

CHAPTER FOURTEEN

WHEN NURSING A BROKEN heart, it really sucked to live next door to the person who'd done the breaking. Kate found that out late Monday night when she lay on her mattress bed in Aunt Flo's duplex, listening to Jack arrive home next door.

As soon as she heard his truck outside, she bit her lip to stop her tears. She definitely didn't want him to hear her through the wall.

She'd been crying for hours. Whimpering like a sissified baby. Wishing she had someone to talk to, but knowing there was no one. Cassie would be too pissed on her behalf to be of any help. Plus, the last thing she wanted to do on the day of the triumph at the store was to tell Cassie someone she thought she loved still looked at her as unworthy.

When Jack had admitted he'd decided to end their involvement because of who she was—a Tremaine—Kate had wanted to die. All she'd heard were his sister's angry words, the echo of taunts of her childhood, the deeply-buried-but-not-erased voice of her subconscious that had told her she would always be just a trashy Tremaine. Never good enough for decent people. Worthy of sex but not love, fun but not commitment.

Living together, but not marriage.

Even though her heart was breaking, she'd still almost gone back to apologize, to tell him she might have first intended to get involved with him for revenge, but knew she could never go through with it. Because like a colossal fool, she'd fallen in love with him. And it had hurt her to see the pain on his face at her confession.

Pride had kept her walking out the door the same way it had sustained her on prom night when she'd walked home in the rain.

She didn't sleep more than one straight hour all night long. Kate knew she looked and sounded like hell, so when she called Cassie the next morning, told her she wasn't feeling well and would be late coming in to help in the store, her cousin hadn't protested. She felt like a heel leaving Cassie holding the bag at Bare Essentials. Still, she doubted their day would be anywhere near as busy as yesterday had been.

Jack left the house early—before eight. She watched him from the upstairs window, careful not to let him see her. She needn't have bothered. He never spared a glance at her half of the duplex as he got in his truck and drove away.

Once he'd gone, she cried some more. Ate some donuts. Took a shower. Finally, sick of feeling sorry for herself, she pulled her cell phone out of her purse and called the one person she knew would understand.

Her mom.

JACK DIDN'T WANT to see anybody Tuesday. He had no interest in being anywhere near his mother or sister. Nor could he stay at the duplex, knowing Kate was right next door.

Sleeping there the night before had been sheer torture. He had lain awake most of the night, thinking about what had happened, replaying the scene at the store. He'd tried to find some explanation, but couldn't deny the truth. She'd said the words herself. She'd fully intended to get involved with him for the express purpose of hurting him as some kind of whacked-out revenge on his father.

Mission accomplished.

Damn, it was almost easier when he thought he'd never fall in love.

After driving around for a while, he went downtown and parked outside the Rose Café. Across the street, Bare Essentials remained dark, not yet open for the morning. When he went inside the café for breakfast, he took a seat away from the front windows. He really didn't want to see Kate arriving for work.

After he ordered, he tried to figure out just how much more he had to do for his family. There were one or two more legal issues, but the real estate situation was taken care of, as were the banking problems. At this point, all he wanted to do was to wrap things up and go home to Chicago. He frankly didn't care if he never saw Pleasantville again.

Just as the gum-chewing waitress deposited a plate full of artery-hardening breakfast on the table in front of him, the café door opened. As Darren entered, Jack looked away. He did not want to talk to anyone, particularly his ex-brother-in-law.

Unfortunately, Darren had other ideas. "Can I sit down?"

"Do I have any other choice?"

Darren took the seat opposite him in the booth. "I need to talk to you. About Angela. She came to see me last night and told me what happened with Kate."

Jack raised a brow, practically daring Darren to make one slimy comment about Kate. "And?"

"Apparently Kate said something to Angela that made her do some serious thinking. About us."

"You and Angela?"

"Yeah. She asked me if I'd left her because I thought she faked being pregnant to get me to marry her."

Jack calmly took a sip of coffee. "Did you?"

Darren answered with a slow nod. "I was convinced she'd

made it up, that there had never been any baby. Because I'd overheard your parents arguing about it one night. Your father accused Angela of being like your mother, who'd done the same thing to him."

Jack could only shake his head. Kate had been right about that much of the story, it seemed.

Before Darren said anything else, the door to the café opened again and Angela came in. Her face was lit up by a huge smile, and her eyes sparkled as she looked around the room. She spotted Darren and walked toward them. Her steps slowed when she realized he was sitting with Jack. Squaring her shoulders, she sat opposite him, sliding easily under Darren's outstretched arm. The two of them might as well have started cooing like doves.

Jack raised a brow. "I see you've worked things out."

Darren nodded. "Angela made me realize how wrong I'd been."

Angela had the grace to admit, "I had no idea, Jack, about Mother and Dad. It never occurred to me what Darren thought until Kate accused me of it last night. I had to make sure he knew the truth. I wanted to be sure Darren understood how much I grieved for our very real baby." She swallowed hard. "I guess I owe Kate one."

Well, let's give a round of applause for Kate, matchmaker and revenge seeker extraordinaire.

"You should probably know," Angela continued, "Darren confirmed what Kate told me. About Dad and Edie being together before he married Mother. I guess...well, it doesn't make it right, what they did, but I think I can see Kate's side a little better now." Angela cast a quick, nervous glance at Darren. He smiled and nudged her, obviously trying to give her courage. "I also, uh, should tell you, I know you only heard part of our conversation. Kate wasn't the only one who said nasty things, Jack. I was pretty mean to her first."

Angela expressing regret? He could hardly believe it. "If it's any consolation," Jack said, "whatever happened with Armand, whatever revenge you think he got on you? I don't think Kate was involved. He's just very loyal to her."

Angela stared at him. "You're in love with her."

He gave her a rueful look. "Crazy, huh?"

"Wow." His sister bit her lip, looking more nervous. "Jack, one of the mean things I said to her was that you, uh…"

Starting to feel very anxious, Jack leaned closer. "What?"

Darren took her hand, squeezing it to give her courage. "Come on, Ang. New leaf, remember?"

Angela spoke in a rush. "I told her you could never love her. And that you'd never marry a trashy Tremaine woman any more than our father ever would have."

Jack sat silently for a minute, beginning to understand, to make sense out of what had happened yesterday.

Probably without even realizing it, Angela had pushed exactly the right button to hurt Kate the most. Because in spite of how put-together, confident and successful a woman she was today, there was still that vulnerable, defensive, wrong-side-of-the-tracks kid lurking underneath Kate's beautiful exterior.

Kate's childhood had molded her into the striking mix of sweet and tough, gentle and outrageous, smart and self-doubting.

Jack had fallen in love with all of her.

But she didn't believe that.

"I've got to go," he said. Dropping cash on the table for his uneaten breakfast, he barely spared a glance at his sister.

"I'm sorry, Jack," she called as he walked away. "I'm sorry I hurt her."

Not as sorry as he was.

RIGHT AFTER Kate's long telephone call with Edie, she hung up, hearing her mother's words again and again in her mind.

"Oh, honey, don't you think for a minute I regret loving the man I loved. And don't think I didn't know how much he loved *me*. Heavens, John asked me to marry him more than a dozen times over the years, starting all the way back in tenth grade." She'd laughed softly, as if remembering something warm and tender. "After Angela grew up and got married, I started to think we could really be together. Then her marriage failed. As did her second. And her third. Pat blamed John for his bad example and guilt made him stay. But we still loved each other. Why do you think I had to leave Ohio when he died? Do you think some narrow-minded people could have forced a Tremaine out?" Her voice had broken and Kate had somehow heard the silent tears she knew were rolling down her cheeks. "It was too painful to stay, Katey. Knowing he was gone."

After she hung up, Kate shed more tears. This time not for herself. But for Edie.

A short time later she grabbed her purse and keys and went to find Jack. One thing her mother had said rang true…if she loved the man, pride had no place in the equation. Any chance for happiness was one worth grabbing.

She took a deep breath as she slowly drove by the Winfield house on Lilac Hill. No truck in the driveway. Thank God. She needed to see him, but she wasn't ready to face his family.

She tried the downtown area next, cruising along Magnolia, looking for his golden hair shining in the bright morning sun. She still didn't see him. Finally, thinking hard about where he might have gone in this town, she turned down a side street toward the Rialto.

Bingo.

Parking her SUV behind his truck, she walked to the front doors and entered the lobby. The overhead fixtures were off out here, but she saw a sliver of light from the main auditorium area. Pushing through the swinging doors, she paused in the back of the theater, looking around in the murky shadows of the cavernous, dimly lit room.

Jack sat in one of the old plushly covered seats in the back row. She saw him there at the same instant he saw her.

"What are you doing here?" she asked.

"I was looking for you. I went to the house, and the store. I finally figured you'd show up here. So I sat down to wait."

He was right. Eventually, even if she hadn't gone looking for him, she would have shown up here.

He remained seated, while Kate stood. She didn't know what to say, now that she had finally found him. There didn't seem to be an easy way to apologize for admitting what had once been the truth. She really had thought she could set out to hurt this man. This amazing man who'd captured her heart and soul.

It now seemed almost inconceivable.

Finally, as if realizing she couldn't find the words to begin, Jack stood and extended his hand. She stepped closer, taking it, letting him pull her into the seat next to his own.

Finally she heard him say, "I'm not J. J. Winfield, Kate." She bit her lip.

"Maybe J. J. Winfield was someone you once wanted to get even with. But that's not me."

"I know," she admitted. "Jack, as soon as I saw you, as soon as I realized who you were, I dropped any idea of revenge. I knew I was too vulnerable to you." She lowered her voice. "I already liked you too much. I knew from the beginning I could care for you."

"I knew it, too," he said. "I never would have believed it if it hadn't happened to me, but I knew from the first time I saw you something amazing was going to happen between us. I started to fall in love with you before I even heard your voice or knew your name."

Her name. Yes, back to the issue at hand. Kate thrust away the thrill of pleasure that had raced through her body at hearing the word love on Jack's lips. "My name. Who I am. That's the issue, right? The reason you didn't call."

She felt his level stare as he carefully answered. "Kate, finding out your name, learning you were a member of the *infamous* Tremaine family, had absolutely nothing to do with me staying away from you." He sighed, shaking his head. "You want the truth? Here it is. I couldn't handle the guilt. I really thought my father had used and abused your mother, and I wasn't about to follow in his footsteps. In case you didn't know it, I don't have a great reputation as a stick-around kind of guy."

There was no question of doubting him, the sincerity in his voice was matched by the look in his eyes.

"So, when you asked me to live with you..."

He cocked his head. "You were upset about that?"

She glanced at her fingers. "I just figured it was history repeating itself. Tremaines are good enough to live with..."

She almost expected him to react in anger, but instead he laughed, long and loud. "God, have we ever been at cross purposes." Turning in his seat, he grabbed her around the waist and lifted her over the armrest, pulling her onto his lap. "I'm crazy about you, Kate. I want the whole nine yards. Marriage, kids, P.T.A. meetings."

Marriage? Kids? She choked on a mouthful of air and had to hack into her fist. When she could breathe again, she said, "P.T.A. meetings?"

"We'll go together, unless, of course, you're busy peddling sex toys at your store."

She couldn't even laugh, still too amazed to see what she wanted was truly within her grasp. "You're serious? You want all that?"

He brought her hands to his lips, kissing her palm. "I absolutely want all that." He pulled her closer, until her head rested on his shoulder. "I figured you'd laugh in my face if I started talking about that kind of stuff, though. You, Miss Lusty Vibrating Fingertip, seemed to not only enjoy doing things backward, but you seem to want to make them as outrageous as possible. I kinda figured love and marriage stuff would turn you off…make you think I thought you were sweet or something."

She sat up and punched his shoulder. "I am sweet, damn it."

He gave her a hopeful smile. "Hopefully not too sweet for those slut-puppy boots."

She lowered her lashes, giving him a coy look. "If you're good. But in the meantime, get back to the L word you mentioned."

"Lusty?"

Their laughter faded as Kate stared intently into his fine green eyes. "Love. Did you mean to use that particular word?"

He reached up and slipped his hand into her hair, caressing her gently as he tugged her mouth toward his. "Yeah. I meant to use that particular word. I love you like crazy, Kate."

Just before her lips touched his, she whispered, "I love you, too, Jack."

EPILOGUE

Six Months Later

LYING IN THE UNFAMILIAR king-size bed in their hotel suite, Jack listened to Kate get up and go into the bathroom. He'd thought she was asleep. Heaven knew, she should be after their strenuous evening. But maybe she was still too keyed up to sleep, too happy, excited and relieved that they'd actually made it. As he was.

Jack waited for her to come back, then smiled in the darkness as he heard the sound of the faucet turning and the gush of water in the tub.

A late-night shower.

What a way to start off married life.

He didn't get up to join her right away, content instead to listen to her from the bed. He waited for the pulling of the plastic curtain, the clink of the rings on the metal rod. The gurgle turning to a hiss as the shower jets came on. Kate's light, off-key humming.

Remembering lying in bed at the house in Pleasantville, listening to her all those months ago, he had to laugh. They'd come a long way. Physically and emotionally.

Unable to hold out any longer, he got out of bed, almost tripping on Kate's white sundress and shoes, which he'd tossed to the floor earlier that evening in his rush to make her his wife in every sense of the word.

Her wedding dress. And the flip-flops she'd worn for the small beachside ceremony.

They'd had a perfect sunset wedding with two bartenders at the couples-only resort serving as official witnesses. A beach vendor had made Kate her bouquet and a housemaid had caught it. A steel drum player had riffed in the background, competing with the sound of the surf and the low, lyrical voice of the island minister who'd married them.

Considering their two mothers couldn't stand one another, they'd thought it best to fly to the Caribbean for the ceremony. Maybe someday they'd all have to be together—probably when he and Kate started having kids. But for now, long-distance family relationships seemed the wisest solution.

Their families certainly wished them well, for which they were both grateful. Edie and her new boyfriend had thrown them a big engagement party at the retirement community in Florida at Thanksgiving. And his own mother—who had decided to give Mayor Otis a run for his money and seek her late husband's seat—had done the same on New Year's Day a few weeks ago in Pleasantville.

Jack still cracked up remembering the expression on Kate's face when his sister Angela had hugged her, telling her how sorry she was her pregnancy would prevent her from being maid of honor. He'd had to cover his mouth so Darren wouldn't see him snort with laughter.

The best party of them all, however, had been the bridal shower at Bare Essentials, hosted by Armand and Cassie. He hoped to God Kate had packed some of the gifts they got *that* night.

Unable to wait any longer, Jack walked into the bathroom. Seeing several conveniently placed candles and matches, he lit a few, then turned out the light. Kate's silhouette shimmered through the shower curtain in the soft glow of candlelight.

She said nothing, obviously waiting for him in the semi-darkness. When he stepped inside the tub, pulling the curtain closed behind him, she leaned back against his body and turned her head to look up at him. "I thought you were asleep. I didn't mean to wake you."

"I wouldn't have missed this. Our first married shower."

She was hot and wet, slippery and lithe. Jack wanted to touch her everywhere. Pulling her closer, he knew she felt his hard-on slipping between her thighs. He groaned as she rocked back on it, rubbing her curvy backside against his groin. Sliding his arms around her waist, he held her tight as he bent to press his mouth to hers for one long wet kiss after another.

"Hope they paid the hot water bill," she said when their lips finally parted.

Remembering some of the other showers they'd shared over the past few months, he hoped so, too.

"I love you, Kate," he said as he pushed a long, dark strand of wet hair off her brow.

She rubbed her cheek against his palm, whispering, "And I love you."

He kissed her again, sweetly, cherishing her tonight as his wife as much as he already cherished her as his mate. Finally, spying a bottle of body wash on the edge of the tub, he reached for it. "Want me to wash your back?"

She nodded, giving him a look of sultry heat. "And my front."

Oh, without question.

"It's a deal." He grinned. "Just remember the rule…"

She rolled her eyes and gave him a disgruntled look. "Okay, I know. No singing in the shower." Then she raised a brow. "Just don't you forget your rule, either, *angel*."

Remembering their first time together back on the stage at the Rialto, he chuckled. "No wings until I ring your bell."

Their laughter, their loving…and their shower…lasted long into the night.

* * * * *

WICKED & WILLING

To Julie, Lori and Tony...terrific writers, even more terrific friends! Thanks for making this project such a wonderful experience. And to my readers. Thanks for hanging in there with me for another wild ride.

CHAPTER ONE

"WHAT WOULD YOU SAY if I told you it's possible you're the long-lost granddaughter of a millionaire?"

Venus Messina snorted as she twisted the cap off a bottle of Bud, then flipped it into the trash with her thumb. She didn't even look over her shoulder at the uptight old windbag whom she'd dubbed Mr. Collins—Tom Collins—since that was his drink of choice. He sat at the end of the bar and had been trying to engage her in conversation since the moment he arrived.

Granddaughter of a millionaire. Right.

Lemme guess…my Granny is Miss Manners. Cause everyone can see I'm just like her. She chuckled under her breath.

The man persisted. "…and his direct heir?"

Though his voice grated shrilly over the noisy chatter in the crowded room, nobody even glanced over in curiosity. It was late into Happy Hour on a hot Friday night in June, and everyone knew Friday nights in an Irish pub were as good a place for outrageous stories and high drama as any movie theater.

Tonight was the third time this week the man had parked himself here at Flanagan's, her foster uncle's bar, where she'd been working until she could find a full-time job. The first night, the man had been so quiet she almost hadn't heard his drink order. He'd looked as out of his element as a nun in a strip club. Not so much in the way he dressed, though. After all, Flanagan's catered to a lot of ambitious, wealthy businesspeople who spent their days bowing down to the almighty dollar in one of the many huge office buildings in downtown Baltimore.

No, he didn't look out of place because of his pricey dark suit, which even Venus could tell probably cost more than she made in a month—or more than she *had* made in a month when she'd actually been employed full-time. Instead, it was his stiffness, the upturned tilt of his pointy chin, the way his nose flared in that irritating way when somebody stepped too close. The way he combed one long strand of graying hair over the top of his head to hide a bald spot, because, after all, rich people were much too refined to ever wear something as gaudy as a toupee.

Nope, she couldn't say she liked Mr. Collins, even if he was a damn good tipper.

"Are you even going to answer me, young lady?"

The imperious tone said he'd given up on easy friendliness, something he'd tried last night and failed at miserably. Mr. Collins's face looked like it was going to crack from his smile—obviously he didn't use it very often.

Tonight he'd skipped friendly and gone for nosy. He'd been trying to engage her in conversation and had been asking way too many personal questions—none of which she'd answered, of course. After she'd spent the past hour ignoring everything he said that wasn't prefaced by the standard, "Bartender, get me a...," he'd finally blurted out his ridiculous millionaire comment.

"Well?" he prompted, impatiently tapping his perfectly manicured fingers on the top of the pitted, sticky bar.

Sliding the bottle of Bud and a Fuzzy Navel—a disaster of a drink if ever there was one—to the yuppie couple seated at the bar, she muttered, "I'd say somewhere a village is seriously missing its idiot."

Yuppie man grinned. His date, with the pisspoor taste in drinks, gave Venus a quick frown, warning her away from spoken-for territory. *As if, lady.* Guys in ties were definitely not Venus's bag these days. As a matter of fact, she'd lately sworn off all men in general. Her last relationship had burned her—*badly*—leaving her not only brokenhearted, but jobless to boot.

Besides which, Venus had decided thirty was too old to keep playing the field. She looked forward to her thirtieth birthday the way a condemned prisoner looked forward to the executioner.

Thirty. Less than a year away. *Now, doesn't that suck?*

Venus didn't so much mind the number. She *did* mind not being where she'd thought she'd be by age thirty—in a great job, a stable relationship, a house, maybe even with a couple of rugrats running around. Her upbringing had made her desire *The Brady Bunch* life as an adult.

At the rate she was going, she'd be lucky with *The Osbournes.*

"It would behoove you to take a brief break and speak with me," Mr. Tom Collins said, still red in the face from her previous comment.

"Behoove?" She paused to finish pulling a draught of Guinness, complete with the requisite "G" swirl of foam on top. She pushed it toward the waitress, and grinned as Janie rolled her eyes behind the annoying man's back. "It would also behoove me to earn my paycheck, don'tcha think, Janie?"

The woman snorted. "You call what that cheapskate Joe pays us a paycheck?" Venus took no offense. Janie was Joe's on-again, off-again girlfriend. This week they were off-again.

Besides, Janie was right. The pay was pretty abysmal. It was the tips that had kept her clothed and fed for several months. For some reason, the regulars at Flanagan's seemed to like Venus's caustic wit and in-your-face attitude. Plus, she made a damn fine Bloody Mary, if she did say so herself.

But bartending wasn't exactly her dream job. Up until eight months ago, Venus had had the job she'd always hoped for, complete with the kind of salary that had enabled her to actually open a savings account. Starting out in the typing pool of a financial company right out of high school, she'd worked her way up for ten years. She'd scraped and studied, taken college night courses when she could. She'd put in long hours and kept the right attitude, including keeping her mouth shut when the occasion warranted it. Eventually she'd ended up in management in the HR department.

Then she'd been stupid enough to let down her guard, to get involved with Dale, one of the executives in the company. She'd fallen in…well, not love, but at least infatuation. He'd fallen in lust. Unfortunately, she'd gotten over the infatuation a little sooner than he'd gotten over the lust. When she'd broken it off, he hadn't been pleased.

In fact, he'd been so displeased, Dale had made sure Venus ended up on the unemployment line three months later.

Hence, her dislike for guys in ties.

Without a college degree to go with her experience, Venus had simply been unable to find a new job—unless she wanted to start all over again at the bottom of the ladder.

She might reach that point. If she hadn't had this job at Joe's place to fall back on, plus the remainder of that nearly empty savings account, she probably already would have. But holding out for a better-paying job wasn't just about taking care of herself. She needed to make enough to get back to helping Ma. Her foster mother had insisted she was doing fine, but Venus knew more than most the way Maureen struggled. Until her layoff, Venus had managed to send enough back to Trenton to make a real difference for the four kids currently living in her old home.

She wanted to be able to do so again. Soon.

"Imagine not having to worry about a paycheck," the man said, sounding almost desperate. "Please, Ms. Messina, give me a few minutes of your time." The word "please," and the urgency in his voice, made her pause and really look at the man.

"Go ahead, V," she heard from behind her. Glancing over her shoulder, she saw the sardonic look on her uncle Joe's craggy red face. "And if you're a millionaire heiress, don't forget who taught you to ride a bike."

"That woulda been Tony Cabrini, the boy in 6A," she replied with a saucy grin.

Joe wagged his index finger at her. "And who taught you how to deal with Tony Cabrini and boys like him when he got fresh on your fourteenth birthday?"

Venus fisted a hand and put it on her hip. "Ma did."

"Well, who do ya think taught *her* that knee trick, hmm?"

Laughing helplessly, she said, "Okay, okay. Thanks for teaching her the knee trick, Uncle Joe."

Not that she'd ever used it on Tony Cabrini. The last time she'd seen him, her knee definitely was *not* the body part she'd reacted with when he "got fresh." She'd lost her virginity to Tony in the laundry room of their building when she was sixteen.

Venus still had a real fondness for the spin cycle.

"Now, take a break," Joe said. "You can use my office." He turned toward the stranger. "Don't try nothing funny. You try to run a con on her and I'll make sure you have to drink your vodka through a straw for the rest of your life."

Venus gave Joe a quick hug, noting his start of surprise. Though not a real blood relation, he was as close as any uncle one could want. His sister, Maureen, had been Venus's foster mother since age eight. She remembered looking forward to Joe's visits to Jersey the way she'd look forward to Santa in

December—even if Santa had usually brought only sensible clothes and donated secondhand toys, rather than the Barbie stuff and play makeup Venus had asked for.

Heck, when she thought about it, Joe's visits were probably more entertaining than Santa's anyway. Joe had taught her to play poker when she was ten. He'd taught her to spit like a boy when she was twelve. He'd taught her how to fake a fever to avoid a big exam when she was fourteen.

He'd also taught her that being poor was nothing to be ashamed of, and used himself as an example of how you could get what you want if you were willing to work for it.

She'd never forgotten the lesson.

Joe had also been the one who helped Venus when she'd come to Baltimore looking for a job right out of high school. And he'd been her closest family member ever since.

"Okay," she said over her shoulder to her impatient customer. "You've got five minutes."

Leading him through a swinging door, Venus walked into the cement-floored storage room, piled high with boxes and crates, broken bar stools and lined with shelves full of premium liquor. At the back of the room was the desk Joe referred to as his office. Sitting in Joe's well-worn chair, Venus leaned back, crossed her arms over her chest, and watched as the stranger sat in the metal folding chair opposite her. "Now why don't you tell me who you are and what the hell it is you want?"

Though he stiffened, she didn't apologize. He was on her dime. And if he didn't like her attitude, that was too damn bad. To Venus, attitude was everything.

"My name is Leo Gallagher," he finally said. "And, to confirm, you are Venus Messina, born in Trenton, and your parents are Trina O'Reilly and Matt Messina?"

"So they tell me, not that I know for sure since I never laid eyes on my father," she said. Then she narrowed her eyes. "Any particular reason you've been checking up on me?"

He ignored her question and mumbled, "The hair is a surprise. But the eyes, that deep green…"

Venus watched as he looked her over again, knowing what he saw—a tall redhead with a big mouth and the kind of figure that could turn horny men into drooling idiots and jealous women into shrews. Venus had long since stopped feeling self-conscious about her height or her very curvy figure. But she began to fidget as the man continued to study her.

"Your parents weren't married."

It wasn't a question, but she answered anyway. "Nope. Shocking, huh? My mother used to joke about how awful her name would have been, Trina Messina."

He ignored her sarcasm. "You never knew your father, and lost your mother to cancer when you were eight."

Venus clenched her back teeth, fighting the impulse to stand up and walk out of here. "What do you want?" she bit out.

He seemed to sense her patience was nearing its end. "Ms. Messina, I believe your father, who called himself Matt Messina, may actually have been my cousin, Maxwell Longotti, Jr."

Her heart beat a little faster, but Venus took a deep breath, ignoring it. "Why?"

"My cousin left my uncle's estate in Atlanta thirty years ago, determined to make it as a stand-up comedian. He stayed in New York for a while, using a stage name—Matt Messina."

Her heart quickened even more. "My mother met my father in New York, but she never mentioned a stage name." *However, she did say he'd made her laugh like no one else she ever knew.*

"She might not have even been aware of it. I don't believe they could have known each other very long. He was in New

York City for only a few weeks, and then he went out to California."

Unable to help it, she asked, "Where is he now?"

"He was killed in a car accident less than a year later."

Venus closed her eyes, angry with herself for allowing a tiny spark of hope to burn for the briefest moment. "Oh."

"He planned to return to New York, but was going to stop in Atlanta first to try to make amends with Uncle Max. They'd parted rather bitterly, you see. He phoned, said he wanted to mend fences. Something amazing had happened, he said. Something that made him reevaluate the importance of family."

Like finding out he had a baby with a woman he'd had a fling with back in New York? She thrust the thought away.

"The next day we heard Max had been killed. When his father went out west to settle things, he found a card in Max's apartment. It simply said, 'Congratulations, Daddy.' Inside was a photo of a baby with the name Violet written on the back."

"My name's Venus," she immediately countered.

The man shrugged, as if unconcerned. "Possibly a nickname? Perhaps your mother changed her mind?"

"No *way* would my mother name me Violet. Besides, I think I would know my own name."

Leo glanced away, not meeting her eye. "Are you certain of the name on your birth certificate?"

"I've never seen it. There was a robbery at my foster mother's place back when I was in high school and a bunch of papers got stolen."

He raised a brow.

"But," she insisted, "my driver's license, social security card and school records all say Venus. I think by now somebody woulda figured it out if I'd been using an illegal name."

"Perhaps. But no matter." The man—who thought he could be her what...uncle? Second cousin?—smiled thinly. "The point is, there is enough circumstantial evidence to think it is *possible* you are my cousin's illegitimate daughter."

She remained silent, absorbing his claim. Her heart no longer raced, and she didn't tremble with excitement. If she hadn't just been told Max Longotti Jr. had died nearly thirty years ago, perhaps she could have allowed herself a moment of hope...a moment of that familiar longing to find out who her people were. Now, she felt only anguish. Whether the man spoke the truth or not, she was no closer to having a real father now than she'd ever been.

Deep down, she prayed he was wrong, this so-called relative. She'd long imagined her real father living a great life, being the great guy she liked to think he was. She'd pictured his happiness when he'd learned about the existence of his daughter, who he must never have known about since he hadn't come for her when her mother died. Her mother told her she'd tried to contact him about Venus's birth, and she'd never stopped believing he'd return to them.

But what if he hadn't gotten the news? Messages got lost. Phone numbers changed. Postmen went postal and didn't deliver the mail. Her father could very well be out there somewhere, living his life, as wonderful as her mother had said he was.

No. Venus didn't want to imagine him dead. Not now. Not ever.

"Okay, Mr. Gallagher," she said as she stood and squared her shoulders. "You've said what you wanted to say. It's a nice fairy tale, but I don't believe it. My name is not Violet. Matt Messina is not exactly an unusual name. New York's a big city. And I think it's time for you to leave."

His jaw dropped and his eyes widened. Obviously he'd

expected her to fall at his feet in gratitude. Right now she wished she'd never laid eyes on him.

"B-but, you have to admit it's possible," he sputtered.

"Why? What difference does it make if the man is dead?"

"Well," he said, "because I want you to come to Atlanta to meet your grandfather."

She began to shake her head. Accepting this Longotti character as her grandfather would mean accepting that her real father had died decades ago. It would mean accepting she really had no parents and the father she'd fantasized about all her life had been in his grave before she took her first steps.

No thank you.

"And I will pay you a great deal of money to do so."

Venus paused. Then she slowly lowered herself to her chair.

TROY LANGTREE sat in his new office at Longotti Lines, nodding with satisfaction at the tasteful decor and the magnificent view of downtown Atlanta off the balcony. His office at his family-owned department store in south Florida had been just as nicely appointed, but its view had been of swaying palm trees and bikini-clad beach goers.

"Well, that had its benefits, too," he murmured with a wry smile. Still, he found himself appreciating the look of Atlanta. The skyline spoke of big-city energy and excitement. In the week he'd lived here, he'd found himself growing energetic and excited, too.

He still couldn't quite believe he was here. His move to Atlanta had been rather a shock, even to him. If someone had asked Troy a year ago where he saw himself on the day of his retirement, he would have firmly replied that he'd still be heading up the Langtree store chain in Florida. He'd never pictured himself doing anything else.

After his father had retired six years ago, he'd worked with his twin brother, Trent, until they both realized Troy liked the store and Trent hated it. When Trent struck out on his own to start a landscaping business, Troy had moved into the executive position with ease. He'd enjoyed his job, and if he sometimes felt bored, closed-in, well, he'd had other outlets to pursue in his off-hours. Mainly outlets of the female variety. As a wealthy, and, to be honest, attractive bachelor, he had never lacked for female company.

But about a year ago, his well-laid plans began to wrinkle. His brother's marriage had been a surprise, though a pleasant one. Watching Trent go crazy over his wife, Chloe, Troy had wondered, for the first time in his life, if he might ever meet a woman who could turn him into a complete idiot, like his brother had become.

"Doubtful."

His sister-in-law's subsequent pregnancy had thrilled the entire family, Troy included. It was, probably, why he'd been foolish enough to get briefly involved with someone not at all his usual type. By dating a friendly, personable young woman who reminded him a little of his brother's wife, had he been subconsciously trying to follow Trent's lead?

Maybe.

Whatever the reason, it had ended in disaster. Because, for once, Troy had gone out with a woman who hadn't played the dating game. She'd fallen and fallen hard. Troy hadn't.

Oh, sure, he'd liked her. She'd been nice and attractive.

And she'd bored him beyond belief.

Their breakup had devastated her, and she'd definitely let him know about it. Troy had never meant to hurt her. He'd certainly never made any promises and they'd only gone out a few times. Hell, they'd never even *slept* together—which should have been his first indication something was wrong.

Looking back, he couldn't even fathom why he'd thought

he could be interested in someone who didn't make him crazy with lust from the first time they met. Love might be the greatest thing since the invention of the wheel, but if it wasn't accompanied by a serious case of the hots, Troy didn't think it would ever be for him. Any woman with whom he fell in love would have to inspire some immediate thoughts of hot, sweaty bodies and long, erotic nights before she could ever inspire images of diamond rings or whispered promises.

"It will never happen," he'd often told himself, especially after that last dating disaster.

In any case, the damage had been done. For the first time in his life, he'd hurt someone who hadn't deserved it.

Lots of women had called him a heel over the years, but this was the first time he'd ever actually felt like one.

Worst of all, the situation had made him cautious about his relationships with women. He hadn't so much as wanted to kiss one in a good three months! That was pretty long for a man who hadn't gone without *sex* for three months since losing his virginity at fourteen to his grandmother's house-maid.

His twin said occasional breaks from sex could be good for a man. Frankly, Troy thought he'd rather lose an arm than his sex drive. "You can teach yourself to write with your other hand," he mused. But you couldn't teach other body parts to have orgasms.

Still, even his suddenly barren love life couldn't compare with the upheaval in his career. The job in which he'd felt so secure had suddenly disappeared.

I think you're crazy, Dad.

After six years of retirement, his father had decided he wanted his job back. He had to hand it to his old man. Most fifty-eight-year-olds who'd had a minor heart "episode" would take it as a sign to slow down. His father had decided his early retirement was going to kill him, and that he'd been much healthier when working. So back to Florida he and Troy's mother had come. Back to the store. Right into Troy's job.

His father certainly hadn't pushed him out. They'd be partners, he'd insisted. But when Troy had thought it over, he'd realized he was being given a chance to do something he never thought he would—go outside the store, maybe move somewhere else altogether, try another line of work.

Freedom from Langtree's had been shocking—but also intoxicating. He'd finally understood some of the choices his twin had made. Though, God knew, he'd never fathom Trent's delight in planting bushes or mucking around in fertilizer.

Fate had stepped in to make his decision a simple one. Max Longotti, an old friend of his late grandfather, had told Troy's grandmother he was thinking of selling his nationally known catalog company. He wanted the Langtrees to consider buying it. To that end, he asked Troy to come work with him at his Atlanta headquarters for a few months, so the board could get to know him before Max asked them to vote on the sale.

Troy had leapt at the chance. He'd closed up his beach-front condo and driven to Georgia. Max Longotti, a crotchety old soul who reminded Troy of his grandfather, had welcomed Troy into his own home until he could find another place. He'd be moving into a furnished apartment in a few days. Until then, the Longotti estate was quite comfortable—if large and rather deserted.

One thing Troy had learned so far during his brief stay in Atlanta…Max Longotti was a lonely man. A rich, lonely man who seemed surrounded by scavengers just waiting for him to kick the bucket so they could sink their claws into his money. Troy shook his head in disgust.

Remembering Max had mentioned he'd be in late in the

afternoon due to a doctor's appointment, Troy glanced at his watch, noting it was nearly four. He should have just enough time to read over the marketing projections for the latest sales circular before meeting with Max at the end of the day.

He reached for it, but froze when something else—a bright flash of red outside—caught his eye.

A woman. "Who the devil..." He stood, walking toward the sliding glass door which led out to the small balcony. A nice touch, the balcony. Troy had become accustomed to sitting outdoors when he had reading to do or reports to peruse.

Obviously no one had come through his office, so the intruder had to have come out the other door, which exited off Max's. Knowing Max hadn't yet arrived, he wondered why the older man's efficient secretary had left the woman alone. And, more importantly, why was she here to begin with? Watching her out the glass, he doubted she was here on business.

The woman had to be tall. She sat in one of the two tasteful, wrought-iron chairs, her long legs crossed and her feet resting on the waist-high balcony railing. She seemed completely unconcerned about losing her slip-on sandal, as she tapped her toe against the air in some unheard rhythm. The heel of the shoe swung against her bare foot as it dangled ten stories above Peachtree Street.

Troy followed every swing of her foot, nearly spotlighted in the sunlight. Her open sandals revealed bright red-polished toenails and a splotch of color—a tattoo—just above her right ankle. *Definitely not here on business.*

He continued to stare. Her legs, completely bare, went on forever. And ever. Troy swallowed hard as he studied the smooth skin of her calf, the slimness of her pale thighs. Her tiny jean shorts interrupted his visual assessment of her legs. His gaze skimmed past them to the clingy white tank top she wore, which hugged a generously curved chest.

His heart skipped a beat.

Then he saw her face, complete with full lips and a pert nose. Long lashes rested on her cheeks since her eyes were closed. And her thick mass of auburn hair caught the sunlight and shone like red-hot flames.

Seeing her lips move, and her head nodding in rhythm with her tapping foot, he leaned closer to the door. Even through the glass, he could make out the words she was singing.

"B-b-b-b-ba-ad. I'm bad to the bone."

The sudden rush of familiar heat as his libido returned in full force brought a smile to Troy's lips. Reaching for the handle of the door, he nearly sighed in relief. He hadn't felt this good for a long time. Three months, to be exact.

"Thank you, God," he whispered.

Now it was time to meet the woman who'd so effortlessly awakened him from his long, sexless sleep.

CHAPTER TWO

"HELLO, ATLANTA. Scarlett has come to pay a visit," Venus Messina murmured to the sky as she reclined on the balcony of the high-rise office building. "Aunt Pitty, hide the silver. And Rhett, if you're out there, call me, baby."

She closed her eyes, thinking she could almost fall asleep in this bright patch of sunlight. Considering the whirlwind of her life over the past seventy-two hours, she supposed it wasn't surprising. She hadn't gotten much sleep lately.

If anyone had suggested last week that within days she'd be in another state, preparing to meet a man who may or may not be her grandfather, she'd have laughed in his face. Or, more likely, cut him off, taken his keys and called a cab.

Yet here she was.

Leaving had been remarkably easy. Joe had insisted he could do without her at Flanagan's. She'd also arranged for her best friend, Lacey, to look after her spoiled cat and her half-dead houseplants. The cat she wanted to come home to. The plants she didn't really care about—but Venus didn't like to admit defeat, and if those dumb ferns were going to die, they would do it at her hand. Lacey would probably have them all healthy and blooming by the time she got back, anyway, just the way she had when she'd lived next door to Venus in their Baltimore apartment complex.

Venus had missed her friend since she'd moved out a year ago. If Lacey were still her neighbor, she probably would have gotten Venus to spill the truth about this trip. Since Lacey was a newlywed, though, it hadn't been hard to keep her in the dark. Lacey was easily distracted by any question about her much-adored spouse, Nate.

Venus wiggled in her chair slightly, the wrought iron hard against her backside. "Pool boy, bring me a froufrou drink and a more comfortable chaise lounge," she whispered with a grin.

A beach vacation would have been nice. But she had a feeling she was going to like Atlanta, especially with the way things had been going in Baltimore.

She hadn't had a second thought when she'd deposited Leo Gallagher's five-thousand-dollar check, nor when she'd taken a cab to the airport and boarded a plane heading south this morning. Venus still hadn't figured Mr. Gallagher out yet. Either he was one heck of a nice nephew who really wanted to see his uncle happy…which she doubted. Or he was running some kind of scam…which seemed more likely. What her part in the scheme was, she really couldn't say. And for five grand—which would go a long way toward rent, not to mention summer clothes for the foster kids back in Jersey—she wasn't asking many questions.

After all, she wasn't doing anything illegal. She'd simply agreed to visit this Longotti guy for one week, to explore the possibility that she was his long-lost granddaughter. Just because she personally had serious doubts that she was—and didn't particularly *want* to be—did not mean it was entirely impossible. The odds were better than, say, getting struck by lightning. Or winning the lottery.

Or finding a nice guy who wanted to get married and have a house in the suburbs and a few babies before Venus was too old to enjoy them. She sighed at that cheery thought.

Anyway, whatever Gallagher was up to was on his head, not hers. She was just along for the ride. A well-paid ride.

She had, however, been curious enough to call her foster mother and ask her about the birth certificate. Maureen had told her she'd lost the original in the break-in, but had also said the Child Welfare Agency had forwarded a box of things after Venus had turned eighteen. Confirming she still had the box somewhere, she told Venus she'd mail it to her in Baltimore.

Nearly purring in the warmth of the sun, Venus began to hum, then to sing, a favorite old rock-and-roll song that fit her mood perfectly. When she heard the soft slide of a glass door opening, however, she stopped singing and opened her eyes. She expected to see Leo, accompanied by an old man.

She was almost afraid to look. Would his face seem familiar? Would his smile look like her own? Would he see something in her that reminded him of his long-lost son?

Stop it, Venus. It's not true and you know it.

When she saw a younger man standing there instead, her heart raced faster, anyway.

Good lord, they grew men well in the south!

Shading her eyes with her hand, she studied the stranger in the gray suit. A guy in a tie. Her first impulse should have been to leap off the balcony in self-preservation. But somehow, after months of relative apathy when it came to men, Venus remembered what she so very much liked about them.

Just about everything.

Besides, she was in Atlanta for one week only. How much damage could even a guy in a tie do in one little week?

First things first—was he tall enough to meet her number-one requirement on her man list? At just a smidge under six feet herself, Venus never went for guys she'd tower over in spike-heeled do-me shoes. A girl had to have her priorities.

All lean, muscled male wrapped up in an elegantly tailored package, this man obviously stood a few inches over six feet tall. *Meets height requirement. Check.*

He was also dark-haired, another personal preference. His thick, chestnut-brown hair was cut conservatively, but ruffled a bit in the strong breeze blowing between the high-rise buildings. It would probably be tousled like that when he woke up in the morning.

Her mouth went dry. She swallowed and continued staring.

His face was magazine-model handsome. Lean jaw, straight, strong nose. Heavily lashed to-die-for eyes the color of springtime leaves. And one of the most kissable mouths she'd ever seen on a guy.

Kissing was one of her personal favorite things to do, and got her vote for being the all-around best activity for the mouth. It ranked even higher than eating rich, dark chocolate, which was probably in her top five. As for the rest of the list…well, that was flexible, depending on her mood, the time of the month and her romantic status. With someone like this incredible man, however, she could definitely picture the possibilities. She nearly moaned at the image.

Her gaze moved lower, to his left hand. *No ring.*

Perfect.

"Good afternoon," she said lazily, her mouth widening in welcome, a signal no man alive could miss.

He smiled back just as lazily, just as aware. Those eyes darkened and his smile faded as they stared at each other for a long, heady moment. Then, taking his cue from her, he expressed not a hint of surprise about finding a strange, casually dressed woman sunning herself out here on the balcony. "Good afternoon to you. Enjoying the sunshine?"

She nodded and turned her face to the sky, drawing in a deep breath. "Love it."

"Be careful," he warned as he sat on the other chair. "It's deceptive with the breeze. Redheads tend to burn, right?"

She raised a brow. "Who says I'm a natural redhead?" At

this point in her life, Venus could barely remember what her natural hair color was anymore, though she thought this was pretty close. She'd run the full color spectrum in the past several years. But red was definitely her favorite.

"Whether you are or not, stick with this," he murmured, glancing at her hair with a look so intimate it felt like a touch. "A woman with eyes as green as yours *should* be a redhead."

His quiet flattery hit home. The man was a charmer.

"And a man with a face like yours is usually wearing a wedding ring," she murmured, needing to make sure he was available before they went any further. Venus might like men, but she never went after the taken ones.

"Not married. Not involved," he replied easily.

She wondered if he heard her audible sigh of relief.

When he didn't respond by asking the same question, Venus paused. Was he not interested? Or was he *so* interested he simply didn't give a damn whether she was available or not? Hoping it was the latter, she offered the information anyway. "Me, neither."

Far below them, the traffic rumbled by, evidence of the bustling city life during a hectic Monday rush hour. But up here, high above it all, Venus felt completely separated. Alone. Except for this sexy stranger with the mouth she felt she had to soon kiss or die trying.

He gestured toward her sandal. "That could probably kill someone if it fell from this height."

She intentionally flipped it harder, setting a tapping rhythm with the shoe.

He grinned. "Okay, so I've got ulterior motives for wanting you to move your legs." He leaned forward, resting his elbows on his knees, and stared intently at her foot. "What is it?"

"I think it's called a shoe."

He chuckled. "No, I meant *that*." He pointed toward her ankle. Leaning even closer, he reached for her leg and gently tugged her foot off the railing. Venus sucked in a breath at the feel of his warm fingers on her calf, wondering if he heard the crazy pounding of her heart within her chest. She heard it—it roared to life in her head as she focused every bit of her attention on the brush of his skin against hers.

"This," he said softly as he placed her foot on his knee, completely disregarding any possible damage to his expensive trousers. Then he leaned over to look at her tattoo. He touched the tiny hummingbird she'd had put on as an unemployment present last year. "Very pretty. Did it hurt?"

She could only manage to shake her head. If she tried to make a sound, it would emerge as a whimper. Or a plea.

He continued touching her, tracing the shape of the blue-green bird with the tip of his finger, cupping the back of her calf with his other hand.

The chair suddenly felt harder against her bottom. She shifted uncomfortably in the suddenly too-tight jean shorts. And her breath barely made it into her lungs as she focused on the way he looked at her. The way he touched her.

"Why a hummingbird?" he asked, still not letting go.

She didn't answer at first, not quite able to. She couldn't even think of anything but the way his gentle touch would feel, sliding up her leg, beneath her shorts. Touching her where she suddenly felt hot and achy.

Finally, drawing in a ragged breath, she whispered, "I like hummingbirds. They're aggressive as hell, but still delicate and small. Just like I always wanted to be."

Shaking his head reprovingly, he tsked. "Why do women always want to be the opposite of what they are? Even when they're stunningly beautiful?"

She snorted a laugh, drawing his stare to her face. Okay, she *was* the opposite of delicate and small. But she didn't think she was the opposite of aggressive. Or so she'd been told. Then she focused on the stunningly beautiful part.

That worked.

"I've suddenly discovered I really like tall women."

Oh, yay!

"Any other tattoos anywhere?" he asked, letting his gaze travel across her bare shoulders and neck.

Her body reacted, her nipples hardening beneath her shirt. Feeling them scrape against the cotton, she wondered if he noticed. "No," she said. "But I'm thinking about it. I'm not sure I'll like my next choice once I turn seventy-five or eighty."

He raised a questioning brow. "Next choice?"

She nodded. "Jessica Rabbit."

When no look of understanding crossed his face, Venus gestured toward her top. If he hadn't seen her body's reaction to the way he'd held her foot before, he'd surely notice it now.

She tugged the cotton tight, revealing the sexy, red-haired cartoon character vamping it up on the front of her T-shirt. In a bubble above the bombshell's head were the words, "I'm not bad. I'm just drawn that way."

Venus liked the sentiment.

"Ahh," he said, staring hard at her shirt. His voice sounded thick. Yeah, he'd noticed.

"She doesn't look like a rabbit," he offered, still delicately stroking her ankle, absently caressing her calf until she nearly writhed in her chair.

"She's, uh, not…" Venus managed to reply. "That's her married name."

"What about you? Are you bad? Or are you just drawn that way?"

She closed her eyes, leaning back in her seat, silently asking him to continue the tender stroking of her leg. "Maybe I'll let you figure it out for yourself," she murmured.

He finally let go of her foot, as if realizing they were moving *really* fast for a couple of people who hadn't yet introduced themselves.

"I've thought about getting one," he admitted, gently shifting her foot off his lap. Then he chuckled ruefully. "Not that anyone would believe it."

"Why not?"

He answered with a secretive smile. "Let's just say people see me in a certain way. A tattoo wouldn't go with the image."

"I know how that goes," she muttered, not even able to count the times someone had been surprised by her intelligence, or the business sense hidden beneath the exterior package and smart mouth. "But you don't exactly look like Mister Boring Businessman." Gesturing toward his tanned skin, she mused, "Looks like you're no stranger to the sun yourself."

"I actually live on the beach in south Florida. Or rather, I did, until last week."

"You moved here? To Atlanta?"

"Not permanently. I'm not sure where I'll end up. I've recently found myself with a lot more freedom than I expected."

She couldn't resist. "So you made parole, huh?"

Deadpan, he nodded. "Certainly. Amazing how quickly they let us homicidal maniacs out nowadays."

"Tell me you didn't get sent up the river for throwing red-haired females over balconies."

He shook his head, a twinkle in his pale green eyes. "Only natural redheads."

She gave an exaggerated sigh of relief. "Whew."

"So," he continued. "Should I ask who you are and what you're doing here? Or should we just leave now and go straight to…dinner?"

She liked his directness. And she suspected his pause had been quite deliberate. They'd exchanged only a few dozen sentences, but she'd mentally substituted another word for "dinner," and she'd bet he had too. As surely as she'd bet that word was "bed."

Venus, you swore off men, remember? Even before this whole long-lost granddaughter business.

Somehow, she couldn't bring herself to care. The instant chemistry between her and the stranger was something she hadn't experienced before. Ever.

Sure, she'd had her fair share of relationships with men. Probably enough fair shares for two or three women, if she wanted to be completely honest about it. That had been part of the reason she'd decided to take a break from them after losing her job.

Other reasons had probably included Lacey's blissfully happy marriage. Plus Venus's brief fling with Raul, a hunky young guy who worked with Lacey. She'd dated Raul in the brief period between dumping Dale, the loser at work, and getting paid back by him with the loss of her job.

Raul, though a good bit younger than she, had been a doll, and she'd found herself caring about him quite a lot. If he'd been older, and at a different place in his life, Venus could have fallen in love with him. But they were moving in different directions and realized they worked best as friends.

Still, having pictured love, she almost found herself wanting it. True love, marriage, the whole shebang...with the right person. Eventually. After she'd gotten over what dickhead Dale had done to her.

Eight months seemed just about long enough to get over backstabbing and betrayal. Besides, she'd missed some parts of her former lifestyle. Particularly men. Venus liked men. She liked dating. Liked going out dancing, or to ball games, or just for walks at the Inner Harbor back home in Baltimore.

And she liked sex. Really liked it. *So sue me.*

As much as she'd enjoyed getting to know men—usually the wrong ones—she'd never felt such an instant, sudden, overwhelming desire for one. Especially not while stone-cold sober. So she at least ought to find out his name.

"My name's Venus," she said. She scooted her chair closer until her bare knees nearly touched his blue trousers.

"How appropriate," he murmured.

"I think so. You would be…"

"Troy."

"How nice to meet you, Troy. I'd love to go to *dinner* with you, but unfortunately tonight's not possible." She gestured toward his tasteful necktie and gave him a flirtatious grin. "Besides, I've recently sworn off guys in ties."

He shrugged. "Easily remedied. I'll take it off."

"And suits," she said, knowing he could hear a suggestive purr in her voice.

"It can come off too." His tone was just as suggestive.

She raised a wicked brow and glanced at the other buildings nearby. "Hmm, that could be interesting. But aren't you worried some of these executives in their cubbyholes keep binoculars around? I know I would if you were in the habit of standing out here, taking off your…tie."

He laughed out loud, a warm, rich laugh that rolled over her body and made her tingle. She liked the sound of it as much as she liked the curve of his lips.

Taking a deep breath, she suddenly wondered what other interesting sounds the man was capable of. Sighs. Moans. Shouts.

She nearly shuddered at the thought.

"I didn't mean here," he said.

She pouted. "Aww, gee."

"Tomorrow?" he asked. "I promise not to overdress."

Or dress at all? Oh, yes, the man knew how to play this

game. But before she could go any further, she needed to find out just who he was. "So, are you here today for a meeting or something?" she asked, hearing a hopeful note in her own voice. *Please say yes.* She hoped like crazy that he didn't work here, in the suite of offices used by Max Longotti's catalog company, Longotti Lines. Because she really didn't want to start off her relationship with her supposed/could-be/maybe grandfather by seducing one of his employees.

Not that she'd have to do the seducing. If she was any judge—and she *was*—the man looked fully capable of seduction. She shivered slightly, in spite of the heat of the brightly lit afternoon.

"Actually, that's my office." He pointed over his shoulder to the door through which he'd emerged moments before.

Moments? Had she really discovered the existence of this man who made her heart pound like crazy and her legs feel weak and boneless mere moments before?

She finally thought about his reply and her heart sank, along with her plans. "Your office. Right there. So, uh, you work here? For Max Longotti?" When he nodded, she tried to contain a disappointed sigh.

"I'm Max's new V.P. For now," he continued.

Perfect. Just perfect. She'd met a man who'd finally made her rethink her "men aren't worth the trouble" stance, and she couldn't have him. It simply would not be smart to get involved with this man, no matter how delicious he was.

Leo would not be happy if she did what she really wanted to do with this handsome, charming stranger. He seemed intent on "pleasing" his uncle by presenting him with his sweet and lovely long-lost grandchild.

Sweet she wasn't, which is exactly what she'd told Leo. So he'd settled for bright and lovely. Still, he had insisted that she be as discreet as possible, and she'd agreed.

And even Venus—who'd been called everything in her

life, *except* discreet—knew sleeping with Max's executive might not be the height of discretion.

As a matter of fact, the guy would have to be completely off-limits. Starting right now.

Hell.

TROY SENSED IT the moment the stunning redhead began to withdraw. Her smile faded, her eyelashes lowered and she turned away in her chair to stare at the skyline. Because he worked here? Interesting…

"Now, why don't you tell me who are you, and why you're here, Venus?"

"I'm just visiting."

Her voice was cool, when it had previously been warm. That didn't concern him. The heat in her eyes two minutes ago could have melted solid ice. "From where?"

"Baltimore."

She swung her feet up on the rail again, silently dismissing him. Troy almost laughed, seeing through the maneuver. He paused to appreciate again those long-enough-to-wrap-around-him-twice legs and had to shift in his seat.

No. The cold shoulder wasn't going to change the way they'd reacted to one another from the start. Or the way he was reacting to her now.

If she worked for Max and was worried about a no-fraternization policy, he might just have to quit his new job. It was a small enough sacrifice. What job could compare to getting his libido back?

"Have you been to Atlanta before?"

She merely shook her head.

Getting answers from her was like pulling teeth, but Troy was not about to give up. Not now that he'd met her, now that he'd seen those beautiful green eyes of hers up close, caught a whiff of her exotic perfume and heard the husky timbre of her voice. He could still feel the smoothness of her skin on the tips of his sensitized fingers.

He wanted her, not knowing who she was or why she was here. And she wanted him too.

It was just that simple.

"What do you do?"

She glanced at him out of the corner of her eye and said, "Right now, I'm a bartender."

He nearly chuckled until he realized she was serious. Then he shrugged. "Remind me never to offer to make you a drink."

"I don't imagine you'd ever have reason to," she replied firmly. "I'll only be in town for a week."

Ouch. A definite rebuff. But Troy hadn't earned his reputation by being easily rebuffed. "Where are you staying?"

"At the Longotti estate." Then, she grudgingly added, "At least, I *think* so. I'm supposed to go over there this afternoon."

He hid a grin. Max hadn't mentioned another houseguest. He could hardly wait to bump into her coming out of the shower or knock on her door at night to borrow some toothpaste.

He wondered if she slept naked. Then he wondered just how long it would take him to find out. Not long, he hoped.

It was too bad he'd be moving out in a few days. Then again, maybe his new apartment wouldn't be ready for a week. Maybe he'd make damn sure it wasn't. "So, why aren't you sure you're staying with Max? He knows you're coming, doesn't he?"

As she nibbled her full lower lip, the heat in his gut shot up another notch. She had a mouth made for kissing. And other things.

"Not exactly," she mumbled. "Leo dropped me off here, then went to find him. He's, uh, setting things up, I think."

"Leo? Leo Gallagher, Max's nephew?"

She nodded.

Not good. Leo was a white-haired weasel, as far as Troy could tell. Not that it was his place to judge, of course. He barely knew the man, who had some high-level job in this company, though no one seemed sure exactly what he did. But he did know Max's nephew had been vehemently opposed to Troy's arrival, and to the possibility of the company being sold.

Apparently, from what Max said, Leo had fully imagined himself to be heir apparent and had been angling for more than a decade for Max to retire so he could step in. Max referred to him as the pencil-necked leech and said he'd retire when they pried his office keys out of his cold dead hand. Or when he passed them over to a new owner—which somehow made Troy think Leo's job aspirations weren't going to pan out.

Venus must have noticed his sudden silence, and his frown. "You know Leo?" she asked.

"Barely."

"You barely know him, but you know you don't like him?"

He hedged. "I don't *dislike* him, I only met him last week when I started working for Longotti Lines."

Her eyes widened and she finally turned to give him her full attention again. "You just started your job? I thought maybe you'd just gotten a promotion and transferred in from Florida or something."

"Today is my one-week anniversary." Leaning closer, he went for smooth charm, since honest conversation hadn't gotten her to relax, the way she had at first. "I never imagined perks like beautiful redheads sunning themselves right outside my door when I took the job. Maybe I should stock up on sunscreen. Would you like me to do your back?"

She rolled her eyes. "Save it. I liked you better when you weren't being oily. Besides, you're not very good at it."

He straightened, not sure whether he felt amused or offended. Then a reluctant chuckle crossed his lips. "All right, Venus. In the interest of being strictly sincere, I personally think Leo Gallagher is a shifty, spoiled man with abominable taste in shoes and a need for a good barber."

She grinned. "My, my, from oily to pompous. You are a contradiction, aren't you?"

Pompous? She'd just called him *pompous?* He raised a brow and leaned closer. "You're one to talk about contradictions. From sultress to iceberg in under a minute."

He stared into her brilliant green eyes, daring her to disagree. She didn't even try. "It's a woman's prerogative to change her mind."

"So you don't want to have dinner with me?" He dared her to deny it, knowing damn well she did.

She raised a skeptical brow. "Oh, you mean we were really talking about dinner?"

"What else could we have been talking about?"

"I was thinking more along the lines of dessert." Her voice held a note of challenge.

"I hadn't even asked about dessert," he said, his voice holding a hint of playful challenge.

Her creamy cheeks began to grow pink with obvious embarrassment. He doubted this woman blushed very often and he found the heightened color in her face extremely attractive.

He let her sweat for a moment. Then, unable to lie to her any more than he could to himself, he said, "But I would have."

Her answer was equally as honest. "Five minutes ago the answer probably would have been yes."

"And now?"

"Now it's got to be no."

"Why?"

She merely shook her head, unable or unwilling to answer. Troy, however, wasn't one to give up without a fight. "Can you give me one chance to change your mind?"

She eyed him warily but didn't refuse. Letting her see his small confident smile, he leaned closer, catching her exotic scent. Then closer, until he saw the pulse beating wildly in her neck. And closer still, until their lips were a breath apart.

"You think you can change my mind with a kiss?" she whispered.

He responded with a slow nod and a lazy drawl. "Yes."

She visibly stiffened at the certainty in his tone.

"You think I can't?"

She responded to his challenge with a raised eyebrow and a taunting look. "You can try."

He did, slipping his fingers into her hair, tangling his hands in that thick mass of living fire. He touched his lips to hers, gently at first, tasting her, savoring the softness of her mouth. Only when she moaned low in her throat did he go farther, sliding his tongue between his lips, letting it mate lazily with hers in a hot, intoxicating dance that sent intense sensations rushing through his body.

She tasted sweet and ripe, like summer fruit. But warm, like fine whiskey. She moaned again and tilted her head, kissing him back just as deliberately, just as invitingly.

He tugged her closer, until, somehow, she was sitting on his lap, her arms wrapped around his neck, his around her jean-clad hips. He skimmed his fingers beneath her cotton top. Lightly touching the bare flesh at her waist, he heard her sigh against his kiss as skin met skin.

Finally, he moved his mouth from hers, kissing the corner of her lips, then her cheek. Her jaw. Her neck.

"Changed your mind yet?" he growled against her throat.

"Uh-huh," she whispered.

"Good. Tell me what time we can get together tomorrow

night." He scraped his teeth along her collarbone, feeling the way she jerked against him in response. "If you're *sure* tonight's out, that is."

She groaned in frustration. "It's definitely out."

Before he could attempt to cajole her, she pulled back. "I think I hear voices."

She was up, off his lap, standing at the rail so fast, he thought he'd imagined their heated kiss.

"Are you sure? I don't hear anything," he said, wanting her back in his arms. Immediately, if not sooner. He stood and joined her at the railing.

Before she could answer, a sliding glass door opened behind them. Max stepped out, followed by his nephew, Leo. Max looked tense, appearing very much the seventy-four-year-old man he was. Leo, on the other hand, looked positively euphoric.

Max glanced briefly at Troy, dismissed him, then focused on Venus. "Is this true?"

She stood up straighter. Beside her, Troy could easily see the way her hands trembled, until she clenched them together in front of her. Her mouth opened, but she didn't speak.

"Is what true?" Troy asked.

"Of course it is," Leo said.

Max ignored them both and stepped closer to Venus. "Is it possible? Is it really you... Violet?"

Confused, Troy said, "Her name's..."

"Yes, I told you, I'm certain it's true," Leo interjected, stepping between Troy and Max. He took Venus's hand and pulled her forward, looking as happy as a kid with a surprise cereal box toy. "Uncle Max, meet your long-lost granddaughter."

CHAPTER THREE

OF COURSE? CERTAIN? TRUE?

Venus wanted to strangle Leo Gallagher. So much for his assurances that this would just be a "visit" to see if it was "possible" she could be the person he claimed she was. He'd obviously presented it to the old man as a done deal.

Well, it wasn't a done deal, not in her book. Five grand or no five grand, she'd never agreed to outright lie.

"Actually, my name's Venus," she said, hearing an edge in her own voice. She shot Leo an angry look before turning her full attention to Max Longotti. "Venus Messina."

The old man, with a thick head of brilliant white hair and piercing gray eyes, met her unflinching stare. "Messina. I see. How old are you, Ms. Messina?"

"That's a nice way to start a conversation with a woman," she tossed off, still annoyed at being manipulated. "You gonna ask me my bra size next?"

Out of the corner of her eye, she saw Leo wince, then draw his brow into a frown. He'd warned her to be discreet.

Not a good start. Especially since if it weren't for her really keen sense of hearing, she would have been caught making out with the hired help three minutes ago.

"I'm not so old that I can't make a fair guess at that," the old gentleman said, his tone droll and amused.

Venus chuckled. Score one for Grandpa.

Beside Leo, Troy watched silently. He leaned casually

against the balcony railing, arms crossed in front of his chest, absorbing every word they said. The bright sunlight cast bits of gold on his dark brown hair, and she was again struck by the sheer handsomeness of the man. Amazing to look at, and hands down the best kisser she'd ever known. Her lips and tongue still tingled.

As if he read her thoughts, he met her eye and smiled slightly. *We have a secret, don't we?* his smile seemed to say.

She wondered what he must think of this whole thing. It seemed like science fiction even to her.

"Now," Max Longotti continued softly, "will you *please* tell me exactly when you were born, young lady?"

She rattled off her birth date, hating to admit being almost thirty in front of Troy. Not that it mattered, she reminded herself. Before that unreal kiss, she'd decided he was off-limits. And after it, well, he'd still be off-limits…after she got at least one more kiss from the man…or two…or…

Max nodded. "And you say your father was actually my son?"

"I didn't say jack," she retorted, dragging her attention away from the hottie with the intense look on his face. "Since I never laid eyes on my father, he coulda been Jimmy Hoffa for all I know." She gestured toward Leo. "But your nephew here seems to think it's possible."

Leo's subsequent frown would have scared small children.

"Maybe I should excuse myself," Troy finally said. "This appears to be a family matter."

"Yes," Leo began.

"No," Max Longotti insisted. "An outsider's viewpoint might be useful here." He turned back to Venus. "I know what my nephew thinks. I want to know what *you* think, Ms. Messina."

Sensing her answer was very important to the man, who suddenly appeared a little less strong and sure than he had at first, she admitted, "I suppose it's *possible*. Stranger things have happened. I mean, who'd have ever thought fat-free potato chips would actually *not* taste like cardboard?"

She saw Troy's lips curve slightly.

"But you personally don't think it's true. You don't believe my nephew's claims," the old man prodded.

Leo touched his uncle's arm. "Max, the evidence..."

Max ignored him. "What happened to your mother?"

"She died when I was eight."

"Then who raised you?"

"I was lucky enough to be placed in a really good foster home. My foster mother raised me until I left home at eighteen."

"Your mother had no family?"

Venus shrugged. "None who wanted *me*."

She didn't glance at Troy, not wanting to see a look of pity on his face. She'd never pitied herself, and she'd damn sure never wanted it from anybody else. Especially not a man with whom she was in serious lust.

"So, judging by your birth date, it is very likely you were conceived during the weeks my son spent in New York. If he was, indeed, your father, your parents' relationship would have to have been a very...brief one."

She tensed, waiting for him to make one crack about her mother's morals. Venus might not know much about her biological father, but she'd adored her always-smiling mother until Trina had drawn her last breath. If this stranger spoke one negative word about her, Venus would be out the door so fast he'd think she'd fallen off the balcony.

He didn't. "So it is possible that your mother never knew my son by any other name than the one he adopted for the stage."

"There's that word again...possible," Venus said, surprised at the relief flowing through her veins just because the old man hadn't passed judgment on her mother.

He continued softly, talking almost to himself. "And it's also possible she had difficulty reaching him to tell him about you. She must have been desperate." He glanced at the sky, continuing to formulate his theory aloud. "Perhaps she sent your picture, with the name Violet on the back, to a club in Los Angeles. The letter might have had only his stage name on it. It could have taken a long time for it to catch up to him." He returned his gaze to Venus. "But when he did receive it, it changed everything. He was coming back."

"More could haves and might haves," she insisted, knowing the man was speculating. She still couldn't bring herself to believe this scenario. It was too far-fetched. Too co-incidental.

Too damned heartbreaking.

Venus didn't *want* to believe her father had died within days…maybe hours…of finding out about her. She didn't *want* to think of her mother—who'd said she'd fallen ass over elbows in love with the man when they'd bickered over a cab in the rain—wasting the last eight years of her life waiting for someone who was already long gone. She couldn't bear to think of Trina pining for a man who'd gotten her message, planned to come back to them…and then died before ever being able to do so.

No, the whole thing was too sad. And Venus wasn't into sad.

Feeling moisture in her eyes, she swung around, turning her back to the three men. She stared out at the sky, blinking rapidly, groping for control. Then, she felt a hand on her shoulder, a supportive squeeze, a tender offer of reassurance.

Turning her head, she saw Troy standing there. He didn't say anything, didn't offer trite, nurturing words. He just let her know she wasn't alone, with a small nod and a look of intense concern on his face. She took a deep breath, sucking up his silently offered strength. Then, crossing her arms in front of her chest, she faced Max again. "Let me ask you something now."

He waited expectantly.

"If all this is true—and I think that's a big humongous if—why'd it take almost thirty years to find me?"

Max glanced at Leo. "My nephew apparently thought of something I never did all those years ago. We assumed Max, my son, had been involved with someone in California. We focused our search efforts there. And, of course, we used his real name."

Leo smiled. She thought he was going for self-deprecating, but his expression looked self-congratulatory instead. "I'm so sorry I didn't think of the possibility of him meeting someone in New York long ago. Nor of having a private investigator search birth records in the northeast to see if Max Longotti *or* Matt Messina turned up as a father during that time."

She immediately latched on to his words. "Birth records. So you *have* seen a copy of my birth certificate?"

Leo's jovial expression never faltered. "No, I left it in the hands of the investigator. He is the one who obtained those records, then tracked you down. I simply utilized the address he provided."

Smooth. Reasonable. But she didn't completely buy it.

"Is he going to send you those records?"

A slight narrowing of his eyes indicated his annoyance. "I'm sure I'll receive them now that the case is concluded."

Wanting to gauge the man's reaction, Venus said, "My foster mother said she does have some paperwork, after all. She's digging it out and mailing it to my home in Baltimore."

Leo stared at her for a moment, then his smile thinned. "Good."

Troy, who'd been standing quietly for several moments, cleared his throat.

"You have something to contribute, Troy?" Max asked.

Troy raised a brow. "It seems you're at an impasse," he offered. "You may discuss dates, pseudonyms and birth certificates all afternoon and never come to an agreement."

He sounded like a businessman brokering a big deal. Venus almost rolled her eyes, wondering where the flirty hunk who'd kissed her until she was brainless and limp had gotten to.

"Wouldn't it be simpler to just conduct a DNA test?" he finally concluded.

"I've already thought of that," Leo interjected. He touched his uncle's arm. "Of course, knowing your mistrust of newfangled science, I made sure to contact one of the experts in the field. When I hear back from him, we'll bring him to Atlanta and have him conduct the test."

"Yes, yes, of course," Max agreed. He raised a quivering hand to his brow, looking out of sorts. "Splendid. That's much more conclusive than any birth records, which aren't entirely reliable. DNA. Marvelous thing."

DNA tests? Conclusive proof? Things were going too fast for Venus's taste. She hadn't decided if she liked this old guy, and she definitely hadn't decided if she even wanted to know the truth!

She cocked her head and raised her hand, wiggling her fingers in a little wave. "Hello? Anybody going to ask *me* if I'm willing to roll up my sleeve and let some stranger poke needles into me? What if I don't particularly like needles?"

"Actually, I think they swab your cheek," Troy explained.

She shot him a glare that told him to mind his own business. "Oh, you've undergone these tests before? Have lots of potential illegitimate junior executives running around out there, do you?"

As he stiffened, Venus cursed her quick temper and sarcasm. Troy had only been trying to help, after all.

Her barb had obviously angered him. His eyes narrowed. "You don't seem very anxious to confirm your claim, Ms. Messina."

"It's not my claim."

"Perhaps not," he admitted. "Or perhaps you *want* Max to think you don't believe it. Throwing your arms around him and calling him Grandpa might have made him suspect your motives. This insistence that you're not may make him more sympathetic." He stepped closer, until the tips of his shoes almost touched her toes. She forced herself to stay still, so close to him she could smell his warm cologne and see the beating of his pulse in his neck. She could think of nothing except the way his mouth had tasted against hers, just minutes before.

"And generous," he finally concluded.

Venus didn't follow at first. She was too focused on her instinctive reaction to him. The heat radiating from his body, the coiled strength concealed beneath the conservative suit. And, unfortunately, the absence of the warm, tender concern that had been in his eyes just minutes before.

"Generous?" she asked, hearing the breathiness in her voice.

"I wonder what your motives were in coming to Atlanta," he said softly, as if merely speculating aloud. "They didn't have anything to do with money, did they?"

Money? He thought she'd come here to try to scam money off the old man? She was about to tell him to take a flying leap off the balcony when she remembered she *had* been paid—and paid well—to take this trip. She swallowed her angry words and lowered her eyes, her whole body stiffening as she acknowledged the partial truth of his accusation. He made a sound that could have been a sigh, then stepped away from her.

"Mr. Longotti," she said, turning her back on the annoyingly handsome man who suddenly had such a low opinion of her, "I'm being straight with you here. I don't think I'm who your nephew says I am. I don't even know if I *want* to be, if you can dig that." She shot a look over her shoulder at Troy, who still watched with suspicion and distrust. "But I am willing to talk to you about it some more. And, perhaps, to consider a test if we *both* decide it's what we want."

The elderly gentleman blinked, then stared at her, his gaze looking sharper and more direct. He seemed to be looking for something in her eyes, a gauge of her honesty, perhaps? Or some reminder of the son he'd lost? Finally he nodded. "Agreed."

"Yes, excellent. These things do take time," Leo murmured, holding his elderly uncle by the arm. "Uncle Max, you look very pale. Perhaps we should go now?"

"I'm fine," he snapped. "I want to visit with my…with Ms. Messina here."

"But your doctor's appointment," Leo continued. "You said you were supposed to see the doctor this afternoon."

"Oh, yes," he murmured. "I'd forgotten. That's what I was planning to do until you almost shocked me into a heart attack with this news." Max frowned at his nephew. "I can reschedule. I want to get her settled in at home."

"I can take Ms. Messina over," Troy interjected. "Max, you go keep your appointment, then head home and meet us there. I think it might be good for everyone to have a little while alone before any further conversation, don't you?"

He shot Venus a look daring her to disagree. Not that she would. She wanted to be alone, to reconsider just what she'd gotten herself into here. Things suddenly didn't seem as simple as they had this morning, when she'd thought she'd take advantage of a paid vacation in the south.

More than ever, she thought Leo Gallagher was up to no

good. It looked like he planned to use her for whatever it was he wanted. The way he'd presented her to his uncle—so unlike how they'd agreed—was a clear indication he couldn't be trusted.

For the first time in ages—probably since she'd first been taken into custody by the state, been told that her mother's distant family didn't want her and that she had to go to a foster home—Venus began to feel very alone. In Baltimore, at least, she had friends—Lacey, Uncle Joe and many others. She was completely comfortable in her world, even if that world consisted only of her apartment, her cat and Flanagan's. There were a dozen people there she could call if she needed help…or just a sympathetic ear.

Here, though, she had only three men, three near strangers. Leo, who apparently wanted to use her. Max, who likely wanted her to be someone she was not. And Troy, a man she was incredibly attracted to, but couldn't have. A man whose kiss had made every thought flee her brain and made her body willing to do absolutely anything so long as he kept touching her. A man who, at this moment, wasn't too impressed with her.

That knowledge, more than anything, made her stomach knot and her body tense. She had a sinking feeling Troy was going to be the most difficult situation of all.

TROY WAS GLAD to get Max Longotti and his undoubtedly scheming nephew out the door. He wanted to be alone with Ms. Venus Messina, or whatever her name was. He had a few things to say to her. A few things to get straight.

The woman was easy to read, almost an open book. She wore her feelings on her face, and was obviously ruled by her emotions, as many passionate people were. As an observer, a thinker, Troy had long ago learned to pay attention to other people's expressions and body language. He gauged reactions of others before deciding on his own actions.

Hers—when he'd confronted her about the issue of money—had been damning. Troy couldn't shake the strong feeling of disappointment he'd felt when he'd seen a flash of guilt in her eyes. She hadn't been able to meet his stare for more than ten seconds. Her shoulders had stiffened and her lush bottom lip had disappeared as she sucked it into her mouth in dismay.

Yes, money definitely had something to do with Venus being in Atlanta.

And no matter how much he wanted to take her in his arms and kiss her again, he knew he couldn't do it. Maybe the old Troy wouldn't have given a damn if he'd gone to bed with a thief or a liar. This Troy did. As much as he wanted her— *really* wanted her—he wasn't going anywhere near the redhead until he figured out what the hell she was up to.

Troy remained silent as they exited the building. Good manners dictated that he hold the door for her, and the sight of her folding her long legs into his low-slung sports car hit him in the gut with the intensity of a punch. Five more minutes on that balcony and he might have felt those legs wrapped around him.

Enough. More than likely, the woman was a con artist. Or else she was Max Longotti's grandchild. Either way, she was off-limits. If she was Max's granddaughter, having a hot affair with her would likely ruin his relationship with his new boss.

If she was up to no good with Max's nephew, they could hurt the old man, whom Troy had grown to care about. Max reminded him of his own grandmother, Sophie, whose strict, controlled exterior hid someone fiercely loyal to family. Unlike Sophie, Max had no close family. With the exception of Leo, a few assorted cousins, and now this mysterious redhead, he had no one.

Given Leo's attitude since Troy's arrival in Atlanta, any plan would probably also involve the company. Meaning it involved Troy directly. He liked Longotti Lines and saw tremendous potential for a merger or an outright sale to his family.

Troy had been paying careful attention to a major merger that had taken place last year between a national retail chain and a popular outfitter catalog company. This current deal could have the same result, each firm benefiting by tapping into the other's strengths. Longotti Lines was known for its southern-themed products for the tasteful home, but had all the standard problems with distribution and marketing as any mail-order business. Langtree's was quickly becoming renowned as an upper-crust department store in south Florida, but wasn't as far-reaching as it should be due to its geographic limitations.

A merger could be a perfect marriage. It could also be the perfect opportunity for Troy to bring something new and fresh to the Langtree family business. Since his father had returned to manage the stores, Troy wanted something of his own, something to take on and make successful. It wasn't that anybody in his family expected him to prove anything to them, and he didn't feel the need to. This was more a matter of proving something to *himself.*

He wanted this catalog acquisition to happen. And he wanted to make it a triumphant success for both companies. Because if he didn't, he honestly didn't know what he would do with his career.

After pulling out of the parking lot of the office building, he kept his eyes on the road, not on the sexy legs of the woman in the passenger seat. He had no intention of getting into an argument with her here in the close confines of his car. Hell, just the warm smell of her musky cologne was enough of a distraction—he didn't want to kill them both in a wreck. They would have time to talk when they got back to Max's estate up in Buckhead.

She, apparently, had no such reservations. "You've got a fat lot of nerve, mister," she snapped.

He shot her a look out the corner of his eye. She was turned in the seat, facing him, arms crossed and steam practically coming out of her ears. "I beg your pardon?"

"You think I'm a con artist, don't you?"

Focused on navigating the traffic-filled street, he shrugged. "I didn't say that."

"You didn't have to. Your attitude said it. You think I'm up to something, just because I'm not falling all over myself to get tests to prove I'm related to someone I haven't even decided I *want* to be related to."

"A very wealthy someone," he replied easily, not allowing her to bait him into raising his voice.

"All the more reason for me to not want to be here. Do you think I don't know how out of place I am with the Max Longotti types? You think I intentionally want to throw myself to a pack of rich wolves who'd tear me apart because I don't know a salad fork from a dessert fork?"

"They're interchangeable, unless they have distinct triangular points at the ends of the outmost tines," he explained, not even thinking about it. "Then it's a salad fork."

Silence. He glanced at her, seeing her staring at him as if he had two heads. "Gag me," she finally muttered.

Troy bit his lip to hide a grin, entertained again by her forthright personality. He couldn't make sense of the woman, who outwardly appeared very open and sometimes shockingly honest. That just didn't gel with the image of a deceptive con artist.

They rode in silence for a few minutes. Then, stopping at a traffic signal, he finally turned to meet her stare, forcing himself to focus on what she was up to, not the way she looked—not the pale curve of her cheek, the fullness of her lips or that tantalizing hollow in her throat.

He stiffened, mentally ordering his body to stop reacting to her when his mind didn't trust her one bit. "You must admit, money is a large motivation for a lot of things, Ms. Messina."

She held his eye, not turning away or blushing. "I'm not after Max Longotti's money, Mr….Vice President!"

Her reaction was different than when the money issue had come up before. So either he'd misread her earlier, or else she'd better prepared herself to answer the question. He honestly couldn't say which he believed more. "My last name is Langtree."

She snorted. "Figures."

He was almost afraid to ask. "Why?"

"Because it sounds rich and uptight. Like you."

"I didn't seem too uptight for you up on that balcony when we met," he said softly, daring her to disagree.

"No, then you were oily and pompous."

He couldn't prevent a small laugh from spilling across his lips. The woman was damned stubborn and fiery as hell. Surprisingly, he found himself liking the combination, even when she was hurling insults at his head. "So," he asked, "which was I when we kissed? Uptight, oily or pompous?"

She didn't say anything at first, and Troy almost regretted baiting her. Neither of them needed to be reminded of the sexy conversation they'd shared on the balcony, nor of their erotic kiss. Had the circumstances been different, they may very well have been driving to a hotel right now. And they both knew it.

He could almost hear her breaths deepening in spite of the sounds of traffic and the purr of his car's engine. A quick look confirmed her sudden confusion—obviously she was thinking of that sultry, electric connection they'd felt from the first moment. Her eyes were wide, her lips parted. Seeing the tightness of her nipples under her clingy cotton shirt, Troy suddenly felt hot in spite of the steady stream of cool air emerging from the car vents. He remembered how her breasts had felt against his chest, the way his mouth had hungered for them. His body hummed as he reexperienced the way she tasted, the softness of her skin. He shifted in his seat, willing himself to forget her deep, seductive laugh, and the way the sun turned her long hair into living, red-hot flames.

Off-limits or not, con woman or heiress, she still attracted him like no one had in a very long time. "Cat got your tongue, Ms. Messina? Just whose lap do you think you were sitting on less than an hour ago?" he finally said, almost regretting the suggestiveness of the words as soon as they left his mouth.

"A body double," she finally mumbled.

Considering he was an identical twin, that amused him. "My body double wouldn't have asked at all. Trent tends to go for what he wants without thinking about it first."

She edged closer to her door, giving him a wary look. "Do you have a split personality? Like that guy in *Psycho?*"

He laughed again. "No, just a twin. He lives in Florida."

"Oh, great, two of you. Is he quick to judge, like you?"

Quick to judge? That's what she thought of him? The accusation was almost funny, considering how he and Trent always viewed one another. Trent leapt without looking. Troy viewed a situation from every angle before deciding on a course of action. "We're not much alike," he admitted, "other than physically. What about you? I take it you have no siblings?"

"No biological ones. I stay in touch with some of the other foster kids I grew up with. And my foster mom has four great kids right now who think of me as a big sister. I get back to see them as much as I can."

The note of affection in her voice couldn't have been feigned. She made no attempt to hide her background, seemed completely accepting and comfortable with the way she'd been raised—another detail that didn't quite gel with the image of her as a clever con woman. "So, you say you don't want money. Why don't you tell me what it is you're really after?"

"I'm not after anything. Leo asked me to come, to meet Max and consider the possibility of us being related." She turned in her seat, facing forward and shaking her head. Her voice dropped to a whisper. "It sounded simple."

"A simple con?"

She groaned in frustration. "*Not* a con. At least not by me. Leo made it sound like it could be true, and I owed it to myself, and Max, to check it out."

He raised a brow. "Checking it out. Yes, that would certainly explain the big reunion scene, culminating with the introduction of the long-lost granddaughter."

"You really can be a snot, can't you?" she snapped back.

Though he'd just changed lanes in heavy traffic, Troy couldn't help jerking his head to look at her. "Did you just call me a snot?"

She answered only with a smirk.

As he had from the moment he'd met her, Troy felt completely unsure how to react. The woman was outrageous and confident. Brazen and funny. Cocky with moments of vulnerability. A complete contradiction. She confused him. She aroused him. She angered him. He'd never met anyone like her. He still wanted her so much it nearly caused him physical pain.

As if completely oblivious to his reaction, Venus reached for the stereo and flipped it on. She punched a few buttons until a loud rock song filled the car. Then she closed her eyes and crossed her arms, silently dismissing him.

Troy reluctantly shook his head and focused on the road.

He'd been called a lot of things in his life, by a lot of different women…some of whom had been hurling objects at him as well as words.

But he'd never known a woman whose insults made him want her even more.

CHAPTER FOUR

VENUS GOT HER FIRST real indication about just how much Max Longotti might be worth when she saw his house. House, though, probably wasn't the right word. Friggin' mansion would be more appropriate.

Her jaw fell open as they drove up the long, tree-lined driveway of the estate, which was just north of the city in a pretty, trendy area called Buckhead. "Holy crap, the old guy with the mail-order business lives *here?* Or is this a hotel?"

"No, Max lives here. Alone. Longotti Lines is a little more than a mail-order business," Troy replied, sounding amused. "It's one of the top catalog retailers in the U.S. Right up there with Land's End and the other biggies."

She whistled, tilting her head back to look to the top of the graceful, two-story house with the thick, round columns across the front. Maybe her Scarlett act hadn't been so far off. The place did remind her of an old-fashioned plantation house, surrounded by rolling green lawn and lush landscaping.

A small balcony with an intricate lattice railing ran across the entire front of the building, above the porch, and curved around the sides as well. Huge French doors provided access from what were probably upstairs bedrooms.

A queasy knot formed in her stomach. She could already picture a forty-foot-long dining-room table, each place set with a dozen metal torture devices masquerading as silverware. There'd probably be an obsequious waiter standing behind every diner, ready to swoop down on anyone who dared to lick a little drop of gravy off her finger or, heaven forbid, sneeze into a pressed linen napkin.

"I feel sick," she whispered.

Though she was speaking more to herself, she realized Troy had heard when his hand touched hers. The contact was fleeting, over so quickly, she almost suspected she'd imagined it. But when she saw his warmly concerned expression, she knew she hadn't. "You'll be fine, Venus. It's just a house."

She shook her head. "I know that," she said, trying to sound confident. "I just don't particularly care for the highbrow set."

He looked like he didn't believe her, as if he'd seen the moment of panic she'd tried to hide.

She laughed lightly. "Believe me, this is no sweat. But I am much happier slinging beer at Flanagan's, and I should be pounding the pavement to find a new job."

"Who are you trying to convince? Me or yourself?"

She shot him a glare and crossed her arms. "I should have known better than to accept a free trip from a guy I knew was too smarmy to be legit from the minute I laid eyes on him last week. Because this free vacation obviously came with a whole bunch of pricey strings attached."

He stared at her intently. "You just met Leo last week?"

She nodded, glancing back at the house. "Last Wednesday. And I knew from the minute I saw him he was up to something."

"Yet here you are."

She shrugged. She wasn't about to explain to this man, who already thought so badly of her, that she'd accepted Leo's five thousand dollars for this trip. Whether she'd taken the money to help Maureen and the kids and to keep a roof over her own head or not, he'd still think her an opportunistic money-grubber, especially if she admitted she really did not believe she was this old guy's long-lost grandchild.

Who cares what Mr. Stuffed Shirt thinks?

As much as she hated to admit it, even to herself, Venus did care. That was a strange feeling for her, considering she seldom gave a rat's ass what other people thought of her. She'd long ago decided she was comfortable in her own skin, happy with the person she'd turned out to be. Maybe a little loud. Maybe a little too friendly with too many guys. But still, a smart, hardworking, loyal woman who, until right now, had never been intimidated by anything as silly as a big ol' house in an unfamiliar city—which probably had diamond-studded chandeliers and gold-plated toilets.

"I need a drink," she muttered.

"Good, you can make us both one," Troy answered as he opened his door to step out. "Let's see how good you are at your job."

"It's just a night job," she clarified as she got out, not waiting for him to open the car door, though he'd come around to do so. "A temporary one until I can find something more permanent again." Then she thought about what he'd said. "You're staying for a while, then?" She nibbled her lip, glancing back and forth between Troy, who was at least somewhat familiar, and this house, populated probably by a bunch of absolute strangers.

He answered with a secretive smile, "Oh, yes, I'm staying."

"Suit yourself," she murmured, trying not to let him know she was pleased at not being dumped at the door.

Max Longotti had obviously phoned home and informed his housekeeper, Mrs. Harris, of Venus's arrival. The woman was welcoming and professional, greeting Troy with familiarity and Venus with unexpected warmth. Venus managed to

keep her mouth closed and her eyes in her head as they walked
through the huge tiled foyer. Fancy sculptures stood on tiny
tables. Even fancier pictures hung on the walls. The predom-
inant color seemed to be bluish-purple, even right down to
some immense flower-filled vases that stood as high as her
chin.

"Wonder if that's where they stash the bodies," she
muttered.

Mrs. Harris gave her a curious look over her shoulder, and
Venus bit her lip.

When Troy informed Mrs. Harris they wanted to step into
Max's office for a drink, the woman took them there, telling
Venus she'd be back shortly to show her to her rooms.

"Rooms?" Venus said when she and Troy were once again
alone in an office that was bigger than the apartment she'd
grown up in. She walked around it, trailing her fingertips
across the spines of dozens of leather-bound books lining
built-in mahogany shelves. The room was furnished with ex-
quisitely detailed antique furniture; she was almost afraid to
sit down.

"There are some nice guest suites upstairs. I'm sure Max
has left instructions for you to be given one of them."

"Do you think he told the servants…" She lowered her
head and glanced away.

He leaned a hip against a brown leather sofa, watching her,
looking as comfortable in these surroundings as anyone born
with a silver spoon in his mouth. Unlike Venus, in her too-
skimpy, too-tight shorts and her suggestive shirt, who
probably looked like she should have come in through the
service entrance.

"Told them what?" Troy asked. "Who you are? Or, who
you *might* be?"

She nodded, hoping he'd say no, that she wouldn't have
to act out this charade in front of a bunch of servants who

might very well have known Mr. Longotti's long-lost son. The last thing she needed was to be watched by every person in the place, her every move evaluated, her every word analyzed.

"I doubt it's common knowledge," Troy said, making her hopes rise. "But I would imagine Mrs. Harris knows. She's worked for Max for decades."

She sighed and glanced at the closed door through which the housekeeper had exited. "She was awfully nice. Do you think she knows…knew…Max's son?"

He nodded. "I would imagine."

"Great," she muttered. "No wonder she was friendly."

"So," he said, raising a questioning brow, "you're trying to tell me you're really *not* anxious to be greeted as the prodigal granddaughter?"

She snorted and shot him a look telling him just how stupid he was even to have asked. He didn't seem offended. Instead, he walked toward her, crossing the room in a few long strides. His hard body did lovely things for the well-tailored suit.

Though she'd more often dated men who wore jeans and leather, there was something intoxicating about seeing a thoroughly male animal—with an occasional hint of wildness in his eyes—wrapped up in an elegant, sophisticated package like Troy's conservative gray suit. It almost challenged a woman, as if luring her into stepping closer to a beautiful but caged tiger. Until the woman found out the cage door was open and the magnificent animal ready to spring.

She'd tried to tell herself Troy Langtree was a stuffed shirt. But she couldn't erase what had happened on the balcony when they first met. He'd been smooth, charming, intense. Sexy as pure sin. His kiss had completely seduced her. While safe in his arms, she'd wanted to make love with him more than she'd wanted to draw another breath.

Just because he'd repressed that part of himself ever since finding out who she was didn't mean it no longer existed. She saw it in his eyes, in the self-assured way he carried that long, lean body. For some wicked reason, it only made her more determined to find it again. Someday, when she had her confidence back.

"Are you curious about him?" Troy asked. "Max's son?"

Crossing her arms tightly over her chest, Venus forced herself to take a deep breath. She sat on the arm of a high, wing-backed chair and feigned nonchalance. "I suppose. Wouldn't anyone be?"

Instead of answering, he gestured toward a massive wooden desk near one of the huge arched windows overlooking the side lawn. The late-afternoon sunlight dripped in, illuminating the fine grain of the wood on the desktop, which was almost the same color as his thick hair. She noticed the back of a decorative, silver picture frame just as Troy said, "There's a photo of him on the desk."

She tightened her arms, almost hugging herself. "I don't think so. Maybe later."

Venus was the one who was supposed to make the drinks, but instead Troy moved to a discreet corner bar and poured two shots of whiskey. After returning with them, he handed her one. "You can impress me with your bartending skills another time. You look like you could use this."

Though she hated confirming how wildly unstable her emotions were, she took the crystal glass gratefully. She tossed it back, feeling the warmth of the amber liquid ooze through her body almost instantly. Closing her eyes, she took a deep breath.

"Good Scotch."

"Another?"

She shook her head.

When he took the empty glass from her hand, his fingers

brushed against hers, sending more heat rushing through her body than the alcohol had. He seemed just as aware, standing close, holding the empty tumbler in his fingers and staring at her intently. Finally, he leaned over to place their glasses on a small, decorative table. His body was so close to hers, for a brief moment she could feel his breath on her cheek and his pant legs brushing her thigh.

He straightened, but didn't move away. "I would think if you were really curious you'd want to see what he looked like," he said softly. "So do you really not care?" He narrowed his eyes. "Or is it that you're afraid?"

"I'm not afraid," she insisted.

But even as she said the words, she knew she was lying.

She *was* afraid—though probably not for the reason Troy thought. She couldn't explain it to him, though. Hell, she could barely admit it to herself.

He might think she feared looking at the picture and seeing a stranger with not one feature like hers. Feared not having any support for Leo's claims. In actuality, Venus dreaded the thought of her own eyes staring back at her. She didn't *want* to recognize the curve of the man's smile, or think his chin resembled hers. She couldn't bear it if the widow's peak on her forehead had been inherited from him.

This whole idea—a fat paycheck for an all-expenses paid vacation—had never seemed more dangerous than right now.

No, she was nowhere near ready to look at that man's picture. Not when seeing it might provide more evidence of the death of a parent she'd never met. She'd remain happily in the dark for as long as she could. Hopefully long enough to fully earn the five grand and hightail it back to Baltimore, with a nice, friendly wave to an elderly gentleman who was *not* her grandfather!

Stepping within inches of her body, Troy made a quiet assessment of her face, looking searchingly into her eyes, which, she suspected, were overly bright right now. Finally, he tilted his head and said in an almost wondering tone, "You're afraid you'll see something you recognize, aren't you? You really *don't* want it to be true."

He didn't say another word, letting his words hang there between them. He didn't expect her to answer, obviously knowing what she'd say.

"Why, Venus?" He shook his head, still appearing surprised by his own insight. "I don't get this."

She had no doubt of that. Troy wanted to figure out why a woman from the wrong side of the tracks wasn't rubbing her hands together in glee at her current situation. Most women would probably be thrilled to discover they could be an heiress. Most would at least be happy finally to know the truth about their parentage.

But Venus wasn't like most. Never had been. Never would be.

"I don't fit in here. I belong in this world about as much as a priest belongs in a synagogue," she said with a dry chuckle, giving him only part of the explanation. She wondered why she bothered trying to make him understand even that much, why she cared what he thought. "I don't know the language. I don't know the customs. I don't have the right clothes, the right speech, the right hair or the right attitude." She shook her head. Voicing these minor misgivings almost made her forget the major ones. "At this moment, Troy, I'm seriously wishing to God I'd never come. This was a stupid idea and I was nuts to go along with it."

He didn't say anything for a moment, just continued to look at her. It was unnerving, having all that intense, masculine attention focused squarely on her face. His shimmering green eyes darkened as he stared at her. Her heart sped up in her chest, reacting to his closeness, to the warmth of his body and his spicy scent.

Remembering the way he'd tasted on her tongue.

Venus had never once, not in her entire life, wanted to melt into a man's arms only to be held and taken care of. She'd been in men's arms for passion. For possession. For desire. For need. And yes, she knew she wanted all those things from this man she'd only known a matter of hours.

But, right now, his tender concern seemed pretty damned attractive, too. Particularly when he reached up to brush a long strand of hair off her brow, his touch innocent yet crackling with electricity.

He leaned closer. "I understand." Then, to her further surprise, he continued. "You're not alone, Venus. I'm going to help you."

AN HOUR LATER, while taking a long shower that did nothing to cool his overheated skin, Troy still couldn't believe he'd offered to help Venus.

"Help her do what?" he muttered as he reached out to turn the spray from lukewarm to cool. He know what he *really* wanted to help her do.

Have a whole bunch of screaming orgasms.

But that was out. No screaming orgasms loomed in the future for either one of them. Not even here in a large, dual-headed shower where he probably should have blown off some sexual steam before he saw the beautiful redhead again.

Troy didn't want to blow off steam with his hand. He wanted to create some serious steam…with her.

Why he wanted her so much, he really couldn't say. She was amazing to look at, sure, but he interacted with attractive women all the time. And for the past three months, none of them had come close to luring him out of his unintentional celibacy. Venus had done it with a flick of her ankle as she tapped her shoe into the air on the balcony.

His suspicions about her should have tamped down on the

desire. They hadn't. The fact that she was a mystery—a cocky, confident mystery—had only added to the instant heat he'd felt when he first laid eyes on her.

Well, not entirely confident. Obviously the woman's self-confidence had taken a real hit when she'd arrived here at Max's home. In the library, when he'd attempted to look at it from her point of view, he'd felt for her. Not that Max would care—if she really were his granddaughter, he wouldn't give a damn whether she fit into his world or not.

Venus, however, quite obviously cared. It couldn't have been easy for a proud woman to admit she couldn't handle the situation in which she found herself. The confusion and hint of fear in her eyes had affected him more deeply than he'd ever have imagined possible. He saw a hint of vulnerability in her which she'd probably never admit to having.

And, to be honest, he admired her. She didn't seem at all bitter, despite the bits and pieces he'd managed to glean about her life. She'd been orphaned, raised in foster care and had had to fight for every single thing she got. Yet it hadn't made her greedy or grasping, nor had it made her resentful. She had a genuine smile and an infectious laugh. Her smart mouth was buoyed by an innate sense of humor that said she didn't take anything too seriously.

Completely unlike him.

Troy was well used to being around money. He, more than anyone, knew he'd been incredibly fortunate to have always been part of a wealthy lifestyle. Still, he liked to think it hadn't ruined him. He might have a reputation as a playboy at night, but fifty-hour workweeks had been a part of his life for the past several years. He didn't mind hard work though, since he had never aspired to be a useless rich guy with fast cars, fast women and no ambition.

He also liked to think he could do exactly what his twin had—make it completely on his own, without a penny of

Langtree money. Though until recently his paychecks had come from a family-owned business, that's essentially what he'd done. His salary had certainly been in line with any other retail executive, and it had supported him just fine. He wore nice clothes because he liked them and got them at a discount. He drove a Jaguar because he enjoyed going fast. Otherwise, he was pretty conservative with his money.

Not, he imagined, that Venus Messina would believe it.

Whatever she believed, she had to know he was in a position to help her deal with her new surroundings. If Leo's claims proved true, if she really was Max's granddaughter, she'd have to deal with them for the rest of her life.

Tending bar at a Baltimore pub was a long way from interacting with the elite of Atlanta. She was right—she'd be crucified the minute she attended her first social function. Not by Max, of course. If Venus really turned out to be his son's daughter, Max wouldn't care if the woman got up and danced the limbo on the bar at the country club.

"She won't, though," he muttered as he rinsed his hair. Because Troy had said he'd help her and that's exactly what he intended to do. At least until he found out for sure what she was up to. Until then, helping her learn to fit in would be the perfect excuse to keep her within his sight and try to make sure Max didn't get hurt. The tricky part would be keeping her in his sight...but out of his arms and out of his bed.

Which was exactly where he most wanted her to be.

She was funny and beautiful. Irreverent and bawdy. But at some moments so damned vulnerable, he wanted to just take her in his arms and hold her. Pretty unbelievable for Troy Langtree, whose own twin had on occasion called him a louse when it came to women.

Twisting the knob close to ice-cold, he let a jet of frigid water cascade down his body, then turned the shower off.

After opening the glass door, he stepped out onto the mat, then reached for a towel he'd dropped on the counter earlier. Before he could take another step toward it, however, he realized he had company.

Venus.

Standing just a few feet away, inside the bathroom, she froze, just as he did. Their eyes met, their stares held. They both sucked in their breath and held it. Each stunned. Each unsure what would come next.

Troy noted the shock on her face. He didn't imagine Venus Messina was shocked by much. Now, though, her wide eyes and gaping mouth said his presence had taken her by surprise.

"Ever hear of knocking?" he asked in a lazy drawl, making no effort to grab the towel. Hell, if she wanted to stand there staring at his naked body, instead of beating a hasty retreat, he'd accommodate her.

She wore only a fluffy towel sarong style, that barely covered all the essentials. Her hair was piled loosely on her head, with a few long, tempting curls hanging loose. In one hand she held a small bottle of bath oil and a paperback book. Her other hand was pressed flat against her heart, the bright red tips of her long nails stark against the white terrycloth and her smooth, creamy skin.

Her eyes remained wide and appraising. Without so much as an apology, an embarrassed explanation, and certainly not a quick exit, she moved her gaze over his body, head to toe. Even from here he could see the strong, fast pulse in her neck and the rush of color on her face. Her every deeply inhaled breath loosened the towel she wore. His heart skipped a beat, as he wondered if the loose knot would give way, revealing her body to his hungry gaze, as his was to her.

On someone shorter, the towel might have done an

He looked pleased, as if her words had led her directly into his trap. When he continued, she realized they had.

"There's one way to prove it," he murmured, his eyes holding a recognizable spark of mischief.

"Drop the towel."

CHAPTER FIVE

VENUS NIBBLED HER LIP, noting the amused challenge in his voice. He almost certainly didn't think she'd do it. After all, she'd walked in on him by accident, and he hadn't intentionally exposed himself to her.

This was different. What woman would simply drop her towel in broad daylight and show her naked body to a man she'd known for only a few hours? A man with whom she had no relationship and had never been intimate?

Nudity with a new lover was intimidating enough. This bordered on exhibitionism.

It would take a lot of confidence, and a lot more nerve.

Fortunately, Venus had been blessed with both.

She reached for the knot over her breast, never taking her eyes from his. He raised a brow, silently egging her on.

"You think I won't?"

"I think you want me to *think* you will," he countered.

She wondered if the naked hunk had retained any of his normal executive, suit-wearing inhibitions now that his clothes were off. If so, she'd be able to tell by his reaction. Right now.

Untying the towel, she removed her hand and let gravity do the rest.

A slow, pleased smile spread across his parted lips as he studied her from head to toe. Not a hint of shock appeared on his face; he never even pretended to look away.

Question answered. No inhibitions in the man.

Venus remained still, letting him look his fill, knowing what he saw. Full breasts, slim waist, flat tummy as a result of way more sit-ups than any one person should have to endure. Her hips were a little rounder than she'd like, but not bad for a woman pushing thirty. And she already knew he liked her legs—he'd been eyeing them since the minute they met.

She heard him draw in a ragged breath. He obviously approved.

"You didn't think I'd do it, did you?"

He tilted his head and raised a brow. "Oh, I *knew* you'd do it, Venus. Why else do you think I suggested it?"

He wasn't kidding. He'd known damn well she wouldn't back down from his challenge. He hadn't known her long, but he already knew her better than most other people ever had.

"Okay, you got me naked. Now, big shot," she said, narrowing her eyes in challenge, "are you going to wow me with your expertise on women?"

He stepped closer, moving noiselessly across the bathmat, until they were less than a foot apart. She could feel his warm breath on her cheek and see the pulse in his temple. That gorgeous erection was within inches of where she wanted it. Her body arched forward the tiniest bit, of its own will.

Schooling herself to remain calm, she figured her tightly clenched fingers on the counter were about the only indication of the inferno raging inside her body.

"Your eyes are glassy, your pupils dilated and your lids half lowered."

She blinked twice. "Bad lighting."

He laughed softly at the lie.

"Your lips are pursed," Troy said, his voice low and

soothing, almost melodic. "You're thinking of being kissed. Of kissing back. Of using your mouth for something other than talking. Lots of somethings."

Score one for the men's team.

"Pursed lips can also be a sign of attitude," she countered weakly.

He nodded. "Oh, honey, there's no question you've got miles of attitude." Watching as he moistened his own lips with his tongue, she nearly moaned. "But it's not your attitude at work when your lips are full and ripe and parted like that. It's another part of Venus altogether."

Yeah. The empty, aching part that badly needed to be filled by him.

He stared into her eyes for a long moment, and she knew he saw the truth she couldn't possibly hide. Then he looked lower. His breaths grew more labored—she heard each one as he drew it into his mouth and slowly exhaled, as if striving for control when there was none to be found.

He stared at her bare throat. Her shoulders. The nape of her neck, where one long curl brushed her collarbone.

Then he studied her breasts, which felt heavier and tighter under his hungry gaze. "It's not too cold in here," he murmured, "so you couldn't have a chill."

True, she acknowledged silently. Her nipples tightened even more, drawing into pointy tips as she imagined him using his mouth on them.

"That's almost too easy, though," he continued. "So let's move on. There's a pink glow on your skin. You're flushed and breathing in shallow breaths, because you're so excited."

She closed her eyes, trying to relax, but unable to.

"Your stomach is quivering slightly with the effort it's taking you to keep your body stiff and unyielding when it wants to be loose and pliant."

She moaned softly, but didn't open her eyes. She kept

focusing on his voice, trying not to think of how much she wanted to reach out a few inches and let her fingers do some walking.

"Though you're trying to stand straight, your legs are shaky. I can see the muscles straining beneath your skin."

When she felt a butterfly-light touch on her thigh, her eyes flew open. "I didn't think touching was part of the demonstration," she said between ragged breaths.

"It's not. I don't have to touch you to know how much you want me." He moved his hand again, the tips of his fingers scraping ever so delicately across the curls concealing her womanhood. "Though, if I did, I think we'd both see just how much you do."

She nodded, knowing exactly where he could touch her to prove his point. She was so wet and throbbing, she'd come apart at his slightest touch. The mere thought of him sliding his fingers into her made her moan slightly.

"Do you concede?" he whispered, still holding his hand no more than a centimeter from her curls. "I am correct in thinking you're incredibly aroused right now?"

She nodded, unable to lie to him any more than she could to herself. "I concede."

Oh, yes, she was definitely aroused right now, so aroused she would have gone for it, right here and now, hard and fast up against the sink. Then slow and languorous in the bathtub. Even having only known him for only a matter of hours, she would have. If it weren't for three things: location, location, location.

"So I want you. And you want me too," she whispered.

He didn't try to deny it. "I've wanted you since the moment I saw your pretty ankles when you were sitting on the balcony outside my office." The smooth words couldn't hide the intensity in the man's voice.

Venus had been desired before. She'd had sex before.

She'd even had relationships before. But she'd never felt like someone wanted to inhale her completely, to indulge in her body and give her every bit of primal passion a man was capable of.

Until right now.

"Point taken. We want each other," she said raggedly. "But this would really complicate things with the old man, wouldn't it? For both of us." Part of her wanted him not to care. A bigger part knew he couldn't.

At his frustrated groan, she continued. "This was a pretty damn stupid thing to start when we know we're not going to finish it." *Are we?* She heard the tone in her voice that almost made her comment sound like a question.

He looked at her for one moment longer, then his eyes shifted away. She heard him mutter a curse under his breath and nearly echoed it.

"You're right. Incredibly stupid." He thrust a frustrated hand through his still-wet hair, sending droplets of water onto her hot skin, providing instant, shocking sensation. He picked up a towel from the counter and slung it around his lean hips.

"I'm sorry, Venus."

Hearing him acknowledge that, no, they were not going to finish the way they both wanted to, she sighed heavily. Not wanting to tempt fate by retrieving the towel she'd dropped by bending down in front of this gloriously erect man, she grabbed a fresh one from a rack behind her. Quickly, she wrapped it around her.

When covered, she forced a laugh. "Considering I haven't had an orgasm that didn't involve a vibrator in so long I've forgotten what one feels like, you're probably not as sorry as I am."

His mouth opened and he gaped at her, as if completely unable to believe she'd said what she'd said. *Okay, that was probably a little crass for Mr. V.P.*

Then she realized he hadn't been shocked by her language.

"You can't tell me you haven't had a lover for a long time. You are the most sensuous, desirable woman I've ever met, Venus. I have trouble believing you couldn't have any man you wanted, any time you wanted him."

I can't have you.

"It's been a long time. Since last fall," she admitted, lowering her lashes and wondering why she'd confessed something so intimate. Maybe because her heart had skipped a beat or two when he'd called her the most desirable woman he'd ever met.

Flattery had been known to make women do foolish things before.

He didn't answer right away. Instead, he stepped closer, then closer still. His expression was intense, focused. His eyes flared with heat and determination. Wary, she took a tiny step back, but was blocked by the vanity countertop behind her.

"That's too damn long," he said, his voice thick and husky.

Before she knew his intention, he'd slipped his hand into her hair, tangling it in his fingers. He drew her close, catching her surprised cry with his lips.

His kiss was hotter than the one they'd shared earlier, on the balcony. Hot and hungry, and Venus melted against him. He made love to her mouth with his tongue until she began to whimper, needing more, wanting more than they'd just agreed they could have.

He slid his palm down her bare arm, slowly, his fingertips creating heat and electricity on her skin, then lower, until his hand brushed against her towel-covered hip.

She jerked and gasped. He only kissed her deeper. When his hand moved between the edges of the towel to brush against her naked thigh, she knew what he was doing, what he wanted to give her. She had one second to wrap her mind around it before his hot fingers slipped between her legs. "Oh, God," she managed to cry, feeling the pressure. She arched into his hand, growing even more mindless when she heard his groan of pure male satisfaction at feeling how wet she was. For him.

"Oh, Troy...*please*," she whispered brokenly.

He teased her, sending her higher as he made tantalizing circles around her throbbing clitoris. When she thought she'd burst with frustration, he gave her a little more, slipping his finger inside her, mimicking the movement with his tongue.

She began to shake, until finally he whispered against her lips, "Now, honey. Right now."

Finally he zeroed in on her hottest spot. With just a few perfect strokes on the delicate flesh, he gave her exactly what she'd been missing. She cried out as waves of pleasure ratcheted through her body, the orgasm literally making her shake so hard he had to support her in his arms.

He kept kissing her, taking her cries against his lips as she gradually returned to sanity. It took several long moments. The intensity of her climax had been like nothing she'd ever experienced before.

"It's funny," he whispered as he moved his mouth to kiss her cheek, then her eyelid. "Right before you came in, I'd been thinking about how much I wanted to give you a bunch of screaming orgasms."

"One down," she managed to mutter, not sure where she got the strength to use her voice.

He chuckled. Pressing one more kiss against her temple, he stepped back. She instantly missed the hot, hard feel of his body against hers. "Troy?"

"You should go," he murmured, gently pushing her toward the open door. She couldn't even protest as he gently shuffled her out into her bedroom. Then, he stepped back inside the bathroom. "I somehow think I need to take another shower. A long one." His eyelids lowered slightly, as did his voice. "I can pretty much guarantee what I'll be thinking about for every minute of it." He shut the door before she could protest.

Venus stood there, listening to the lock click, then the shower turn on. She knew what he was doing.

And she wished like hell she was the one doing it for him.

AFTER TAKING another long and equally unsatisfying shower, Troy dressed for dinner. Though an easygoing man, Max did enjoy the niceties and, so far, every night Troy had been here they'd had a full-course dinner in the dining room. Tonight, he found himself hoping the salad forks weren't too confusing. The quiet, elegant dinner hour might never be the same once Venus got through with it.

Venus. He closed his eyes, pausing while shrugging on his pressed white shirt. He still couldn't get her image out of his mind. Like her namesake, she was the epitome of woman, so damned seductive he had been barely able to shut the door behind her after pushing her away earlier.

He'd known full well she wouldn't be able to resist his challenge when he practically dared her to drop the towel. Probably not his wisest move. It had been bad enough when he'd only imagined what she looked like under her clothes. Now, having seen her, all he could think about was what it would be like to go farther. Her body was the kind men fantasized about—lushly curved, sleek and supple. He wanted nothing on earth as much as he wanted to cup her breasts, to suck those tight nipples into his mouth, to press hot kisses on her stomach…and hotter ones between her long, pale thighs.

Not taking her while she still shook from her orgasm had required every bit of self-control he possessed.

"Cool it, jackass," he muttered aloud, knowing there was

no time for yet another shower this evening. Hell, when his sex drive came back, it came back with a vengeance.

He was dying to make love to her. Kissing her, touching her, catching her cries of pleasure in his mouth may have given *her* a little release from the tension, but it had only added to his. Troy knew he'd be able to think of nothing else but making love with Venus every time he was with her.

And when he wasn't with her he'd have the memory of how she'd looked when she'd dropped the towel. Not just her glorious body, but that spark of devilment and outright confidence in her eyes that he'd never before encountered with another woman.

No question, if she'd been anybody else, he would have made love to her right there on the bathroom counter an hour ago. They'd probably be in the middle of their second or third encounter right now.

"Not happening," he reminded himself. *Unfortunately.*

A few minutes later, after he was dressed and back in control of his raging hormones, Troy left his room. Noticing Venus's open door and empty suite, he headed downstairs alone. The house was quiet, and he wondered if Max and Leo had returned. Spying Mrs. Harris in the foyer, he asked her.

"Mr. Longotti is in with *her*," the gray-haired woman said in a loud whisper, nodding toward the closed office door.

"Is he all right?"

She frowned, nearly clucking in disapproval. "He looked very pale and tired when he and Mr. Gallagher returned." The way the housekeeper said Leo's name hinted at what she thought of the man. "Too much excitement."

"I would suspect Ms. Messina's arrival was quite a surprise for him," Troy said, not wanting to put the woman in an uncomfortable position, but needing to see if she could provide any useful information. After all, she knew Max better than just about anybody else. "I'm sure it will make him very happy, though, if it turns out to be true, and she is his grand-child."

"Of course it will," the woman replied. "Never was a man who loved his son more than Mr. Longotti. Losing him the way he did, so soon after he'd lost Miss Violet…it wasn't fair."

Troy tilted his head in confusion. "Miss Violet?"

The woman nodded. "Mrs. Longotti."

That explained why the name Violet had been important on the back of the mysterious baby photo. And why Max had been so keenly interested in Venus's name.

"She passed on when Max Jr. was in high school," Mrs. Harris continued, "just a few years before he left. I often thought that's why he went. Mr. Longotti couldn't let her go. He repainted the house, filled it with different shades of violet, and Max Jr. couldn't stand the constant reminders."

Troy knew Max was a widower, but didn't realize how long ago he'd lost his wife. No wonder the man seemed so alone. He *had* been for a very long time. "Sad," he murmured.

Mrs. Harris nodded and lowered her voice further. "Yes, it is. Which is why I'm hoping Mr. Gallagher knows what he's doing. I don't think Mr. Longotti could handle another loss. He's not been well, anyway. If he grows to care about this young woman, and she turns out not to be Max's daughter, he's going to be badly hurt. He could break down again…."

She quickly glanced away, as if realizing she'd said too much. Troy certainly wasn't going to pry.

At that moment, movement in the front living room caught his eye. Leo stood there, staring absently out the window.

Perfect. Troy very much wanted to speak with the man. After thanking Mrs. Harris, he joined Leo, pausing to make himself a drink at the well-stocked wet bar.

"How was Max's appointment?" he asked, keeping a note of casual interest in his voice as he took a seat on one of the overstuffed sofas.

"All right," Leo replied, his lips twisted into what probably was supposed to be a smile. "He has to have some more tests later in the week. He's too old to work himself as hard as he does and the doctors are concerned."

The man still stood at the window, moving his gaze between the lawn and Troy.

"Quite a shock he got today."

Leo nodded. "Oh, yes. I haven't seen Uncle Max quite so pleased in a long, long time."

"Yes, I'm sure. How fortunate you were to find the missing child after all these years." Troy paused to sip his drink. "When did you say you came up with the idea to have an investigator look in the New York area?"

Leo visibly stiffened. "Recently. I didn't want to raise Uncle Max's hopes, though, which is why I didn't mention it until I had all the information."

"And everything happened to occur last week." *Just two days after I arrived.*

"Yes." The man smiled thinly. "How unfortunate that you came up here to Atlanta for nothing."

"Oh? I don't understand," Troy said, though he understood full well where Leo was headed.

"Well," the man explained, "it's possible Max will rethink his strategy. He does, after all, have a grandchild to think of."

"You mean you don't think he'll sell?"

Before Leo could answer, a door opened and warm laughter filled the foyer. Troy watched intently, seeing Max exit his office with Venus on his arm.

Venus. Troy had to lower his head to hide a chuckle when he saw her. She looked positively wicked in a short black leather skirt that showed off long bare legs to perfection. A flouncy white peasant blouse hung right at the edges of her shoulders. Her high-heeled black shoes made her tower over Max. And her hair was poufed up in a mass of curls which added another couple of inches to her already considerable height.

Judging by the look on his face, Max didn't seem to care. He looked completely delighted in her company.

"Troy, Leo," he said as they entered the room, "you must have Venus tell you how she and her foster family used to use the Longotti Lines catalog to decorate their home."

Leo raised an arrogant brow. "I didn't imagine your childhood home to be the type in need of interior design."

Troy stiffened, wondering if the guy had to work hard at always sounding like a pretentious ass.

Max ignored his nephew and took a seat on a sofa near the front window. "Troy, as I was saying, Venus and her foster mother were big fans of our catalogs. They used to cut out the pictures and tape them to the walls. They'd redo the look of their entire apartment every season."

Venus grinned. "Can I confess that it wasn't always the Longotti Lines catalog?"

Max put his index finger over his lips and frowned. "Shh. Don't ruin the story."

"Sorry. But, frankly, we were limited to the catalogs the doctors had on the tables in the waiting room at the health clinic—because we had to steal 'em, of course."

"Very nice," Leo murmured.

She smirked, obviously enjoying goading Leo, who was so blatant in his disapproval.

"Don't you need to get home?" Max asked Leo, giving him a pointed stare. "Your mother said you were supposed to take her to the club this evening."

That was another thing Troy couldn't stand about Leo. The man still lived with his mother, for God's sake.

"Yes, I should," Leo replied. "Now, Uncle Max, don't forget to take your pills," he said. "And please you mustn't forget again about your next appointment."

He left quickly, pausing only long enough to bid a pleasant goodbye to Max and Venus and a not-so-friendly one to Troy.

"He makes my teeth hurt," the old man muttered once Leo was gone.

Venus snorted a laugh, as if she understood exactly what Max meant. Considering the number of times he'd clenched his jaw when Leo was around, Troy thought he did, too.

"Treats me like I'm an imbecile," Max continued. "I tell myself he means well. He took over quite a lot—a little *too* much—when he said I kept forgetting appointments or missing deadlines." Max glanced at Troy and gave him an approving nod. "Now, I have you to do that, though."

"Yes, you do," Troy said, "and I'll update you after dinner on some of the meetings I had this morning."

Max shrugged, as if uninterested. "I tried to like Leo when my brother married his mother. He was five or six then." He stroked his jaw absently as he stared out the front window. "But I just couldn't take to the kind of kid who'd constantly torment my boy with wet willies and arm burns, or run and tattle whenever Maxie did the slightest thing wrong."

Maxie. Max Jr. Beside him, he saw Venus stiffen ever so slightly. No one else would even have noticed. But Troy was very much in tune to her every movement right now, particularly because of what they'd shared in his bathroom earlier.

Max gave a rather evil-sounding chuckle. "Not that my Maxie couldn't hold his own. He might have been a few years younger, but he was a quick one. Talked circles around Leo." Obviously lost in memory, he slapped his own knee in delight. "Tricked Leo into playing cowboys and tied him to a telephone pole down the road one day, just so he could get some peace from the whining, he said."

Even Venus smiled briefly. Then she glanced away, still obviously uncomfortable. Max didn't seem to notice. "I had to punish him, a'course. But my Maxie didn't have so much trouble with Leo after that day."

Before Max could comment further, Mrs. Harris stepped in to tell him he had a phone call. He picked up the receiver on a side table and quickly became engrossed in a conversation.

Informing them dinner would be ready shortly, Mrs. Harris exited, leaving Troy and Venus alone, staring at one another.

"So," Troy said, determined to steer the conversation away from Max's late son, "you covered your bedroom walls with pictures from catalogs. My twin brother always preferred those Pamela Anderson-type posters."

The tension faded from her face as she snickered. "Oh, you mean there's actually blood running through the veins of someone in your family?"

He laughed softly at the jibe, glad he'd distracted her. "You weren't complaining about me being cold-blooded an hour ago." In a soft whisper, he mimicked her. "Oh, Troy, *please.*"

"Screw you," she said with a good-natured grin.

He tsked. "I thought we already discussed that."

Apparently unwilling to be drawn into a sensual conversation, she ignored him. "I suppose you decorated your room with wide panoramic views of Fort Knox or perhaps mountains of dollar bills."

"Certainly not ones," Troy replied smoothly.

She rolled her eyes. "But, I'm sure, nothing as tasteless as pin-up girls."

"From fourteen on, I didn't *need* posters," he said, daring her to figure out what he meant.

She didn't even try. "Well, I did. When I hit my teenage

years I started swiping the *People* magazines and covering my walls with pictures of Kevin Bacon and Tom Cruise."

"I assume that was before you'd reached your current height?"

"Hey, no short jokes about my honey Tom," she retorted with a chuckle. "For him, I might just rethink my 'no guys shorter or lighter than me' rule."

Troy stepped closer, until they stood nearly eye to eye. Even with her heels and poufed-up hair, she still couldn't quite match his height. He shook his head and murmured, "No, I think you're better off sticking with your rule. You need someone bigger who can keep you from walking all over him."

Her lips curved. "Better men have tried, darlin'."

"Oh, I'm sure *some* men have tried, but not *better* men." He let her see the confidence in his stare and drove his point home. "At least not for the past nine months or so."

A slow flush rose in her cheeks. Damn, he loved that he could make this unflappable woman blush. She was obviously thinking about exactly what he'd wanted her to—the way she'd felt in his arms an hour before.

She wouldn't give up, however, and whispered, "Coulda been anyone."

The dig didn't phase him. "But it wasn't, Venus." Turning slightly to block Max's view—not that the man was paying them any attention—he ran the tip of his index finger down her cheek to the corner of her full lips. "It was me."

Not giving her a chance to reply, he walked away and took a seat opposite Max. The man finished his conversation and hung up the phone. His eyes shone with interest as he stared speculatively between his houseguests. Maybe he'd been paying more attention than Troy had thought.

Troy mentally kicked himself for letting Venus get to him in front of Max. He needed to be more discreet. Unfortunately, the return of his sex drive wasn't taking into account that it wasn't very appropriate to lust after your boss's potential family members right in front of your boss.

"Can I help myself at the bar?" Venus asked Max, still looking flushed and slightly confused. Troy liked that he'd put the hungry look on her face, even as he wondered whether Max noticed.

"Please do," Max said.

Venus made her way over to the bar and poured herself a glass of wine. She glanced over her shoulder at Troy. "I owe you one, don't I?"

Glancing at his empty glass, he shrugged, wondering about the spark of mischief in the redhead's eyes. "All right, thank you," he murmured, more than ready to take her challenge.

In a few moments, she walked toward him, carrying two glasses. She pressed one into his hand, leaning close enough to whisper, "Now we're even."

They weren't anywhere close to even, not that he was going to call her on it in front of Max. Before he could think of a way to discreetly remind her of the way he'd made her come with just a few kisses and caresses, he noticed the wicked look on her face. Then he glanced lower, at the view of her perfect breasts, fully revealed when she bent over in the loose blouse.

Her bra was tiny and black. Completely wrong with a white top. Not apparently that she gave a damn. It plumped up. Pushed out. Tempted beyond belief. He almost hissed as he tried to breathe.

Her confident smile as she finally straightened and took a seat next to Max told him she knew it, too. Yes, she was definitely capable of some payback. She knew just which of his buttons to push. He apparently hadn't been very subtle in his visual appreciation of her lush breasts when she'd dropped her towel up in the bathroom.

Not that any red-blooded man could have been.

Striving for control, he finally sipped his drink. The strong flavor seemed very appropriate. Sweet, milky and creamy. Luscious but with a kick of heat—just like he imagined her soft skin would taste.

He sipped again, meeting her eye, as he licked the liquid off his lips. "It's very good," he said, making no effort to disguise the true direction of his thoughts. "I'm thirstier than I thought."

"I'm glad you like it. I'd be happy to give you another," she replied, her voice sounding a little breathless.

"So, exactly what is it?" Max asked, leaning over to stare suspiciously at the concoction.

Troy shifted in his seat, barely listening as Venus listed the ingredients. "One of my favorites. Irish Cream, coffee liqueur, almond liqueur and vodka," she explained. Then she paused, catching Troy's eye, making sure she had his undivided attention.

He had to ask, because she so wanted him to. "What's it called, Venus?"

Her wicked stare gave him a five-second warning. Then she lowered her voice to a sultry purr. "It's a screaming orgasm."

CHAPTER SIX

THOUGH THE BED was huge and comfortable, Venus slept fitfully her first night in Max Longotti's house. The comforter was one of those fancy fluffy ones that she was scared to actually use, so she folded it up and put it on a chair instead. Her window was just above a dramatic fountain on the side lawn, which gurgled and gushed all night, so she had to get up to go to the bathroom at least a half-dozen times. She sourly hoped the constant flushing kept her next-door neighbor awake.

The sheets were slick and satin instead of percale, making her wonder if she was going to slide right off the bed and knock herself unconscious. What a picture that would make for the maid in the morning. Naked Venus out cold on the floor, with a robin's egg knot on her head.

Not Venus on the half shell...Venus on a gurney.

To top it all off, the scent of lilacs wafted from a flower arrangement on the dresser. Lilacs always made her think of dead people. Not a good mental image before sleep.

No, she didn't fit in here, in spite of how much she'd enjoyed the hour she'd spent with Max Longotti in his office yesterday afternoon. The room made that obvious. As had, of course, dinner the night before.

Dinner? More like disaster.

She pulled a pillow over her face and groaned into it.

The silverware hadn't been too bad. She'd remembered

what Troy said about the salad forks. And there hadn't been an army of servants, just Mrs. Harris and a maid. The table had been big, but not so huge that she couldn't talk with Max, who sat at the head, or Troy, who sat directly across from her.

But who on earth could have known the soup was supposed to be cold, the fish supposed to be raw and the pretty fruit garnish supposed to be for decoration only, not for eating? After scrunching up her nose and wondering why Max wasn't complaining about the temperature of the soup, she'd followed the lead of the men at the table and suffered through it.

There was no way, however, she could suffer through raw fish. They might call the appetizer sushi, she called it bait. She'd—very delicately, she thought—spit a mouthful of the stuff into her napkin, hiding the maneuver behind a cough.

Troy had seen, of course. When he'd rolled his eyes in disapproval, she'd considered sticking her tongue out at him, but had settled for a haughty chin lift instead.

By the time they reached the main course, she'd been so determined not to make any more faux pas that she tried to force herself to eat the undercooked roast beef, even though it was bloody enough to still be mooing.

Venus was a well-done woman.

She'd tried holding her breath while chewing really fast and had ended up nearly choking. Knocking over her wineglass while reaching for her water, she'd said a prayer the meat would cut off her oxygen supply quickly, so she'd pass out and avoid any further mortification.

No such luck. Troy, Mr. Hero, leapt around the table, hoisted her out of her chair and Heimliched her so fast she barely even saw the hunk of raw meat flying out of her mouth and into the pretty carnation centerpiece.

"At least it didn't hit Max in the head," she muttered aloud. Thank goodness for small favors. And, thankfully,

Max had seemed to accept her claim that she'd had a really long day and wanted to go to her room right after dinner. Bad idea. She'd been trapped in here for hours, needing sleep the way a politician needed votes.

Though it was now only seven-thirty, she knew there was no point staying in bed. Remembering Max had said to feel free to use the pool, she decided to put on her suit and start the day with a little exercise. Though she considered exercise one of the worst words in the English language, it wasn't as bad as another of the worst words—cellulite. She'd just sat up in bed when she heard a knock on the door. "Venus?"

Troy.

Great, what a way to start the day. Face-to-face with the guy who'd seen her naked, made her have an orgasm she'd dreamed about during her pitifully few hours of sleep and sent a piece of half-chewed beef flying out of her open, drooling mouth with enough force to bruise her ribs.

"Just a sec!" She reached for the T-shirt she'd put on before going to bed last night, which, since Venus always slept naked, had been flung off within ten minutes. Unfortunately, she reached too far, and felt herself slipping right off the stupid sheets, hitting the floor with a thunk and a surprised shriek.

The door opened before she'd even had time to lift her face off the floor and see if she'd broken anything. Like a lamp. Or her nose.

"Are you all right?" Troy crouched next to her, touching her bare shoulder.

"Maybe I'm looking for something under the bed," she muttered as she glanced up at him, hoping she was still asleep and this was just another bad dream.

He cast a leisurely look down her naked back, grinning as he frankly perused her ass. "Perhaps your underwear?"

"I don't wear them," she snapped. Grabbing a sheet from the

bed, she tugged it down and wrapped it around herself as she stood up. "Didn't you get enough of seeing me naked last night?"

He shook his head. "Is that a trick question?" Continuing to stare her up and down, he murmured, "You know, like asking a woman if she can ever own enough shoes? She might try to lie, so she doesn't look greedy, but deep in her heart, she's dying for one more pair of Prada's."

Considering Venus was a shoe woman all the way, she found the comparison immensely flattering. "What do you want?" she asked.

She looked him over as she waited for his reply. He wasn't dressed for work. He wore a pair of gym shorts and a sleeveless muscle shirt, which should have looked out of place on Mr. V.P., but instead looked damned sinful. He'd either just showered or gone swimming. His body glistened with a sheen of moisture that accented the rippling muscles of his arms and chest.

Perfect. Here she was with hair flying in twenty directions, a serious case of morning breath and probably a fat lip where her face had hit the floor.

Femme fatales worldwide must be quivering in mortification.

"You're a little accident prone, aren't you? Remind me to never let you drive my car."

"No. I absolutely am not," she retorted, holding the sheet against her chest while she ran her other hand through her hair, trying to smooth it down. "And, besides, I don't like your car."

His eyes widened in disbelief. "Okay, that's going too far. You just insulted my Jag."

Men and cars. Who could figure? "It's too small," she explained. "Or I'm too tall. We just don't fit well together."

Now, there was an understatement. She fit in with his car about as well as she fit in with this man or with this house.

That'd be a big fat zero percent.

"It's a convertible. I can put the top down."

"Wouldn't that do wonders for my hair?"

He cast a doubtful look at her head. "Oh, yes, that would be a tragedy."

Venus thought about letting go of the sheet long enough to punch him in the gut, but figured the sheet would fall and he'd get yet another chance to see her stark naked and vulnerable. "Exactly what is it you want?"

"What size are you? Ten? Twelve?"

"Excuse me?"

Instead of answering, he walked around her, studying her head to toe. "Probably a ten…but with those hips…"

"I'm a perfect eight," she snarled, wondering how her day had gone from so-so to lousy in a two-minute time span.

He snickered. "Yeah. Right. Okay, have a good day." Then he turned toward the door.

She grabbed his arm, almost tripping on the sheet tangled around her feet. "Why do you want to know my size?"

He paused, smiling gently. "You went to bed so early last night, you didn't get a chance to hear Max's plans. He wants to take us to some charity dinner at the country club tomorrow."

Though Venus hadn't eaten much the previous night, she suddenly felt as if she had a full stomach. A full stomach on a roller-coaster ride. She raised a shaky hand to her lips. "His country club?"

He seemed to see her nervousness immediately. "It's all right, Venus. I'll make sure you have something to wear."

"All the better to spill on, my dear?"

He stepped closer, pushing her wildly curling hair off her face with a touch so tender she almost sighed. "You'll be fine. We'll talk tonight, okay? And we'll get you ready."

"Ready to enjoy eating cold soup and meat with a pulse?

I doubt it," she said as she flopped on to the bed, lying on her back. She stared at the ceiling. "I want to go home."

"Home is better than designer clothes and country clubs?" he asked, sitting beside her on the bed, taking her hand but making no attempt to move too close.

She somehow doubted the role of comforter came naturally to the man, but he was pretty darn good at it, anyway. "Home is beer and pizza. Laughter at Flanagan's, my uncle's pub. Games of darts. Betting on the Orioles." Still lying next to him on the huge bed, she turned to stare at him. "What's home to you?"

"Sales circulars," he murmured. "Meetings. New lines." He chuckled lightly. "Battles with my grandmother about the suitability of the date I brought to the last holiday party."

"That sounds interesting."

He glanced at her out the corner of his eye and admitted, "My grandmother doesn't seem to approve of my taste in women."

"Oh?" she asked, trying to hide her keen interest. "You have a certain type you like?"

He laughed softly. "The breathing type."

She slowly rose on the bed until she sat next to him. "Are you trying to tell me you're a dog?"

He narrowed his eyes, obviously thinking about it. Then, slowly, he nodded. "I suppose that's as accurate as anything."

"I don't believe it." She crossed her arms in front of her chest, careful not to dislodge the sheet, and gave him a look of pure skepticism. "Dogs don't admit they're dogs."

He shrugged. "Ex-dog? Reformed dog?"

"Neutered dog?" she said with a wicked grin.

He raised a brow, daring her to remember how totally bogus that claim was. She giggled, saying, "Okay, that one's out."

"I should say so."

Though it was early in the morning, and she was in a strange house, having a conversation with a man she'd known less than a day—and, oh, yeah, almost naked—Venus wanted to know more. "So does the respectable, conservative, suit-wearing businessman by day live a double life?"

He took a moment before answering. Then, finally, he sighed. "I guess I did, though I didn't really see it at the time. Trent is convinced my romantic troubles came about as a result of having to be the good twin growing up."

She raised a dubious brow, remembering the naked man who'd made no effort to grab for the towel yesterday afternoon. "You're the good twin? Lordy, I think I wanna meet your brother."

"I said growing up," he clarified. "We switched roles somewhere along the line. He's now settled down, happily married and soon to become a father."

"But it wasn't always like that?"

"No. Trent used to be the one in trouble for skipping school. The one who wrecked cars as a teenager. He took up every dangerous sport there is—skydiving, mountain climbing, street racing."

She began to understand. While she'd always thought it would be kinda cool having a twin, she now saw the flip side. Imagine being pressured from a young age to be the opposite of a person who physically looked just like you? "And you were the good son, great student, the suck-up rich kid who was supposed to honor the family name and make dad proud, right?"

He shifted on the bed, turning to face her. "Suck up? You've got the most colorful vocabulary."

She ignored him. "So Trent was the troubled teen, while by day you lived your dutiful, assigned role, and by night…"

He shrugged. "I snuck women into my room."

Sounded like her kind of guy. Too bad she'd already

decided she couldn't have him. Now, though, sitting in her rumpled bed, still lethargic and warm from her sheets, she could hardly remember *why* she couldn't have him. "I suppose your brother's theory makes sense, and it could be part of what's driven you…."

"But?" he asked, looking very interested in her opinion. More interested than she'd have expected.

"But isn't it possible, Troy, that, uh, you also just really…like sex?"

He started to laugh, genuinely amused. "Yeah. That's what I always figured," he admitted. "How funny someone I've known for less than a day would understand." His laughter gradually faded and he simply looked at her face. He studied her intently and repeated, "How funny."

"Maybe I understand it because I'm a lot like you," she admitted softly. "There's plenty of stuff in the world that can stress me out or bring me down. Should I feel ashamed because sex isn't one of them?"

He instantly reminded her of their conversation the night before. "Then why has it been since last fall for you?"

She answered his question with a question of her own. "Well, why are you now 'reformed'?"

They stared at each other, both realizing the conversation had somehow gotten more intense and personal than they'd ever intended. Certainly it had on Venus's part. She had no problem talking to this mouthwatering man about sex. But about silly things like family and babies and a fast-approaching thirtieth birthday? He didn't need to hear about how she'd awakened one day and decided she wanted real emotion and commitment for the first time in her life. He'd probably laugh in her face.

"All I can say," he replied, "is that if we'd met a year ago, we wouldn't be sitting here just *talking* right now."

His mouth curved into a knowing smile, and all Venus

could think about was the way he'd tasted when they'd kissed. She focused on a bead of sweat on his jaw, which drew her attention to the strong beat of his pulse in his neck. His skin would taste salty right there, his heart would beat hard against her if she fell back onto the bed and pulled him down on top of her.

When he met her eyes, his expression told her he knew exactly what she was feeling, and felt the same.

No. They wouldn't be talking. They'd be all over each other. She wasn't fool enough to try denying it even to herself.

"We'd be...."

"Yeah," he said with complete certainty. "We would."

She nervously licked her lips, wincing slightly as she touched her tongue to a tender, swollen spot. He leaned closer, close enough that she could feel his breath on the side of her face. Then he gently touched his mouth to hers, delicately licking the sore spot.

"You're gonna have a fat lip," he murmured as he teased her with incredibly light touches of his tongue.

She moaned deep in her throat. "Are you kissing it to make it better?" She shifted on the bed to face him more fully.

"Uh-huh. Is it helping?"

No. Not helping. He might be making her mouth feel better, but other body parts were beginning to feel distinctly uncomfortable. Needy. Hot. "I might have bumped myself in one or two other places, too."

He laughed softly. "I'd love to kiss all of those places and make them feel better, Venus." Then, he reluctantly pulled away. "But I guess I should get out of here. Because if I start, I'm not going to be able to stop."

For the rest of the day? Or forever? He pulled away before she could ask him to clarify.

Finally, in a shaky voice, she said, "Okay, size ten. Twelve if it's cut narrow in the hips and bust."

He smiled slowly as he rose to leave the room. "I'll see you tonight, Venus."

AS HE DROVE through downtown traffic on the way to the office, Troy dialed his brother's home number on his cell phone. Trent would probably be long gone, of course. No doubt he'd been up with the sun, out digging holes in the dirt, planting trees and mucking around in fertilizer. *Lovely.*

He'd often wondered where Trent got that earthy streak, Not that Troy disliked being outdoors. As a matter of fact, so far the one thing he hated about life in Atlanta was losing out on his mornings on the beach. In Florida he'd started every day with a run, watching the sunrise, enjoying those quiet, silent moments, disturbed only by the never-ending churning of the surf and the lonely calls of gulls and osprey. Here, he had to run down winding roads in the elite community where Max lived. Still beautiful scenery, if he counted mansions and BMW's. But not the same, not at all.

When his sister-in-law answered, he couldn't help flirting. She'd expect nothing less. "Hey beautiful, ready to leave that dog-faced gardener you're married to yet?"

She sighed. "What can I say? I've grown rather attached to those rough, calloused hands, even if he's not much to look at."

"How's my niece or nephew?"

"No longer making me throw up every morning, at least," Chloe responded. "This is awfully early for a social call."

He quickly explained what he wanted her to do. Since Chloe now worked full-time in management at the store, having finished up her education last year shortly after she and Trent had married, she was the perfect person to ask. "And don't say anything to anyone else, please. Just charge it to my account."

"Are you going to tell me why you need this stuff? Or should I use my imagination?"

"Let's say I'm helping a friend prepare for an elegant dinner for Max tomorrow night."

She snorted. "Tell me you're not bringing a hooker to your boss's dinner."

He grinned, wondering what Venus would say to being called a hooker. Considering she was one of the least judgmental people he'd ever met, he doubted she'd be too offended. "No, actually this person might be a long-lost member of the family."

"Oh? As in long-lost distant cousin or something?"

"No. Possibly Max's granddaughter."

Chloe whistled, then zoned in on the key issue. "Max's granddaughter? Someone who could interfere with the merger?"

"You're too quick," he said as he cut down a side street to the parking lot of his building. "I think I liked you better when you were dressing windows."

"Even when you starred in them?" she quipped, referring to the display windows she'd done at Langtree's last summer, when she and Trent had met and she'd mistaken him for Troy. She'd been pretty obvious about her feelings, and the displays had reflected that.

A lifelong habit of intentionally trying to get under his more emotional brother's skin had made Troy intentionally pretend an interest in her, even though she'd really wanted Trent from the start. "Look, don't worry about it, Chloe. Max is still planning on going ahead with the deal. Venus is…a distraction, that's all. Even if she does turn out to be Max's granddaughter, I don't think she'd want any part of Longotti Lines."

He spoke the truth. He honestly didn't picture Venus having any desire to pick up and move to Atlanta to run her grandfather's company. She'd know better than anyone that she had no experience, no qualifications, and would be better off if Max sold out. The sale would bring a whole lot more cash into the family, which would no doubt seem beneficial to someone who might prove to be his main heir.

"Venus?" his sister-in-law asked doubtfully.

"I'm pulling into the parking lot right now. I'll talk to you later," he said, cutting the connection. He did not want to try to explain Venus to his sister-in-law. He didn't think he could do her justice, though he imagined Chloe would just love hearing about a woman who'd called him a snot to his face.

Venus was the kind of woman who had to be met in person to be appreciated. No way could he describe the way her aggressive attitude and smart-ass personality hid a vulnerable woman underneath. He shouldn't be so sure of that, not after such a short relationship, but he was. As much as she'd hate to admit it, Venus could be very easily hurt.

It would also be impossible for him to talk about her to Chloe without revealing some of the crazy feelings he had for the woman. Lust, well, that was a given. He'd been hot for Venus the moment he set eyes on her.

But he also liked her. He liked the way her brilliant green eyes glittered when she was angry. Liked the way she didn't back down to anyone—not him, not Max, not Leo. Liked her honest ability to talk about her own shortcomings. Liked the fond way she spoke of her foster family. He liked that she didn't moan and groan about her situation, other than worrying about not fitting in. Liked the way she tried to act more tough when she was afraid or nervous.

Basically, he liked the way he felt when he was with her.

"Alive," he murmured. Alive and anticipatory, never quite knowing what she was going to do next, or how he'd react to it.

He'd never in his life felt like that with another woman.

Troy somehow managed to put Venus out of his thoughts for most of the work day. Still new to his job, he had a lot of reading to do, meetings with manufacturers and a union rep. Their telemarketing contract was up for renewal and he was charged with drawing up the short list of companies. And, of course, in the back of his mind during every decision was the constant thought about the potential merger.

As he packed up to leave at the end of the day, he asked Max's secretary if she needed him to bring anything home to the elder man. Max hadn't come in that day—he'd been busy entertaining his house guest. After bidding the woman and some of the other office staff good-night, he paused in Leo's doorway. The man's office was dark and empty, as it had been all day.

Obviously Leo had taken the day off, too. One of these days, Troy really did have to find out what the man did to earn his six-figure salary. Other than hover over Max, pushing pills in his hand and taking him to doctor's appointments.

As he exited the building and flicked the alarm button on his key chain, he glanced appraisingly at his car. The memory of Venus's words from this morning made him chuckle. "Sorry she doesn't like you, sweetheart."

A woman who flat-out told him she didn't like his car— that was a first. And almost as bad, in Troy's opinion, as telling a man he wasn't good in bed, or had a little… He shuddered.

Troy had certainly never been told either of those things. Uh-uh. Never in a million years. But the car comment had definitely stung, almost as much as it had amused him. Particularly because of the adorable way she'd looked wrapped up in the silky sheets, all rumpled and warm from her bed when she'd said it. And the way she'd looked flat on her face on the floor, bare-ass naked when he'd entered her room.

"That was pretty good too," he said with a nod as he unlocked the car.

He wondered where Max and Venus had spent their day. Last night, before the unfortunate choking incident, Max had offered to take Venus to one of the premier shopping complexes nearby. The center was filled with exclusive stores including Sak's and Cartier, that should, ideally, make any con woman's eyes light up with anticipation.

She'd instead told Max she preferred to visit Margaret Mitchell's house.

He wouldn't have pegged Venus for a big southern romance nut. Then again, maybe she saw something of herself in Scarlett O'Hara. He had the feeling Venus fancied herself a man-eater, a hard, ruthless seductress. Maybe some other people pictured her that way, too.

"Wrong." Troy shook his head ruefully as he started the car and drove out of the parking lot.

As far as he was concerned, Venus was as ruthless as a kitten. Sure, she exuded confidence and brazen sex appeal. Yeah, she had guts. Certainly she'd done something most women wouldn't have had the nerve to do... dropping that towel yesterday.

He took a moment to appreciate the mental picture.

Still, underneath it all was a sensitive woman who, he believed, wouldn't hurt anybody intentionally. How he could be so sure, he couldn't say. Intuition? Years of experience with so many women he'd come to understand the sex? Maybe even a little wishful thinking? All of the above?

He didn't know for sure, but he truly believed it.

Troy wasn't fool enough to completely rule out the possibility of Venus being involved in some kind of scheme with Leo Gallagher. But he would bet that if it came down to actually hurting somebody, she would never go through with it.

He just hoped she didn't prove him wrong.

When he arrived back at the house, he immediately looked around for Max and Venus. Following the sound of laughter into the entertainment room, as Max called it, he stopped in the doorway to look at them.

Venus and Max were sitting opposite one another over a huge coffee table, trying to bounce coins into a mug of beer. Max's face was tight with concentration as he focused on flipping his wrist just so to get the quarter to land in the mug. "Ah-ha!" the man cried when he was successful.

"See?" Venus said with a triumphant grin. "It's all in the angle of your fingers."

"Drink," Max ordered.

Shaking his head ruefully, Troy entered the room. "I haven't played quarters since my frat house days."

Venus glanced at him out of the corner of her eye. "Oh, do they play such low drinking games at the University for the Uptight and Pretentious?"

Max snickered.

"Nice to see you too," Troy replied. "Have a good time on your shopping trip?" He cast a long, studying glance over her tight jeans and tank top. "I see you didn't shop for clothes."

She stood and struck a provocative pose, fisting her hand and putting it on one jean-clad hip. The jeans fit her like a second skin, drawing attention to her long, slim legs and the curve of her rear. The cotton top was also wickedly tight and was low cut enough for him to see the tops of her lush breasts and a tempting hint of cleavage. "You don't like my clothes, Troy? Aww, that hurts my feelings."

As she intended, her exaggerated pout looked sultry and inviting, reminding him of the way they'd kissed. He swallowed, trying not to let her see how she so easily affected him. The look of triumph in her eyes told him he'd failed. This was definitely not a woman to whom he wanted to give the upper hand. She was quite used to walking all over men—but, Troy wasn't like most other men. He'd done some walking of his own.

"We didn't go shopping," Max explained, the twinkle in his eye negating his grudging tone. "Venus dragged me to that writer's house, then we went to have lunch at a terribly touristy restaurant called Melissa's Tap Room."

"'That writer,'" Venus muttered in disgust. "And it was *Melanie's* Tea Room." She turned to Troy. "Can you believe this man has lived in Atlanta for seventy years and has never seen or read *Gone with the Wind?*"

"Sacrilege," Troy mumbled as he loosened his tie.

Venus nodded, not acknowledging his sarcasm. "I mean, imagine, living in Atlanta where it all took place—while you were living here—and not seeing it!"

Max tilted his head and raised a brow, obviously trying to look insulted. "I know you told me this morning I'm…how did you put it? Older than dirt? But I must say I'm offended you think I'm old enough to have been around for the war between the states."

She rolled her eyes. "I didn't mean the actual war. I meant the movie release, the big premiere, all that stuff."

"Older than dirt?" Troy asked, again amazed at the easy camaraderie between the pair.

Venus grimaced. "The man has Liberace CDs in his car."

"Oh, that certainly explains it," Troy said. "Two strikes, Max. Liberace and a *Gone with the Wind* virgin."

"But not for long," Venus replied with a Cheshire cat smile as she sat back down.

Almost afraid to ask, Troy glanced at Max. The older man let out an exaggerated sigh. "We stopped and bought a copy."

"We waited to order the pizza until you got here."

"Pizza?" Troy asked, hearing her merriment.

Venus grinned. "If Max is going to drag me into his club tomorrow night and a fancy party Friday, he can do something I want to do tonight."

Pizza, beer and a video. Sounded good to Troy, especially after his long day, though he would never have chosen the mother of all chick flicks. "All right, do I have time to change?"

She nodded. "Grab a box of tissues before you come back." She told Max, "This is a real tearjerker, with a killer ending."

"If you ruin the ending of the movie, young lady, you can forget this idea right now," Max replied tartly. "That's as bad as people who read the end of a book first."

Venus looked at her own hands. "Uh, guilty."

Max's eyes widened in horror. "No."

"Well, what's the point of reading a whole book if it's going to have a sucky ending?"

"There's such a thing as the journey," Max said. "Oh, dear, I see I'm going to have to introduce you to some books worth reading simply for the sake of the words."

Venus snorted. "Great words can't make me like a book." She glanced at Troy through lowered lashes. "Though if it's got some great sex or some bloody bodies or, better still, a bit of both, I might be interested."

Max shook his head in amusement. Tapping his finger on his cheek, he said, "I think I might have a few that would meet your requirements. And they might even have an ending you'd approve of." He gestured toward the DVD case. "Though the ending to this is so awful, I can't imagine why you insist we see it."

Troy hid a smile, liking the liveliness in Max's eye and his obvious good mood. The man looked ten years younger than he had last week. He had to give Venus credit for that—she could breathe life into any house.

"Ignore her, Max," he said as he turned to leave the room. "It's got a great ending."

"What do you mean, great?" Venus asked, looking highly annoyed. "It's tragic."

Max covered his ears and glared. "I'm not listening."

Troy grinned. "As far as I'm concerned," he said in a loud whisper, "it's a happily ever after. Any man who stayed with *her* would be completely insane within a month." Her eyes narrowed. Before she could reply, Troy said, "Back in a minute…Scarlett."

CHAPTER SEVEN

VENUS GLANCED at the clock yet again, noting it was nearly 1:00 a.m. Though she'd gone to bed over an hour before, she still felt wide-awake. She told herself her insomnia was a product of the pizza. She knew better, however.

Men, she decided, were usually the best reason to remain awake late into the night. But the man ruining her sleep this night wasn't in her bed, keeping her up with long, slow, erotic lovemaking that would curl her toes and leave her limp and sated. He was on the other side of the wall, probably sleeping peacefully, as comfortable and relaxed as a baby. Probably naked and warm, rumpled and ready.

She groaned.

Venus had wanted him terribly when they first met, and even more when she saw him naked—whoa, mama, had she wanted him when he was naked! But somehow it was the Troy she'd sat next to on the sofa tonight, drinking beer, licking cheesy pizza off his fingers, teasing her mercilessly about the schmaltzy sentimentality of the movie they were watching, who really had her too confused to sleep.

Damn. She enjoyed being with the man. How bizarre was that? Lust was one thing—she knew lust, she trusted lust. It was reliable and instinctive, easily assuaged. Or *usually* easily assuaged—just not in this case.

But liking? A man she enjoyed being around for the sheer pleasure of seeing the sparkle in his eyes when she baited him? For the sheer joy of exchanging sassy barbs? She'd only ever *liked* one other man with whom she'd been involved. Raul, and that hadn't ended well. She'd pulled back as soon as she started liking him too much, knowing they had no future and she could get hurt if they continued.

There was even less of a chance of anything lasting happening between her and Troy Langtree. Sure, he wanted her. Sure, she amused him. But as for anything long-term? Impossible. He was not only in a different social stratosphere, he'd also readily admitted to being a dog when it came to women. Temporarily reformed or not, she didn't imagine he was ever going to be the type to settle down to just one.

Besides, with Troy, having to pull back wasn't even an issue, since they weren't really involved. Well, unless she counted their few kisses, and the shattering orgasm he'd given her. "Don't start thinking about that," she told herself.

She glared at the clock, trying to push the picture of Troy Langtree out of her mind, desperate to think of something else.

Unfortunately, her thoughts easily segued to someone equally troubling to her peace of mind. Max—another man she'd never expected to like. But she did. She really liked the old guy, with his keen sense of humor—almost as wicked as her own. During the hours they'd spent together today, he'd teased her, instructed her, even joined her in pure cattiness on occasion, particularly when it came to anyone he deemed "too big for their britches."

Max really had a dislike for condescending people. Probably explained why Leo made his teeth hurt. It was funny that he liked Troy so much. Troy, however, wasn't so much arrogant as he was confident. And in spite of his occasional haughtiness, he'd never been condescending toward her—even when he'd practically accused her of being a con artist.

He hadn't mentioned it once today, and she wondered if he'd let go of his suspicions. She hoped so. For some reason she really didn't want the man to think badly of her. And she hoped he never found out she'd taken money from Leo to come on this trip, no matter how good her reasons had been.

Now, having spent some time with Max, she had to wonder if those reasons had been good enough. "Hell, yes, they were good enough," she muttered, tamping down any uncertainty and aiming for practicality instead. Max would be the first one to say keeping a roof over her own head and helping her foster family out were good enough reasons to take money from a weasel.

She didn't, however, know that Troy would agree. Max was a much more pragmatic man than Troy. Perhaps because he'd suffered a lot of loss in his life. That made as much sense as anything, mainly because Venus felt pretty much the same way about herself.

In any case, it hadn't made him bitter, and it hadn't made him self-pitying. Instead it had made him understanding. He'd also proven to be very interested in the people around him.

Today, he'd asked her about her childhood, seeming to enjoy hearing about what an unholy terror she'd been as a kid. He'd demanded to know her favorite foods, and whether she liked roller coasters. He'd asked her about her first date…and said he was going to put a hit out on Tony Cabrini for never calling her again after relieving her of her virginity in the laundry room.

She still couldn't believe she'd told that story to a seventy-something-year-old man. Max, she had to admit, was incredibly easy to talk to, and completely nonjudgmental.

Most importantly, he seemed to respect her unspoken desire to avoid talking about his late son. It was as if Max knew Venus was poised to bail, ready to head back to Baltimore if things got too hairy. Confronting her about the man who could be her father might be enough to put her feet in motion.

Max had somehow understood without being told. He'd been content to spend the day with her, getting to know her, enjoying her company like any two people who'd just met and believed they might have a few things in common worth exploring. Aside from that little bit of reminiscing the first evening, he hadn't brought up his son at all.

She looked at the clock again. A whopping three minutes since the last time she'd checked. Finally realizing there was no way she was going to be able to fall asleep, she decided to go for the swim she hadn't taken that morning. Sure it was late—one in the morning—but Max had said the pool was heated. And he'd said she was welcome to use it at any time.

Not turning on a light in her room, she pulled her swimsuit out of her suitcase and quickly donned it. She grabbed a towel out of the bathroom and silently made her way through the house, pausing only briefly outside Troy's bedroom door.

Silence. He was probably happily dreaming about boat-loads of money and lots of willing women. She wondered what he'd think if one slipped into his room right now.

Enough.

She made her way through the big house, finding her way through the downstairs with the low lighting left on by the housekeeper, who'd watched the last hour of the movie with them.

She grinned when she remembered it. Max and Troy had applauded Rhett, while Venus and Mrs. Harris had haughtily informed them that he would be back.

"He should have married the other one," Max had said. "The nice one."

Venus had been unable to prevent a snort. "Oh, please. That's such a crock. Just like those old-fashioned romance novels."

Troy had smiled. "I'm sorry to admit I haven't read one lately. Do enlighten us."

"There was always a wicked hero reformed by the love of a sweet, virginal ingenue who wouldn't say crap if she stepped in it."

Max had grabbed his handkerchief to cover his laughter. Troy had simply waited.

"And he always chose the sweet nitwit over the evil wicked other woman who was horrible enough to admit she liked sex and had a brain in her head."

Troy had given her a knowing look. "You're saying opposites might attract, but they don't stay together?"

"Exactly."

"So two wicked people are a better match?" Max had interjected, looking back and forth between Venus and Troy as if aware of the undercurrents flowing between them.

"Absolutely." Venus had practically dared Troy to deny it.

"Even if she—how did I hear Troy put it when I didn't cover my ears enough?—drives him completely insane within a month?"

This time Troy had answered, his eyes never leaving Venus's, holding her stare until she'd felt a little dizzy. "But, Max, I didn't mean it. They were perfect together. Because insanity is better than boredom any day."

Now, slipping quietly through the sun room to the French doors, Venus though about Troy's comment. She agreed. Insanity was way better than boredom. But she suspected Troy had simply been flirting with her and hadn't really meant what he'd said.

As she walked out the back door, her eyes quickly adjusted to the near darkness. Small garden lanterns illuminated the shrub-lined patio surrounding the huge free-form-shaped pool. The bright moon added its glow to light her way.

Still, it was almost dark enough that she didn't see the man in the water until she'd reached the steps.

She heard the splash first. Freezing where she stood, Venus scanned the pool and was finally able to make out the body slicing through the water. Strong arms and shoulders lifted in a steady rhythm. Thickly muscled legs kicked efficiently as the swimmer steadily traversed the length of the pool and back. Even before she recognized the wet, dark hair and the unmistakable body, she knew who it was. Troy.

A quick burst of doubt urged her to go back inside, knowing this might well be a very dangerous situation. Every time the two of them were together, sparks flew. Even clothed, in public, in daylight, they couldn't resist any opportunity to dance around the attraction so thick between them it could be spread on toast.

Now, late at night, half clothed, completely alone…it would be pure temptation. Definite danger.

Play it safe for a change and get out of here. Now.

But she couldn't. Instead, she stood there, watching the way his body moved, wondering how a man could look so masculine when doing something as basic as exercising.

Finally, after a few long, voyeuristic minutes, she watched as he paused for a breath at the ladder beside her feet. That's when he saw her. He was nearly concealed in the water, but she could see the way his chest heaved with deeply inhaled breaths as he watched her. His eyes glittering in the moonlight, he looked her over, from head to toe, his stare deliberate and appreciative.

She still held the towel in the tips of her fingers but it did nothing to cover her body, clothed, only in the most basic sense of the word, by the skimpy, royal blue bikini.

He looked his fill, then finally murmured, "Hello, Venus."

"Hi."

"We both had the same idea, I see."

She nodded. "I didn't know you were out here." Then, swallowing, she said, "Do you want me…to leave?"

"I want you…to do whatever it is you'd like to do," he responded, his pause every bit as provocative as hers had been.

She dropped the towel and stepped down one rung on the ladder, sighing at the feel of the water on her feet. "Warm."

"Very. I love swimming at night," he admitted, looking at the flecks of moonlight shimmering on the surface of the pool. "I do this a lot at the beach at home."

Still holding the rails for balance, and still facing him, she stepped down again, until the water reached her knees. "Night swimming in the ocean. Sounds a little too much like a blatant invitation to an all-you-can-eat buffet for any great white creatures swimming around down there."

He laughed softly. "Actually, I think I'm more afraid of jellyfish." Then a look of pure devilment widened his smile. "Especially because I like to swim naked."

In the process of stepping to the third rung, she froze and stared at him. Her eyes shifted and she glanced at the water, trying to see beneath the dark surface. "You're, uh…"

"What?

"You like to swim naked?"

"Nothing feels better," he assured her. His voice was low and sultry, as smooth and silky as the fabric of her bikini.

She raised a brow. "Nothing?"

"Well, one or two things," he admitted with a soft chuckle. "But there aren't a whole lot of physical sensations that can compare to the feel of liquid warmth against your bare skin."

Parting her lips, she drew in a shaky breath, fully grasping his underlying meaning. She knew exactly what liquid warmth a man wanted against certain bare skin. Considering she got wet just looking at the man, she didn't think that would be a problem.

"Don't tell me bad, bad Venus has never skinny-dipped?"

She hadn't, not that she'd admit it. "You think I won't?"

He only answered with a tiny shrug as he put his head back and looked up at the star-filled sky. When he straightened, he swiped a lazy hand through his wet hair. Long streams of water glittered against his tanned skin, highlighting the corded muscles of his arm and shoulder as he moved. Another rush of pure desire spread through Venus's veins, warming her, making her even more achy and aware with every breath she took.

It really shouldn't be legal for a man to look so good.

"Coming?" He swam away from the wall in an easy backstroke.

As usual, when challenged, Venus reacted with bravado and instinct. Once she was sure she had Troy's full attention, she sat down on the top rung of the ladder, nearly cooing at the pleasure of the water against her thighs and bottom. Not saying another word, she reached around her back, feeling for the tie of her bathing suit top. She undid it slowly, so intent and focused, she could almost hear the wisp of the material as the strings gave way. Then she dropped her hand, feeling the warm night air brush against the bottom curves of her partially uncovered breasts.

Troy watched from a few feet away, never taking his eyes off her. He didn't urge her on, or try to stop her. He simply waited, more patient—more *confident*—than any man she'd ever known.

Giving him a sultry smile, she reached for the string at the back of her neck. Neither of them blinked. Venus hardly even breathed as she carefully untied the fastening. Then she let the top fall off her body, into her lap.

Though his only reaction was a slight widening of his eyes

and a parting of his lips, Venus knew he liked what he saw. He couldn't take his gaze off her.

Feeling very wanton, and very sure of her own power as a woman, Venus dipped her cupped hand into the water. She slowly raised it to her throat, pouring a trail of liquid down the front of her body. Sighing at the cool relief against her heated skin, she closed her eyes to savor the sensation.

A moment later, she reached in and drew up another handful. Again, she gently poured it on her body, focusing on the pleasure of it as the gentle droplets slid down her throat, across her collarbone, then over the curve of her breast.

A drop of water reached her puckered nipple and hung there, practically inviting him to come taste it. She wanted more than anything for him to lick the drop off her, to warm her cool skin with the heat of his mouth, to take her nipple between his lips and suck deeply on her flesh.

He swam closer, silently, cutting expertly through the water. His piercing stare never left her body. And almost before she'd fully realized what she'd started, he was there, holding on to the rails on either side of her. He stayed below her, one rung down, his chest between her parted thighs.

"You're wet," he murmured. Then, as if he simply couldn't help himself, he leaned close and licked away a bit of moisture in the hollow of her throat.

She moaned. "Troy."

He ignored her protest. Or maybe it was a plea. She couldn't think straight enough to decide.

"I didn't get it all yet." He followed the trail of the water, his tongue and warm breaths sending a path of pure fire across her skin. She didn't move, could only clutch the metal handrails, her fingers close to his, so close, but not touching. Just his mouth. His tongue. On her chest. Until, finally, his lips were at the curve of her breast. She whimpered as he moved lower. Then, finally, he licked the single drop of water from her nipple with one slow, deliberate flick of his tongue.

She almost came right there on the step.

"Thank you," he said. Then, with a sultry smile, he extended his arms behind him and leisurely swam away.

Venus watched, slack-jawed, ready to order him to get back over here and finish what he'd started. He paused a yard or so from the side of the pool, treading water again. Watching her, he waited for her next move, as if he'd lobbed the ball back on her side of the court and wanted to see if she had the guts to hurl it back toward him.

Not about to let him think he'd nearly shattered her with his much-too-brief caress, Venus moved her hand down her body, following the path his lips had taken. She paused for a fleeting moment as her fingers reached her nipple, moving it as lightly and deftly as he had moved his tongue. She knew he understood she was mimicking what he'd done.

She felt sure she heard a tiny groan, but supposed it could have been the breeze blowing through the branches of a tree.

Then she lowered her hand under the water. Standing on the last rung, she bent and pushed the bathing suit bottoms off. Naked, she tossed both pieces of wet material to the pool deck.

"You're right," she whispered as she felt the liquid sluicing between her thighs, cooling her where she was most hot. "This feels amazing."

Submerging completely beneath the surface, she kicked off the wall and swam for several yards, toward the shallow end of the pool. The feeling of being naked, enveloped by warm, gentle water, was incredibly sensual. She'd never felt more free while swimming and loved the way her body slid so intimately through the surrounding wetness.

When she finally came up for breath, she found herself standing in thigh-deep water. She made no effort to go deeper, or to cover herself. She wanted him to look at her. Wanted him to want her every bit as much as she wanted him.

Troy surfaced a few feet away, concealed from the waist down. "Venus rising from the waves," he said. She saw his breaths deepen as he studied her, his gaze lingering on the curve of her throat, then her breasts. He looked lower, to her waist and hips, then at the shadowed curls between her thighs brushing lightly, with delicious sensitivity, against the surface of the pool.

"You do look beautiful." His voice was thick, revealing his reaction to her. "As wanton and desirable as any goddess of love should look."

He approached her. She held her breath and made no effort to move away. Then, as his body emerged, she noticed a band of black fabric around his hips. She couldn't prevent a tiny laugh, knowing she'd been tricked. "You're wearing trunks."

He shrugged, completely unrepentant. "I never said I wasn't."

"So why did you dare me to take off my suit?"

"I didn't dare you, Venus," he replied with a knowing smile. He moved closer, until they stood only inches apart. "You are perfectly capable of doing whatever you want to do, whenever you want to do it."

True…except when it came to him. Because what she really wanted to do was reach out and tug that suit off him, to see if he was as aroused and ready as he'd been in the bathroom. As she was right now. Then she wanted to wrap her legs around him and let their bodies move together in the gentle flow of the water.

He continued. "Do you blame me for understanding you well enough to know you'd take off your clothes and swim gloriously naked in the moonlight if given the slightest provocation?"

She shook her head, tsking. "You didn't even try to stop me, when you knew what I thought."

Lowering his gaze to her bare breasts, he whispered, "What kind of fool would do that?"

Making a split-second decision, she reached for the waistband of his trunks. "Maybe the same kind of fool who would have handed you the towel in the bathroom?"

He laughed softly.

"Or the kind of fool who *wouldn't* insist turnabout is fair play," she murmured, determined to even the stakes.

Troy had only intended to tease her a little, to taunt Venus into doing exactly what she'd done. He had no compunction about tricking her into removing her clothes. After all, he'd been remembering her naked ever since the moment she'd dropped the towel in the bathroom. He'd wanted to look at her stunning body again almost as much as he wanted to lose himself in it.

He hadn't, however, counted on being completely unable to control his reaction. He'd managed to back away after one quick self-indulgent taste of her supple skin.

He'd tried to keep his desire for her in check, not wanting her to see the intense storm of need almost making him shake. But when she reached for him, when she brushed the tips of her fingers against his stomach in a long, slow caress, he couldn't prevent a deep groan.

"Oh," she whispered, obviously hearing his need and seeing the coiled tightness of his body. "You're not quite as unaffected as you wanted me to think, are you?"

He shook his head, unable to lie about something so damned obvious. "No." He slipped his hand into her hair, tangling his fingers in the wet strands. "Venus, I've wanted you since the minute I laid eyes on you."

She moved her cool fingers lower and grasped the waistband of his suit. He leaned closer, making it easier for her to remove the trunks.

"That's your answer?" she asked, apparently recognizing the move for the confirmation it was.

"Yes."

She didn't hesitate, not that he'd expected her to. Troy waited, watching her nibble the corner of her lips as she pushed the suit down his hips until he could kick them off under the water. He hissed when she cupped his ass, squeezing him tightly, pulling him closer. His wet erection slid against her bare stomach, making them both quiver.

"So we do this, we do what we've wanted to do since the minute we met, we, uh, get it out of our systems, and that's the end of it?" she asked as she slipped her arms around his neck and pulled him closer for a kiss.

He chuckled, truly amused. "Hell, no, Venus." He gently tugged her head back, still cupping it, still stroking her hair, touching her soft earlobe, scraping his fingertip along her nape. Her green eyes were wide and excited, full of anticipation as she met his stare.

"We do this," he told her, pressing his body suggestively against hers in an instinctive male question that she answered silently with a feminine thrust of her hips. "And then we do it again." He kissed her temple. "And again." Moving lower, he lightly nipped her earlobe. "And again." After sampling her neck, he moved his way to her mouth.

Just before their lips touched, she gave a helpless groan and whispered, "Works for me."

Then he was kissing her deeply, tasting her, feeling her warmth and acceptance. Their tongues danced and mated as she melted against him, her naked body warm and vibrant. The scrape of her pointed nipples against his chest nearly made him lose his mind as her hands stroked his back and then her nails dug into his shoulders.

"Do you know how crazy it's been making me, wanting to touch you like this?" he whispered when they parted for breath, hearing the hoarse need in his voice that he couldn't possibly disguise.

"Like this?" she asked, drawing his hand up to her breast, offering that perfect, puckered flesh to him.

He knew what she wanted as she pressed against his hand. Instead, he drew out the tension, moving his hand away to delicately rub her collarbone and the hollow of her throat. He built the fire, even though he knew it was already hot enough to burn them both up.

He should have known Venus wouldn't respond with similar restraint. She pushed him back until he lost his footing and almost fell under the water. When he rose again, she kissed the surprised laughter off his lips. "No more teasing, Troy. I just can't take it," she said, making no effort to play coy.

She wanted what she wanted. And she wanted it now.

God, he loved a woman who didn't play games when it came to something as elemental as sex.

"Fine," he promised her. "No more teasing. But I reserve the right to some serious foreplay at a future date."

"Deal."

"By the way, I really *like* foreplay, Venus."

Venus heard a note of something in Troy's voice and saw his amusement segue to pure male drive. Before she realized what he intended, he'd picked her up by the hips and tugged her legs around his waist. The warmth of his erection slid between the wet folds of her body, coming close, so close to where she wanted him. Beginning to pant and quiver, she arched closer, trying to take what he wasn't yet giving her.

"Not yet," he muttered just before he lowered his mouth to her breast, as if he had to taste her, now, or die.

She jerked when he captured one sensitive nipple and sucked it deeply into his mouth—hard. Yes. *This* was what she wanted, what she'd demanded moments ago.

He completely supported her weight, easily holding her with one arm as she arched back invitingly. He thoroughly tasted both her breasts, nibbling and suckling one while he playfully stroked and cajoled the other with his fingers. She wriggled and writhed against him, not wanting him to stop, but wanting more than just his hands and mouth.

"Are you protected?" he asked raggedly, his tone telling her she'd damn well better be.

"Yes. The pill."

"Good."

Then, with one agonizingly perfect thrust, he plunged deep into her, filling her up until she cried out at the pleasure of it. He caught her cries with a wet kiss as they both absorbed the sensations. Hot bodies. Cool water. Deep... *deep* penetration.

She'd never felt anything more pleasurable in her life.

"This is just the first time, right?" she somehow managed to say, almost crying at how good he felt, so thick and solid inside her. "There's an again?"

"Absolutely." He cupped her head, pulling her close for more of those slow, hot kisses that completely melted her and made her want to devour him at the same time. "Several agains."

"Oh, thank heaven," she managed to whimper, needing him to move, faster, deeper, harder. "Then could you please, *please* go slow next time. Right now I want...I need..."

She didn't have to finish. He seemed suddenly as out of control as Venus, catching her around the waist and pounding into her with deep, soul-shattering thrusts. The water gushed against her in never-ending, undulating liquid caresses. His mouth licked hungrily at her own. He filled her so deeply she imagined she'd feel him inside her forever.

And finally, when he dropped his head back and shouted out his completion, he gave her another of those screaming orgasms.

CHAPTER EIGHT

LESS THAN TWO WEEKS on the job and he was going to be late for work. Troy glanced at his watch, seeing it was after nine, and hit the gas. He didn't imagine his new boss would care for his excuse. *Sorry, Max, I overslept because I was up until four having the most amazing sex of my life with your granddaughter. Man, we did things I didn't even know were possible.*

No, he didn't want to have to explain. Especially because he couldn't think about last night without getting hard again.

Venus. She'd been incredible. He'd never known a woman as completely in tune with her own body, and her lover's. They'd read each other's moods, known what each other wanted. When to slow down, or when to pound forward. Every touch had been savored, every stroke answered in return.

After that first frantic encounter in the pool, Trent had carried her out and gently dried her off. They'd curled up on a padded lounge chair, exchanging kisses and caresses for an hour as the night shadows deepened. More lovemaking, this time sweet and languorous, had followed.

They didn't come inside until almost three. After he'd placed her in bed, Venus had sleepily whispered, "When you mentioned those *agains,* did you mean all of them tonight?"

He'd chuckled and held her until she fell asleep. Then, not wanting to risk discovery in the morning, he'd left her warm bed and gone back to his own. As much as he'd wanted to say goodbye to her this morning, he hadn't gotten the chance. He'd call her from the office in a while, just to hear her voice. Of course, that sounded sappy as hell, so he'd have to pretend to be calling to see if his package had arrived.

Venus would know, anyway. The woman could read him better than anyone ever had.

While thinking of the package he was expecting today, he reached for his cell phone. Max had mentioned another event—a semiformal party—scheduled for Friday night. Venus would be no more prepared for that than she would for tonight's dinner at the club. He quickly dialed his brother's home number.

"This is starting to become a habit," Chloe said when he identified himself.

"I'm glad I caught you. I was afraid you might have left for the store already," he replied.

"Doctor's appointment." He heard a crunching sound and knew she was eating while holding the phone. Trent had told him Chloe had constant cravings for apples. He hoped his godchild liked them since that and Doritos were about all Chloe had sent down to the poor kid in the past several months.

"What's up?" she asked.

"Did you get the stuff for me?"

"Uh-huh. It'll be there by three."

"Great. I need another favor." He told her what he wanted.

She whistled. "Very nice. I've seen that dress and thought about using my employee's discount myself."

"I think you need to be shopping in another department," he teased.

"Yeah, the beached whale department," she said. "I swear to God, if the doctor's wrong and this is twins, I'm going to kill you and your brother."

"Whoa, I didn't have anything to do with it."

"Damn right you didn't." Trent's voice. He'd picked up on another extension.

"Aw, hell, why are you home?" Troy asked. "Shouldn't you be out pulling weeds or something?"

"I'm taking Chloe to the doctor." Then, as expected, his twin tossed an insult right back at him. "What about you? Sounds like you're stuck in traffic. Shouldn't you be sitting at a desk getting fat and pasty?"

"Oh, and Troy," Chloe said, ignoring the insults, "I nixed the stockings. The shoes you picked cry out for bare legs."

Venus with bare legs. That worked.

"Tall woman?" Chloe asked, quite obviously fishing.

"Yeah. How'd you know?"

"The shoe size. Is she a blonde?"

"Redhead."

She let out a long "ahh," which probably meant something to her, or to anyone with a uterus, but which he didn't get at all.

"Does this mean your self-imposed celibacy is over?" Trent asked. "And you're out of this miserable mood you've been in?"

He frowned. "I haven't been in a miserable mood."

"Yeah, you have," Chloe said. "Ever since that dingbat got you all tied up in knots because you asked her to lunch and didn't show up with a wedding ring."

Troy was so startled by Chloe's comment that he nearly cut off a semi loaded with beer in the next lane. The driver laid on his horn, and Troy jerked the steering wheel. He gave the guy an apologetic wave and got flipped off in return.

"You there?"

"Sorry," he muttered. "Now, what are you talking about?"

"Oh, come on, Troy. You've been doing the self-flagella-tion thing for months. I could understand if you'd done anything to deserve it." She muttered something under her breath, which sounded suspiciously like *as usual*. "But this time you didn't. You took her out, it didn't work, and she got all whacked out about it. You just wanted to spend some time with someone you thought was 'nice'—for a change—and she turned out be a loony." She crunched her apple again while Troy thought it over. "What I don't get is why you went out with her in the first place," she mumbled between bites. "You must have caught some of my pregnancy hormones and temporarily lost your mind."

"They're catching?" he asked.

"Oh, yeah," Trent said. Troy had forgotten he was on the extension. "Women turn into goo-gooing know-it-alls who want to rub Chloe's stomach and tell her how to breast-feed."

He could definitely get into the breast thing, but that's about as far as he could relate.

"And men look at me like I should be strutting because the whole world knows I actually had sex with my wife at least once."

"Hopefully not in the store after hours," Troy said with a wicked chuckle, reminding them of one of their premarital dates.

"Trent Langtree, you are a dead man," Chloe said, suddenly sounding incensed. "How could you tell him about that?"

Troy let his twin sweat and sputter for a minute. "I didn't say he told me." He heard Trent's relieved sigh, then decided to pay his brother back for the fat and pasty crack. "Maybe he just forgot to turn off one of the security cameras."

He hung up as Chloe shrieked, figuring he'd admit he'd lied later. Trent would never kiss and tell—he'd always played his romantic cards close to the chest. Troy had put two and two together when the security guard had admitted Trent had bribed him to leave them alone in the store one night last summer.

Picturing his twin trying to convince his wife of that, he laughed all the way to work. Damn, he really missed his brother.

When he arrived, the first thing Troy took care of was a quick call to the rental office of his new apartment building. They expected him to move in tomorrow, but he made an excuse and put off the move until Monday—*after* Venus left.

Since he'd only known her a few days, he couldn't quite understand the flash of dread he felt at the thought of her leaving. Still, it was undeniable. He might not have known her long, but he knew he wanted every minute he could get with her. So he'd have to stay at Max's through the weekend. Max wouldn't mind. He'd been trying to talk Troy into staying on anyway. After last night, he didn't think Venus would mind, either.

Hit with a crisis involving a flooded mailing center at their north Georgia warehouse, Troy got so wrapped up with work that he forgot about calling Venus that morning. He thought about it while heading out for a lunch meeting, but since he was with the sales rep of one of their big textile providers, he decided to wait until he got back. They'd just sat down at their table in a nice restaurant in the Atlanta underground when he heard the trill of his cell phone, which he'd been about to turn off. He apologized and hit the answer button.

"Troy Langtree."

"You got a big package," Venus said.

He couldn't prevent a truly amused chuckle from escaping his mouth. His lunch companion eyed him curiously, and he turned slightly for privacy. "Thank you. Glad you approve."

She snorted. "Ha. I meant in the mail."

"Sure you did. Come on, you set that one up on purpose." He practically dared her to deny it.

"Okay," she admitted. "I did. And you went right for it, you dirty-minded thing."

"Just call me Mr. Black Kettle, Miss Pot."

She feigned offense. "Are you calling me dirty minded?"

"I would never do such a thing," he replied, knowing he sounded every bit as insincere as she had.

"While we're on the subject…"

"Yes?" he prodded.

She paused, then lowered her voice to a sultry, very satisfied-sounding whisper. "Wow."

He turned farther, almost covering the mouthpiece of the phone with his cupped hand. "Wow? Is that a good wow?"

"A most excellent wow." She sighed so deliberately it was almost a purr. He could suddenly picture her stretching out, extending her long, slim arms over her head, making her beautiful breasts rise up for his mouth, as she had last night.

He cleared his throat. "Wow works."

Seeing the sales rep glance at her watch, he murmured, "I should go. As for my…ahem…package, don't open it."

She sighed audibly. "It's from your department store."

"I know."

"It says it's from the Ladies' Department," she hinted.

He held back a chuckle. "I know."

Silence. She was probably trying to think of a way to get him to let her open it. Finally, she went for bluntness. "How will I know if I want to wear it if I don't get a chance to see it?"

"You're wearing it." His tone allowed for no argument.

Obviously not the tone to use with Venus. "Well, for your information, if it's a boring, typical little black cocktail dress, I'm so *not* wearing it."

Before he could reply, the sales rep leaned over and asked him if he knew where the ladies' room was. When he pointed, she got up, leaving him alone at the table. He knew Venus had to have heard the woman's voice. And of course karma was never kind enough to provide a bad cell phone connection when he needed one. Sure, it'd die out during an important business call, or if he broke down in the middle of the night somewhere. But certainly not right now when he had a woman on the line prepared to leap to the wrong conclusion.

"Where are you?" Her voice no longer sounded playful.

"At a lunch meeting. With a sales rep."

"A sales rep. A female one. Is she sixty and wrinkly?"

"No," he said, almost enjoying the flash of jealousy. "Probably thirty. Petite."

"Oh, thanks so much for sharing," she snapped.

"You asked."

"Which I shouldn't have. It was none of my business. I was just curious about whether last night released you from your spell, and you've gone back to your full dogginess."

He didn't know whether to be amused or offended. Knowing Venus could be a lot more easily hurt than even she would admit, he replied with honesty. "Venus, she's happily married with kids, and she's a nice lady. This is a business lunch."

"Okay," she murmured, not sounding completely convinced.

"I'm damn sure not a saint…"

"No question," she muttered.

"You wouldn't want me so much if I were." He dared her to deny it—she stayed quiet. "I can honestly tell you, however, that I'm not interested in anyone except you."

She harrumphed into the phone, obviously not believing him. "It's not like it's any of my business, anyway. We had sex. We're not lovers or anything."

That really made him laugh. "Oh, honey," he said between chuckles, "we are *definitely* lovers. We've been lovers since the moment I touched your foot on the balcony Monday afternoon."

He heard her slow breaths as she absorbed his words, took them in, accepted them. They were, after all, nothing but the truth.

Then, finally, she whispered, "I won't open the package."

But he knew she would.

VENUS SWEATED for about nineteen and a half minutes after her conversation with Troy, then she finally tore the brown wrapping off the damn package. "He knows I will. He expects me to," she told herself. The realization should have made her more determined not to open it. Uh-uh. She just couldn't resist.

When she opened the box and found a plastic-wrapped bundle of emerald-green silk, she cooed. She pulled the dress out, breathless as she admired what Troy had selected for her.

She should have known the man would never go for something as simple as a little black cocktail dress. This was a glittery silk sheath. Slick and straight, it would fit like skin. Shot with gold threads, the fabric caught the light and sparkled like a jewel. It wasn't low cut, in fact it would fit tightly up around her neck. Judging by the high slit, however, what it didn't show in cleavage, it would make up for in leg.

The box contained everything else she'd need for tonight. Strappy, high-heeled sandals, along with a green silk bra and underwear so soft and silky they would feel like liquid against her skin. The man had very good taste.

Though she was dying to try everything on, she decided to shower first. It was already after one, and Max said they'd need to leave for the club by six. So, really, she'd done Troy a favor. Imagine she had waited for him to get home from work, and the dress hadn't fit? It wasn't as if she could have just pulled something out of her suitcase. *Hmm, the red spandex catsuit or the leopard-print halter and black leather miniskirt?*

That would have made for an interesting evening.

Besides, when Troy saw her in the dress, he'd forget he'd asked her not to open it. She hoped.

After showering, she dried her hair and took her time doing her nails. As she reached for the dress to try it on, someone knocked on her door. When she opened it, she saw the housekeeper, Mrs. Harris. The older woman smiled. "I wanted to see if you needed anything for tonight."

Surprised and touched by the offer, Venus shrugged. "Well, I don't think so. I have the dress." She nodded toward the closet door, where the dress was hanging.

"Beautiful," Mrs. Harris said with an approving nod. "Absolutely the perfect color on you."

"I do love emerald," she admitted, wondering how Troy had known her exact favorite shade of green.

"Of course, with your eyes, you would," the housekeeper replied. "Just like Miss Violet."

Venus raised a confused brow. "Who?"

"Mrs. Longotti."

"Her first name…was Violet?"

"Yes, didn't you know?"

No, she hadn't known. Max had never said anything. Then again, he'd been going out of his way to avoid talking about his son, or their possible relationship. So, of course, he hadn't talked about his wife either. "She died a long time ago?"

The woman nodded. "Yes, very long ago."

Venus sat on the edge of her bed. "She had green eyes?"

Mrs. Harris's expression conveyed her fondness for the woman. "Exactly the same shade as yours. And Max Jr.'s."

Max Jr. The reason she was here.

Somehow, in the excitement of getting to know Max, and, of course, of becoming involved with Troy, she'd nearly forgotten why she'd come to Atlanta. Since Leo hadn't been around for the past couple of days to remind her, she'd almost been able to convince herself this was simply a vacation. She hadn't sat down to think about what she was doing here—to determine if Max Longotti really could be her grandfather.

Somehow, though, as she considered the idea right now, in this home where she'd been so warmly welcomed and where she'd met two men who had become special to her, she couldn't say she minded the idea as much. That didn't mean she completely believed it. For the first time, however, she was willing to concede it might not be so awful. Yes, finding out it was true would mean giving up on her dream of someday finding her real father. But it would also mean that Max really was her family.

She honestly couldn't say she preferred to hold on to a phantom father when it was possible she might have a very alive, very real, very lovable grandfather. Venus swallowed hard. "Thank you for offering, Mrs. Harris, but I think I'm covered."

The woman began to walk out of the room, but paused to glance over her shoulder. "Would you like me to do your hair for you, Ms. Messina? I used to do Miss Violet's, and I believe I can still remember a few tricks."

Venus couldn't remember the last time anyone had done her hair for her. Other than color jobs or cuts, it had been ages since she'd sat still while someone brushed and curled and put her hair up. She nibbled her lip. "To be honest, I'm pathetic when it comes to anything except a basic braid or big, puffy curls. I'd love to put it up and do something fancy with it."

The broad smile on the other woman's face told Venus she hadn't been offering just to be polite. She really wanted to do this. She stared at Venus's head, lifting a long strand of hair, and nodding her head. "Yes, up in the back, with long tendrils beside your face. Perfect with the neckline of that dress."

"I should warn you, use a ton of spray on it," she said as Mrs. Harris led her to the vanity table. "This southern humidity has been killing me and it'll probably all be flat in no time."

"Oh, you'll get used to it," Mrs. Harris replied as she began going through Venus's hair supplies. "The best thing to do for the heat is to go for a late-night dip in the pool."

Venus felt a blush rising in her cheeks, but saw no secret meaning in the other woman's expression. "I'll have to do that."

If all her swims were as fabulous as the one the night before, she had a feeling she'd be doing a lot of swimming.

Over the next couple of hours, they joked and gossiped. As carefully as she could, Venus tried to draw the woman out about Max's family. His wife. His son. The kind of life they'd shared. The kind of man Max Jr. had been.

Apparently, quite a wonderful one.

Hearing stories about Max Jr.'s childhood—the way he could set anyone at ease, make even the most reserved person laugh—she very much wished she'd had a chance to get to know him.

Venus found herself enjoying the housekeeper's company. Mrs. Harris might have claimed not to have much experience with hair, but she knew a lot more than Venus did. She managed to create the kind of style Venus had never even attempted before—namely, simple, elegant and classy.

"Perfect," the woman said when Venus emerged from the bathroom, dressed, made-up, curled and primped to within an inch of her life.

Venus turned to look at herself in the full-length mirror, and froze. She knew the face, knew the features, but felt like she was staring at a stranger. She'd started the day as a bartender, and ended it as a red-haired Grace Kelly. "Well, Fairy Godmother, I think you should call me Cinderella. Wow."

The hairdo was a mass of swirls and curls, all tucked in at the back of her neck, with the exception of two long tendrils hanging over her shoulders. Her makeup was more subdued than she usually wore, but made her face look smoother, her lips fuller and her features more refined. The dress was a dream, as she'd known it would be, and it emphasized the green of her eyes.

"Wow, is right," a man's voice said. Glancing toward the door, Venus saw Troy standing there, watching from the hallway.

Surprised, she sucked in a breath. She hadn't even known he was home yet. Judging by his damp hair and smoothly shaved skin, as well as the crisp, navy suit he wore, he'd been back and getting ready for a while.

He looked amazing. As a woman who'd usually avoided guys in ties and instead dated men in hard hats or leather jackets, Venus didn't know that she'd ever fully appreciated how utterly perfect a man could look in a suit until she'd met Troy. He was a wicked Cary Grant, a modern Rhett Butler. A man who would look completely at home in a roomful of businessmen, but would secretly make every woman there want to slowly pull off that tie and undo the buttons of his white dress shirt with her teeth.

She was no exception.

Wondering if he was angry she'd opened the package, she gestured at the dress. "Thank you."

"You're welcome," he said as he strolled into the room. He walked around her, surveying her appearance from head to toe. Then he looked into her eyes. "You look absolutely beautiful, Venus. I figured that color would be great on you."

"You're not mad at me for opening it?"

"I knew you would."

She grinned. "I knew you knew I would."

Their smiles faded as they stared at one another. This was

the first time they'd been face-to-face since Troy had left her bed this morning. Venus understood why he'd gone, but had missed him when she'd awakened. She'd almost needed that awkward morning after to try to get a hint as to where they were going from here. Were they, as he claimed, really lovers? Or would they revert to the tentative friendship they'd begun to form before last night?

"I think I'll go let Mr. Longotti know you two are ready," Mrs. Harris replied. Before she left, she took Venus's hand and gave it a squeeze. "Have a wonderful time tonight."

Venus thanked her yet again, then waited as the woman walked out, leaving her alone with Troy.

"Did Mrs. Harris help you with the makeup too?"

"Yes. Is it okay?" She cast a nervous glance at the mirror.

"Think you can put the lipstick back on by yourself?"

Knowing what he meant, she nodded and tilted her head back for his kiss. His lips touched hers gently, with tenderness she hadn't expected and wasn't quite prepared for. He cupped her cheek, then caressed her neck, all while tasting her lips like he'd never kissed her before.

Slipping her arms around his neck, she pressed against him, remembering the way his naked body had felt against hers. He obviously remembered too, and responded by deepening the kiss. Venus nearly whimpered as their tongues met and danced in a lazy, intimate kiss that sent warmth shooting through her body. When they finally parted, she stared into his eyes and whispered, "Thank you again. Can I confess I'm really glad you're going to be there with me tonight?"

Keeping his arms wrapped around her waist, he raised a brow. "You're not nervous, are you?"

She shrugged. "Shouldn't I be? I can't dance very well, and obviously my food preferences are a little limited."

"Just don't spit anything into your napkin," he said with a teasing laugh. "Besides, you don't have to try anything you don't think you'll like. Plenty of women who go to these things are too worried about their dress or their figures to eat much, anyway."

Venus cast a horrified glance down at her body encased in the outfit. "Okay, that cinches it—I'm not eating a bite."

"Babe, you have absolutely nothing to worry about." He gave her a look that could only be called a leer. "Your figure is perfect. After last night, I should know better than anyone."

"You knew that better than anyone on Monday. Remember your bathroom? Speaking of which, I haven't yet had a bath in that sunken tub of yours."

"Maybe tonight? I can wash your back." His eyes made it a promise, rather than an invitation. "Or would you rather meet me for another late-night swim?"

"Let's not limit ourselves. Both sound good." She pressed another quick kiss on his lips. "Now, I'd better fix my face."

Troy stayed and watched, leaning casually against the wall, his arms crossed in front of his chest as Venus reapplied her kissed-off lipstick. The scene felt surprisingly domestic, and it flustered her. She had to force her attention off his reflection in order to focus on applying her makeup.

"Okay," she said, squaring her shoulders and taking a deep breath. "The imposter is as ready as she'll ever be."

He tensed slightly. "Imposter?"

Suspecting he thought she'd been talking about her supposed relationship with Max, she clarified. "You know, the mouthy bartender dolled up as an elegant, sophisticated lady?"

"You're not an imposter."

"Yeah, I am. I'll be a fish out of water tonight, in spite of the fact that I look all…nice. Classy." She frowned. "Good."

Stepping closer, until their bodies were just inches apart, he kissed her temple. "Aww, don't worry honey. You're not good. You're just dressed that way."

She laughed at his reference to her Jessica Rabbit T-shirt.

"So, which is it?" he murmured as he kissed her again, this time on her cheek, close to her hairline. His whisper sent shivers of anticipation through her body as his warm breath touched her skin. "Are you not good? Or are you not bad?"

Swallowing as her senses filled with his closeness, with the amazingly tender way he kissed her face, as if she were the most perfect woman he'd ever seen, she said, "Maybe I'm both?"

He nodded. "Maybe that's why I like you so much."

He moved his lips to hers and kissed her lazily, ruining her lipstick again. Not that she cared. When he kissed her like that, so thoroughly and erotically, he was showing her the things he wanted to do with his mouth on other parts of her body.

Finally, she regained her senses and pulled away. "I'm sure Max is waiting, and now I'm going to have to fix my makeup again. You might want to, uh, do some repair work yourself," she said. Grabbing a tissue, she wiped the traces of mauve off his well-kissed mouth. He nibbled lightly on her fingertip before she could draw her hand away.

"Behave," she scolded. "We've got to leave in a few minutes, and the last thing I need is for you to get me all hot and bothered before we go downstairs to meet Max."

She should have known better than to offer him such an irresistible temptation to be bad. He took her hand and brought it back up to his lips, kissing her knuckles, then her palm. "As I recall, you owe me some serious foreplay."

"Stop." Even to her own ears her voice sounded completely soft and unconvincing.

"We never did do everything I wanted to do last night."

Remembering some of the things *she'd* wanted to do, Venus wobbled on her high heels. To get him to stop seducing her with his words, not to mention his mouth, she tried to make a joke. "If I'd done some of the things I wanted to, I would probably have drowned."

"We were only in the pool the first time," he whispered as he pulled her hand up to encircle his neck, and leaned close to taste the skin just below her left ear.

"The first time. We...uh..."

He moved his hand to the small of her back, lightly stroking his fingers just above her backside. "Were frantic?"

"Uh-huh," she managed to whisper.

His leg slipped between hers, given easy access by the slit that bared her thigh almost to the very top. "Insatiable?"

"That too."

Before she realized what he was doing, he'd flattened his palm and run it down her body, pausing ever so briefly on her breast, before moving down to her stomach. Lower.

She shuddered.

"I needed to be inside you so much that first time, I didn't get a chance to explore you. To taste you like I wanted to."

Closing her eyes, she dropped her head back, picturing what he'd said. Moisture gathered between her legs. She leaned into him for support. "What about the other time?" she managed to ask.

"Wonderful," he said before kissing the corner of her mouth and nibbling on her lip. "But quieter. Sweeter."

Yes, it had been. Heartbreakingly tender, slow and delicious. "So," she murmured as he kissed her jaw, "we've done fast and frantic. And sweet and tender. What next?"

He lifted his head to stare down at her, and his answering smile was wickedly anticipatory. "Intoxicating and erotic."

A myriad of possibilities flooded her brain at that sultry promise. Troy was a sensory man, a deliberate man. A patient and confident man. He'd give his full attention to anything he attempted, in business...or in bed. The spark of heat in his eyes told her last night had merely been the beginning of something intense and mind-blowing. Another burst of lethargic desire spread through her body, warming her belly, loosening her limbs until she felt sure she couldn't remain standing.

Before she could respond, however, she heard a sound outside the bedroom door. Troy obviously did, too. He smoothly stepped back, just as they heard a knock. Max popped his head in and saw them together. "Almost ready?"

"Absolutely. Please, come in." Venus busied herself by reaching for the purse that had come with the dress.

"You're going to be the most beautiful woman there tonight, Venus. Troy, you're a lucky rascal."

Venus glanced back and forth between the men. "Troy?"

Max shrugged. "I'm afraid I'll have other responsibilities and won't be able to stay by your side all evening. One of which is to arrive an hour early, so I'm on my way now. The car is downstairs. Troy, can you bring Venus and find your way?"

Troy nodded. "Of course."

"And I don't want Venus having to fend off all those no-good, lazy playboys at the club. So you'll stay by her side?"

Straightening his tie, Troy gave Venus an intimate look. "I can promise I won't let her out of my sight for a minute until she's back here in this bed, safe and sound."

And he'd be right here with her. *Intoxicating and erotic.*

She wondered if Max could sense the current of excitement snapping between them. Not that she worried Max would disapprove of their involvement. In fact, when she thought about it, she had a feeling he wouldn't mind a bit. In spite of his wealth, Max was a very down-to-earth person, with a sharp wit and a true appreciation for other sharp-minded people. The way he often spoke about Troy had made her realize he liked him very much.

Still, she didn't want the old gentleman to think badly of

her. Her concern had absolutely nothing to do with Leo Gallagher's demand that she be discreet. Instead, she simply found herself caring about Max's opinion.

Maybe she was too reckless on occasion. Or, at least, had been when she was younger and hungry to be loved. Maybe so wanting to have a family of her own, to belong to someone, had made her sell herself short when it came to relationships.

But what was happening between her and Troy was different. Because, whether he realized it or not, whether they admitted it aloud or not, in some ways they were two of a kind. They spoke the same language, even though they used completely different words. They had the same drives, though they were on different paths. They'd fallen into a perfect harmony the moment they'd met, though they argued whenever they were together.

They were, she believed, very well matched. Whether that equaled a relationship for a week, or a lifetime, she couldn't say. Nor, right this minute, did she much care. For tonight, at least, she was going to be Cinderella enjoying the ball. And enjoying what happened when she got back home even more.

How appropriate for a Jersey princess with a checkered past to hook up with a prince charming who was a self-confessed dog.

"Mrs. Harris told me what color dress you were wearing tonight," Max said. He cleared his throat and tugged at his tie. "I have had these things lying around for years, with no one to wear them. You might get some use out of them." He reached into his suit pocket and pulled out a velvet box, handing it to her. "It's up to you. If they're too old-fashioned…"

Seeing what lay inside the box, Venus immediately shook her head and took a step back. She raised her hand, palm out.

"I can't. That stuff probably costs more than I make in a year."

No way could she wear the dangly emerald earrings and stunning emerald-and-diamond bracelet. Fancy dress and hairdo or not, she was not cut out to wear jewels fit for a princess.

"I'm a walking catastrophe when it comes to jewelry," she said with a forced laugh. "If I dropped an earring down the sink or lost the bracelet in a punch bowl, I'd never forgive myself."

"I doubt you're going to be seeing any punch bowls at the club," Troy murmured with a wry chuckle.

"I was speaking figuratively," she snapped.

A knowing, completely understanding smile widened Max's lips, and his blue eyes held such an expression of tenderness, she nearly cried. "Refuse them if you don't like them, Venus. But, please, don't refuse them because you think you're not worthy." Placing the box on the table beside the bed, he took her hand and snapped the bracelet onto it.

Seeing that he would not be dissuaded, Venus put one, then the other, of the beautiful dangly earrings on her ears. "Thank you, Max. I promise you I'll take good care of them. And I'll return them the minute we get home."

Max nodded. "I know you will. Just avoid the punch bowl."

She rolled her eyes at the joke.

"Now, would you mind if Troy or Mrs. Harris took a picture of us together?" the old man asked, sounding slightly unsure of how she'd react. "I'd like to have one…but only if you agree."

Venus stared at the man, usually so confident and strong. "Of course I don't mind." At his look of visible relief, Venus drew in a deep breath. This obviously meant a great deal to Max.

"Thank you again for the use of the jewelry," she said as he gallantly offered his arm to lead her out of the room.

"They're as perfect on you as I knew they'd be. Your eyes, just the same..."

Though almost afraid to, she wanted to be sure of what he'd been about to say. "As?"

"As hers," he replied, his voice soft and reminiscent. A gentle smile softened his craggy features. "As my Violet's."

Venus didn't say another word as they proceeded downstairs.

CHAPTER NINE

THE COUNTRY CLUB wasn't all *that.*

It was okay, Venus decided when they arrived, But no fancier than any four-star hotel in Baltimore. The white columned entrance didn't seem quite as grand as Max's house. The chandeliers were normal size, not tremendously ornate. The furniture was standard banquet issue—round tables for eight, padded metal-framed chairs. The food she worked up the nerve to try was pretty good, but the drinks were definitely a little too heavy on the mixer and the ice.

The people, however, were just about what she'd expected. Max introduced both her and Troy as friends from out of town, nothing more. He didn't clarify that they were friends from *different* towns, and some people seemed to assume they were a couple. A misconception Troy didn't go out of his way to correct, she quickly realized. She liked that he didn't.

They were dressed tastefully and spoke serenely, but Venus couldn't miss the speculation in the eyes of some of those she met. The wealthy women judged her dress, noted the emeralds and greeted her warmly. The unattached men judged her figure *under* the dress, noted the absence of a ring, and tried to pick her up. On the few occasions when she found herself alone she came across the typical smooth-talking, flirtatious guys and their sharp-eyed, possessive dates. Seemed like things were pretty much the same with the rich set as they were with the Flanagan's crowd.

"Having a nice time?" Troy asked as he returned from the bar, carrying a glass of wine for her. She was standing near the patio doors, watching the dancers in the center of the tastefully decorated banquet room.

"It's okay."

"So far no one's called you an imposter, have they?"

"The night is still young."

An anticipatory smile was his only answer. She suddenly knew what he was thinking. Yes, the night was still young, and he'd made some rather suggestive promises about how it would end. *Intoxicating. Erotic.* She shivered in anticipation.

"Are you chilly?"

"No, fine," she replied.

"Good, let's dance."

She shook her head. "Sorry, dancing's not one of my strong suits. I'm about as graceful as a clown on roller skates."

He took her drink from her hand and set it down on a table, along with his own. "Just follow me."

She remained rooted where she stood. Hiding her absolute terror of going out onto the dance floor in front of all these people, she tried to go on the attack. "In case you haven't figured it out yet, I don't follow any man."

Taking her arm, he leaned closer. "I know that about you already. Just follow my lead on the dance floor. It's a legal excuse for me to have you in my arms in front of these people."

Well, when he put it that way…

Venus caught Max's eye as she and Troy walked on to the dance floor. He gave her a small nod, still chatting with the club set, who'd given him an award earlier in the evening for some of his charitable work. Another reason to admire the man—apparently, from the glowing remarks of the head of some committee or another, Max had spent a fortune helping to finance a summer youth camp program for underprivileged kids.

"Venus?" Troy asked, waiting patiently for her to step into his arms. She did so, immediately slipping her arms around his neck. He paused, then gently pulled one hand into his, and laced his fingers with hers. The other he placed on his shoulder.

"Look, my dance experience is the type where the girl wraps her arms around the guy's neck and he plants his on her butt," she said with a sigh. "Then they rub against each other to the music while they make out and wait for the lights to come up."

He chuckled, easing her closer until their bodies nearly touched from neck to knee. "I wouldn't mind that kind of dancing. But try it my way this time, okay?" Troy said. Then he began to move, indicating by the brush of his thigh against hers, or a slight squeeze of his hand, which way he was going.

Venus almost surprised herself at how quickly she was able to catch on. The song was strictly Muzak, but she found herself almost liking it, feeling the rhythm as she began to relax in Troy's arms. Catching sight of the two of them in the reflection of a mirror over the bar, she hid a smile, thinking she did feel very much like Cinderella.

Troy probably wouldn't appreciate the comparison to Prince Charming, who, even she had to admit, had been something of a wimp. Troy wasn't the kind of man who'd rely on a glass slipper instead of his own eyes to track down the girl at the end of the story. Actually, when she thought about it, Troy probably would have seduced the poor thing into his palace bachelor pad, making her miss her midnight curfew altogether.

She probably wouldn't have given a damn.

"You must do this a lot," she said. "You're good."

"Believe it or not, my mother forced us to take lessons when Trent and I were kids."

She should have known he'd dance as well as he did everything else. As they moved to the music, she began to count the number of women who eyed him approvingly or, in some cases, hungrily. She lost count when she ran out of fingers. And toes.

"You're doing very well, too," he said. "Though, sometime, I'd like to try your kind of dancing. You've definitely put an image into my mind." He lowered his voice. "Particularly since I know better than anyone what you have on under your clothes."

Knowing he was referring to the underwear accompanying the dress, Venus bit her lip and lowered her eyes. "Uh, sorry to break it to you, but I'm not wearing them."

He missed a step. "You have nothing on under that dress?"

She practically snorted. "Puh-lease. I haven't gone braless since a month after I hit puberty."

He sighed.

"But," she admitted, "I'm not wearing the panties."

Troy honestly tried to focus on the dance. Particularly since they were in the middle of a floor crowded with other couples, some less than graceful and prone to bumping into anyone in a ten-foot radius. But at Venus's saucy announcement, he missed another step. "You're really bad."

"I thought we'd already established that," she said, tossing her head and raising a brow.

"And I thought you were kidding when you said you don't wear underwear."

"Oh, you remember that, do you?"

Remember it? Remember her lying on the floor beside her bed, her sweet, naked butt the first sight he'd seen when he walked into her bedroom the other morning?

Yeah. He definitely remembered.

"I was kidding," she finally admitted, her green eyes still sparkling with merriment.

"When were you kidding? Tuesday morning?" He glanced down at her dress, looking for any seams. He saw none. "Or now?"

Though it was probably wicked, he couldn't help hoping she didn't mean now. The idea of having her in his arms, in public, wearing a dress that felt like silky skin beneath his hands, bare from the waist down beneath it, was incredibly erotic.

"Tuesday," she admitted, her smile sultry. She obviously knew what he'd been thinking. "I do wear them most of the time."

"And tonight?"

She shrugged, drawing out the expectation with her silence. Then, finally, she shook her head.

He moved one hand down her back, continuing the dance. Resting his palm below her waist, just above the curve of her backside, he pulled her closer, letting her feel the way he'd reacted to the provocative image her confession had inspired.

Her eyes widened and he thought he heard a sound almost like a whimper. "I think I like your kind of dancing, too," she admitted, pressing her body even closer.

"Good. Because I can't walk off this floor right now," he growled into her ear. "Are you going to tell me why you're not wearing…anything?"

"They were very pretty, but I don't do thongs."

"Oh?"

She shook her head. "A friend of mine swears by them and got me to try them once. Frankly, I just don't like feeling as if my cheeks are being flossed all night."

He couldn't prevent laughter from spilling out of his mouth. A few people on the dance floor looked over, but he ignored them.

"I suppose you had nothing else you could have worn?"

"Nope," she said, completely unapologetic. "A dress this fabulous required something more special than anything I had in my suitcase."

He nodded. "I agree with your reasoning. Much more special this way. There's only one problem, the way I see it."

She raised an inquisitive brow.

"That dress is silk. It tends to show moisture." He brushed his lips across the tendril of hair at her temple, letting her feel his breaths. Moving his hand lower, until his fingers caressed the curve of her rear, he continued. "So you'd better be very careful not to get it wet."

Her body tensed. This time, it was Venus who missed a step. He moved his hand around to her hip. "Or is it too late?"

"It was probably too late before we left the house," she admitted, her voice thick and husky.

He swallowed, imagining her wet and ready for him. He remembered how slick and sweet she'd been the night before, the way she'd cried out when he'd caressed that hot flesh between her legs. Right now, he wanted to be inside her again more than he wanted to keep breathing. "Let's get the hell out of here."

"What about Max?"

"We have two cars."

She smiled slightly. "Lucky thing."

"If Max hadn't found a reason for riding separately, I would have."

"Oh? How?"

"I have no idea," he admitted. "But I would have come up with something."

Pressing against his body, she could feel the hard-on straining against his suit trousers. "I think you've already come up with something."

"Yeah," he growled. "It's going to stay that way, and we're going to have to keep dancing, if you don't knock it off."

No way were they sticking around any longer than necessary. She stepped back so quickly she nearly bumped into someone dancing behind them.

He grinned. "Anxious?"

"Dying."

"Ditto."

Luckily, Venus managed to behave herself for the next dance, until Troy felt in control enough to walk off the floor. They stopped to tell Max they were heading out, and he didn't seem to mind at all. In fact, he went out of his way to tell them to enjoy themselves at the house, since he would have to stay here for another couple of hours. This wasn't the first time Max had looked at him and Venus with a hint of understanding in his eyes. Troy liked knowing he had the elderly man's silent blessing.

They waited quietly while the valet brought his car around to the front entrance of the club. Troy didn't so much as hold her arm, not trusting himself to put one finger on her because his need for her was so great. She appeared to be having a similar problem. She held her body straight and rigid, not meeting his eye, not until after they were in the car, pulling down the long driveway.

Troy made it about fifty yards away from the entrance before pulling off the side of the road. He stopped the car and reached for Venus. "I can't wait."

She unfastened her seat belt, leaning closer as their mouths met in a hot, frenzied kiss. "Me, neither."

"God, I want you so much," he muttered, tugging her closer. He lifted her right off her seat, placing her sideways in his lap. She wriggled her bottom against him, whimpering as she felt the raging erection that had returned.

They kissed again and again, their tongues hungrily mating as the heat in the car went from simmering to explosive.

"I told you this car is too damn small," she muttered with a wince when they parted for air.

Glancing down, he saw the gear shift digging into her hip. "Here." He slipped his hand down her body, until he reached her thigh. While he shifted her so her back was pressed against his chest, he tugged her dress up and her legs apart, then placed one of her sandal-clad feet on the seat she'd just vacated. The other was on the floor, right next to his own.

The high slit in the front of the dress fell open, revealing those beautiful toned legs, invitingly splayed open, the gear shift between her parted knees.

"Better?"

"Oh, much," she said with a sigh as she turned her face to stare at him, her eyes hungry.

He agreed. The position was perfect. Her warm bottom fit snugly on his lap. She lifted her arm behind her head and turned her head up, tugging him down for another one of those wet, frenzied kisses. His own hands were free to explore her.

She nearly purred as he slid his palm higher up her thigh. "Checking to see if I was lying?"

"I know you weren't lying, Venus," he said. "I'm just accepting the invitation you issued when you left your underwear at home."

She silently invited him again, parting her legs wider, urging him on. When he finally reached the apex of her thighs, he found her warm, wet, and open. And, of course, unclothed.

Slipping his fingers between her slick folds, he heard her breath catch in her throat. He kissed her again, absorbing her whimpers and moans with his mouth as he slid one finger deep inside her and toyed with her clitoris with his thumb.

"You're going to make me come right on the side of the road, where someone could drive past at any second," she said, sounding both indignant and excited as hell.

"Yeah," he replied, completely unapologetic. "I am."

She smiled, then kissed him again, rocking her body against his fingers. The heady smell of sex filled the quiet car, the silence interrupted only by the sounds of their harsh breathing and her helpless whimpers. She was beautiful, open and responsive beneath his hands. Completely trusting. Intoxicatingly feminine.

Entirely his.

When her frenzy intensified, he took her higher until she shuddered and moaned her completion. She shook beneath his hand, her muscles contracting as her body was overcome with her rush of pleasure.

Troy watched her, saw the flush rise in her face, and her lips part as she gasped for air. Her eyes were nearly closed, her head tilted back. She bit her lip as she shook with her powerful climax. Venus was an incredibly responsive woman, and it took all his willpower to avoid following her over the edge.

He moved his hand to lightly caress her thigh and hip. Then, kissing her jaw, he whispered, "You're incredible."

Her breathing hadn't even yet returned to normal when she turned around and reached for his zipper. "So are you."

"I think in this instance you're right—the car's too small," he said with a heartfelt sigh, wishing right now that he'd bought a damn station wagon. Or a minivan. Or a bus.

She shook her head, undeterred, and eased the zipper down. Scooting off his lap, she knelt in the passenger seat and gave him a wicked look. "Fair's fair."

When she freed him from his trousers and cupped him in her hand, he jerked up, unable to resist the touch of her cool fingers against his heated skin. "Venus…"

"Shh," she said as she reached across him, her upper body in his lap, her curvy rear sticking up in the next seat. He paused to appreciate the view until she pushed the seat release lever. Troy fell back in the car to a reclining position. He had to laugh at her determination. Then she moved over him, again sitting on his lap, but this time face-to-face.

"Hot, fast sex in the car. This isn't exactly as intoxicating and erotic as I'd planned," he told her.

"This is erotic as hell," she replied with certainty. "Besides, considering we've been having verbal foreplay for hours, I have a feeling this is just going to be an appetizer. You need to blow off steam to get ready for the main course."

He groaned, picturing all the things he planned to do to her when they got home. Main course was a pretty apt description, as he planned to feast on every inch of her long, luscious body.

Venus slid down, closer now, holding her wet opening just out of reach of his straining erection. Unable to resist, he thrust up, entering her the tiniest bit. Her eyes widened. "Impatient, are you?"

He responded by encircling her head with his hands, his fingers twisting into her hair as he pulled her down for a slow, wet kiss. "You're not?" he whispered against her lips. Their kiss was carnal, filled with promise, heat and desire. He moved again, surging a little deeper.

But not nearly deep enough. "Have mercy," he whispered.

Before she could reply, a bright flash of light lit up the interior of the still-running car. Venus's eyes widened in panic as she rose to peek out the back windshield. "A car. Coming from the country club."

She was off his lap and in her seat so fast, he wondered if he'd imagined he'd been an inch inside her eight seconds before.

He groaned, then grabbed the seat lever and brought himself up to a sitting position. "I think we'd better go. Another near miss and I'm not going to give a damn if it's Max, or the president of the charitable society, or the state police."

They sat silently, watching a car drive by, its occupants staring out the windows in abject curiosity as they passed.

"I think you're right. Let's get home," she murmured, obviously still as aroused and ready as he.

He threw the Jaguar into gear and hit the gas, turning toward Max's estate. The thick silence in the car remained heady with expectation as they drove.

He'd never known a more erotic woman, and had never imagined the intoxication of being with someone so fully in tune with her desires. He just didn't know quite *how* anxious she was. At least, not until she reached into his lap again. "What are you…"

"Shh," she whispered. "You have to blow off that steam, or my night is just going to be ruined."

He only knew what she meant when she bent down over his lap and put her lips over him.

"Holy hell," he muttered, managing to keep the car on the road as she engulfed him with her warm, wet mouth. "You can't…"

"I can," she whispered as she pressed kisses all over his erection and reached into his pants to gently stroke him. "And I am. So get used to it and get us home."

Get used to it? Get used to heat and warmth and silky wetness sucking him deeper and deeper toward absolute bliss?

Okay, yeah, he could get used to it. He just didn't know if he could concentrate on driving long enough to stay alive to get used to it! "Venus, you have to stop," he said as she wrung a deep moan of pleasure from his throat. "I could crash."

"Think of how that'd look in the papers," she whispered, her breaths tickling his sensitive skin. She nibbled, licked again, then sucked him deeper. "New Atlanta executive crashes during oral pleasure with plucky Baltimore bartender."

His laugh segued into another long, guttural groan. He pressed the gas pedal harder, seeing the exit for Buckhead, dying to get home to end this incredibly erotic torture.

He'd just spotted the gates outside Max's driveway when he felt the signaling waves of anticipation roll through his body. He was close. Very close. "Holy mother…"

"Are we home yet?"

"You have to stop," he told her, his voice ragged and nearly out of control as he cruised the car up the driveway. He was hardly mindful of the trees lining the drive, maneuvering by instinct rather than sight.

"Oh, but I don't want to stop," she insisted as she lowered her mouth over him again.

He hit the brakes beneath the porte cochere, throwing the car into Park and grabbing her by the shoulders about ten seconds before too late. Hauling her up, he pulled her mouth to his and kissed her, absorbing her taste and her frenzy.

She tasted erotic. Of sex and intimacy. And endless, mindless pleasure. Their tongues tangled and met even as she moved her hand to his lap in order to coax him into that final, body-rocking climax.

When it was over, when he was drained and spent, he sagged back in his seat. Troy waited for an outside light to flip on, for the housekeeper or a maid to open the front door and catch them in the car in this incriminating position.

Frankly, my dear, I don't give a damn.

"I'm sorry, I think I ruined your pants," she whispered.

"Screw the pants."

She smiled lazily. "Okay, Troy, that was the appetizer. But don't think for a minute you're off the hook for the intoxicating and erotic."

"Deal," he muttered. "Now, give me five minutes to get my brain working again and we can go inside and get started."

Merciless, Venus grabbed for the door handle. "You've got five seconds." She hopped out of the car, anxious to get up to her room, or Troy's, and get naked with him. Oral sex and orgasms were lovely. But she wanted more. A lot more.

Biting a cheek to hide her grin, she watched as Troy adjusted himself, then took his suit coat off and draped it over his arm. The coat did an effective job of covering the crotch of his pants. But she doubted anything could disguise the smell of passion they both exuded. Thankfully, they didn't run into Mrs. Harris or anyone else when they entered the dark, quiet house.

His was the first doorway off the top of the stairs, so that's where they stopped, by unspoken consent. Once inside, he shut and locked the door, then dropped the coat.

"Do you still need five minutes?" she asked. She reached for her zipper, knowing he didn't. She'd learned the night before that Troy wasn't one of those men who needed a lot of down time.

He shook his head and took her into his arms, pulling her hands down to her sides and holding them there. "Now we're on my clock, honey." He kissed her lightly, licking her lips in a quick tease, then pulling away to nibble on her cheek, her earlobe and her neck. "So it's time to slow down." His whisper sent warm breath against her flesh and tingles down her spine. He kissed her again, still teasing, still building this at his own pace. "The pool was yours, Venus," he whispered against her throat. Then he laughed softly, a wicked laugh full of anticipation and seduction. "So was the car…"

He almost dared her to dispute his final words. "But the rest of the night's all mine."

She grabbed the dresser to steady herself on legs that felt as limp as jelly. Her pulse roared in her ears and she moaned, certain of one thing: Troy was going to take his time and deliver everything his self-confidence had promised he could from the moment she'd first set eyes on him. Like a cocky baseball player pointing to the grandstand as he took the plate, he was promising her one hell of a home run.

"You're in control all night?" she managed to ask through harshly indrawn breaths.

He nodded, allowing for no argument. "All night."

His anticipatory expression told her he intended to use his time very wisely. He would not be rushed like their first time in the water. Nor would he be as slow, tender and sweet as he'd been the second time they'd made love on the chaise lounge.

Slow, yes. But sweet, oh, no. His eyes didn't promise sweetness. They promised wicked, sensual torture.

She shivered in anticipation. A Troy frenzied with desire and desperate to have her she could handle. Because that's how he made her feel. But a Troy deliberately seductive, painstakingly thorough and completely in control, would likely be the most intensely erotic experience of her life. She could either fight for a more equal footing by trying to seduce him until he was as mindless and needy as she. Or, she could give up, let him take over and do every delightful thing he could imagine to her.

Hmm, life's full of tough choices.

This sure as hell wasn't one of them.

"All right, Troy."

He nodded, as if he'd never had any doubt about her response. "Come here," he ordered, walking away toward the bed. He didn't turn to see if she'd follow, knowing, of course, that she couldn't resist. He undid his tie, pulling it off and throwing it to the floor, then he unbuttoned the top few buttons of his shirt.

Venus slowly approached, nibbling on her lip, nearly unable to breathe because of the excitement roaring through her veins. "Here?" she asked when she reached the king-size bed.

He nodded, then made a turning motion with his finger. She obeyed, turning around until her back was to him. His touch was deliberately light, barely brushing the sensitive spot on the back of her neck as he reached for the zipper of her dress and began tugging it down. The zipper opened slowly, the hiss of the separating teeth the only sound in the room.

As every inch of skin was revealed, he followed the path with his mouth. He kissed her lightly, nibbling on her spine, inhaling deeply as if savoring the scent of her body. He tasted every bit of her, memorizing her with his lips and tongue.

The zipper was a long one, ending well below her waist, almost between the curves of her rear. By the time he had it all the way down, Troy was kneeling on the floor behind her. Her breath caught in her throat as he continued to kiss her, and Venus forced herself to relax. To accept what he wanted to give her. To be patient enough to enjoy the delight of each step, rather than rushing to the climax, in spite of how much she ached to have him inside her.

"Have I told you yet I'm glad you didn't wear the underwear?" he asked as he moved his mouth lower, his warm breaths reaching the top curves of her bottom.

She moaned, dying to see him, to watch him, but forcing herself to stay still. "I think I figured that out in the car."

"Ahh, the car. That's one for you." He gently nipped at her hip. "And one for me. Let's check the score in the morning."

Score? He meant orgasms. Lots and lots of them.

She began to shake.

"Drop the dress," he murmured, continuing to press hot kisses across the small of her back.

With a lift of her shoulders, the fabric fell away, puddling at her feet. He lifted her foot, letting her step out of the dress, then tossing it aside. Circling her ankles, he slid his hands up her legs, touching them from foot to hip. "Mmm," he whispered, as if delighting in the texture of her skin, the way one would enjoy the sensory feel of soft velvet or satin.

She couldn't see him. But she felt each touch, each scrape of his finger on her body. Every exhalation he made against her flesh was another caress. Every dip of his tongue made her arch back toward him in invitation.

He continued to stroke her legs, moving down with such slow precision she ached, waiting to see where he'd touch her next. Finally, he gently eased her foot out of one shoe, then the other, taking time to caress even her toes. He seemed to take great delight in nibbling the back of her hip, and the curve of her bare backside. She hissed when he moved lower, kissing the vulnerable spot where her right cheek met the back of her thigh. Then he nudged one of her legs forward, pushing it up until her knee rested on the bed. A gentle push with his hand told her he wanted her to bend forward slightly, and she complied.

Venus realized what he intended one second before she felt his tongue slide over her hot, wet flesh.

"Oh, God," she moaned, dropping her head back and closing her eyes. He was below her, tasting her, drawing all the nerve endings in her body together in one wet, throbbing spot that he suckled and tasted with perfect precision and obvious delight. And when she shuddered and cried out with her orgasm, she thought she heard him whisper against her inner thigh, "That's two."

CHAPTER TEN

TROY TOOK PITY ON HER over the course of the night and stopped counting out loud at five. But, as he gradually awoke the next morning, knowing by the angle of the sun slanting into his bedroom that he'd overslept again, he had to figure Venus had hit at least seven or eight on the orgasm meter. He chuckled.

A most satisfying night.

Not just for her. Definitely not. Troy didn't think he'd ever had a more erotic experience in his life.

He couldn't get enough of her. He'd loved every kiss, every taste and worshipped every inch of her. The sound of her cries and moans had thrilled him as much as the look of heady delight on her face. Venus had been so trusting, so responsive, so open to everything, from gentle teasing to erotic massage. When he took her to the heights of pleasure, she'd playfully challenge him to take her higher—a challenge he couldn't resist.

Their entire night had been one enticing moment after another as they'd made love for hours. Troy had used all of his control to focus only on her. Touching her. Tasting her. Indulging in her while keeping himself in check. He'd managed to bring her to the point where she was sobbing in desperation before he finally took her. And that, too, had gone on forever because she'd so wisely helped him "blow off steam" in the car.

Troy thought of himself as someone who knew his way around the bedroom. Lord knew, he'd had enough experience. But last night, in Venus's arms, when he'd realized how much he loved looking into her eyes, realized that he'd never felt anything as perfect as the smoothness of her skin, he knew it was about more. There had been desire, yes. But also, he had to admit, emotion.

"Crazy," he told himself as he got out of bed, eyeing the pile of blankets on the floor where they'd kicked them.

Crazy maybe. Still, it was true. He liked her more than he'd ever liked any woman. He wasn't crazy enough to call it love, because, after all, he'd only known her for a few days. Besides, Troy had never truly believed he'd ever fall in love.

So his feelings for Venus confused him. If not love… what?

He'd wanted her from the moment they'd met. More importantly, he'd liked her wit, liked her sharp, sassy comments. He'd admired her self-confidence and her attitude. He'd enjoyed her company, been challenged by her, always wondering but never quite sure just what she was thinking or what she'd do next.

Probably most telling of all, he absolutely dreaded the thought of her leaving on Sunday.

Then again, if she turned out to be Max's granddaughter, she could end up staying in Atlanta for a while. Though Max and Venus hadn't talked any more about DNA tests or birth certificates, Troy found himself wanting them to hurry things along. "So she'll stay," he whispered.

Damn. Maybe he really was falling in love with her.

He didn't spend a lot of time evaluating that thought. It was too early in the morning to wonder if his horndog days really were behind him and he would be able to settle down to one amazing, vibrant, sensual woman. "Venus."

Missing her, though she'd left his bed only a couple of

hours before, he tugged on some shorts. He washed, then went to her room, noting the open door. Peeking inside and seeing her empty bed, he figured she'd already gone down to breakfast.

Instead of showering and getting dressed for work, as he should have, Troy headed downstairs, too, still wearing only a pair of shorts. Something Max had said during the party last night, about how much Venus loved roller coasters, had stuck with him. Judging by the look in Max's eye when he'd planted the idea in his head, he didn't think the older man would mind him taking a day off. Venus would probably really enjoy a trip to a local theme park just outside Atlanta.

That is, if she had the energy to walk today.

His own step was light as he descended the stairs, a whistle on his lips. Hearing voices in the dining room, he turned toward it. Then, however, a flash of red caught his eye through the French doors leading to the family room.

Only one thing on earth with that particular shade could make his heart speed up.

He pushed the door open, preparing to greet a sexy, thoroughly satisfied Venus. Instead, he froze just inside the door. She was here all right, dressed scantily in a sexy bikini.

And in the arms of another man.

IN SPITE OF HER LONG, sleepless night Venus had awakened early, still too keyed up, physically and emotionally, to remain in bed. *What an amazing night.*

Troy had not only delivered what he'd silently promised since the moment they'd met, he'd hands-down blown her out of the ballpark. Grand slam couldn't begin to describe it. *Wow.*

It was during their 2:00 a.m. bath in his sunken tub, when she'd been reclining between his legs—her back against his chest, her head on his shoulder—that she realized she was going to have to leave him soon. Just a few more days and she'd be out of Troy's life, back to Baltimore, back to her own world.

Whatever happened with Max, Venus truly couldn't see herself staying here in his home. If she did turn out to be his grandchild, an idea that somehow didn't seem so horrifying anymore, she hoped they could develop a good relationship in spite of the physical distance between them. She just couldn't picture herself living here permanently. This was a fun vacation, playing Cinderella at the castle. But all vacations had to come to an end. She had to go back to her real world.

Besides, she missed her friends and her apartment—surly cat, dying ferns and all. She missed Uncle Joe and Flanagan's.

But she was honest enough to admit one thing—she suspected none of that would compare with how she'd feel leaving Troy on Sunday. It amazed her that someone she hadn't known a week ago could now seem to be the most important person in her world. She hadn't expected it, but somewhere along the way, she'd fallen head over heels in...*something* for Troy Langtree.

Real love? What Venus knew about real love she'd learned from her mother and foster mother. She knew next to nothing about romantic love, so she couldn't be one hundred percent sure.

But it felt pretty darn close.

She'd lain awake this morning, marveling at that fact, until she finally had to get up and go do something. Figuring Troy would still be sound asleep, she'd donned her bikini and gone out to the pool to swim some laps.

Afterward, feeling much more ready to face the day, she'd headed back inside to change for breakfast. She'd paused when she spied Troy standing inside the family room. He'd had his back to her, and she'd hidden a mischievous chuckle as she snuck up on him. She'd paused long enough to admire the view from the rear. She'd never seen Troy dressed in faded jeans and a tight black T-shirt like what he wore this morning. "Why don't you wear jeans more often?" She reached out and squeezed his taut butt. "You definitely do some *fine* things for them, darlin'."

He'd jerked, as if startled. Before he could say a word, she'd slipped her arms around him and pressed her mouth to his.

He sucked in a breath, probably shocked that she'd risk kissing him where someone could walk in at any time, but Venus couldn't help it. Since she'd quietly left his bed just a few hours before, she'd begun to acknowledge how she felt about the man. She'd fallen for him, big time, and wanted nothing more than to be in his arms to revel in her newfound feeling.

Unfortunately, she realized almost instantly something was wrong. Troy wasn't kissing her back.

She tried again, cupping his cheek, turning her head to the side as she tangled her fingers in his hair. Then something bright and shiny caught her eye. A small, gold hoop dangled from his pierced earlobe—an earlobe which had *not* been pierced when she'd been sucking on it just hours before.

"What the hell is that on your ear?" she asked, shocked enough to drop her arms and take a step back.

"That would be an earring," a woman's smooth voice replied. "My *husband's* earring."

Completely in shock, Venus turned toward the doorway. Standing there, looking utterly shocked, was another Troy.

He was still tousled from his bed, all warm and rumpled. Definitely the man whose chest she'd nibbled on enough to leave a visible love bite—which she could see even from here. Directly behind him stood a petite, obviously pregnant, brunette.

"Oh, crap," she muttered. Pressing a completely humiliated hand over her eyes, Venus took a step away from the guy in jeans—who had to be Troy's twin brother, Trent.

Trent started to laugh. So did the pregnant woman—his wife, obviously—who sidestepped Troy and walked across the room. She extended her hand. "Hi, I'm Chloe. You must be Venus."

All Venus could do was nod and shake the woman's hand. If the situations had been reversed, and she'd walked in on her husband in the arms of a half-naked woman trying to stick her tongue down his throat, Venus didn't think she would have been quite as friendly. Her hand wouldn't have been extended for a shake. More likely for a slap. Or a punch.

"I'm so sorry," she whispered, still feeling awful, in spite of the genuine smile on the pretty young woman's face. "I honestly thought..."

"That Trent was Troy," Chloe finished. "Don't sweat it. You're not the first, and you probably won't be the last. It took me a long time to tell them apart, too."

"That's an understatement," Trent murmured as he slid an arm across his wife's shoulders.

Venus finally worked up the nerve to look at Troy. He didn't appear too happy and certainly wasn't handling the situation with the same good humor as his sister-in-law. In fact, his usually bright eyes were somewhat stormy.

"Troy, I'm really sorry. I feel like an idiot."

He slowly crossed the room, his mouth tight and his jaw set. Ignoring the other two, he focused only on Venus. Taking her chin in his hand, he lifted her face to his. "You can always tell us apart," he said, his tone controlled and confident. "I'm the one who tastes like *this*."

Then, completely uncaring of the other couple, or the still-open door, he brought his mouth to hers in a hot, insistent kiss. His lips parted as he ravenously tasted her tongue with his own, igniting liquid flame in her body.

Moaning, Venus met every sweet stroke. She pressed against him, curling her fingers into the crisp hair on his chest. Forgetting everyone else in the world, she could only think about what this man had made her feel the night before. What he'd made her feel since the moment they'd met.

Her heart pounded in her chest and her knees grew weak. She almost collapsed against him, unable to focus on anything except how much she adored being exactly where she was—in Troy's arms.

"I think she gets the picture," someone said with dry amusement. The wife. Chloe? Was that her name? Heck, she could barely even remember her own right now!

Troy finally began to pull away, pressing one or two more sweet kisses against the corner of her mouth before stepping back. He kept his arm around her waist and turned to face his brother and sister-in-law. Venus sagged against his side, limp and boneless, just as he'd obviously intended.

"What is it with you two guys, both kissing your women in front of other people?" Chloe asked, looking back and forth between the brothers. "Ever hear of keeping it in the bedroom?"

Troy gave her an evil grin. "You've got a lot of room to talk, Miss After-Hours-in-the-Store."

Chloe glared. "All right, that's enough. How did you find out? I tortured Trent and he still swore it wasn't him. Did he really forget one of the cameras?"

Venus couldn't completely follow the conversation. But she did see the sparkle of satisfaction in Troy's eyes at his obvious attempt to get his brother in trouble with his wife.

Men. What totally strange creatures.

"I can't quite recall," Troy said with a deliberate shrug. "I thought for sure Trent had mentioned it."

"Bull." This from his brother, whose expression demanded his twin tell the truth. "Don't forget, paybacks are hell." He cast a knowing look toward Venus, as if warning Troy that he, too, now had a weak spot.

Never having considered herself anyone's weak spot before, Venus found herself liking the feeling.

"Oh, all right," Troy said with a phony-sounding sigh. "The security guard dropped some details about you paying him to leave for the night. I figured it out for myself." Glancing at Venus, he quickly explained about his brother's date with Chloe in the store after hours, concluding by saying, "He's such a cheapskate. Chloe, I'm amazed you ever went out with him again."

"He has his good points," Chloe said.

Troy glanced at Trent's clothes. "Obviously not when it comes to his wardrobe. I don't know which is worse," he said to Venus, "that you were kissing my brother, or that you mistook him for me to begin with. I wouldn't be caught dead in those jeans or work boots."

Trent snorted, staring pointedly at Troy's rumpled shorts and bare chest. "Oh, right, Mr. Style Plate. What's the matter, forget to forward your *GQ* subscription when you moved?"

Chloe raised a suggestive brow. "I don't know, honey. Your brother definitely has the legs for this look." Then she pursed her lips and gave a wolf whistle. "Not to mention the chest."

Troy smirked at his twin as Trent tightened his arm possessively. "Still playing the caveman, I see?"

Trent's gaze shifted to Venus, then back to Troy. "I'd better move over to make some room for you. Go ahead and grab a mastodon leg and sidle on up to the fire, little brother."

"Are they always like this?" Venus asked.

"Always," Chloe replied. "But if anyone else criticizes one of them you're in for a brawl."

Trent turned to his wife. "Damn straight. No one tells my brother he's a pompous, arrogant ass except me."

"And me," Venus quietly interjected.

"Oh, I knew I was going to like you," Chloe said with a grin. "You've looked past his hotshot facade though, haven't you? I hope so. Because there's something rather endearing about these two, in spite of the exterior package."

Venus gave Troy a long, assessing look, knowing the others could see her frank appreciation for his looks. "Can I admit I'm one shallow woman and have grown rather fond of the exterior package?"

Chloe gave Trent a look every bit as appreciative. "I guess that makes two of us."

Trent crossed his arms in front of his chest. "Now, are you going to apologize for believing I'd tell my brother about our date in the store? Are we finished with the cold shoulder?"

Troy looked truly amused. "You really got in trouble?"

Trent glared. "I had to take a day off and fly up here at the crack of dawn this morning with Chloe just to get this straightened out."

"Oh, baloney," Chloe said. She turned to Troy. "We came to meet Venus."

"Me? Why?"

"We've been waiting for this day," Chloe informed her. "I could hear in his voice that it had finally come. And getting a glimpse of this guy so jealous he could barely see straight? That was worth ten times what we paid in airfare. We wouldn't have missed this for the world."

Venus began to wonder if pregnancy affected the brain cells, because the woman wasn't making much sense. "Missed what?"

Chloe plopped into an overstuffed chair and lifted her feet onto a footrest. She crossed her arms over her swollen belly and stared at them, like someone waiting for a show to begin.

"Well, missed seeing some woman turn Troy into a complete driveling idiot. And here you are." Chloe nodded in satisfaction. "I'm so *very* happy to meet you."

WHEN TROY HAD PICTURED taking Venus to a theme park for the day, he'd imagined them holding hands, riding rides until they felt sick, eating a bunch of junk food and stealing hot, passionate kisses in dark tunnels. Lots of smiles. Lots of laughter. Lots of that wonderfully wicked attitude of hers.

He hadn't pictured his twin being in the third seat on every roller coaster, and his pregnant sister-in-law watching over them from any shady spot they could find for her.

Such was their day at Six Flags.

"A double date at a theme park," Venus said late in the afternoon. The four of them sat at an outdoor table, eating drippy ice cream. Chloe had to sample all their cones, insisting the baby hadn't yet decided what flavor was his or her favorite. "This is just so utterly..."

"Fabulous?" Chloe offered.

Trent sighed and two-pointed his balled-up napkin into a nearby trash can. "Sappy?"

Troy raised a brow. "Middle class?"

"I was going to say unexpected," Venus said with a chuckle as she gave Troy a light elbow to the ribs. "But how about we settle for all of the above?"

"I don't think we've double-dated since freshman year of college," Trent said. He shot Troy a taunting look. "Those blond twins in my lit 101 class."

Troy instantly knew what his brother meant. "Don't."

"I owe you for the store."

"Say one more word and I'll tell Chloe about Penny Marsden."

"Penny Marsden?" Chloe said, perking right up.

Trent groaned. "Jeez, that was eighth grade!"

"Good grief, Troy. Don't tell me Trent was as much of an early Don Juan as you," Venus muttered. "Two horny fourteen-year-old twins on the prowl? Your parents must have gone nuts."

Chloe sat up straight and put her hands flat on her belly, as if protecting the ears of her unborn child. "Fourteen?"

Trent looked like he wanted to reassure her, but Troy's confident smirk made him shut his mouth, just as he knew it would. His ten-minutes-older brother hated like hell to admit Troy had beat him at anything, including losing his virginity.

"Trent?" Chloe prompted.

"Aw, hell," his brother finally admitted. "So, for once, he did something first. I was sixteen."

"And a good thing, too," Venus said. "You were quite busy crashing cars, from what I hear. You didn't need the succession of women sneaking out of your room at night."

"Cars?" Chloe asked, fisting a hand and putting it on her hip. "As in *plural?*"

"From his street racing," Venus informed the other woman helpfully. Troy began to feel a hint of sympathy for his brother, who was going to have a really ticked-off, emotionally whacked-out pregnant woman to deal with when they got home.

This time Chloe almost snarled. "Street racing? Dammit, Trent Langtree, you said you never drove fast!"

"You're dead meat," Trent promised, looking ready to send some fists flying in Troy's direction for telling Venus about his wild teenage years.

"Venus," Troy asked, standing and tossing his napkin in the trash. "Care to risk death on the Superman ride again?"

Casting a quick, assessing look between Trent and Chloe, Venus nodded and leapt to her feet. "Less dangerous than here!"

Wrapping her fingers trustingly in his, she willingly followed him away from the other couple.

They spent the rest of the afternoon and early evening at the park, heading home at dusk. Troy couldn't remember when he'd had a better, happier, less stressful day.

It wasn't just being at a park designed for good times and fun. They'd all instantly taken to one another, and the four of them had spent most of the day in the kind of comfortable, friendly companionship which usually required years to cultivate. Trent and Chloe obviously really liked Venus. And she seemed to like them, too. She also seemed to like being away from the estate, able to be herself and not worry about wearing the right clothes or using the correct eating utensil.

The only serious moment came in the car when they were driving back to Max's estate late that night. "I'm so sorry we have to leave tonight on the red-eye," Chloe said. "I'd love to visit with you some more, Venus. Next time."

"Yes," Venus agreed. "You'll have to come up to Baltimore. We'll catch an Orioles game."

"Baltimore?" Trent said, looking surprised. "You're not staying in Atlanta?"

Troy tensed, waiting for her answer.

"No, of course not. This is just a vacation. A...trial run."

"But I thought you'd be staying here with your grandfather," Chloe continued. "He'd love that, I'm sure."

Beside her in the car, which they'd borrowed from Max for the drive to the park since his was too small, Troy waited to see what she'd say. They hadn't spoken about Venus's possible relationship to Max since the day she'd arrived, both seeming to want to take things as they came.

"I don't know how much Troy has told you," Venus explained.

"Not much," Troy assured her.

She took his hand, lacing her fingers with his on the vacant seat between them. "I don't honestly know if Max is my grandfather. You know, I suppose, about his son?"

Chloe didn't, but Trent and Troy told her about the man's death. When they'd finished, she said, "So Leo has found some kind of evidence that made him believe you were Max Jr.'s long-lost baby, making you Mr. Longotti's granddaughter."

"Yes," Venus said. "But, to be honest, when I got here Monday, I truly didn't want him to be."

Just as Troy had suspected. He wondered if she'd explain why.

"Really?" Chloe asked, not pressing for more information.

Venus nodded. "It seemed easier to not believe it. You see, I've held on to this fantasy for a long time."

Trent leaned forward from the back seat, where he sat with his wife. "Fantasy?"

Venus's answering laughter was soft and sounded almost sad. "I've thought about my father since I was a little girl. Who he was, what he looked like, where he lives now. I guess I convinced myself that one day he was going to show up at my door, having just found out about me."

Troy tried to focus on the highway and not on the hint of hurt in the voice of someone he truly cared about.

"When Leo showed up at the bar last week with his crazy story, I…well, my first reaction was to wish I'd never laid eyes on him. I didn't want to believe it."

Troy was about to ask why she'd agreed to come to Atlanta with the man, if that were the case, but Chloe spoke first. "And now? Have you changed your mind? This morning, it seemed like you and Max were very close."

"He's great," Venus admitted. "I've never known anyone who could make me laugh so hard or who had more common sense. He's incredibly generous. And while he can be caustic and tough, he's much more vulnerable than he'd ever want anyone to realize."

Trent could sense her smile, though he couldn't see her face well in the shadowy confines of the car. "You love him," he stated, believing what he'd said, "even though you just met him."

She didn't deny it. "Max is a wonderful man. I wish I'd gotten to meet him long ago."

The woman had opened up her heart and let Max in after only a few days. She'd let her feelings for him ease into the empty part of herself that had been reserved for her lost father for decades. For all her toughness, Venus had again confirmed her innate sensitivity and capacity to care.

Troy had to ask. "So, Venus, if you've come to that realization…do you plan to stay? Permanently?"

After a long pause, when she glanced out the window to watch the approaching lights of oncoming cars, she softly murmured, "I honestly don't know, Troy."

He didn't lose heart—well, that wasn't correct since he suspected he'd already *lost* his heart. To her. But it was only Thursday night. He had three more days to change her mind.

Because, if he had his way, Venus wasn't going anywhere.

CHAPTER ELEVEN

ON FRIDAY, Venus agreed to spend the entire day with Max. Troy had gone into the office early, saying he needed a day of work to recover from their trip to the theme park. Troy's teasing hadn't disguised his uncertainty. It had been evident since last night when he'd asked whether she'd be staying on in Atlanta. He hadn't asked her to. He'd said nothing to make her think he wanted her to, but she suspected he did.

How she could be so sure, she honestly couldn't say. She didn't delude herself that he'd fallen madly in love with her and couldn't bear for her to leave. They had a serious case of the hots going on. Their physical relationship was the most intense she'd experienced in her life. Venus wasn't ready for that to end any more than Troy seemed to be.

Late during the previous night, however, as she lay in his arms exchanging lazy kisses and whispers, she'd again acknowledged there was more than desire—on both their parts.

Guys who wanted only to nail a woman didn't typically introduce her to their families or take her on the floorless coaster over and over until they both thought they were going to be sick. Women who wanted only sex didn't automatically feel cherished because of the man's hand on her waist or his knowing smile.

He liked her as much as she liked him. With her track record for dating losers, finding a man she just enjoyed being with—holding hands or sharing a cold bottle of water on a hot day—left her confused. She felt the way she had with Raul last year. Attraction had segued to liking. Then the realization that they could never have anything more permanent had made her walk away. She'd understood she couldn't risk losing her heart over someone moving in a different direction in his life.

Like Troy? Yeah. Like Troy.

Considering how soon she'd started feeling this way, she suspected Troy was a much bigger threat to her heart than Raul ever could have been. She'd *thought* she might eventually love Raul. She already *knew* she was falling in love with Troy. Not good when she was going back to Maryland in two days.

So stay here, a little voice told her.

A few days ago, she would have said no, absolutely not. Now she had to wonder. What was there to go back to in Baltimore? She had no job, not much of a home. Her friendships were strong enough to last in spite of distance and time between visits.

Max might well be her only living blood relative—a relative she'd liked on sight and now could honestly say she cared deeply about, as Troy had suggested last night. Max wasn't a young man. At times over the past few days he'd seemed tired and a bit confused, once even calling her Violet. Yesterday morning he'd mentioned Max Jr. being in the backyard playing ball, as if mixing up the events of the present with events forty years ago.

Who knew how long she'd have to enjoy him, her final connection to the father she'd never seen? If she left, she might be leaving behind much more than she'd ever expected to find when she'd boarded that plane from Baltimore on Monday morning.

As she walked outside to meet Max for breakfast, she paused in the doorway. He sat at a patio table beside the pool, sipping his tea, watching a pair of blue jays winging in and out of the leaves of a huge magnolia tree. Looking beyond him to the pool and the rolling lawn, she pictured what Max was seeing.

Max Jr.

On a sunny summer morning like this, he'd be swimming or perhaps playing baseball—breaking a window, getting scolded by his mother, and secretly praised for his swing by his father.

She could imagine him, visualize him, almost hear his voice. She was beginning to know him through Max's loving memories. Maybe in allowing *his* father into her heart, she'd be able to know her own father. And finally let the fantasy fade away.

Feeling more sure than she'd ever felt about anything, Venus walked to the table and kissed Max on the cheek. "Good morning."

Looking incredibly pleased, he took her hand. "Good morning to you. Ready for that shopping trip?"

Venus poured herself a glass of raspberry iced tea and shook her head. Then she told him what she wanted to do today.

He blinked twice, glancing down at his own clenched fingers. Max's voice shook slightly as he asked, "You're sure?"

Taking a deep breath, she nodded. "I am. If you don't mind, I'd really like to see some photos of Max Jr. and your wife."

He nodded again, still averting his gaze. As he reached for his cup, Venus touched his hand. When he looked up and met her stare, she saw moisture in his eyes. "And Max, if it's all right with you, I'd like to go ahead and schedule that DNA test."

THE SUN WAS BRIGHT in her room the next morning when Venus awoke. She noticed one thing immediately—the weight of Troy's arm across her waist. "Troy, you overslept," she hissed, glancing toward her bedroom door.

Max might like the idea of her and Troy as a couple. He'd hinted at it again last night when the three of them had blown off the party and gone out to play miniature golf instead. But she didn't know how he'd feel about finding out they were already lovers…and had been since her second day in town!

She giggled, remembering how offended Max had been in the limo on the way to the party when she'd claimed golf was not a sport, but a way for rich guys to pretend to be athletic. Ordering the driver to detour to the nearest mini course, he'd challenged her to a game. Ten bucks a hole. He'd beaten the pants off her, as had Troy. But at least neither of them had collected on the bet.

Lying in Troy's arms, she still couldn't imagine what the other golfers—a mix of families with kids begging for tokens for the nearby video game, and teen couples on first dates—had thought of them. Two men in tuxes, her in the glorious red silk dress Troy had gotten for her, laughing as they argued their way through the course.

"What time…." Troy mumbled.

"It's after eight."

"Saturday," he replied, not even opening his eyes.

"Max's golf morning, which we know he takes very seriously. He could be knocking on my door to say goodbye at any moment."

That got his eyes open. He sat up in bed, giving her a quick good morning kiss and a slower goodbye one. "I think we need to stop sneaking around and come clean with Max," he whispered against her lips before finally pulling away to get out of bed.

"I know," she agreed. "But let's tell him, not *show* him." She couldn't resist casting an appreciative glance over his naked body. She sighed audibly, wanting him again already.

"Maybe I'd better take the back way out." He quickly donned a pair of briefs, which didn't fit well considering his body's reaction to her stare. "It would be bad enough running into anyone coming out of your room. I don't think there's any way I could hide *this*."

"I'd love to help you *hide* it," she whispered with a saucy smile, eyeing the morning erection straining against the cotton.

"Oh, please," he said with an exaggerated rolling of the eyes. "Spare me the 'hide the salami' jokes, especially since you just kicked me out of your bed."

She lifted one shoulder, dropping the sheet lower until one breast was completely bared. "I didn't exactly kick you out…"

"Yeah, babe, you did, so don't go trying to tempt me back into it." He leaned down to give her one more hungry kiss and a playful stroke of her breast. She sighed and arched toward him, deepening the kiss, knowing she was tempting him to stay.

He finally pulled away with a groan and a softly muttered curse. "You're really bad," he said as he grabbed his clothes. "And damn, I'm crazy about you." Without another word after his shocking announcement, he grabbed his clothes. After crossing the room, he opened the person-high window. He waved and grinned his wicked, heartbreaking grin before ducking out onto the balcony connecting their two rooms.

After Troy left, Venus lay still for a full five minutes, thinking about what he'd said. Crazy about her, huh? She could live with that. For now, anyway.

A few moments later, she got up and showered. She spent several minutes under the pounding jets mentally reliving their long, sensual night. Finally, knowing she was going to get herself hopelessly aroused if she didn't knock it off, she forced herself to focus on something else. Like the previous day.

She and Max had spent hours going through album after album. She'd loved hearing every story as Max shared his memories of his family. Venus had never considered herself the emotional type. She didn't cry at weddings—except when she thought of the bucks the poor bride's parents had to put out for a one-day party with a bunch of near strangers too cheap to bring good gifts. Ditto on movies—with the exception of *Gone with the Wind.*

But seeing Max's life unfold on the pages of his albums, she'd cried. Particularly when gazing into the vivid green eyes of Violet Messina, and Max Jr. Those eyes, more than anything else, had convinced her she'd made the right decision about the DNA test. Staring into those photos had been like staring into a mirror.

At some point, while examining the photos, or perhaps while laughing nose to nose with Troy when he'd picked her up to swing her around after she'd made her one decent shot in mini golf, or maybe even twenty minutes ago when he'd told her he was crazy about her, she'd come to a decision.

She was staying in Atlanta. For herself. For Max.

And for Troy.

After drying off, she dressed and began to brush out her hair. When she heard a knock on her door, she figured Max was popping in. She was surprised to see Leo Gallagher instead. "The prodigal nephew returns," she said. "I thought you were Max."

"I passed him downstairs as he left for his golf game."

Venus felt a twinge of disappointment that he hadn't stopped in for a morning chat. Continuing to brush her hair, she glanced at Leo and raised a brow. "You've been rather scarce."

"And you've been rather busy," he said, a small smile on his lips. The smile instantly put her on guard.

"What do you mean?"

"I noticed someone leaving through your window a little while ago when I pulled up."

Great. Leo had seen Troy. "I know we agreed on discreet…"

"Don't worry about it," he said. Not waiting for an invitation, he sat in a delicate antique chair in the corner. "I have to admit, with his reputation and your appearance, I rather suspected the two of you would…get along."

He didn't seem to mind. That bothered Venus more than anything else the man had said. It seemed so…un-Leo-like.

"So, you told Uncle Max you want the DNA test?"

She nodded warily. "Is that all right with you?"

Leo shrugged. "It's not necessary, but I have got someone lined up to take care of it."

Not entirely sure she wanted to know, she quietly asked, "Why is it not necessary, Leo?"

A slow satisfied smile crossed his lips. "Well, dear, because I have medical records listing your blood type and Max Jr.'s. I already know the truth. I've known all along."

She waited, her heart skipping a beat as she suddenly suspected what he was about to say.

"You are *not* Max Longotti's granddaughter."

AS TROY SHOWERED, he wondered if Max had already stopped in to say goodbye to Venus. He hadn't heard the older man walking by his room, but suspected he wouldn't leave without a quick visit. Frankly, judging by the buoyant mood they'd both been in last night, he had a feeling the two of them had reached some kind of understanding about their relationship.

And that could mean Venus wasn't going home tomorrow.

He didn't stop to think too much about the big smile that possibility put on his face as he dried off and got dressed. He'd evaluate the feeling later, once he was sure she wasn't flying out of his life within twenty-four hours.

Wanting to see her again already, but not wanting to interrupt if she was with Max, he decided to visit her the same way he'd left. He opened his window and stepped out onto the balcony. The curtains flowing in the gentle morning breeze told him her window was still open as well.

As he approached, he was easily able to distinguish two voices—Venus's and a man's. Assuming she was with Max, he decided to leave them alone. Then he paused, hearing a word sounding like the kind often used by sailors.

It had been spoken by Venus.

"You selfish bastard," she continued, sounding furious.

"Don't take the high road," the man replied.

Troy recognized the voice of Leo Gallagher. Leaning closer, he saw the other man sitting stiffly in Venus's room.

"You can't tell me you don't want the money."

"I *don't* want the money," she snapped.

Money? Troy's jaw tightened.

"You wanted it a week ago, didn't you? You were quick enough to cash my check and come down here, even though you didn't believe what I'd told you was true."

"Shows how right my instincts were," Venus said. Troy couldn't see her—she obviously stood in a corner near the bathroom, out of his range of sight. "I can't believe you knew all along I couldn't be Max Jr.'s daughter and did this anyway. Or that I was stupid enough to cash your check."

Troy drew in a deep breath, shaking his head as a wave of disappointment washed over him. Venus had been paid to come here. No matter how angry she was at Leo now, she'd accepted his money to meet Max. Troy couldn't help feeling betrayed. Not so much because she'd done it but because she'd been lying about it. In spite of what had happened between them, she hadn't trusted him enough to come clean.

"Get out, Leo. I'm packing up and going home. I will

not be used by you so you can get your grubby hands on Max's business."

The man didn't seem concerned. "Be sure to tell him goodbye before you leave."

"You bet I will." Her words were almost snarled. "I'll be sure to tell him all about his loyal nephew, who brought me down here to try to run a scam. What did you think, that you'd talk me into convincing him not to sell to Troy's family?"

Troy wondered the same thing. He frankly couldn't see what Leo had to gain out of this whole scheme, with the exception of time. A DNA test would have proven the truth, and Max would still have sold. It just might have taken longer.

"That was one option," Leo said. "It still can be, if you stop and think of the money you could make. I have someone lined up to run the DNA test in our favor. You can stay and live happily as Max's granddaughter. Make him happier than he's been in years." Though he was obviously trying to appear concerned, he was unable to hide the note of self-satisfaction in his voice.

"The two of you can be together and you can convince Max to retire, keeping the company in the family—with me at the helm."

"What was the other option?" Venus asked, sounding weary.

Leo appeared to visibly relax, and Troy wondered if something in Venus's expression had led him to think he was getting through to her.

The man obviously didn't know who he was dealing with.

"Many people know about Max's medical problems, including the board of Longotti Lines." Leo stood and approached the window, though not coming close enough to see Troy outside. "He's also not in the best emotional shape. But he's grown very fond of you, hasn't he? Pinned all his hopes and dreams on your pretty shoulders. Finding out you're not his little Violet, such a severe disappointment...well, he could break down. *Again*."

Troy closed his eyes briefly, remembering what Mrs. Harris had let slip the other evening about Max's previous breakdown. His fingers clenched into fists and he wanted nothing more than to slam them into Leo Gallagher's self-serving face.

"You cruel man." Venus's voice was low and thick with emotion. Troy knew her well enough by now to recognize the fury buried in the sadness. "I have to say, in spite of the things I've seen in my life, I can still be surprised by how damn vicious some people can be."

Leo continued as if she hadn't spoken. "I don't think I'll have much problem convincing the voting board members Max isn't competent to make major decisions about the future of the company." He shrugged in satisfaction. "So, you see, Ms. Messina, either way, I'll get what I want. All that remains to be seen is whether you care enough to keep an old man happy in his final years. Or if you prefer to tell him the truth and make him fall apart, after which I'll step in and take over the company anyway."

"I won't lie to a man who's been nothing but kind to me."

"Suit yourself," Leo replied. "By all means, tell him the truth. Might be quicker that way." He stood and plucked an invisible piece of lint off his navy sport jacket, still seeming perfectly content with the way his plan had progressed.

"You won't get away with it, Leo. I'll tell the board what you did," she said, her voice regaining its steely tone.

Leo chuckled. "Who would believe you? I have the cancelled check you cashed. I was your dupe, the pawn of a grubby foster kid turned bartender who tried to con us all. Poor Uncle Max."

Troy had heard enough. Pushing through the billowing

curtains, he entered Venus's bedroom and strode across the room. He grabbed Leo by the collar of his designer jacket.

"Langtree!"

"They'll believe her," Troy snarled. "Because I heard every miserable word, you lousy little prick."

Before Leo could respond, before Troy could even give the man a good hard shake, the bedroom door was pushed in from the hall. "As did I."

Venus, who still couldn't quite believe Troy had just stalked in here like an avenging god, watched in dismay as Max entered, looking pale and shaken. And very, very angry.

"Max, how long have you been standing there?" She went to his side to take his arm.

He patted her hand. "Long enough. Don't worry, dear. I'm fine." He turned to his nephew. "Get out of my house. Remove your belongings from my offices. With four witnesses, I think we'll be able to convince the board that you're completely unsuitable for any type of responsible position."

Venus followed Max's glance toward the doorway, seeing Mrs. Harris standing there. She'd obviously heard every word, too.

"Uncle Max, I…" Leo attempted.

Max held up a steady, unshaking hand, silently ordering him to stop. "Out. Right now, before I call the police."

Obviously knowing he couldn't twist this situation to suit himself, Leo cast a glare at Venus. He swept out of the room, brushing past Mrs. Harris. The housekeeper turned to follow him, her arms crossed over her chest. She appeared to want to ensure Leo didn't pick up any souvenirs as he left.

When the three of them were alone in the room, Venus slid her arm around Max's waist. "I feel so awful."

"None of this was your fault, Venus. You were used as much as I was by the slimy weasel. I'm so glad we're not actually blood relatives. Never could stand the little peckerwood."

Venus bit the corner of her lip.

"I was this close to introducing him to my fist," Troy said. "I don't think I've ever felt such violence toward anyone in my life."

"Just as well you didn't," Max replied succinctly. "He'd have found the nearest ambulance chaser and sued you but good."

Seeing the man trying so hard to joke, to reassure her, Venus felt tears rise in her eyes. "I'm so sorry, Max." He shrugged, obviously about to tell her again it wasn't her fault. She hurried to explain. "What I mean is, I'm so sorry I'm not *her.*" Her voice broke and she cleared her throat. "I wish more than anything that I was really your granddaughter."

"So do I, honey," he murmured, still patting her hand. "Can I confess that in my heart, you always will be?"

Troy edged toward the door, probably thinking they wanted to be alone. "I think I'd better go down to the office and make some phone calls. Leo's going to try to twist this his way and we need to cut his legs out from under him right up front."

"Let me start here at the house with some of the long-standing members of the board," Max said. He glanced back and forth between Venus and Troy. "I should go downstairs now and make sure Mrs. Harris isn't having any trouble with Leo. Troy, I'll see you shortly?" Before he left, he pressed a kiss to Venus's temple. "Come visit me later, when you're feeling better, all right? We'll talk things over."

She nodded, blinking rapidly. She didn't want him to see her cry, not when he'd been so strong. As soon as he was out of the room, with the door shut behind her, however, she felt the moisture on her cheeks.

Without a word, Troy pulled her into his arms, twisting his fingers into her hair to cup her head and hold her tight.

"It's all right," he whispered. "Max is going to be okay. Leo didn't give him enough credit—he's a tough old guy."

She let the tears come, crying for Max. For herself. For the fantasy father she'd let go of while she'd tried to embrace an unexpected gift of family. Now that family had been yanked away too, leaving her with nothing.

Though she was glad she'd gotten to meet Max, part of her wished she'd never come. Once again, love seemed to be a blessing and a curse. She'd begun to love the old man. And, like nearly everyone else she'd ever loved, she'd lost him. At this moment, she couldn't say whether the emotion was worth the heartache.

Troy tugged her down to sit beside him on the bed. She kept her face buried in his neck, sucking up his comfort and warmth like a kid burrowing into a parent.

"Venus, baby, don't," he whispered, stroking her hair, her back, and kissing her temple. "Max doesn't blame you."

"He should. I should have trusted my instincts about Leo."

He shook his head, and finally Venus took a deep breath and pulled away. They remained on the bed, face-to-face. Troy looked concerned and understanding, but she thought there was also a hint of something else in his eyes. It was as if a veil had dropped over them and just a bit of the warmth with which he'd looked at her before had been lost.

"Did you hear everything?" she asked.

He nodded. "I knew Leo had you all wrong and you wouldn't do it. Once you began to love Max, you couldn't have betrayed him."

Though his trust warmed her, she again noted something remaining unsaid. Then she began to understand. "But before I got to know him…I took Leo's money."

Troy stiffened so slightly, she almost wondered if she imagined it. But she knew she hadn't.

"Max isn't angry about the money."

"You are."

He didn't answer with words. His eyes were telling enough.

"I shouldn't have lied about it," she admitted.

"I wish you hadn't. I'd hoped you'd started to trust me enough to tell me the truth."

She glanced away. "I guess I'm not used to trusting people."

"Me, neither," he admitted with a rueful sigh.

"Maybe that's why we got along so well from the start." She paused. "And why it's best for me to leave now."

"You don't have to go," he said. "You heard Max—he doesn't blame you. He cares about you. He'd be glad if you stayed."

She waited for a few seconds—the length of a heartbeat—for Troy to continue. Would he admit he cared for her, too? Did *he* want her to stay? When he said nothing, she sat up straighter, more resolved. "I was leaving tomorrow anyway." Her voice didn't catch at all on the lie. "I'll stay in touch with Max."

He raised a brow, waiting for her to continue. When she didn't, he said, "And me? Will you stay in touch with me, Venus?"

Would she? Could they maintain a long-distance affair, with occasional trips for hot, exciting weekends filled with passion and laughter? A day or two ago, she might have said yes. But that was before. Before she'd realized she was in love with him. Before she'd been reminded just how heart wrenching love could be.

If she really thought they had a future, she might have risked it. But they didn't. She was *not* the long-lost heir to a millionaire. She was not going to be living in an Atlanta mansion, mingling with the kind of polite society Troy was used to. She was the one who couldn't dance, had wild taste in clothes and didn't know one utensil from another. She was the unemployed, broke bartender from Baltimore with a mountain of debt and a string of bad relationships trailing along behind her.

I'm the woman who took money from a stranger to come play on the hopes of a sad, heartbroken old man.

The memory shamed her. How could Troy not be ashamed of her, too? She'd seen that look in his eyes. She knew he no longer trusted her. They wouldn't end up together in the long run. So, for her own protection, she needed to walk away now.

"I don't think so, Troy. This has been amazing. But we both knew it was short-term. Lust. Not…not love. We're too different for it to be anything more than physical. And physical seldom survives long distances." She forced a humorless laugh. "Out of sight, out of mind, as they say."

His jaw stiffened and intensity flashed in his eyes. "I don't think I'll ever get you out of my mind, and I don't want to try." He lifted a brow in that confident, sexy expression of his. "Have you forgotten? I agree with you about Rhett and Scarlett. Insanity is better than boredom any day. Opposites attract, but don't stay together. Like belongs with like, Venus."

She almost smiled, knowing he still wanted her, knowing she felt the same way. He just hadn't yet seen the flaw in his logic.

"Don't you see, Troy?" she asked softly, admitting the truth to herself, as much as to him. "We *are* opposites."

If this were really *Gone with the Wind,* he'd be Rhett and she'd be Belle Watling, the madame with the heart of gold who could never fit into the hero's rich highbrow world.

She'd thought they were alike, and perhaps in some ways, they were. But not enough for forever. Not enough to prevent eventual heartache.

He opened his mouth to reply, but before he could say a word, the door opened and Mrs. Harris looked in. "Mr. Longotti thinks you should come down now," she said to Troy, giving them both a sorrowful look. "Apparently Mr. Gallagher has been making some calls on his cellular phone already. Mr. Longotti doesn't have the numbers for all the board members here at the house and thinks you should go into the office right away."

Troy looked torn. Finally he stood. "This isn't finished, Venus. We'll talk about it later, when I get back, all right?"

Later, when he got back, she intended to be gone. But she didn't say anything.

Troy turned to follow Mrs. Harris out. Before exiting the room, however, he turned back to the bed. Cupping her cheek in his hand, he tilted her face up and pressed a hard, insistent kiss on her mouth. "This conversation isn't over."

She had to disagree. Two hours later, after a heartfelt goodbye to Max, who tried to convince her to stay, Venus got in a cab for the airport. As she flew away from Atlanta, she whispered, "You're wrong, Troy. It's definitely over."

CHAPTER TWELVE

VENUS SPENT her first two days back in Baltimore wallowing and eating lots of chocolate. Max called twice, both times telling her she was always welcome in his home. He'd also mentioned Troy. "He's angry, and, I think, hurt," Max said Sunday night. "He can't understand why you left. I can't either. I have eyes—I know something happened between you two."

Knowing Max was only trying to be helpful, she admitted the truth. "He thinks we're a lot alike. I think we're opposites. Maybe it wouldn't matter if we were both a little right, or both a little wrong, *if* we really loved each other."

At her pause, Max prompted, "And you don't?"

She couldn't answer. Instead, she changed the subject, making Max chuckle while she told him stories of her moody cat, who'd repaid her for being gone by leaving yucky presents all over her apartment her first day back.

He *hadn't* laughed when she'd told him someone had broken into the vestibule of her apartment building twice last week, vandalizing the mail boxes. Luckily, Venus had arranged to have her mail held before she left, meaning there'd be a bunch of bills to pick up at the post office Monday morning.

"Funny," Max said. "It turns out Leo was in Baltimore last week, while you were here. He was meeting with a P.I., whose name has turned up on some checks from Longotti

Lines over the years." He sniffed. "My accountants spent the day in the office. They think the sneaky little bastard's a thief as well as a liar."

Venus's first thought was to wonder if Leo had thought to steal his money back from her. She thrust it out of her mind—Leo had told her he had the cancelled check, so he knew she'd cashed it. She had absolutely nothing else that he needed, and he'd only known about her for a matter of weeks. So the P.I. had to have been working on something else that didn't involve her.

The pile of bills at the post office was bigger than she'd feared, so Monday she went straight to Flanagan's. She needed money. Since she'd sent the entire five thousand dollars she'd gotten from lousy Leo to her foster mother—unable to even consider keeping a dime of it for herself—she needed cash *now.*

"Tell you what," Joe said when she showed up. "You tell me where I can find this Leo guy so's I can break both his legs, and you can come back to work right now."

Venus kissed his grizzled cheek and got to work.

On Wednesday afternoon, Joe's waitress had an appointment and Venus leapt at the chance for an extra shift. Wednesdays were the slowest day at Flanagan's, so after lunch Venus assured Joe she could handle things while he ran to the bank. He'd been worried about keeping cash on hand because of a rough-looking stranger who'd hung around a lot last week.

"Hey," he said before leaving, "I forgot. There's a package for you. Maureen sent it here since she knew you were away. It's under the bar."

Remembering her foster mother had promised to send some old papers, Venus glanced at the package. Not wanting to open it until she was alone, she left it on the shelf.

Right now, two businessmen occupied a corner booth.

When they weren't hitting on her, they were busy whispering, probably about their plans for world domination, or for screwing over their shareholders. An elderly woman and her two middle-aged daughters, who said they were on a shopping spree, were in another booth.

The only other person in the place was a silent, dark-haired chick dressed all in black, who sat at the bar. She faced the door, able to see everyone who entered. Venus had the feeling she didn't trust anyone enough to present them with her back. With her pale skin, striking hair, dark clothes and unsmiling expression, she reminded Venus of Tuesday Adams from the old Adam's Family show.

None of them were conversationalists, which left Venus time to wallow in self-pity because she hadn't heard from Troy. She shouldn't have cared—she was the one who'd left without a goodbye. But, dammit, he could have at least made the effort.

"Probably moved on to the next willing female before my plane left the ground," she muttered.

Taking a damp rag to a stubborn dried stain on the surface of the bar, she glanced up when the door opened. About two grand worth of designer clothes, wrapped around a stunning redhead, walked in off the street. A lifetime worth of antipathy for the wealthy sent a tiny shot of stiffness up her spine.

Then Venus paused. She'd just spent a week with a rich man, Max, whom she now truly loved. Besides, this woman had a simmering look of intrigue and a boatload of attitude. That made anyone okay in Venus's book. She greeted the newcomer with a smile.

"Cool shirt," the woman said. She took a seat at the bar, crossing her legs in a way that most women in a short dress would consider a requisite for modesty, but which Venus recognized as a subtle sign to any man within drooling distance. A glance at the dweebs in the booth confirmed the Pavlovian response.

Venus looked down at her favorite old T-shirt, complete with saucy mascot. Troy might not have known who she was, but any self-respecting redhead sure as hell would. She grinned, then glanced at the other woman's designer outfit. "You don't look like the T-shirt type."

The woman's warm laugh continued to draw the eyes of the two businessmen, as she'd almost certainly intended, probably more due to nature than design. "Believe me, sister, I don't dress this way every day. And I certainly don't do it for myself."

Frankly, if Venus had buckets of money, she'd dress *only* to please herself. Except, perhaps, in the bedroom. Hell, for Troy, she might actually have given in and tried a thong again!

The woman had continued speaking, still talking about Venus's shirt and Jessica Rabbit. "I'd like to think I have a lot in common with her. Not bad, just drawn that way."

Venus nodded. "Ditto." Without being told, she instinctively knew the woman with the smoky voice would be a whiskey drinker. She poured her a shot of the good stuff and slid it over. "My name's Venus. Venus Messina."

The woman extended her hand. "Sydney. Sydney Colburn."

Venus instantly recognized the name, which was on the spine of several of her all-time favorite novels. "Sydney Colburn. No kidding? The writer?"

After Sydney tasted the whiskey, she nodded that it was to her liking. "One and the same."

Sydney Colburn's books had provided many nights' escape during the past year. Venus might have sworn off men physically, but she'd been addicted to reading about the kind of fabulous guys this woman created with such thrilling—*throbbing*—detail.

After telling Sydney how much she'd liked her heroes,

saying it was too bad more men couldn't live up to her standard, she added, "And my favorite thing about your books—no wimpy heroines!"

"Men who meet my standard do exist," the author said softly. "The trouble is finding them."

Venus almost snorted at that one. "Finding men has never been a problem for me." Hell, she'd been finding men who'd attracted her since she had been old enough to look up the word orgasm in the dictionary! "Keeping them? That's another story."

"The good ones or the so-so ones?"

Venus sighed. "Good or even so-so wouldn't be bad. Unfortunately, the only ones I seem to manage to hang on to are the creeps who cost you jobs or empty your bank accounts. Not the green-eyed dreamboats with chestnut hair and the kind of wicked, sexy grin that oughta be illegal." She glanced away, trying to thrust Troy's image out of her mind.

Sydney obviously noticed and made a knowing sound.

"What?"

"You got it bad, sister."

Venus scowled. "Speak for yourself."

After Sydney admitted she *was* speaking for herself, Venus poured her another drink.

"We bad girls have it tough, you know?" Venus said. "Those Goody Two-shoes have saying 'no' down to an art form, blaming morals or past hurts. We say yes because of those *same* morals or past hurts! We can't seem to give up on the idea that the next handsome stud who comes along might erase what the last one did."

"Handsome studs are a dime a dozen."

The lady in black, whom Venus had nearly forgotten about, had obviously been following their conversation. Venus approached the attractive young woman, whose demeanor, clothes and attitude sent off one signal: mysterious. "Hey, girl, I almost forgot you were here. Come join us. Bad girls need to stick together."

The woman looked back and forth between them, still wary, but considering. Then her lip curled, possibly in jaded amusement. "Bad girls. Are we forming a club here?"

Venus snorted at the very idea. "Last club I belonged to was the Girl Scouts. I got kicked out when I was eleven." As Sydney raised a questioning brow, Venus explained. "Summer camp. I got caught sneaking into the boys' cabin to play Seven Minutes in Heaven. The troop leader came in just as I was heading into the closet with Tommy Callahan." She shook her head and sighed at the memory. "He had the cutest dimples. And cool braces."

Sydney nodded, wearing a similar look of reminiscence.

A grin suddenly brightened the features of the woman in black, softening her face and making her look younger than Venus had figured her to be. "I never made it past Brownies. I kept altering the uniform in a way that, well, didn't meet with the troop leader's approval. But the boys liked it." She winked. "Besides, brown isn't my color."

"Hell," Sydney proclaimed, "my mother never let me forget I got tossed outta preschool for showing the boys my underwear."

Venus snickered. "Hey, why was she complaining?"

"Yeah," the brunette said with a knowing look at Venus. They finished the thought in unison. "At least you were wearing 'em."

The three of them, strangers until ten minutes before, but sisters just the same, shared a moment of soft laughter. Seeing the understanding in their eyes, Venus wished she'd met them long ago. "I guess we've been members of the bad girls club since birth, huh?"

Sydney silently lifted her glass in salute, and the other woman followed suit. Venus popped the cap off a beer and joined them in an unspoken toast to wicked women everywhere. *God love them.*

The door opened again. This time, two young women in proper business attire entered to join the men in the booth. The suit-clad oglers promptly sat up straighter. "Oh, no, a good girl's in sight, reign in the lust," Venus whispered.

The stranger in black picked up her drink and moved next to Sydney, introducing herself as Nicole Bennett. They chatted for several more minutes, until the ring of Sydney's cell phone interrupted.

Venus left to wait on the two newcomers—white wine spritzers, she coulda predicted that a mile away—then returned to find Sydney disconnecting her call. The woman drained her glass and dropped a bill on the counter. When Venus realized it was a hundred, she picked it up. "I'll get your change."

Sydney, however, refused. She ordered Venus to keep the change and get Nicole good and drunk. Then, with a cheery wave, she walked toward the door, easily moving out of Venus's life as quickly as she'd moved into it.

Or, not so easily, considering her way out the door was blocked by someone coming in. A man. A big man. A big chestnut-haired man with the kind of sexy grin that oughta be illegal.

Troy.

TROY WAITED for the jolt of awareness that always shot through his body when an attractive female passed by. The redhead exiting Flanagan's bar was certainly attractive—and knew it—but caused no familiar blast of heat to rush through him.

Only one woman did that now. The one standing behind the bar, looking ready to do one of two things: slug him, or jump on him. "Hi, Venus."

"What are you doing here?"

"I'm thirsty," he said as he slid onto a bar stool and tapped his fingers on the pitted wood surface of the bar. "What do you recommend? A Screaming Orgasm? Sex on the Beach?"

She smirked. "A Screaming Orgasm Up Against the Wall is always a good choice."

He swallowed, hard. Damn, he'd missed the woman. "How about a Screaming Orgasm Up Against the Bathroom Counter? Or In the Pool?" His grin dared her to remember. Before she could say a word, however, they both heard a tiny wolf whistle from a dark-haired woman sitting at the bar. Troy had barely noticed her, though she was striking enough to garner attention on her own.

"Yep. Definitely oughta be illegal." She nodded at Venus, then walked out.

"Who was that?"

"A new friend," Venus said softly. "Now, why are you here?"

He answered with a question of his own. "Why did you leave?"

She busied herself pouring some unshelled peanuts into a wooden bowl. "What was the point of staying?"

"Maybe because Max wanted you to?" When she didn't answer, he leaned closer. "Okay, how about because *I* wanted you to?"

She paused, not meeting his eye. "Did you want me to? Why?"

He sighed, wondering how such an intelligent woman could be so blind to her own appeal. Finally, tired of watching her pretend to swipe at the counter with her dingy rag, he grabbed her hand and made her stop. Then he waited until she met his eye. "Yes, I wanted you to. I told you I'm crazy about you."

Her eyes narrowed. "That's nice. But I have my own life,

back here. We knew I was going to have to leave sooner or later."

"You could have stayed in Atlanta. With Max." He hesitated, then pushed harder, wondering if she was any more ready to hear this than he was ready to say it. "Or with me."

She raised a questioning brow. "You?"

"I moved into my own place Monday, between meetings with lawyers, the board and a P.I. It's downtown, near a Marta stop and some great shopping." He glanced around the pub and continued to try to tempt her. "There's even an Irish bar."

She nibbled one corner of her lip, moistening it with the tip of her pretty pink tongue. "You want me to live with you?"

He nodded. "There. Or here. I told Max I might be resigning from my job. It all depends on you."

"Because...you're crazy about me?"

Hell, he'd already gone farther with Venus than he'd ever gone with any woman—asking her to move in. Having gone this far, he figured he might as well jump in feet first. Leaning across the bar, with his elbows on the wood, he tugged her other hand in his and pulled her closer. "Because I'm in love with you, Venus."

She yanked her hands back. "Get *out!* You are *so* not in love with me."

Not quite the reaction he'd hoped for the first time he told a woman he loved her. He grinned. Maybe that was why he'd fallen in love with her in the first place. "No lie, babe. It's love."

"You can't love me."

He didn't know who she was trying to convince, but it sure wasn't going to be him. "I do."

"We're too different."

"No, we're not. We're the same."

She flung the rag down and crossed her arms in front of her chest. "No, we're not the same. A guy can be a total dog and still be a wealthy, respected businessman. A woman makes a few…dozen…mistakes, and she's a bad girl for life."

He snickered. God, she was just priceless.

Troy saw that they'd drawn the attention of the other people in the place, including two couples who'd walked in behind him. But he didn't give a damn. "Venus, we're a hell of a lot alike in every way that really matters. Besides, honey, you are not nearly as bad as you like to pretend."

Her spine stiffened at the tossed gauntlet. "I seduced my dentist when I was nineteen."

Okay. One-upmanship. He could handle that. "I slept with the mother of one of my college buddies when I was nineteen."

Her eyes narrowed. "I did it to get out of paying for a crown."

"I did it to get laid."

She glared, then thought about it. "I flashed the boy's soccer team from the top of the bleachers when I was a freshman."

"Did they win the game?"

She rolled her eyes.

"I had the entire senior cheerleading squad at each other's throats before soccer season even started because I'd been dating four of them at the same time," Troy admitted.

She harrumphed. "I started sneaking out with guys before I'd even hit puberty."

He chuckled. "I think we already discussed this. I didn't have to sneak *out,* because I was too busy sneaking females *in.*"

An elderly woman, sitting in a booth nearby with two middle-aged ladies, tittered. "Sounds like you two are made for each other."

Troy gave her a quick smile of thanks. "I agree."

Venus still didn't look convinced. "So we were both rotten little sex fiends. That's not all." She began to tick off her fingers, cataloguing her badness. "I refuse to pay parking tickets. My picture's on a wanted poster at the library because I return books so late. And," she continued, dramatically slapping her hand on the surface of the bar, "I quite often have more than ten items at the express checkout at the grocery store."

"I hate it when people do that," the old lady muttered.

Troy took her hand again. "I love you."

"You can't."

"I *do*."

She lowered her eyes, until her lashes brushed the curves of her lovely cheeks. When she looked up again, her green eyes were suspiciously bright. "I took money from Leo to come to Atlanta, never even stopping to think I might be hurting a wonderful old man who'd never done a thing to me."

He understood. Finally, he understood. Not answering, Troy walked around the bar, pushing through a swinging half door designed to keep customers away. Venus watched him, wide-eyed, backing up until she was blocked by a huge silver vat of beer.

"You didn't keep the money, did you." It wasn't a question. He knew without asking what her answer would be.

She shook her head slowly. "I sent it to my foster mother. How did you know?"

He brushed a long tendril of red hair off her brow, gently tucking it behind her ear. Lightly caressing her earlobe, he then ran his fingers across her jaw, down her neck, until his hand rested on her strong, stubborn shoulder. "Because I know you, Venus Messina. You're honorable. You're honest."

He leaned closer, inhaling to breathe in the sweetness of her cinnamon-tinged perfume. "And you're too damn good for me."

She tried to shake her head in denial, but he caught her chin and held her still. "You're too good for me," he repeated. "I don't deserve you. But the truth is, I'm a selfish enough bastard to want you anyway."

Not giving her another chance to throw up any more ridiculous obstacles, he pulled her close and pressed a sweet, gentle kiss on her lips. She softened in his arms, returning his kiss, then pulled back.

"We're still opposites," she whispered, stubborn to the last. Studying him from head to toe, she rolled her eyes. "Look at us." She pointed down to her tight-as-sin jeans and sexy-as-hell T-shirt. "I'm a walking advertisement for a thrift shop. And there you are in your designer shirt and pants that probably cost more than I paid for my couch."

"I can take off the shirt," he said, reaching for the top button, letting her see the mischievous look in his eye.

She glanced at the bar crowd. "Oh, yeah, right."

"You think I won't?"

"Maybe you want me to think you will," she taunted.

He slipped the button free. She kept watching, silently egging him on, never moving her gaze away from him as he slowly unfastened every single button. He tugged the shirt free of his waistband and shrugged it off his shoulders, dropping it to the floor. He knew every person in the place was watching them, him, standing shirtless behind the bar, but he didn't care. Venus, with her hot, devouring eyes, was all he cared about.

"You didn't think I'd do it."

A wicked smile widened her beautiful lips. She tapped his chest with the tip of her index finger, until he was the one backing up. "Oh, I knew you'd do it, Troy. Why else do you think I suggested it?"

He turned the tables on her, picking her up by the waist and turning around to deposit her on top of the bar. Then he stepped easily between her long, jean-clad legs and tugged her closer, until her parted thighs rested on his hips. He ignored the flurry of whispers and a definite sigh or two from the women seated in the place. "Tell me you love me."

She continued to stare at him, both amusement and sensual awareness in her eyes.

He pulled her closer, feeling the warm dampness of her jeans against his stomach. Sliding his hands up under the bottom of her shirt, he caressed her waist, then reached around to stroke the delicate bones of her spine. Leaning forward, he pressed a hot, moist kiss in the hollow of her throat. "I won't stop until you tell me," he threatened.

She dropped her head back and moaned. "I won't tell you if you stop."

"I'd tell him absolutely *anything*," a woman's voice said in a loud whisper.

They both began to laugh and finally Venus took pity. Her brilliant emerald eyes glittered with happiness as she dropped her arms over his shoulders and met his unflinching stare.

"I love you, Troy." She leaned down to kiss him, parting her lips to let him sample the sweetness of her mouth. She sighed as their kiss ended, and whispered, "Now, take me home."

"To Atlanta?"

She shook her head. "No way can I make it to Atlanta today. We'll go tomorrow. But when my uncle gets back, you can take me to my apartment before I rip off the rest of your clothes and get us both arrested."

THAT EVENING in her apartment, after three solid hours of the most incredible lovemaking of her life, Venus asked Troy to fill her in on what had been happening in Atlanta. "Max sounds okay. Is he going to be able to keep Leo in line?"

Troy grabbed another egg roll from the mountain of carry-out spread all over the coffee table in her living room. "Yeah. Max has got enough on Leo to force him out of the company and he could press criminal charges if he wanted to. But I still can't help wondering what Leo's been up to with this P.I. in Baltimore."

Feeling a little silly about it, Venus admitted her earlier suspicion. "If I had anything worth stealing, I might have wondered if he was responsible for the mail thefts."

"Wait a second," Troy said, casting a quick glance toward the door, where they'd dropped their clothes, her purse, and the package she'd brought home from Flanagan's. "You said that box was delivered to you at the bar last week, right? And your uncle Joe was worried about some shady character hanging around?"

It sounded crazy. "It was just a bunch of paperwork from my foster mother. You don't think…"

He glanced again toward the door. Finally, curious herself, Venus got up and brought the shoe-box-size package to the table. She tore off the brown paper, then removed the lid. A note rested inside. "From Maureen," she said as she scanned it. "She said most of her paperwork was taken in the robbery when I was in high school. But DCF sent these things to me at her place after my eighteenth birthday. I'd already come to Baltimore. She told me she had it ages ago, but I completely forgot."

Troy looked at the pile of papers, and a small red leather-bound book. "A diary?"

Venus recognized the book. "My mother's. I didn't know what had happened to it. I guess the state kept everything for me until I was of legal age, since no other family came forward."

"Maybe you should read it later," he said, a look of intense concern on his face.

Knowing she might regret it, she reached for the diary, anyway. She trusted Troy more than she'd ever trusted anyone in her life. And if reading her mother's words was going to be painful for her, she could think of no one better to be right beside her, holding her hand, than the man she loved.

An open envelope containing some legal-looking papers was stuck to the book. As she retrieved it, the papers fell out, fluttering to the floor beside Troy. Focused on the diary, she barely paid attention as he reached for them to put them back.

Just as she opened the faded, aged cover of the diary, she heard Troy make a strange confused sound. She barely had time to register what was taped on the inside cover of the diary—a strip of photos, like those taken at photography booths in the mall—when she heard him say, "Oh, my God."

"What's the matter, Troy?"

His eyes were wide with shock. "Honey, Venus…"

"What is it?"

"I was trying to fold them to put them back," he explained, as if he feared she'd think he was snooping.

She glanced at the legal document in his hand. "What is it?"

He handed it to her. But before she even glanced at it, she felt a strange tingling of something in her spine. Recognition. Culmination. Understanding. Because in that brief glimpse at the photo strip in her mother's diary, she'd seen a face she'd never expected to see.

Letting the document fall to her lap, she opened the book again and looked at the photographs. Her mother's smiling face was easily recognizable…as was the face of the laughing man, mugging it up for the camera beside Trina.

Max Longotti Jr.

She knew it was him. She'd seen enough pictures of the handsome young man at Max's place the week before to instantly know the thick dark hair, the green eyes, the dimple in his left cheek.

Tears spilled out of her eyes.

Troy shoved the table out of the way, ignoring the cartons of food tumbling onto the floor. He pulled her into his arms. "It's all right, Venus. It's okay," he murmured as he stroked her back.

"It's Max Jr." She felt numb and almost couldn't grasp the words she spoke. "In the photos. With my mother. It's him."

"I know." Troy kissed her brow. "The paper was a registered document showing your name was legally changed to Venus when you were two years old." He held her tighter. "From Violet."

She closed her eyes, letting it sink in, accepting the truth. Trina really had met and loved Max Longotti Jr. Even without reading the diary, she understood what had happened. Their whirlwind love affair. Trina's inability to contact the mysterious "Matt" after he'd gone off to California. Her birth. His death. Years of not knowing. Finally Trina losing hope and changing Venus's first name, but not having the heart to go that final step and change the last one.

She understood just about everything. "Leo…"

"I'm gonna kill that son of a bitch," Troy muttered.

"He's known for a long time, I suspect."

Troy nodded. "Probably for years. I imagine he kept it from everyone, not wanting you found. Then I came along. He started worrying Max would sell the company and he'd lose everything he'd worked so hard to steal."

She thought about the robbery at her foster mother's place more than a decade ago and wondered if it would be possible for someone to be so deceitful and duplicitous for so long.

Yeah. Unfortunately, when it came to Leo Gallagher, she believed it was possible.

"Leo was standing right there last week when you said your foster mother had some documents she was going to mail you," Troy said. "He probably panicked and came up here, trying to intercept the package."

"You think his P.I. was the guy who spooked Joe at Flanagan's?" When Troy nodded, she continued speculating. "And the DNA test…he probably did have someone lined up to falsify it. To make it turn out exactly the way he wanted it." She lowered her voice, shaking her head in disgust. "He would have used me, or bribed me. Either way, he never intended to let me find out the truth."

Troy cupped her face and brushed a few tears off her cheek. "Are you all right?"

She nodded. "A little numb. A little shocked." She bit her lip, thinking of all the lost time. "A lot sad."

He obviously understood, not finding it strange that the truth would seem so incredibly tragic to her. Then again, Troy truly cared for Max, too. So maybe his first thought, like hers, had been for all the years they'd wasted. Those years had made Venus stronger, helped mold her into the woman she'd become. But they'd been awfully lonely for Max Longotti.

"Troy, will you take me home tomorrow?"

He nodded. "I'd do anything for you, Venus. Anything."

She stared into his eyes, knowing he meant it. This man, this wonderfully wicked man, loved her with every ounce of his big bad heart.

As she did him.

She smiled and kissed him, almost in awe that she'd been given back the people she most wanted, all within a matter of hours. Troy. Her father. And her grandfather.

Still wrapped safely in the arms of the man she loved, she reached for the phone. "Max?" she said when the old man answered. "It's Venus." She took a deep breath and blinked back fresh tears.

"And," she told him softly, "it's Violet."

* * * * *

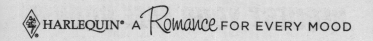
HARLEQUIN® A *Romance* FOR EVERY MOOD

If you enjoyed these passionate reads, then you will love other stories from

HARLEQUIN® *Presents*

Glamorous international settings...
unforgettable men...passionate romances—
Harlequin Presents promises you the world!

HARLEQUIN® *Blaze*

Fun, flirtatious and steamy books that tell it
like it is, inside and outside the bedroom.

Silhouette *Desire*

Always Powerful, Passionate and Provocative

**Six new titles are available every month
from each of these lines**

Available wherever books are sold

REQUEST YOUR FREE BOOKS!

**2 FREE NOVELS
PLUS 2
FREE GIFTS!**

HARLEQUIN®

Blaze™

Red-hot reads!

YES! Please send me 2 FREE Harlequin® Blaze™ novels and my 2 FREE gifts (gifts are worth about $10). After receiving them, if I don't wish to receive any more books, I can return the shipping statement marked "cancel." If I don't cancel, I will receive 6 brand-new novels every month and be billed just $4.24 per book in the U.S. or $4.71 per book in Canada. That's a saving of at least 15% off the cover price. It's quite a bargain. Shipping and handling is just 50¢ per book.* I understand that accepting the 2 free books and gifts places me under no obligation to buy anything. I can always return a shipment and cancel at any time. Even if I never buy another book, the two free books and gifts are mine to keep forever.

151/351 HDN E5LS

Name _____ (PLEASE PRINT) _____

Address _____ Apt. # _____

City _____ State/Prov. _____ Zip/Postal Code _____

Signature (if under 18, a parent or guardian must sign) _____

Mail to the **Harlequin Reader Service:**
IN U.S.A.: P.O. Box 1867, Buffalo, NY 14240-1867
IN CANADA: P.O. Box 609, Fort Erie, Ontario L2A 5X3

Not valid for current subscribers to Harlequin Blaze books.

**Want to try two free books from another line?
Call 1-800-873-8635 or visit www.morefreebooks.com.**

* Terms and prices subject to change without notice. Prices do not include applicable taxes. N.Y. residents add applicable sales tax. Canadian residents will be charged applicable provincial taxes and GST. Offer not valid in Quebec. This offer is limited to one order per household. All orders subject to approval. Credit or debit balances in a customer's account(s) may be offset by any other outstanding balance owed by or to the customer. Please allow 4 to 6 weeks for delivery. Offer available while quantities last.

Your Privacy: Harlequin Books is committed to protecting your privacy. Our Privacy Policy is available online at www.eHarlequin.com or upon request from the Reader Service. From time to time we make our lists of customers available to reputable third parties who may have a product or service of interest to you. If you would prefer we not share your name and address, please check here. ☐

Help us get it right—We strive for accurate, respectful and relevant communications. To clarify or modify your communication preferences, visit us at www.ReaderService.com/consumerchoice.

HB10R

THE HEAT IS ON
by
Jill Shalvis

The attraction between Bella and
Detective Madden is undeniable.
But can a few wild encounters
turn into love?

Don't miss this hot read.

*Available in August
where books are sold.*

---

red-hot reads

www.eHarlequin.com

HB79562

HARLEQUIN® A *Romance* FOR EVERY MOOD™

CLASSICS

Quintessential, modern love stories
that are romance at its finest.

Harlequin Presents®

Glamorous international settings…
unforgettable men…passionate
romances—Harlequin Presents
promises you the world!

Harlequin Presents® Extra

Meet more of your favorite Presents
heroes and travel to glamorous
international locations in our regular
monthly themed collections.

Harlequin® Romance

The anticipation, the thrill of the chase
and the sheer rush of falling in love!

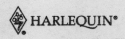
HARLEQUIN®

Showcase™

On Sale July 13, 2010.

Reader favorites from the most talented voices in romance

Save $1.00 on the purchase of 1 or more Harlequin® Showcase™ books.

SAVE $1.00 on the purchase of 1 or more Harlequin® Showcase™ books.

Coupon expires November 30, 2010. Redeemable at participating retail outlets.
Limit one coupon per customer. Valid in the U.S.A. and Canada only.

52609187

Canadian Retailers: Harlequin Enterprises Limited will pay the face value of this coupon plus 10.25¢ if submitted by customer for this product only. Any other use constitutes fraud. Coupon is nonassignable. Void if taxed, prohibited or restricted by law. Consumer must pay any government taxes. Void if copied. Nielsen Clearing House ("NCH") customers submit coupons and proof of sales to Harlequin Enterprises Limited, P.O. Box 3000, Saint John, NB E2L 4L3, Canada. Non-NCH retailer—for reimbursement submit coupons and proof of sales directly to Harlequin Enterprises Limited, Retail Marketing Department, 225 Duncan Mill Rd., Don Mills, ON M3B 3K9, Canada.

U.S. Retailers: Harlequin Enterprises Limited will pay the face value of this coupon plus 8¢ if submitted by customer for this product only. Any other use constitutes fraud. Coupon is nonassignable. Void if taxed, prohibited or restricted by law. Consumer must pay any government taxes. Void if copied. For reimbursement submit coupons and proof of sales directly to Harlequin Enterprises Limited, P.O. Box 880478, El Paso, TX 88588-0478, U.S.A. Cash value 1/100 cents.

5 65373 00076 2   (8100)0 11668

® and TM are trademarks owned and used by the trademark owner and/or its licensee.
© 2010 Harlequin Enterprises Limited

HSCCOUP0710